Jenny Fran Davis was born in Manhattan and spent four months avoiding (but later embracing) millet mountains in a peace- and justice-focused Quaker community in northern California. Fond of big dogs, doo-wop, and Judy Blume, she attended the Chapin School and is a recent Wesleyan University graduate. *Everything Must Go* is her debut novel.

JENNY FRAN DAVIS

Everything Must Go

corsair

CORSAIR

First published in the US in 2017 by St. Martin's Press
First published in Great Britain in 2017 by Corsair

1 3 5 7 9 10 8 6 4 2

A CIP catalogue record for this book
is available from the British Library.

ISBN: 978-1-4721-5308-1

Printed and bound in Great Britain by Clays Ltd, St Ives plc

Papers used by Corsair are from well-managed forests
and other responsible sources.

Corsair
An imprint of
Little, Brown Book Group
Carmelite House
50 Victoria Embankment
London EC4Y 0DZ

An Hachette UK Company
www.hachette.co.uk

www.littlebrown.co.uk

For my fellow wombats, with love and millet mountains

ACKNOWLEDGMENTS

I'm brimming with gratitude. I feel enormously, wildly lucky for everyone who has made this book possible and everyone who continues to sustain me in friendship and mentorship. Thanks first to Miriam Altshuler, my dynamite agent, for your steadfast belief and advocacy, as well as for your patience with my ignorance about all things publishing. Infinite thanks too to Sara Goodman, my wonderful editor, whose incisive comments saved this story many times over, as well as to the entire team at Wednesday Books (especially those who had to deal with this maddening format). I'm also extremely grateful to Carolyn Hessel, the first person who read and believed in this book, as well as to Kiley Frank and Sarah Yeoh-Wang for being its first intrepid editors.

The thorough love and support of my parents, Beth and Michael Davis; my grandparents, Irma and Charles Margolis; my sister, Lucy Davis; and our dogs, Reuben and Bailey, all who were a sustaining force behind this project and behind all that has come before and after it. Uncle Bobby, we love and miss you very much.

At Woolman, screaming and grateful laughter to Jane Davis and Maya Guffey (my fellow residents of "The Pile"); Lulu Dewey, the funniest person I know; Devin Cruz, my improbable prom date; Hannah Durant, the fearless New Yorker; Demetrius Thompson, wise beyond your years; Daniel Freehling, who was nineteen; Ariel Fisher, my English Cottage Garden co-conspirator; Chelsi Torres, sly and darkly funny; Maria Doerr, the most gleeful wood nymph; Max Paris, of the many-colored headlamps; Gregory Terry, a hilarious Tarzan; Savannah Henderson, buzzing and bumbling with life; Brooke Lyons-Justus, sharp and courageous; Lucyanna Labadie, so deeply wonderful in all ways; and to our queenly mentors, Dorothy and Doug Henderson, Grace Oedel, Jacob Holzberg-Pill, Emily Zionts, Katya Thronweber, Jess Holler, Kristin Pearson, Kerstin Martin, Ryan Stennett, Cecelia Watkins, Lewis Maday Travis, and Aaron Schwartz. I wanted to be all of your best friends.

I am profoundly grateful for my generous mentors: Achy Objeas, who told me I should write, as well as Professors Anne Greene, Cliff Chase, Inara Verzemnieks, Sally Bachner, and Eskor Johnson. To my teachers at the Chapin School, particularly Diane Spilios, Lisa Moy, Barbara Minakakis, and Andrea Kassar, thank you for pushing me to take the time to be better.

I must be going on too long, but of course this book is above all by and for my friends, a large handful of which includes Natalie Bolt, with whom watching *ANTM* is a religious experience; Rebecca Brill, a glorious and haunted mind; Hadley Feingold, my steadfast partner in crime in the GoRo, Usdan, and beyond; Evelysse Vargas, my one-woman publicity team and a source of deep honesty and humor; Veronica Harrington, to whom explosive kindness is second nature; Lily Taylor, a divine spring of generosity; Eliza Mellion, vegan guru and Garment District explorer; Nadja Shannon-Dabek, my light in the storm; Amari Tankard, who remembers it all and loves me anyway; Anastasia Almyasheva, my froomie and thick-and-thin love; Sarah Yeoh-Wang, who simply gets it; Paige Martin, guardian of the warmest and most bizarre memories; Avigayl Sharp, with whom I will stage a revolution; Zettie Shapey, who assures me that I'm not too much; Ben Matusow, who laughed with me through it all; Lilly Lerer, the most majestic prancer; Devonaire Ortiz, whose knowing glances in the Argus office sustained me; Hannah Shevrin, the realest housewife; Rebecca Hutman, the sharpest tack in the drawer; Taina Quiñones, source of the quickest laughter and deepest understanding; and Iryelis Lopez, my rope. Your friendship staggers me. It is daily salvation.

Everything Must Go

A Note to the Readers of This Collection

When I was sixteen, I traded my prep school in Manhattan for an alternative boarding school in upstate New York's Hudson River Valley to make Elijah Huck love me.

As is usually the case when one follows an up-and-coming feminist fashion photographer to a remote Quaker boarding school, I was in for a few surprises. These surprises were manifold, but perhaps most poignantly: Elijah broke my heart, I stuffed all my belongings into a vending machine, and I kissed a budding Marxist.

I left for Quare almost three years ago, before Elijah won his one-hundred-thousand-dollar MacDougall innovation grant and opened a gallery on Orchard Street. Before I started my freshman year at this small East Coast liberal arts college in one of those cramped dorm rooms I'm laying out these documents—the letters, journal entries, clippings, forms, and reports that comprise this collection—in chronological order on the floor.

Back then Elijah was a freshman at Columbia who worked part-time in the history department of the Bowen School for Girls, where I was in tenth grade. On an afternoon in late August, three days before the start of classes, I slid into Bowen's darkroom, on the building's eighth floor, to search for a bottle of fluid whose name I've since forgotten. As I stumbled forward, engulfed in darkness, someone called out, "Hello?"

I froze.

"Hello?" I asked, stopping in my tracks. It was still pitch-black. My heart pounded in my ears. "Who's there?"

A pause.

"It's Elijah."

The voice could have been two feet from me, or it could have been ten; in the dark, it was impossible to tell. I did a quick mental recall of the self-defense techniques I'd learned the previous spring as part of Bowen's five-step plan to defend its students from predators, and folded my hands into beaks, should I need them to poke at my would-be attacker's eyes.

"Who's Elijah?"

Step one was to speak in a firm, confident tone, and I was proud that my voice didn't shake too much.

"Elijah Huck."

I paused, hands still in beak formation, waiting for him to elaborate.

"I'm the new history Tutor."

This rang a bell. Bowen had hired three Columbia University history majors as Tutors for the pilot program of the Bowen Tutorial, modeled off the Oxford Tutorial, which basically meant that we sophomores would meet with the Tutors to explore our individual interests in one-on-one intensive sessions.

We were both quiet. I didn't know what to do with this information, and I didn't want to step forward to search for the lights, lest I barrel into him. So I waited.

"Who is *this*?" he asked.

"Flora."

"Flora who?"

"Flora Goldwasser. I go here."

A long pause.

"It's nice to meet you," he said.

I couldn't find my voice.

"I'm holding out my hand." His voice sounded ready to tip over into a gentle laugh, but no laugh followed.

I unfolded one of my beak hands and held it out tentatively, not sure how close he was. My hand collided with his. It was big and soft, slightly warm. His handshake was firm, almost crushingly so, and when he released me, my own hand lingered in the residual warmth.

"Do you have night vision or something?" I asked.

"I've spent a lot of time in darkrooms."

"Dark rooms, or darkrooms?"

A short laugh. "Both."

The lights flickered on.

It wasn't until I saw him that I realized I'd been imagining someone completely different. Someone beefier, taller, someone with thick dark hair and an olive complexion. But there he stood, Elijah in all his five-nine, narrow-shouldered glory. Cuffed jeans, flannel shirt, tiny round glasses. Sandy hair long enough for him to run his fingers through, which he did at that moment.

We blinked at each other. One side of his face curled into a smile.

"Hey," he said. He held a stack of photographs in one hand, which he now pressed against his chest.

I quickly tightened the band of fabric I'd used to tie my hair back from my face. The fabric matched that of my dress: white, spotted with huge sunflowers. I smoothed the dress, too, and tried to discreetly wipe the sweat from my forehead with the back of my hand.

"Hello."

"Do you come here often, Flora?"

His voice was slightly raspy, like he was getting over a cold. He smiled as though he'd caught me mid-transgression, and a twinge of annoyance shot through me. *He*, not I, was the clear transgressor here.

"I'm helping Mr. Greenberg," I said. My words felt heavy and insufficient. "What are you doing here?"

"Just developing some work." The photos were still pressed against his chest, and I suddenly wondered if they were sexually explicit images of a lover, or something.

"Your own work?"

He nodded, still smiling with half of his face. I pressed my lips together to keep from grinning.

"You're allowed to do that here?"

"Not technically."

My heart was racing. We regarded each other. I didn't know what look to give him, so I settled for half-hearted suspicion. His look was pure amusement.

"I should—" Instead of finishing the sentence, I gestured to the room at large.

"Have fun—" Here he mimicked my empty gesture, but he was smiling so hard that I smiled back despite myself. "See you around, Flora."

He nodded once, and then he strode past me and entered the revolving door to exit the darkroom. The air behind him smelled like men's deodorant. It was nothing special—probably the drugstore brand, even—but smelling him, smelling the suggestion of a body that moved and sweat and required deodorant, made my cheeks hot.

I know.

And I promise, it gets way worse.

If I were Molly Ringwald in a John Hughes movie, I would have slid to the ground with my back against the wall, knees at my chest, a hand clutching my throat, and a dazed expression on my face. But I was more of a take-action type of girl, so I grabbed a set of prints that Mr. Greenberg hadn't asked for and hurried through the door. But by the time I reached the art room, Elijah was gone. I worked for the next few hours in a distracted trance, and when

I went home, I organized and reorganized my closet until I was calm enough to slice some strawberries and read *Anna Karenina*.

When school officially started, I scoured the hallways for Elijah, but it wasn't until the end of the first week that we met again. This time, a pair of shoes brought us together.

They were sunflower pumps, and they were gorgeous. (In hindsight, maybe it was the sunflower print that summoned him. Maybe, like a bee, he'd been drawn to both my floral dress and my floral shoes.)

The shoes violated the Bowen dress code, which explicitly stated that all students were to wear white-and-green saddle oxfords. All offenders were forced into the Shoes of Shame, a pair of battered, dirt-streaked saddle oxfords left over from the first Bush administration. As evidenced by my tendency to come to school early to help teachers set up their rooms, I was hardly the rebel type. I wore the offending shoes for no other reason than half-hearted curiosity about whether anyone would say anything. At around noon, Ms. Loren, my English teacher, apologetically sent me to the head of Upper School, Dr. Muamba, an ex-ballerina from the Congo, a slightly embarrassed look on her face, as though she, too, believed the whole saddle oxford rule to be ridiculous.

Journal entry from that fateful September day

Oh my GOD, we had another interaction today.

I was sitting in the office of the head of Upper School, feet bare, the sunflower shoes resting in my lap, when I caught sight of Elijah. Dr. Muamba had gone to fetch the Shoes of Shame. Elijah first walked by the open door of the office so quickly that I caught sight only of his narrow back. In seconds, he did a double take and

appeared in the doorway. He stood, half-smiling again, peering down
at me. I almost passed out.

"Flora Goldwasser," he said. It was a statement, a confirmation,
an affirmation. It was him saying my name. It was everything.

I nodded. My stomach caved in on itself. My chest cramped.

"Those are nice shoes," he said, cocking his head at my lap and
leaning one shoulder against the doorway, knocking one toe of his
loafers into the carpet.

I nodded. I was jumping out of my skin.

"Why aren't they on your feet?"

"They violate the dress code," I said.

Elijah straightened and took a few steps toward me. My heart
jumped up into my throat. The office was small. I held out one of the
sunflower shoes, sensing that was what he wanted, and he took it,
examining it from all angles: the narrow frame, the slightly pointed
toe, the sturdy heel. I stared at him the entire time, not sure whether
he'd been a shoemaker in the old country, or something, and was
interested in the delicate stitching, or whether he was about to pitch it
out the window to start a shoe revolution.

As I'd soon come to learn, Elijah's emotions were inscrutable.

But he didn't say anything about crafting shoes in Lithuania,
and he certainly didn't hurl the shoe. When he was done, he handed
the shoe back to me gently, like it was made of glass. He didn't leave
immediately, but he retreated back to the doorway and crossed his
arms in front of his chest. He smiled wider.

"I knew it was a violation," I said. "I just wanted to see if I
could get away with it."

He was silent for a few seconds. Then he finally opened his
mouth to speak. But at that exact moment, Dr. Muamba appeared in

the doorway, just behind Elijah. She held the Shoes of Shame in her
left hand. My heart collapsed.

"I'm afraid they're in a bit of rough shape," she said, sliding past
Elijah and into her office. She looked expectantly at him.

"May I help you?" she asked.

He shook his head.

"Godspeed," he said, and ducked out.

My heart rate didn't slow down until sixth period. I'm still kind
of wigging out, eating Lael's chocolate-covered cranberries so fast, my
tongue hurts. God, I have it bad.

The next morning, after spending the night furiously exfoliating my feet to slough off all the skin cells that had touched the
Shoes of Shame, I dressed in my Bowen kilt and white collared
blouse in front of my full-length mirror. Tying a white silk scarf
around my waist, I turned to my open closet, fixing my gaze on
my shelf of shoes. I thought of the way Elijah had marveled at the
sunflower pumps and then at me as I sat with my bare feet tucked
around the curved mahogany bar of my chair. I snatched a pair of
red velvet flats, shoved them onto my feet, and ran out the door.

By noon I hadn't been caught.

Let me state again for the record: *I was a kiss-ass.* I was a
straight-A student, the president of my class, the founder of the
Bowen Feminists for Girl Power!, and the managing editor of the
Bowen Bulletin. The day of the velvet flats dragged on, uninter-
rupted.

"Are you sure about those?" one of my best friends, India,
asked as we washed our hands in the second-floor restroom after
lunch. "I mean, they are *red.*"

The Bowen School had a rule that forbid us from wearing
any hue of red or any color with red in it, like orange, purple, or

pink; it was something about their not wanting us to look like Christmas trees, what with our green skirts, and all. I shrugged off India's concerns.

As soon as I opened the bathroom door and stepped outside, Elijah breezed past me. He carried an old-fashioned briefcase, and his tiny round glasses called to my mind a first-year law student at the University of Michigan in the fall of 1962. In my memory, a gentle mist soared past my eyes, clouding my vision, but in retrospect it was probably just a puff of India's perfume.

He'd passed me but then suddenly turned sharply, just as he had the last time we'd met. His eyes immediately shot down to my feet. My chest tightened. I silently berated myself for staring at him, but I couldn't look away. His eyes returned from my shoes to my face. He studied me.

"The revolution marches on," he said.

"It marches," I said.

We hadn't broken eye contact in what felt like four minutes. My heart pounded. I didn't know what to do with my shoulders, my hands, my knees. My whole body felt like it was hanging wrong. So I cocked my head, turned on the non-heel of my flats, and strode away, heart hammering. India scurried behind me, quietly exclaiming, "Oh my God! Oh my God!"

Readers, I was acting more confident than I felt. Maybe it was because while exfoliating my feet the night before, I'd listened to the Shangri-Las and felt empowered. Maybe it was because, even then, I could see that although Elijah looked like a baby bird, a) he was a *man*, b) he was *my teacher (sort of)*, c) those things, in combination, were a certain amount of thrilling, d) the whole baby bird thing was, like, intentional and also a *look that suggested emotional depth and intuition*, and e) I was extremely into it.

In the beginning of October, the Tutorial debuted, and Elijah was assigned to be my Tutor. I wasn't surprised by this development. I was sure he'd request me, just as I'd requested him. After pairing us up, Dr. Levin, my history teacher, allowed us to find locations outside of school that were convenient for both Tutor and Tutee. Elijah and I settled on Thursdays at Margot Patisserie, south of my family's apartment on West Seventy-Ninth Street and his dorm at Columbia.

Before our first meeting, I stopped home and changed into something I thought was more suitable for the occasion: a light blue dress with slightly puffed sleeves that made me feel like a rebellious sister wife. I paired the dress with striped pastel sandals that the brand Classique had made in the eighties, fluffed my hair, and applied rouge to my cheeks on the elevator down to my lobby.

My doorman, Saul, gave me a look when I stepped out of the elevator. I strode out the door and walked leisurely to the café. Elijah was sitting at a table by the window. I approached him.

"*Gediere uff re Bauerei,*" he said, without missing a beat.

My mouth dropped open. "You speak Pennsylvania Dutch?"

He laughed. "Just a few phrases."

"What did you just say?"

"'Animals on the farm.'"

"Where'd you pick that up?"

He took a long sip of his cappuccino.

"A place called the Quare Academy," he said.

"What's that?"

He leaned back in his chair and smiled slightly. "It's a long story."

I tilted my head, waiting for an explanation, but he just opened his briefcase and slid a stack of papers toward me.

"Let's get to it," he said.

We spent the hour talking about peasants in medieval Europe. Elijah knew his history, and despite the flirty stuff that had happened before, when the boy got down to business, he really got down to it. Seeing his intellectual side—in particular, the way he pushed up his glasses and gesticulated wildly when he got excited about the effect of rocky soil on England's economy—made heat rise to my face. When I got home, I tore off my clothes and took a long bath, watching my heartbeat send tiny ripples through the water. If you're familiar with the works of Judy Blume, you'll understand me when I say that I identify with Deenie on a deep level.

So this is where we begin: me, naked and in love in the bathtub, like many a tragic protagonist before me.

I've assembled the documents that follow to make sense of the year that ensued. But maybe *sense* is the wrong word. The year still avoids, in my mind, any sort of stark understanding.

Compiled from my own collection and those of my friends, this project gives a glimpse into the complicated process by which I went from loving Elijah to, if not always loving myself, then at least maybe *becoming* myself. Taken together, the pieces are a portrait of a jumbled contradiction of a person and a place not in their final forms, but very much in progress. One of my aims here is certainly to tell a story. But assembling this collection is really about seeing that story happen in just the way it happened, in all its urgency and all its absurdity.

Part 1

Elijah's uniform:

- *Cuffed, slim-fitting jeans*
- *Dusty brown Blundstones*
- *White T-shirt paired with open flannel jacket*
- *Tiny round glasses*
- *Briefcase*
- *Camera on strap on shoulder*

Elijah on his favorite album, Sean Kingston's 2007 Sean Kingston: *"It's so fucking chill."*

I'm such a confused and sweaty mess right now. Mum and Daddy have been screaming at each other all night about money—it all started when Mum bought those almonds with turbinado sugar, which Daddy deemed to be an extravagance, to which she replied, "WHY DO I WORK SO HARD, ARNOLD, IF I CAN'T HAVE NICE THINGS?" *and then they started this awful argument about why his dental practice is thriving while her obstetrics one is floundering, and now Lael and I are holed up in my room, eating red grapes. Lael is seething. She just put in earplugs to finish her early action application to Harvard. I can't focus on pre-calc right now, so I'm journaling instead.*

When I told Elijah on Thursday that Mum and Daddy have been having awful fights, he just listened for a long time, silently. Then he rose from his seat wordlessly, but with the most delicious little smirk, and bought me a single pink macaron at the counter with a crumpled dollar from his leather wallet. He set the plate down in front of me.

"For the girl who has everything," he said. His smirk reached a breaking point, and his face erupted in a smile.

I wanted to DIE. But also live, you know?

Journal entry, October 18

Oh my God. I just got home from an Elijah meeting, and I am FREAKING out.

Let me start from the beginning.

After we'd settled at a table, he thumped a packet of readings on the table but rested his big hand on it, keeping me from reaching for it.

"Have you ever been photographed?" he asked.

"I mean, yeah," I said. "Hasn't everyone?"

He just shook his head. He wasn't smiling this time, and I shifted around in my seat.

God, he's so intense. I would do anything for him.

"I mean by a professional," he said. "In an artistic way."

"I don't think so."

"You'd know if you had."

"I haven't."

"Can I shoot you?"

His eye contact was sending electric signals to my chest, making my heart beat funny. I had to look away, so I did, down at my calf-length light denim skirt.

"What did you have in mind?" I asked when I'd gathered the strength to look up at him again.

I was flirting with danger at this point, and I knew it. I was nervous, but I was also wearing a vintage Prada blouse (for which I'd paid twenty-eight dollars at a consignment shop, naturally), so I felt a bit unstoppable.

"I'm asking if I can take a series of photographs of you in various outfits for a project I'm doing," he said.

I paused. The moment stretched out before us like a strand of a spiderweb.

"Yes," I said. And then: "Why?"

He laughed. "You have such a look about you," he said. "The clothes themselves, but also the way you wear them. You're, like, reclaiming them somehow. I think it'll translate well on film."

My neck burned. Is there anything quite as delicious as a physical compliment? I don't think there is, and definitely nothing better from Elijah.

"I still haven't seen any of your work," I said.

He rummaged in his back pocket for his phone and extracted it, tapping with concentration. Finally he held it out for me. I stared at the screen. A pale girl with long, shining white hair floated on her back, arms akimbo, in a high-waisted white bikini. White-blond hair glimmered on her legs, under her arms, at the edges of the crotch of her bikini bottoms. Two mossy, dirt-speckled lily pads floated beside her. There was something hauntingly beautiful about the photo. My chest tightened.

"Who is she?" I asked.

"She's a photographer, "I shot her first," he said. "This was last year. Before she got into taking her own photos."

I looked into the girl's big green eyes, which pooled with tears. The name came to me at once.

"I totally know who she is," I said. "She's Ursula Abbot, right?"

Ursula Abbot was one of my favorite feminist Instagram artists. She basically argued, with beautiful shots of her looking sad in mirrors, in hospital beds (Urusla had a life-threatening illness and documented her doctors' visits), and in Victorian backyards, that being visibly sad—emotional, moody, diseased, *upset*—was political and liberating in a world that shames girls for their sorrows about sexism and sickness, about the demands society places on women. That being an unhappy girl could reshape the very idea of sickness itself, exposing it as a capitalist project and crafting it into a weapon against the patriarchy.

After agreeing to meet Elijah at the entrance to Central Park, I ran home, a scream scratching at my throat, and took another bath to hold my body. In the bath I prayed, "Dear Jesus, please, please, make him fall in love with me."

After drying off, I pulled out my laptop and typed "Elijah Huck" into Google. And Elijah Huck, it turned out, was kind of a Big Fucking Deal. I mean, he was hardly a national celebrity, or whatever, but he'd made headlines in the independent online magazine from *Oyster* ("Elijah Huck Documents Upper-Class Underworld"), the teen feminist magazine *Nymphette* ("Urban Hipst-onary: A Conversation with Up-and-Coming Photographer Elijah Huck"), and even a *New York Times* live piece called "Too Cool for Instagram (But on It Anyway)."

Nymphette, by the way, will become much more important later on in the story.

I didn't tell my friends. They would have called him a creep or something (but he wasn't that much older than we were! Only nineteen to our sixteen! And his age was part of what made him so attractive). Like one of my idols, *Clueless*'s Cher Horowitz, I'd made it my policy not to date high-school boys. (Not that I really even *knew* any high-school boys, on account of going to Bowen, but that was beside the point.)

He told me to wear whatever I wanted to the shoot, so the night before, I tried on every item of clothing in my closet for Lael, my sister, who sat on my bed, eating chocolate soy milk ice cream from the carton. She wasn't impressed—by Elijah or by my outfits.

"So he's into your clothes," she said. "Is he gay?"

I shook my head. He'd mentioned a high-school girlfriend, a Polish immigrant named Ivana who'd been a math whiz and, as it had turned out later, a lesbian, a fact he'd shared while trying to illustrate a point about the Wars of the Roses.

"Not gay," I said. "And besides, it wouldn't matter. I'm not interested in him *romantically*. Also, way to dabble in tropes, Lael."

Lael just laughed.

I finally settled on a short apricot shift dress and a matching coat (both made in 1958; I'd bought the set on Etsy from an old woman in Idaho) that didn't make Lael want to gouge her eyes out with her ice cream spoon, which she'd almost done earlier when I put on a busy green Marimekko dress. (About that number, she'd declared, "Pregnant art teacher.")

In hindsight, the coat was a little bit too heavy for the weather. I arrived at the entrance to the Park ten minutes late (my 1950s guidebook called "So You Want Him to Pin You"—not that I wanted Elijah to pin me *yet*, of course—cautioned against punctuality, and though as a proud feminist I obviously read it *ironically,* it wasn't like I was about to read good advice and *ignore it*), sweating more than I cared for him to see.

I saw him before he saw me. He was adjusting the lens of his camera, squinting in the sun a little bit and pursing his lips. I took a deep, shaky breath. I waited until he saw me and waved me over, slowly nodding approval at my outfit.

He photographed me on the street first. It was more awkward than I'd expected to be photographed: I felt like I had to hold my breath the whole time, and I had to make sure none of my limbs were at funny angles. Besides, it was a weekend morning, and the streets were flooded with tourists. People around us stared. A few tourists photo-bombed us, especially as we headed toward Fifth

Avenue, as though we were a famous art monster couple or something.

The shoot lasted for a few hours, into the early afternoon, and it seemed natural to get lunch in a Le Pain Quotidien that had just opened on Fifty-Ninth Street.

It was there, over a vegan fall tart that we shared, that he told me his idea: instead of taking an entire series of photos and uploading them to the portfolio on his website, he'd create a blog in order to share the images every week. The goal was to drum up a robust fan following on social media, a career move his mentor had been urging him to make. I agreed, with two caveats: one, that he couldn't tell anybody that the photos were of me (he agreed to always cover my face somehow, with a big hat or my hair or a sign of some sort), and two, that he had to expand on the Pennsylvania Dutch thing, which I hadn't been able to stop thinking about ever since he'd told me.

"You really want to know?" he asked, setting his fork down on his plate.

I nodded.

"Remember when I told you about the Quare Academy?"

I nodded again.

"That's where I went for my last two years of high school."

"Is it in Amish Country, or something?"

He laughed. "No, no," he said. "It's in upstate New York. In the Hudson Valley. It's an alternative farm school where you learn peace studies and global issues and environmentalism instead of normal English and history and science."

"So how did you know the phrase?"

"Quare offered an elective in Pennsylvania Dutch. Accompanied by a narrative history seminar, part of which took place in Amish Country."

I swallowed a laugh. "That's the long story you couldn't get into before?"

He nodded, crossing his arms. "Are you going to back out of the blog now that you're not satisfied with my answer to your question?"

I pretended to think about it.

It took us a few tries, and a few soy lattes, but we finally settled on the concept. He laughed as he typed out the first post, hyperbolic and wry. Of course he wasn't taking this seriously. He was too cool for that in his flannel and cuffed jeans. He pressed publish. We each took a bite of éclair.

The first Miss Tulip blog post, October 21

misstulipblog.com

HOME   SEARCH   ARCHIVES   PRESS   CONTACT

INTRODUCING MISS TULIP: *A* IS FOR *AUTUMN* AND *APRICOTS*

<      >

Photos c/o Elijah Huck
Click to navigate through photo album

Jenny Fran Davis

Meet Miss Tulip, a teenager who has made it her mission to dress every day like it's 1958. Before you roll your eyes and shake your fist at the whims of this generation, or worry about troubling nostalgia for pre-Civil-Rights-Era America, hear—or, more accurately, watch— her out. You might just be surprised.

I met up with Miss Tulip at the entrance to Central Park on West Fifty-Ninth Street. She showed up in this matching apricot dress and coat from the waning days of the Eisenhower administration, as well as a pillbox hat that she'd informed me had been dyed to match by her tailor on Third Avenue.

The thing about Miss T is that at first glance, she could be the type to reinforce a classic femininity that conjures baking casseroles and darning socks. She's got an in with every vintage retailer in New York. She has an honorary PhD in accessorizing. But don't be fooled by her demure exterior: Miss Tulip is a *rebel*. Recontextualizing outfits from an era plagued by even more bigotry than our own throws the gazer into a new incarnation of the constructed feminine, one informed by, yet working to liberate itself from, its past.

But the clothes are only half of it. After the shoot, we discussed intersectional feminism and modern-day settler colonialism over coffee, two keen interests of Miss T's: at the surface, she's pure 1958, but inside beats the heart of a *Jezebel* editor.

THE LOOK: 1950s WOOL SHEATH-STYLE APRICOT DRESS | |
MATCHING COLLARED COAT | | BLACK STOCKINGS | |
BLACK FLAT SHOES | | CAT-EYE SUNGLASSES | |
APRICOT PILLBOX HAT (DYED TO MATCH)
SETTING: CENTRAL PARK | | WEST FIFTY-NINTH STREET

Daily Elijah interactions:

8 a.m.: The Spence Room, at breakfast, eating half a bagel and sipping coffee.

My heart starts to hammer, and I make a point to pass the table he's at—with a few other teachers, usually, but sometimes alone, sometimes writing in a little notebook—and if he doesn't look up and smile at me the first time, I walk by again and again until he does. If he beckons me over to the table he's at, I make a point to gesture at myself, all fake-surprised, like, Me??? and he laughs and I walk toward him. On the walk, I can't feel the ground under my feet, probably because my toes have gone numb.

1:30 p.m.: Dr. Levin's class, which he sometimes leads.

I literally can't sit still when he comes to observe in Dr. Levin's class. I'm so aware of everything. I've never felt so alive. But it's the kind of alive where I feel like I'm about to die—that's how alive I feel. I can't sleep. My heart is beating too fast. Everyone's voice sounds tinny, like when music plays on a computer.

3 p.m.: Dismissal, when I stroll past Dr. Levin's room to watch Elijah collecting his stuff and preparing to leave.

Which isn't really even that creepy, if you think about it. I mean, I could be a Peeping Tom, or something.

4:30 p.m.: every Thursday: our meeting on the Upper West Side.

On Thursday, at our meeting, he told me about this super-emotionally damaging relationship he was in during high school (post-Ivana) after I gave him a Mum-and-Daddy update, and we just sat smiling at each other behind our lattes despite the pain that we'd just shared. He's just so in touch with his emotions and gets so sad despite the cool front he puts up!!! I have it SO BAD.

He's taking a year off from Columbia next year to teach

an elective on the history of violence at Quare, the peace-
environmentalism-and-arts boarding school he graduated from. So
that means he won't be around next year. The thought of not seeing
him at least twice a week makes me want to die. I hope by that time
I'll have convinced him not to leave, but that's kind of creepy, so I'll
keep that to myself for now.

I want him every hour of the day.

God, if anyone found this journal, I would absolutely DIE. Is
there anything more humiliating than being in love?

Profile in LOTUS magazine, mid-December

TO A T(W)EE:
NEW ARTIST AND MUSE TAKE CENTER STAGE

There's a new sheriff in town, and her name is Miss Tulip. She's
taken off like wildfire, especially with the teen set—specifically,
with teens who've eschewed Forever 21 in exchange for thrift
stores. Elijah Huck, who's made a name for himself in indie
photography, receives over one hundred emails per day about
the series, most of them gushing with praise and thanks for
giving them a fashion resource they can relate to.

In the past few weeks, the *Miss Tulip* blog has spurred doz-
ens of copycats, including *Hex in the City* (a Wiccan teen, Lula
Mikelson, wanders New York in vintage gothic attire performing rituals), *PEARLS* (four young women clad only in pearls
pose with Park Avenue doormen from Seventeenth Street to
the Bronx), and *The Wizard of Bras* (a young designer of feminist lingerie dresses statues of men in all five boroughs in her
custom bras and underwear).

Huck's posts, which regularly attract thousands of visitors, are unique in their ability to evoke both modernity and antiquity, as well as provide a tentative explanation—a subtle one—about why today's young people look to the past for answers about their identities and their futures.

Journal entry from December 22

I haven't even told India and Cora about him, because they'd definitely tell me to snap out of it. Every time something gets written up about Elijah and Miss Tulip, I feel such a sense of pride, but it's PRIVATE pride—like an intimate thing between Elijah and me.
Elijah fantasies:

- *We're in the Met. He pulls me off to the side, into some deserted corner, and starts kissing me.*
- *I'm standing in front of an ornate bookcase, studying it, hand on my chin. He comes up from behind and drapes himself over me. I spin around; we kiss.*
- *We're on the subway. He reaches for my hand; I let him hold it. I look down at my lap and smile. There is electricity at the line where our legs touch.*

Let me pause here and say that I know this seems like the most trivial, most bourgeoisie shit ever. I mean, a *hipster fashion blog* in which I *dress in clothes from 1958*? Please don't lose heart, readers. This was my *old* life, remember. It's as painful for me to relive this time as it is for you to hear about it, if not more so.

Anyway, I was his muse, but he wasn't in love with me. Or was he? Therein lay the problem. He wanted to follow me around the city, photographing me in vintage clothes. He called me interesting. He listened to my problems and opened up about his. He told me that I could really rock a Jackie Kennedy head scarf and that I knew a thing or two about tastefully pairing prints. AND YET. He didn't invite me over to his 107th Street apartment to kiss me. He didn't even touch me, not even once to adjust me during a photo shoot. We took the subway together on weekends from Brooklyn to Manhattan to Queens, even rode the Staten Island Ferry together, but he didn't so much as put his arm around me. There was always a thin barrier between us, which I chalked up to his position of power. And although sometimes this barrier was made of metal, sometimes it was made of a gauze that seemed thin enough to tear.

Let me pause again for one more minute. At age sixteen, just as now, I was a *fucking woman*. It wasn't that I needed his approval to exist. Even in this time of frissons and jittery stomachs, I knew my power without Elijah. I didn't need him to kiss me. I just really *wanted* him to, and that wild desire made my body feel like it was on fire. I was in love, and it was the kind of love that made me forget myself.

So he didn't kiss me, but he talked to me. He told me countless hilarious stories about Quare, academically rigorous and socially conscious, and encouraged me to apply, albeit in a buoyant, slightly jocular way. Until eleventh grade, he'd attended Westwood, Bowen's prestigious brother school. (Quare was for students in the eleventh and twelfth grades only.) He'd grown frustrated, just as I was growing frustrated, with the stuffy, pretentious private school scene. (Even though I would never say that out loud.)

And as I'd mentioned in my journal, he'd be taking the following year off from Columbia to teach photography at Quare. We'd be interesting *together*. Cue fantasy of us picnicking and reading subversive literature in a field. Cue fantasy of Elijah realizing how adventurous I was, professing his love, and kissing me, preferably in a canoe, on a pond at sunset.

One thing happened after another, and before I knew it, I was asking for recommendations and writing my application essay for Quare about the need to make adoption more accessible to same-sex couples.

My acceptance letter

The Quare Academy

Flora Goldwasser
470 West 79th Street, Apt. 5A
New York, NY 10024

April 10

Flora,

On behalf of the Quare admissions committee and faculty, I'm thrilled to offer you a spot in the class of 20— Quare received a record number of close to 250 applications for just 16 spots, and it's a testament to your ambition, creativity, and curiosity that you've been selected.

Please sign and return the enclosed document, along with a preliminary deposit, by May 10 if you wish to attend Quare next year. Please also feel free to call our office should you have any questions at all; I or another member of our team would be delighted to speak with you.

Infinite blessings,
Miriam Row, Headmistress

As soon as I got the letter, I knew that I would go.

Elijah would be going to Chicago to spend the summer as he always did, studying under his photography mentor, the famous Michael Rosenberg, at Chicago Arts, and I'd be interning at Sotheby's.

I hardly heard from him all summer; he was busy in Chicago. So I did my Sotheby's internship, ate my last Maison Kayser macarons with Cora and India—who still couldn't wrap their heads around why I was doing this; I told them I was bored at Bowen and needed an adventure, which I could tell they didn't quite buy, but what could they say?—and packed my nicest dresses, skirts, and shoes—along with my portable mint-green Underwood Olivetti typewriter to compose letters on the go—into two huge steamer trunks.

What follows are the letters, journal entries, and other sundry items from my first year at Quare Academy, where I had gone to follow my One True Love (or for the adventure, depending on who was asking).

But first, the last ever Miss Tulip blog post, from April 30

BREAKING PLAID: RED, WHITE, AND TULIP

<   >

Photos c/o Elijah Huck
Click to navigate through photo album

Morning, cool cats. Miss Tulip woke up feeling a little bit glum, but after stepping into this plaid skirt suit (courtesy of the year 1958), her day got brighter. A whole lot brighter. It's not that she's *materialistic*, or anything, but she knows the power of a smartly cut suit.

And why today to bust out such a number? The three-quarter sleeves are just right for spring, and the fabric is swingy and breezy. But good luck getting your hands on one: the make is Mode O'Day, and Miss T has one of the very last ones ever manufactured. As usual, she knew a guy. What can we say? Not all of us can be so lucky or so fabulous.

Miss Tulip will be on hiatus indefinitely due to her various other social, academic, and political engagements. From both of us, subject and her documentarian, thank you for being such a rapt and reverent audience for these past months. Miss Tulip might be going away for the moment, but keep your eyes open as you wander the streets of Manhattan. You just might find her.

THE LOOK: SKIRT SUIT (COLOR: RED-AND-WHITE PLAID) | |
BROWN STOCKINGS | | BROWN-AND-RED JAPANESE SCHOOL SHOES (RETRO) | |
RED-AND-WHITE-CHECKERED PURSE | | CAT-EYE SUNGLASSES | |
SKINNY BROWN WATCH
SETTING: RIVERSIDE PARK | | MORNINGSIDE HEIGHTS

74 THOUGHTS ON "BREAKING PLAID: RED, WHITE, AND TULIP"

PastelsnPrints MAY 30 7:57 A.M.
WHAT THE FUCK WHY IS MISS TULIP NO MOREEEEE :((((((

Rebel MAY 30 8:46 A.M.
I'M OBSESSED WITH MISS TULIP UGH WHY HAVE YOU NOT POSTED SINCE APRIL

VivianXoXo MAY 30 8:51 A.M.
I think I'm sadder about Miss Tulip's disappearance than I was about my own grandmother's death.

SexyGayKitty MAY 30 11:59 A.M.
Yesssssss Miss T at it again. Looking DAMN good too.

Load 70 more

Letter from Lorelei Winkle, Headmistress of the
Bowen School for Girls

The Bowen School for Girls
A note from the headmistress

Flora Goldwasser
470 West 79th Street, Apt. 5A
New York, NY 10024

June 8

Dear Flora,

It has been my distinct pleasure to serve as your headmistress for the past eleven years. I'm writing to express my regret that you're leaving us at the end of this school year, and also to wish you the best of luck in the future.

Bowen is accustomed to sending girls to institutions such as the Phillips Andover Academy and the Groton School when they choose to depart for boarding school, so I was surprised to learn of your choice. I am not familiar with Quare (though our college guidance team assures me that its college entrance rate is nothing short of spectacular!). I wonder if Bowen, too, might benefit from including Peace Studies and World Issues in its curriculum—you'll have to let us know how it goes.

Perhaps the most bittersweet part of my job is saying farewell to girls I've come to know over the years, especially when those girls are, like you, among our brightest stars, but I am confident that you will find a home at Quare. We hope you keep in touch!

Fondly,
Lorelei Winkle, Headmistress

My Final Bowen report card

The Bowen School for Girls

Final Upper School Report for Flora Goldwasser, Class 10

Precalculus	A	History	A
Orchestra	A	History Tutorial	A
Chemistry	A	French	A
English	A	Drama	A
Physical Education	A	Community Engagement	A

To: Lael Goldwasser <lgoldwasser@bowen.edu>
From: Flora Goldwasser <fgoldwasser@bowen.edu>
Subject: Ugh
June 12, 8:17 a.m.

Lael,

I can't believe this is the last email either of us will send or receive with our Bowen email addresses. And I really can't believe you're already in England. Summer hasn't even begun yet.

I'm getting the weirdest vibes from Elijah. After your graduation, he bolted without saying good-bye. I mean, I'll probably see him around over the summer, and if not, then once we get to Quare in the fall, but still. He is just SUCH a baby bird (like, a hot and confident one), and it scares me how v. v. into it I am. I can't even blame him for acting weird, you know? He's a brilliant artist. He can't exactly be expected to be tethered in any meaningful way to this world, or any petty romances it might contain.

By the way, your graduation was beautiful, your dress was beautiful, and I'm so proud of you. I can't believe you refused to come out to Les Deux with me and India and Cora—we celebrated YOUR graduation without YOU, because you needed to sleep before your flight. You are such an old woman sometimes.

Keep me posted about how it's going at Oxford! I'll be here relaxing as Mum and Daddy throw vases at each other.

Xoxo

Flora

To: Flora Goldwasser <fgoldwasser@bowen.edu>
From: Lael Goldwasser <lgoldwasser@bowen.edu>
Subject: Re: Ugh
June 13, 5:19 p.m.

Flora,

I didn't say anything before, because I was a little bit preoccupied with graduating and also didn't want you to strangle me, but I'm having worse and worse doubts about this whole Quare thing the more you talk about it. So I waited until I got to Oxford to say this.

Don't go to Quare.

You always get these romantic notions in your head about things, and usually, it's charming. But this—following some wimp to this hippie school to make him love you—might take the cake. And his limpid good-bye at graduation doesn't bode well for the future. Abandon it while you still can. Talk to Lorelei Winkle; she'll take you back in a flash. Daddy will be so happy, and Mum will be miserable, which is pretty much worth it in itself. Let Elijah go to Quare alone. It's his home, not yours, and I have a strong feeling that you'll regret this.

I know you're not going to listen to me, but this is my official advice. I'm printing this email now, in fact, so I can tell you the exact day and time that I (quite rightly) warned you about this foolhardy thing you're about to do.

Your adoring sister,
Lael

To: Lael Goldwasser <lael.goldwasser@gmail.com>
From: Flora Goldwasser <flora.goldwasser@gmail.com>
Subject: Ugh
June 13, 9:30 p.m.

Lael! He is not a wimp. I really wish you would stop saying that. Do all men have to be muscle-bound blocks of emotionless concrete? He's SENSITIVE, for God's sake. Stop acting like this is some sort of crime. And read something by Judith Butler about gender, while you're at it. (*Gender Trouble* is my summer reading for Quare, and to be fair, I've only read the back cover, but STILL. Get with the program.)

And please, would you calm the hell down about Quare? It will be an adventure, if nothing else. It's not like I'm doing it SOLELY to be with Elijah, or anything. Jesus Christ.

F

Text received from Elijah on August 24

hey flora, just a heads-up, i decided to stay at columbia this yr & won't be coming to quare after all. but i'm planning to come visit in dec. let's do one last miss t shoot!

The Quare Academy

Flora Goldwasser
470 West 79th Street, Apt. 5A
New York, NY 10024

August 24

Flora,

As the broccoli and cabbage appear aboveground, the eggplant bursts onto the landscape purple and ripe, and the mint springs up in succulent pockets, we prepare ourselves to welcome the sixty-second class of Quare students. You are a member of one of our most vibrant classes yet: sixteen dreamers, poets, dancers, environmentalists, knitters, milkers, and activists selected from twelve states and two countries among hundreds of applicants.

Yesterday, our child, Basilia, mewed at the first sliver of tooth poking through her gums, and we laughed that the first of the visitors had already arrived. We were reminded that with every change comes the possibility for strife, and we invite you to embrace whatever insecurity you might be feeling in the days leading up to your arrival on campus.

I am delighted to inform you that you will be living with Juna Díaz, who hails from Santa Fe, New Mexico. I advise you not to pack more than a couple of bags' worth of belongings: the "love shacks," as we call our cabins, are rather cozy.

We very much look forward to meeting you and celebrating your story.

Infinite blessings,
Miriam

The Frequently Asked Questions page of Quare's website

quare.edu/about/index.html

FREQUENTLY ASKED QUESTIONS

What is Quare?

The Quare Academy is a two-year residential, college preparatory boarding school for students in eleventh and twelfth grades focused on environmentalism, the arts, peace studies, and global issues. Quare occupies 420 acres in the Hudson Valley region of upstate New York.

What are the classes like?

The Quare Academy assigns work at the college level. Five academically rigorous, seminar-style courses yield credit in English, government and economics, math, science, and language, through a combination of research and hands-on experience. In addition, each student earns elective credits that include feminist forms, ethics and the environment, permaculture seminar, and art activism. Students may also choose to take one independent study course during each semester.

What qualities do you look for in prospective students?
High school students entering their eleventh- or twelfth-grade years are admitted based on their academic records, service work, recommendations, and extracurricular activities as they demonstrate motivation, aptitude, and achievement. Specifically, Quare seeks students who feel called to come here—called to challenge themselves, called to engage with the world's ills, and called to join a radically inclusive community of dreamers and thinkers. Admissions cap at twenty students.

Where will I live?
Students live in two-person A-frame cabins circling Quare Pond. The cabins contain a small sofa, a wood-burning stove, shelves for books, and desk space, as well as a drying rack.

Where is Quare located?
Quare is located roughly twenty miles from Woodstock, New York. The town of Main Stream, which is home to just over one thousand residents, is rich in history and culture; many artists, peacemakers, and farmers reside here. Just a five-minute drive, or a twenty-minute hike, to the Hudson River, Quare is fortunate to call such a scenic pocket of New York home.

Where do graduates go to college?
In the past five years, Quare graduates have matriculated Bard College, Brown University, Columbia University, Grinnell College, Harvard University, Macalester College, Northwestern University, Oberlin College, Pitzer College, Pomona College, Reed College, Smith College, Stanford University, Swarthmore College, the University of California at Berkeley and Los Angeles, the University of Chicago, Vassar College, Wesleyan University, Williams College, and Yale University.

How can I communicate with my friends and family?
Because of our limited bandwidth, Quare students in their first year
can email anyone with a Quare email address using our internal
server; however, to communicate with friends and family off campus,
we encourage these students to call or write letters. Second-years can
send and receive email both internally and externally.

The Quare Academy | 2 Quare Road, Main Stream, NY 12497 | 846-552-1304

Journal entry from August 24, minutes after the text message

*I feel like I'm on a trolley speeding down a hill. And for once I
don't even feel like I'm being dramatic in that comparison. I'm going
to QUARE in a few days, and it's entirely too late to back out. I'm
really GOING, and he's not going to be there after all.*

*Holy FUCKING shit. I can't back out. I can't. My stuff is
packed. The papers are signed. I have a roommate and everything,
according to a letter from the headmistress.*

*And now that I think about it, there was that weird look Elijah
gave me in the early days after my acceptance—a look that at the
time I interpreted as adoration, but which now seems a little bit off,
somewhere between a gas pain and a "this is awkward."*

*I'm trying so hard to remain calm. I have three candles burning,
and my blinds are closed so I can't see my creepy across-the-street
neighbor Mr. Cheney. But there's this awful weight in my stomach
that even the lemon-lime seltzer I picked up on the way home isn't
helping. I don't know what to do other than curl up in a ball and cry.
I feel so stupid and pitiful.*

To: Flora Goldwasser <flora.goldwasser@gmail.com>
From: Emma Engelbrecht Goldwasser <emma.goldwasser@
downtown-obgyn.com>
Subject: onward!
August 26, 7:18 a.m.

Darling,

I'm ever so sorry that I won't be able to come with Daddy to drop
you off at Quare. I know you understand, but I hope you aren't
too sad about it. It was absolutely crucial that I spend this week
in West Virginia. The people I've met here in the more depressed
bits of Appalachia are nothing short of heroes: in the face of
mountaintop removal, chronic asthma, and rampant Oxycontin
addiction, they nonetheless find the will and the grace to go on.

And so will you. The future is bright, darling. I am thrilled that you
agree Quare is a much more suitable environment than Bowen,
and I commend you for taking my complaints about Dr. Winkle all
these years to heart—really, her unrelenting focus on Advanced
Placement classes and etiquette seminars denies you the most
important part of yourself: your individuality. I'm so proud of you
for finding this place, and I know that it will soon feel like home.

Love always,
Mum

Lael Goldwasser

Harvard College

2609 Harvard Yard Mail Center

Cambridge, MA 02138

August 29

Lael,

I didn't back out. Even after getting that text from him. I think I was in a state of shock, and besides, my trunks were packed.

So I'm here. At Quare. It's actually happening.

I was one of the first ones here, of course, at least as far as I could tell, because Daddy forced us to leave the city at about five forty-five in the morning, even though I told him about a hundred times that it's only a two-hour drive. So we got here at the crack of dawn, just in time to hear a rooster howling. I'm kidding, but just barely. As we neared Quare, I hardly opened my eyes, not only because I was so tired, but also because I didn't really want to see it—something about seeing it would make it real, I guess.

It isn't that I wish it weren't real, per se. But I've been a bundle of anxiety for weeks, and I simply couldn't deal with the sight of a dirt road at seven in the morning.

And Daddy was so quiet on the drive up here. I mean, it's not that he's usually such a great conversationalist, but he didn't even offer the obvious statement-nod combinations he usually does ("Red house. Blue sky"). I had no idea what to say to him, either, because we hadn't exactly been chatting it up all summer.

Thanks, by the way, for leaving me to deal with Mum and Daddy while you did whatever you do with test tubes at Oxford.

I feel like Daddy's depressed; the divorce funk is only going to get worse now that we're both at school. It wasn't lost on me that he's driving directly to his new house in Rye on his way back from dropping me here. I don't even want to know what the house looks like—I can only assume it has gray walls and a solitary toothbrush (and single tongue brush and single floss container and single tub of mouthwash, of course) in the medicine cabinet. Oh, and maybe a single bottle of Prozac, assuming that he goes to see Dr. Modarressi like I urged him to.

Wow, that image got really harrowing, really fast.

Anyway, I should probably finish—or start—unpacking. Daddy didn't really stick around after helping me get all my stuff into the cabin. We hugged a little, he told me he loved me, and then he was just . . . gone. I felt superlight and had no idea where to put myself, so I sat down and wrote to you.

Can you tell me about Harvard, please? I'm dying to know whether your roommate is really as mousy (in a good way!!) as she seemed online.

XOXO,
Flora

India Katz-Rosen
1025 Fifth Avenue, Apt. 9C
New York, NY 10028

August 30

Dear India,

Do you remember those macarons we used to get from the Seventy-fourth Street Maison Kayser?

Well, I've been having dreams about them.

They fall somewhere between *Casablanca* and that old French movie that Madame Leflore had to turn off because of all the boobs.

I'd definitely rather make out with a macaron than with that old French guy with the weird mole on his face.

You might be wondering why I'm fantasizing about macarons. I can answer that in one word: *quinoa*. Want another? *Kale*.

It's not that I have anything against quinoa. Or kale, for that matter. You know that I enjoyed a spring quinoa salad in the Bowen cafeteria as much as any other girl. And I can't even count the number of times I've opted to add kale into a smoothie at Juice Gen. But it's gotten to the point—and I know it's only been two days, and I should be grateful that we have food to eat, blah, blah, blah—that if I am forced to eat either of these things one more time, I might just lose it, and we both know that my losing it is not something anybody wants to see.

I'll stop talking about food now so you don't put this letter down and watch a video tutorial on doing milkmaid braids, or something, as I know you are wont to do when you're bored.

(I promise I won't tell anyone if you get a prescription for some Adderall. You can reach Dr. Modarressi at 212.547.8923. He got Cora a Xanax prescription when that thing with her dad happened—has that blown over yet, by the way?—and he's superconfidential. Call him, India.)

Oh my God. I just remembered those thin little pizzas we used to get at Sal's on Friday afternoons. Please tell our cute Italian waiter that I miss him. Maybe make it sound like I had some sort of romantic mental breakdown, à la Natalie Wood as Wilma Dean Loomis in *Splendor in the Grass,* instead of the truth, which is decidedly less glamorous.

So anyway, after Daddy dropped me off at Quare like a sack of moldy carrots and then drove off into the sunrise, I was left with two choices: to meet my new classmates or to unpack my stuff.

Obviously, I chose the latter—not because I didn't want to meet new people (okay, if I'm being perfectly honest, I didn't really want to meet new people), but because I had to do SOMETHING to make the crapshack I'm living in more palatable.

Honestly, Inds, you wouldn't believe what it looks like in here. You would be back in your mom's car the minute you peeked your little blond head inside. When I tell you it's rustic, I mean it's rustic—but not in the posh, house-in-the-mountains-of-Colorado way. It's rustic in the shack-in-godforsaken-upstate-New-York-hippie-school kind of way. Not cute.

My pile of bags alone took up most of the floor space. I felt a bit sheepish about having brought so much stuff. It took me and Daddy about twelve trips to retrieve all the little odds and ends I brought. But seriously, like I was going to leave my collection of scents at home? I know it weighs about three hundred pounds, but I swore on the day that we left New York that I would not let myself go, and I stand by that promise. There was this one small suitcase lying on the other bed—my roommate's, I assumed— but there was no further trace of her.

By the way, I've decided to refer to the cabins exclusively as "hovels" from now on. Technically they're "love shacks," for the purpose of "community building" and "honest and judgment-free expression," but really they're hovels. We're talking creaky wooden floors, cobwebby corners, and mildewed mattresses. I opened all the windows to get a cross breeze going, but somehow that just made it worse, maybe because I'm downwind from the communal bathrooms.

But I mobilized quickly. A lone tapestry, probably left by some druggy kid in the seventies, hung from the ceiling when I got there, but I quickly took it down and repurposed it as a dust rag. (And thank God, because otherwise I would have had to untie my silk head scarf—and use that instead.)

Oh, and there was also a squashed beanbag chair, which I imagined reeked of urine—I held my nose as I tossed it unceremoniously out the door, so I didn't actually smell it—perched in the corner like a socially awkward party guest. I cleaned my entire living space with the cleaning supplies I'd brought from home before unpacking a single T-shirt. I replaced my head scarf with a Rosie the Riveter–style bandanna to get down to the (very complicated, as you know) business of unpacking. But I got it done, and now—

Merde. The dinner bell just rang. I'll write soon!

Love forever,
Flora

Transcript of a voicemail recording, August 31, 4:21 p.m.

Hello. You've reached Flora Goldwasser. I regret that I'm not able to take your call right now, but if you leave a message at the tone, I'd be happy to get back to you as soon as I can.

Flora, what the fuck? I just got your letter about Elijah not coming to Quare. Way to not tell me about that until you're at that godforsaken place. Why are you letting him get away with this? He completely bailed, and you're, like, immune to any criticism of him. I guess I just don't get it. Fuck. I have to go to a first-year meeting. God damn it. Call me back.

Journal entry, night of August 31

I haven't even been able to write about my first day because I've been so overloaded with orientation activities. I still can't believe Elijah isn't here. I feel like I'm living in an alternate reality, and it's all I can do to get up every morning (okay, two mornings so far) and put a small smile on my face.

The first person I met here on my first day was Dean, my mentor, who's a second-year. We drove right up to the office, a little gray house, and she was inside, waiting for me with her arms crossed against her chest.

Dean's look is slightly mesmerizing, and as soon as I saw her, I swallowed hard, because she's clearly cool, which I have to say really threw me off. Her hair is straight and black and frames her face perfectly, and her solid line of bangs has zero splits or uneven pieces. And she's got these thick black glasses that are way too big for her face, but they make her look awesome, just like Jenna Lyons. She wore high-waisted jean shorts, a stained white T-shirt, and blocky tennis shoes that made her look like a camp counselor from the early 1990s.

Dean barked out to Daddy that she'd point us in the direction of the first-year cabins and then meet us there. We got back in the car, and she jogged along behind us. When we pulled up to the hovel, she was panting slightly.

It was still around the same time I used to get on the subway to go to Bowen in the morning. I hadn't eaten breakfast before leaving because I was too nervous, so finally, perched on the edge of the mildewed mattress that would become my bed after Daddy drove off, I dug around for a Luna bar in my backpack. Dean stood there watching me, clearly judging my (environmentally friendly!) cleaning supplies; she had refused my insistences that I was fine by myself. I offered her a chunk of the Luna bar, but she just shook her head. Her hair didn't move one inch.

"I'm off sugar," she said.

Dean somewhat grimly offered to stick around and help me unpack, but I politely declined, because a) I needed to be alone to absorb the fact that Daddy had really left me here to die, and b) I didn't particularly want her riffling through my clothes. (I'm such a bitch, I know, but my clothes are the only things I have from my old life. They will not be corrupted by the Quares.)

I felt deflated, but quickly got to work. I was suddenly determined to make this work, if only aesthetically.

A few minutes after Dean left, I was hanging all my dresses on the (tiny, tiny, tiny) hanging bar that I handily installed by dismantling my bamboo lamp and positioning the reed between the two beds (they couldn't have actually expected me to FOLD my dresses, could they?). I looked out the window to make sure my new roommate wasn't coming up the path. She wasn't, thankfully.

Instead I could just make out in the distance someone in another cabin walking out onto her porch: a girl with a mane of coarse yellow hair. That hovel's exterior was strewn with all the trappings of whom I took to be its freakish owner: assorted miniature flags dotting the surrounding lawn, Mason jars of coffee on the ledge of the porch, and broken wind chimes littering the molding steps.

I got this impulse to grab those vintage binoculars I got in SoHo (the really nice ones with the faux leather strap) and watch her, this new person.

And here's what happened—I'm almost too grossed out to write this: the girl suddenly scampered down the porch steps, pulled down her cords and granny panties, squatted in the grass, and released a waterfall of neon-yellow urine onto the grass. In plain sight! In the light of day! The communal, gender-neutral bathroom was forty paces away!

But when I quickly diverted my binoculars' gaze out of sheer disgust, I saw something even more horrifying. Right above where she squatted was a clothesline with about four white cloths dangling from it, each held up by two clothespins. I squinted harder, and I could make out red and brown splotches staining the cloths.

She'd hung up what I can only assume are the cloth-diaper version of maxi pads on a clothesline outside her cabin.

I didn't blink for about forty minutes after that. After I had recovered from the incident—which took a quick listen to the meditation app on my iPhone and copious lavender spray—I went back to unpacking. I was quite proud of myself, actually: once I had hung up some old movie posters, put my sheets and comforter on the bed, and lined up all my shoes by the doorway, it didn't look half bad. Still a hovel, of course, but MY hovel.

Ugh, it's time for a campfire. We have to tell our life stories and roast bananas or something. I feel like I'm radiating with loneliness, sometimes, as though people can feel it coming off me like invisible microwaves.

I can't believe I'll have to wait until December (if Elijah even comes then) to see him. I can't do this I can't do this I can do this I can do this.

Two · lips

*Fashion show & exhibit by six up-and-coming New York designers
September 1, 8–10 p.m.*

ABOUT THE COLLECTION

The styles in today's show are in homage to Miss Tulip, the star of the award-winning blog that rocked the alternative fashion world. Our six young designers hail from all five boroughs of New York City and took inspiration from various blog posts over the course of the past year.

ABOUT THE DESIGNERS

Keisha Miller, an alumna of Brooklyn Heights's Parker School, was born and raised in Canarsie, Brooklyn, and began studying drama at Yale University in the fall.

Lanier Haim hails from Forest Hills, Queens, where she's a senior at Forest Hills High School. She's been taking weekend classes at Parsons since sixth grade.

Joshua Lu, a native of Staten Island, is entering his second year at Williams College. In addition to designing, he enjoys playing water polo.

Frank LeFront emigrated from Haiti to the north Bronx when he was six. All of the fabrics in his collection, *Spring into,* are from his last trip to Port-au-Prince. LeFront attends Columbia University.

Bea Martinez grew up on the Upper West Side and attended the Columbia Grammar and Preparatory School. She entered Vassar College this fall.

Margot Wade-Horowitz is a downtown girl through and through: in addition to growing up in the East Village, she now attends NYU, where she's a sophomore.

ABOUT THE LOOKS

Some enchanted evening: Looks that will keep shining even after the clock strikes midnight.

Jog your memory: Miss Tulip gets her workout on.

Blue: A little winter never hurt anyone's style.

Spring into: Florals, naturally. *"Florals? For spring? Groundbreaking."*

Out to lunch: Lunching with friends and looking good.

Old school: It's no secret that school comes first for Miss Tulip. Watch her rock ten looks, from fifties-inspired pantsuits to plaid skirts.

All proceeds go to the Ali Forney Center, dedicated to helping LGBT homeless youth.

Lael Goldwasser
Harvard College
2609 Harvard Yard Mail Center
Cambridge, MA 02138

September 1

Lael,

I need to tell you more about arrival day! I was putting the
finishing touches on the walls (a bulletin board, a simple vision
board, and my entire 1940s movie poster collection—I hoped my
roommate didn't have any grand plans for the space, because I
was definitely monopolizing it at this point) when the door burst
open. I froze with my thumbtacks in my hand as though I were in
the middle of committing a misdemeanor.

It was Dean, my mentor, unsmiling as ever.

"YOU'VE BEEN SUMMONED, FLORA GOLDWASSER!"
she boomed after stepping inside my newly cleaned hovel. Her
announcement was so loud that I jumped about four feet in the air.

Okay, so you know me. I can't say no to people, especially not
to people I've just met, so I followed her out of my cabin. She
walked so fast that I was practically jogging to keep up with her. I
followed her across a short footbridge stretching over a babbling
brook lined with tall grass, and across the enormous soccer field
(more of a huge lawn with two soccer goals). The blue-green
mountains spread out in the vast beyond almost made me gasp,
but it might have just been that I was out of breath trying to keep
up with Dean.

The dining hall is huge and oddly shaped, with weird parts
jutting out of it where it's clearly been expanded as the years

have gone on. Dean pushed me directly inside the kitchen part of the dining hall, a conspicuous side entrance, before I could examine anything more thoroughly. There she introduced me to a woman named Pearl, who was peeling a mountain of potatoes at a wooden table, letting the skins fall to the floor. I still didn't know what I had been "summoned" for, but I didn't mind Pearl, because her face reminded me of a homesteader or a pioneer— one of those plain potato faces you can just see in the 1860s. It helped that her hair was in two long straw-colored braids, I suppose. Anyway, Pearl said that she teaches women's literature this semester and that she's my academic adviser.

Yes, I have both a mentor and an adviser. I meet with each of them every other week.

It soon became clear that I had been summoned to help Pearl peel the potatoes. So I did, with as much grace as I could muster, given the circumstances. You'd be proud of me: I donned one of the hideous purple aprons and pretended to be excited to meet my fellow students. I even said, and I quote, "Quare seems like a really nurturing place!"

We were peeling potatoes and making small talk, and Dean was banging around on the stove, making what she described as "the tangiest, most mouth-tastic miso soup in human history" when a commotion erupted from the pantry in the back of the kitchen. It sounded like two rain sticks coming down together. Pearl got this worried look on her face and rushed into the pantry, and when she came back out, she was carrying a four- or five-year-old girl with long blond braids just like Pearl's, and only a diaper on. I was the only one who was shocked by the just-diaper situation— the girl was at least four, Lael; everyone else's primary concern was the girl's shattered psyche.

"It's just some spilled rice," Pearl was cooing, swinging the girl by her armpits. "Shhh, shhh, shhh, just some spilled rice."

I mean, Jesus, you'd think she was comforting a girl who had just accidentally stabbed her dog with a steak knife.

Pearl shot me a look that was hard to read. I wasn't sure if I was supposed to join in on the comforting or what, so I just stood there, frozen, the peeler in my hand.

"Flora, would you mind taking her to the garden?" Pearl asked, swinging the child over in my direction. "Cass, go on with Flora. Show her all the cukes that are growing in your garden."

Now, we both know my feelings about children (except for those exceptionally cute, phenomenally well-behaved Lower School girls). Cass, from the looks of it, was not one of those, but I didn't have a choice but to take her hand and let her lead me (humiliatingly enough, I had no idea where we were going) to the garden.

I'll admit that it's a nice garden. There are rows and rows of vegetables, some neat-looking rusty trellises, and a few awesome vintage wheelbarrows with plants just exploding out of them. The soil is all plush looking, and it's oddly peaceful to gaze out at the mountains in the distance. It wasn't until that moment that I realized how QUIET it is here. It's downright scary.

Cass had her own little plot next to the playground—which is more like a wooden set of monkey bars and a few swings—and she told me all about her cucumbers. I stopped listening pretty much immediately, but I was impressed by how she knew every detail about how to grow things, and I'll admit that she turned out to be pretty cute. She's got huge brown eyes and red cheeks, just like Pearl's. Cass wanted to go on the rickety little swing, so I started to push her, getting fancy with the underdogs (you remember how much I love my underdogs).

"Is that Cass all the way up in the sky?"

I spun around to see a slender young woman with a cute bob and a big white quilt in her arms. She smiled a little bit, nodding at me.

"This is Basilia." The girl tipped the swaddled baby so I could see her squashed face. "Miriam's child."

Miriam, as I might have told you before coming here, is the head of school. And yes, she named her daughter—sorry, her child; they're raising this child without gender—Basilia.

Juna and I began to chat. She seemed halfway normal, remarking on the layout of the garden and telling me some of the things she knew about permaculture.

"Why are you taking care of Basilia?" I asked.

"I'm just helping Miriam out," Juna said. "She's got a really bad cold and didn't want Basilia to catch it, and the nanny is training to be a doula this weekend."

I wondered what Miriam's advertisement for a nanny had read. Probably something like this:

> *Middle-aged Quaker seeks caring, compassionate caretaker.*
> *No gendered pronouns. Must be familiar with the body-contact method and be comfortable with harvesting raw goat milk, which we feed our child for its immunity benefits.*

"That's cool," I said, because I wasn't sure what else to say. I had a sudden pang of homesickness, thinking about how little Juna and I had to say to each other.

"Is your dress vintage?" I asked her, trying to make conversation. The dress was bright yellow, tied at the shoulders.

She gave me a slightly pitying smile, and suddenly I felt very, very nervous.

"You obviously didn't know this before now," she said, "but you're actually not supposed to give physical compliments here. . . . You know, 'no shell speak'?"

She reminded me of an ice-cream scooper trying to sound nonconfrontational and buddy-buddy with her coworkers who were swiping gummy bears from the toppings bar. The fondness I'd initially felt toward her dissolved as quickly as it had come.

"I think it's a great rule," she said quickly, as though she were afraid that the swing set was bugged. "It totally takes the emphasis off what people look like and lets conversations go way deeper."

Lael, I could barely stifle an eye roll!

"Why is it called 'shell speak'?" I asked.

"Miriam and the rest of the administration think of the body, physical features, and clothing and accessories, as a shell. It's just protecting and covering up what's inside. So by not commenting on other people's shells, we'll all get to know each other deeply and soulfully."

A small surge of vomit rose in my throat, but I swallowed it back down quickly.

"I wonder what they're doing over there," she said when I abstained from commenting on "no shell speak," pointing in the distance to where a few disembodied straw hats were bobbing up and down among the rows and rows of vegetables, presumably harvesting something. My stomach lurched at the sight of new people; I remembered all the people whom I would have to meet later—and the fact that one whom I had already met I presumed would be none too pleased to see that I'd gone ahead and decorated our whole "love shack" with my own . . . shell.

If India and Cora were here with me right now, we would be making fun of "no shell speak" immediately, but here I can't even bring myself to laugh about it. Juna was clearly very committed to the idea, judging by what she'd just said to me. I made a quick vow to myself that even though I couldn't talk about clothes, I would still never relax my own personal standards of presentation.

"Maybe it's for dinner tonight," I suggested, focusing on the harvesters to curb the nausea. "That's actually what I'm supposed to be doing now. Helping Pearl with dinner. It's funny, because it's only, like noon."

"Is it noon?" Juna's face creased.

"A little after," I said.

"Oh," she said. "I have to return Basilia now. Want to come with me and then head back to the cabin? I haven't unpacked at all."

I agreed, and we dropped Cass off at the dining hall on our way to Miriam's house, which was one of the houses at the edge of campus. There are a handful of faculty houses, and Miriam's is nestled among them. All of the houses are on a dirt road that eventually leads out of campus. Juna let me hold Basilia for a minute as we walked, and it was so cute the way she looked up at me with her little face scrunched up.

Juna rapped on Miriam's door a few times before she answered.
Miriam's forty-ish, with short salt-and-pepper hair. She wore a
grey tunic and grey linen pants and was barefoot. Her toes were
very pale and hunched-looking. I could tell that that she had a
cold by how red her nose looked and how watery her eyes were,
but when she saw us her face broke out in a huge smile.

"I'm Miriam," she said to me, pulling me into an embrace. "It's
so lovely to meet you."

I introduced myself, and her face lit up.

"Roommates!" she said. "I'm so glad you've encountered each
other. Already I'm particularly excited about this match."

Juna and I looked at each other nervously.

Once the door shut, Juna and I set off down the dirt road. We
didn't talk much until we reached our hovel, at which point Juna
swung the door open and gasped.

We stood on the step and looked at the fruits of my hard work:
the posters, the perfume collection, the sunglass shelf, the pastel
carpet.

"You did a lot to the place," Juna gasped.

"Sorry if I went overboard," I said, rushing to move my
typewriter off Juna's dresser.

Juna kept assuring me that it was fine, but I can't shake the sense
that she's miffed by the way she looks around occasionally and
shakes her head slowly before going back to her reading, which is
some obscure book of poetry.

I'd better go, because this letter is ridiculously long and I'm
getting the sense that Juna is annoyed by all the clacking. When

she first saw my typewriter, she gushed all over the place about how cool it is, but now I think all the noise is driving her crazy— from the looks she keeps shooting me.

Please write me back. You are the only thing keeping me sane.

Wait—before I sign off—a note on Elijah: I know you're worried about me, but I'm fine, really. He's an artist. He's got opportunities in the city he can't say no to.

    Love from the farm,
    Flora

India Katz-Rosen
1025 Fifth Avenue, Apt. 9C
New York, NY 10028

September 1

India!

I'm writing to you from my new home at Quare. So far, these are a few things that have gone down:

- I brushed encrusted shit off a pig's back at the farm orientation with a wire brush and then dry-heaved for twenty minutes.
- My peace studies teacher, Allison, who's eight months pregnant and has a mop of curly orange hair, workshopped birthing positions and cathartic noises on the big field in the middle of campus (see attached map).
- One pair of shoes (my suede Carel flats with little apples on them) and one dress (the green gingham one with the white collar) have been stained, nearly irreparably, but that is TBD after the baking soda soak I have going on my desk chair.

That's all for now—I should probably get back to sterilizing this place so I don't mess up my cleaning schedule (twice a day, including the stuff that belongs to my roommate, Juna, which usually makes her glare at me). I'll write you every day. I swear to God, you and Lael are better than diaries any day of the week. Oh, and here's a map I drew so you could picture everything.

Love from the farm,
Flora

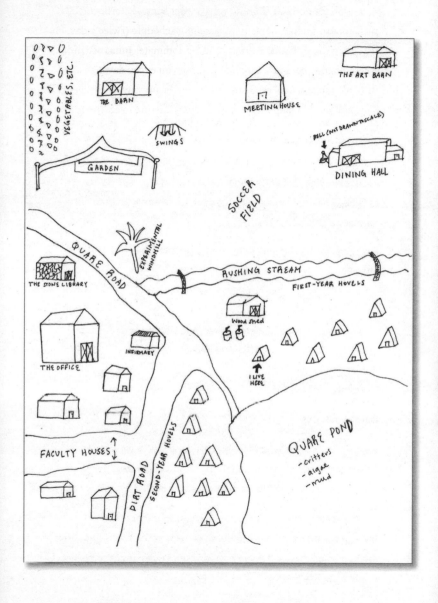

To: Cora Shimizu-Stein <cshimizustein@bowen.edu>
From: India Katz-Rosen <ikatzrosen@bowen.edu>
Subject: Flora!!!
September 4, 12:13 p.m.

Oh my God. I only have a few minutes because Dr. Nadler is breathing down my back, but Blanca just texted me that I got a letter from Flora and that it seems things are NOT going well. (I told her to open anything from Flora IMMEDIATELY and text me the update.) Blanca said something about there being a urine-soaked beanbag chair?? Anyway, she's headed to Maison Kayser to put together a care package ASAP.

I'm honestly worried about Flora. Why did she decide to do this, again??

To: Faculty, staff, and students <everyone@quare.edu>
From: Miriam Row <mrow@quare.edu>
Subject: Welcome back!
September 4, 4:45 p.m.

Dear community,

It's my pleasure to let you know that the gang's all here! The sixteen first-years, of course, arrived a few days ago, but I'm delighted to say that all eighteen second-years are now all accounted for on campus.

I wish everyone the best of luck with classes tomorrow, and I invite you once again to reach out to me (my office hours this week are posted on my door) if you have any questions or concerns—or if you'd just like to chat.

Infinite blessings,
Miriam

Lael Goldwasser
Harvard College
2609 Harvard Yard Mail Center
Cambridge, MA 02138

September 6

Lael,

I realized that I've told you about only two people, and that just
won't do, so here goes.

As other first-years began to arrive at the beginning of
orientation, I watched them settle into their own hovels from my
tiny little porch, disguised by a huge sun hat and sunglasses.

> *MARIGOLD CHEN (my neighbor):*
> *Hometown: San Francisco, CA*
> *Physical description (shell speak be damned):*
> *Tall, wiry, conventionally beautiful*
> *Attire: Crown of daisies in her hair, which miraculously seemed*
> *to be unaffected by the humidity that's making me frizzy (to add*
> *insult to injury). Other than the flower crown, Marigold's not*
> *really a hippie, and her clothes and bags are actually cute—lots of*
> *Free People and Element, and well cared for, none of this tattered*
> *tunic trend that has taken off with everybody else.*

I thought maybe we'd be friends, or at least friendly, but when
she came to my hovel to say hello to Juna (who's way more
popular than I am, by the way), I lowered my sunglasses to smile
and wave at her, but she just stalked right by me. From my perch
outside I could hear her hyena-laughing about some quip of
Juna's.

BECCA CONCH-GOULD, Marigold's roommate:
Hometown: New York, NY
Physical description: Cropped blond hair and a receding chin—
meek as anything, just this whispery voice in a fringy top
Attire: The aforementioned fringy top, accompanied by loose-
fitting cotton pants with a low crotch. She's also been spotted in
quite a few tattered linen tunics with swirling floral patterns.
Ooh, they should all start a band called the Tattered Tunics.
Isn't that a great name?

But I digress.

LUCY AND BENNA WILLIAMS (neighbors on other side):
Hometown: Amherst, MA. Lucy and Benna have been
homeschooled their whole lives on a farm in the Berkshires. Quare
is their first brush with formal education. I asked them a million
questions in spite of myself, and though Lucy answered them
happily, Benna rolled her eyes, as though I were exploiting them
or something.
Physical description: Fraternal twins. Lucy is tall and thin with
a puff of drooping curls, and Benna is shorter and stouter with
longer ringlets.
Attire: For Lucy, unflattering flared jeans and a white tank top.
For Benna, a wrinkled rusty-orange T-shirt dress.

When Lucy saw me sitting on the porch, she asked if she could
come in and see my hovel. I acquiesced, a bit nervous, and
followed her inside, because I didn't know what else to do. But
she thought the old movie posters were cool.

"That's awesome," she said, pointing to *It's a Wonderful Life* and
simultaneously shirking her pants. I tried not to stare. Lucy has

been experimenting with nudism, she explained to me; all I can say is that I'm glad her underwear stayed on. (For now, at least.)

Benna stared at my *The Scarlet Letter* poster for a long time, saying nothing. "That's cute," she finally mumbled.

For the first few days, Juna and I, and our neighbors Marigold and Becca, moved as a clump. We went to dinner together (Kale. Quinoa. Potatoes. Repeat.). We went to the garden tour together. We went to Meeting for Worship together (thirty minutes of silence. Inner truths.). When classes started today (I'll tell you about them in another letter), we headed to those together too. But for the past few days, they've been enveloped in their various cliques, leaving me to fend for myself. Benna has been taken up by the activists; Marigold has been adopted by the artists; Becca has been swooped up by the environmentalists; Juna has become one of the intellectuals. Allow me to explain.

The Quares: A Field Guide

GENUS HIPPIE: tattered tunics, bare feet, untamed body hair (we're talking pits and legs), showers few and far between, usually seen toting musical instruments such as guitars, fiddles, and saxophones

ACTIVIST SPECIES: unequivocal outrage at social injustice, propensity for protests and in-depth discussions about cycles of violence

ENVIRONMENTALIST SPECIES: Mason jars instead of water bottles (nobody uses plastic, but the most popular bottles are canteens), dirt caked under fingernails, sunburns

GENUS HIPSTER: cuffed jeans, flannel, tiny round glasses, groomed facial hair, vintage clothes (not cute like mine, though; more like tablecloths from the 1950s worn as skirts), usually seen with musical instruments such as ukuleles, banjos, and harmonicas

ARTIST SPECIES: "creative" clothes, "interesting" makeup, "experimental" haircuts

INTELLECTUAL SPECIES: dark-framed glasses, pen-stained fingers, furrowed brows, functional clothing, strong necks with muscles strengthened from all the impassioned nodding about Proust

I haven't exactly been chatting it up with my peers. That may come as a shock to you, my being the social butterfly that I am, but I don't want to get too attached.

And it doesn't help my social stock that I've been dressing to the nines every day. Maybe it's a reaction against all the tattered tunics, but my appearance has become my raison d'être. I wake up early for the sole purpose of putting together my outfit du jour. I dress even nicer than I did in the city. Every day is 1962 for me, and my Grace Kelly dresses are certainly getting quite the workout.

Maybe my Bowen shoe rebellion was a sign of things to come: my goal is to make it as hard as possible for the Quares to follow "no shell speak" with me, but they haven't indulged me yet. I get a lot of weird stares, and I can tell that the tattered tunics want nothing to do with me by the way they cluster closer together when I walk into a room. When Juna invites her friends from other cabins over to our hovel, they try not to stare at all the stuff. My twelve pairs of shoes. My collection of white gloves, which as you know keep my hands smooth and ladylike. My vintage parasol. I don't want to be paranoid, but something tells me they talk about me behind my back.

I know what you're screaming at this letter right now: "LEAVE." Right? Part of me wants to do just that. It's not like Elijah is returning my phone calls. Well, the most obvious obstacle is logistical—more specifically, the surrounding woods. I know that Woodstock is half an hour away, but . . . which way? My engraved explorer compass might be gorgeous, but I don't exactly know how to use it.

It's just hard. Write me.

> Peace,
> Flora

To: Grace Wang <grace@nymphettemag.com>
From: Wink DelDuca <wink@nymphettemag.com>
Subject: Fashion show
September 6, 5:22 p.m.

Grace,

I just wanted to check in to make sure you got a writer to cover the Miss Tulip fashion show a few days ago. This is the type of article that will take the features section to the next level!

Besides, it's important that we keep reminding our readers that even though Miss Tulip may have gone on hiatus, she's still (hopefully) alive and kicking. As always, keep forwarding me tips from readers, even if they ARE woefully uninformed, as you receive them.

;)

Wink

Editor in Chief, *Nymphette* magazine

Nymphette is an online feminist arts & culture magazine for teenagers. Each month, we choose a theme, and then you send us your writing, photography, and artwork.

To: Wink DelDuca <wink@nymphettemag.com>

From: Grace Wang <grace@nymphettemag.com>

Subject: Re: Fashion show

September 6, 6:17 p.m.

God, yes. Did I not tell you? I sent Chester, and he said it went great—got lots of interviews with the designers, audience members, etc. He did say that it had slight funeral vibes, though, like it was a final good-bye to Miss Tulip (please lord, let that not be the case, obviously). I wish I could have been in New York for the event!

And yes, I'll keep forwarding you tips, even if most of them are improbable subway sightings. Sigh. Someone needs to explain to these girls that not every young woman in a pillbox hat is Miss Tulip, especially on the train to Williamsburg!

Xo

Grace

Features Editor, *Nymphette* magazine

Nymphette is an online feminist arts & culture magazine for teenagers. Each month, we choose a theme, and then you send us your writing, photography, and artwork.

Lael Goldwasser
Harvard College
2609 Harvard Yard Mail Center
Cambridge, MA 02138

September 6—night

Dearest Lael,

I have to tell you something. I've been trying to ignore this
sinking feeling I have.

Things are not going so well for me.

I wanted to write this in the smallest handwriting I could, because
I'm not exactly proud of my decision to come here. I'm not even
writing on my typewriter, I'm so ashamed to say it. But you're
my sister. If I can't admit that I think I made the wrong choice in
coming here to you, then I can't tell anybody.

You know why I'm here. But I'm getting confused by everything
now, and maybe that's because it's the middle of the night and I
can't sleep, but I want to lay it all out.

What I told India and Cora was that I'd been feeling more and
more last year as though I'd outgrown Bowen. Not outgrown the
two of them, of course, but the school itself. Nothing interesting
happens there, ever—unless you count the odd cheating scandal
or that time the editors of the *Bulletin* broke the "news" that Miss
Bowen was a lesbian.

It wasn't even a total lie. The more I thought about coming
to Quare, at least in the abstract, the more it appealed to
me. Lounging in the grass, reading Naomi Klein's *No Logo*
or Patrick Reinsborough's *Decolonizing the Revolutionary
Imagination*. Setting tomatoes in a straw basket with a plaid cloth

and picnicking on a mountain with my banjo-playing friends. Weaving together prayer flags and knitting afghans. Wearing my cat-eye sunglasses and silk head scarf, striding confidently on a clear trail with the wind at my back, environmental sampling kit in hand, like a regular Rachel Carson.

Needless to say, Quare hasn't exactly been a picnic, and I haven't heard from Elijah. This is all to say that I think I've made a huge, terrible, massive mistake. I mean, I'm assuming he's still coming in December, like he said in his text, to take one last Miss Tulip photo, but even that doesn't exactly help, as it's still the beginning of September. Please write back and tell me I'm being ridiculous.

   Love,
   Flora

Flora Goldwasser
Pigeonhole 44
The Quare Academy
2 Quare Road
Main Stream, NY 12497

September 8

Flora,

Okay, Miss Mopey. Last time I checked, nobody was holding a gun to your head, forcing you to go to Quare, so if you're so unhappy, why don't you just pack up and come home? (And don't give me that bullshit about finding your way through the woods with your ineffectual compass, either.)

You and I both know the reason: Elijah. I didn't trust him last year, and I sure as hell don't trust him now. I know this sounds harsh, but I'm worried about you—I have been for a while, actually, but to be honest I never thought you'd actually go through with it (Quare, I mean).

Face it, Flora. You wanted this to be some grand romantic gesture, and now you're upset that there are bugs and sticks and armpit hair (which, by the way, you really shouldn't shame if you truly call yourself a feminist).

Sorry for the tough love, but I've had about as much as I can take of the whining. You chose this. Make the most of it or get the fuck out.

From,
Lael

PS. Harvard is fine. There are some real dweebs, but overall a bunch of cool people. My mouth hurts from smiling so hard. It's exhausting to be friendly.

India Katz-Rosen
1025 Fifth Avenue, Apt. 9C
New York, NY 10028

September 8

Dear India,

I itch. All over. And I'm going to start bitching about the itching.

I'm pretty sure it's not poison ivy, because there's no rash or anything. But every inch of my skin itches like hell. I changed my sheets (because I know I've been shedding dead skin cells in this weather), but to no avail. I changed my moisturizing regimen to three times a day instead of twice—nada. I even started wearing tights and long sleeves, although it's still warm out, because I figured maybe there were tiny invisible bugs in the atmosphere that I wasn't seeing (it's far-fetched, I know, but believe me, if you were in my place, you would try anything too).

I finally got up the nerve to ask the Oracle of Quare, who doubles as the official spiritual guide of Quare and the maintenance guy (everyone says he and Miriam are hooking up, which, ew, would be superweird because he's in his twenties and she's at least forty—an age difference, of course, that society accepts in heterosexual couples when the man is older but shames when the woman is older), to come and check out our hovel to see if it was infested with bedbugs or termites or some other god-awful thing like that. He tore apart my whole bed (and seriously damaged my mattress pad situation) looking, and destroyed Juna's bed too, but he came back outside a few minutes later and said he hadn't found anything, "nothing but a serious case of bad vibes." I guess I was lucky, because in New York a guy would have charged a hundred dollars for that, but the Oracle just hugged me (he smelled terrible, by the way) and danced away into the sunset, ropy arms akimbo.

So I'm left with no explanation—besides my case of bad vibes, of course—as to why I'm so itchy.

This is all to say, please excuse this letter.

The second-years (the ones who aren't peer mentors like Dean, that is) have descended upon us. They all know each other, of course, so across the dirt road—where their hovels are—came their unbridled shouts of glee and booming laughter.

Also, news flash: Dean is cool. Like, really cool. I'm not even offended anymore that she's about as interested in me as she is in a random twig on the ground.

The night they arrived was Quare Share, which is part of the orientation activities they do at the beginning of every year. It's held in the Art Barn, which is very cool: it's all glass, so when you're on the outside, you can see everything that's happening inside, and vice versa. There are huge solar panels on the roof that make it look like something from a science-fiction movie. It's like a spaceship that randomly landed behind the dining hall.

For Quare Share they moved everything outside, so it was just this massive open space, a glass barn with a wooden floor. I was so itchy that I had so sit with my back against the wall, subtly rubbing it up and down to get the places I couldn't reach. I've turned into a bear, apparently.

Then Dean, who is not only my mentor but also the master player of Guild, Quare's student-run theater troupe, went onto the "stage," a slightly raised platform at the front of the room, and everyone went insane. You know those upperclassmen girls at Bowen who were just effortlessly COOL? Well, Dean is one of those, but to the extreme. She's definitely a hipster, but she's an intellectual-artistic crossover. It suddenly made sense why I'm scared shitless of her: I've always been terrified of people who inspire awe in others.

When Dean assumed the stage, the crowd went wild.

"WELCOME TO QUARE SHARE!" she shouted. She was a rock star, and I stopped itching to watch her perform. She was absolutely hypnotic.

Dean grabbed the microphone and pressed it to her lips.
"Now, as many of you know, Quare Share is the first time in
the year that the entire campus comes together in the name of
performance art. So let's give it up for one another!"

Again, cheering.

"We've got some outstanding acts for you tonight, including
some—let's hear it for them—FIRST-YEARS!" Dean shouted.

When the hoots and hollers died down, Dean explained the rules.
There were no drugs or alcohol permitted, obviously, and no acts
that glorified violence, but everything else was fair game. We could
propose marriage. We could have sex onstage. We could come out of
the closet (as though there was anybody still IN the closet). As long
as we kept it to two minutes, we could do anything.

Then the performances started. There was no set list, as far as
I could tell. People just rose, one after another, and assumed
the stage. Dean would sort of mediate between two pieces with
a remark that made everyone laugh: a joke about how because
she's a lesbian, she's friends with all her exes, or about how her
Samoan mother had said X, Y, or Z to her over summer break.

I have to admit, I was surprised at how . . . well, TALENTED,
people are here. I guess it shouldn't come as a surprise—Quare
is superselective—but some of the performances were scarily
good. I was rather fond of the slam poetry, actually. It always
starts with some big shocking statement, like, "I was twelve when
I discovered I could masturbate with my mom's construction
hammer," and then the poet proceeds to describe all this hurt and
shame with all this flowery language and these motifs that you
have to carefully follow. I'll admit that I got chills once or twice.
You know how I appreciate wordplay.

There were some singing performances, too, and a couple of really cool magic tricks. And then there's the unofficial Quare chant when someone does something unexpected (like when Althea delivered a lecture on invasive species, the topic of the elective she'd be teaching that semester, for her act):

"KEEP QUARE QUIRKY! KEEP QUARE QUIRKY! KEEP QUARE QUIRKY!"

Now that I think about it, maybe the fact that we're in the sticks is the reason I haven't gotten any of your letters yet. I'm writing my address one more time here, just on the off chance that you misplaced it (or maybe Blanca threw it out accidentally while cleaning your room?). It's such a pain that there's no cell service out here and that we're not supposed to overload the fragile Internet connection with streaming (good-bye, Skype) or social networking sites (good-bye, Instagram) or even OFF-CAMPUS EMAIL, at least until next year.

I'd better sign off now and tend to these itches. But please, WRITE ME BACK! I'm dying to hear from you.

Love forever,
Flora

By now you're probably wondering, just like Lael did, why I didn't just leave. I still am not totally sure why I didn't call Daddy to come take me home. The only way I can make sense of it, if only a glimmer, is that at Quare, in those early days, I felt Elijah everywhere.

It wasn't something I could explain, or even something I told Lael, but something about Quare felt infiltrated by him. Even among the annoying hipsters (if Elijah was, in fact, a hipster, he certainly wasn't annoying, and besides, he was *my* hipster), I saw him in the dining hall, smiling widely, serving himself sautéed kale sprinkled with sesame seeds, leaning back in his chair during peace studies, pulling absentmindedly on a rake during shared work. I didn't leave, because I was hanging on to the dogged hope that even though he had yet to show his face, he was *here* somewhere, just around the corner or behind a bale of hay.

The Song We Sang Before Meals

For the Love of Singing!
[To be chanted slowly, in unison]

Simple is what I want to be
To know I'm enough, and enough is me
Others say I should want money, pow'r, and control
But I ought not be fancy; I just ought to be whole

Amsterdam Dental Group
1243 Amsterdam Avenue
New York, NY 10027

Flora Goldwasser
Pigeonhole 44
The Quare Academy
2 Quare Road
Main Stream, NY 12497

September 8

Dear Flora,

I've been trying to reach you on your cell phone, but Lael reminded me that service is somewhat lacking up there.

Mum and I are both stable. She is very much enjoying her apartment in the Flatiron and I am quite happy in Rye. The suburbs suit me, I think. From the bedroom window, I can see the Long Island Sound at the tip of the property.

I know this has all been hard on you, and I want to thank you for your resilience. You're really a great kid. (Between you and me, I'd have preferred you stayed at Bowen, but I knew arguing against your mother would not have been such a good idea.)

I'm sorry if you felt that you had to run away from home. Is that what going to Quare was about? I know things haven't been so pleasant for us as a family recently, but now that Mum and I are both settled in our respective places, we'd love to have you home. Rye is just a forty-minute train ride from Grand Central, and obviously Mum's apartment is just a quick hop on the subway from Bowen and your friends uptown.

If you decide to stay, please let me know if you need anything sent to you on campus, and I will arrange for someone to send it.

Love,
Daddy

Lael Goldwasser
Harvard College
2609 Harvard Yard Mail Center
Cambridge, MA 02138

September 10

Dear Lael,

Just got a letter from Daddy. He thinks I'm here because I wanted to "run away from home," as though there's even a home to run away FROM. And he even had the GALL to act like it's some secret that he disapproves of Quare (because, God forbid, I go to Oberlin or something and not Harvard like him and Mum and you).

I'm lashing out, I know. And I really am trying to be less mopey, like you said. I have no one to blame but myself for my current pickle, especially since, at the rate things are going, Elijah will forget that I ever existed by Thanksgiving.

Besides, how can I be even remotely chipper when we're going to Mum's stupid apartment for Thanksgiving? I want to go to New Jersey, like we always do, but just as usual, Mum and Daddy have been completely selfish.

I wonder why they got married in the first place: it's hard to think of a couple more different from (erratic, spontaneous) Mum and (staid, mild-mannered) Daddy. They're both doctors and everything, but still—even then, all they share is a fondness for orifices.

I'm really trying to be happy about being here. And fine, maybe you're right about ((((Elijah))) and the whole grandiosity thing. I'm actually starting to wonder if I made him up, despite all the evidence to the contrary. Another part of me wonders if this is what I get for trying to realize my hetero-romantic fantasy at a school called QUARE. But something in me is like, "Stick it out, Flora." Just to prove to myself that I can do it, or something.

And okay, yeah, maybe I'm holding out for Elijah to come to

his senses. I'm just so sure it'll happen, that's the thing—I'm positive he'll show up here at some point and realize that I was perfect for him all along.

But taken all together, these present circumstances have turned me into quite the unhappy camper. My mantra these days is "I would prefer not to." (Remember when you were reading *Bartleby* in your junior year, and I read it too?)

I would prefer not to join my entire class of sixteen on an impromptu wilderness hike. I would prefer not to swim in the nasty lake, even though it's sweltering (the reason being that I would prefer not to ingest an amoeba). I would prefer not to strengthen my connections with students by engaging in circles of nonviolent communication practice.

There was one activity last week during the host of get-to-know-you seminars and icebreaking exercises that I wasn't given the chance to prefer not to do. Very little at Quare is required, but this certainly was.

Allison Longfield, the Peace on Earth teacher, is friends with the Woodstock-based poet Ellis Sugarman (you probably haven't heard of him). He's got all these tufts of bright orange hair exploding from his scalp and a long, scraggly red beard.

Anyway, Ellis coached us through a variety of different exercises to get us to acknowledge our privilege—racial, class, gender, religious, etc.—and process them creatively. First he made us stand in a horizontal line on the soccer field, facing the net or whatever it's called. He—wearing a tattered piece of fabric and those tan pants with the crotch that sags to the ankles—shouted a bunch of statements, and if they applied to us, we were supposed to take a huge step forward.

"I CAN WALK AROUND MY NEIGHBORHOOD AT NIGHT WITHOUT WORRYING ABOUT BEING HARASSED," he shouted, and a bunch of kids, mostly the boys, stepped forward, toward the soccer net. "I CAN GO INTO ANY BUILDING AND GET AROUND REGARDLESS OF WHETHER OR NOT THERE'S AN ELEVATOR OR A RAMP." Almost everyone stepped forward. "I AM NEVER ASKED TO SPEAK ON BEHALF OF ALL PEOPLE OF MY RACIAL GROUP." The white kids, about half of us, stepped forward.

I stepped forward for most of the statements, actually, and at the end, when he shouted, "NOW, EVERYBODY, RUN TO THE NET!" I was one of the first to touch it, even though I was wearing my oxfords with the slight heel, which are notoriously difficult to run in.

But I'm far from the only one here with copious privilege. There are some really rich people here. Even though they wear shirts with holes in them and haven't had a professional haircut in years, you can kind of just tell by the way they talk about their families that they're uncomfortable with how much money they come from. We're an economically diverse group, though, thanks to the fact that Quare's rich alumni pledge to pay the full tuition of any student whose family can't afford to send them here.

Afterward, at Allison's—the peace studies teacher—house, we had to write poems about the experience. Juna, my roommate, was all, "I am a stranger, I come / from a strange place / from bone, born of the sea," and got lots of snaps. Ellis's beady little black eyes almost popped out of his misshapen head, he was so excited. I wrote something about the idea of ownership (I'm too embarrassed to say more, unfortunately), and pretty much only Ellis was into it—and it was kind of his JOB to be into everything we wrote.

The only poem he wasn't really into, actually, was by this guy Sam, who's different in a strange way. He's really popular, and makes everyone laugh about all the disparaging stuff he says about Quare and Canada, where he's from, but I can sense that he feels a little bit like an outcast too. His poem was totally off topic in the most hilarious way—it was about being trapped in a shower with a huge spider. Now that I think about it, it was probably a metaphor, but I'm not exactly sure for what.

When the workshop was over—and I'd LIKED the workshop; the privilege stuff was superimportant—Ellis bolted out the door kind of spazzed out in a fit of love. He started twirling and laughing maniacally on the patch of grass outside of Allison's house. We all watched him from her porch. A laugh bubbled up in my throat—it was just like an *SNL* skit, Lael—but I swallowed it down once I saw that everyone else was humming and swaying. (Except Sam, whose eye I caught—he started to laugh but looked away.) Ellis zoomed back inside Allison's house and emerged with a pair of scissors seconds later.

"I WANT YOU ALL TO TAKE THIS BEARD," he said, handing the scissors to Juna, "TO REMEMBER ME BY. TO REMEMBER THIS SPECTACULAR DAY."

When Juna hesitated, he guided her hand toward his face. She gingerly snipped off a little piece of beard and held it between two fingers. He closed her fist around it and pressed it to her chest. She looked like she'd swallowed a cucumber.

"Save it forever," he said. "Promise?"

She nodded.

The scissors made their way around. Agnes—he's a guy, despite the name, a black guy with dreads, and I don't know why his parents named him that—cut a huge, ambitious chunk that made Ellis look like someone had taken a bite out of his face. After that, people really got into it. Sam took an even bigger piece and solemnly promised to plant it sacredly in the ground. I kept escaping from the lineup and slithering farther down, avoiding my turn until absolutely everyone else had gone. Ellis's face was a lot barer now, revealing a receding chin.

"DO IT," he instructed.

"I'm okay," I said lightly, not wanting to offend him.

He orchestrated the group in a chant.

"DO IT! DO IT! DO IT!" everyone shouted at me.

I reached out to touch his face. His beard was crunchy and wiry. My stomach leapt. His black eyes gleamed into my soul, and his little red mouth, now surrounded by awkward strands of red hair, twisted up eagerly at me. I opened the scissors and then pressed down hard. The chunk of beard was between my fingers. Everyone cheered.

I have few acquaintances. It's not that I hate everyone, or anything—I just feel like a turtle whose head is stuck in its shell. I feel, frankly, dull and quiet and uninteresting. I wouldn't mind being friends with my teachers, though. The only thing I WOULD prefer to do is the reading from my classes. I'm such a nerd, I know, but when Juna is out doing whatever it is she does with Marigold, no-chin Becca, and the twins, I'm so happy lying on my bed with a stack of books. Old habits die hard, I suppose.

It's also really woodsy here. I just ordered a mosquito net from Amazon (bad me, using the Internet for nonscholarly purposes and cluttering the bandwidth, but it was an emergency), and the second it comes in the mail, I'm hanging it above my bed. I think our hovel is infested with bugs, and the thought of little creatures climbing into my mouth at night makes me want to fall on a sword.

Tell me all about school! I want to hear about your friends, your professors, your activities . . . everything! Anything to distract me from here.

Oh, and when you're home on fall break, could you search through the boxes in my room at Mum's for a few things? My wardrobe is crying out for variety.

- Yellow-and-white-striped mini-dress—mod style one with slightly torn hem
- Light pink wool dress with cord around waist
- Faux-suede wrap skirt

Lots of love,
Flora

Flora Goldwasser
Women's Literature
Short response: *Jane Eyre*
September 10

> *When Jane leaves Lowood School for her position as a governess at*
> *Thornfield, she marks the change by presenting a new scene and*
> *addressing the reader directly. She narrates:*

A new scene in a novel is something like a new scene in a
play; and when I draw up the curtain this time, reader, you
must fancy you see a room in the George Inn at Millcote,
with such large-figured papering on the walls as inn rooms
have; such a carpet, such furniture, such ornaments on
the mantelpiece, such prints. . . . Reader, though I look
comfortably accommodated, I am not very tranquil in my
mind. (111)

> *Rather than merely addressing her reader—establishing solidarity but*
> *preserving distance—Jane begins to do the analytical work that we*
> *readers are accustomed to doing. Hovering above the page, addressing*
> *form and distancing herself from plot, narrator Jane's voice becomes*
> *larger than the novel itself, and she moves toward her reader while*
> *protagonist Jane remains opaque on the page. Her dissociation—*
> *becoming both character and narrator—is deliberate and measured.*
> *Jane amplifies her narrative voice by achieving duality, a superhuman*
> *feat, and she obscures the distance between us and her by creating one*
> *transparent version of herself to come stand beside the reader: Jane is*
> *behind the "curtain," but she is also on our side of it. We watch the*
> *unfolding scene together.*

COMMENTS:

Very interesting observations, Flora. You seem to be suggesting
that Jane's ability to separate herself as narrator from herself
as character is where she derives strength: what, then, does
this suggest about the role of any woman writer in straddling
the line between acting and narrating—between acting as
protagonists and authors of our own lives? What changes in
ourselves when we write our own stories? And what happens
to the stories we tell about ourselves as we live? —Pearl

Flora Goldwasser
Pigeonhole 44
The Quare Academy
2 Quare Road
Main Stream, NY 12497

September 12

Dear Flora,

I can't believe Daddy said that he and Mum are "stable." That's
fucking hilarious.

Quare sounds just like I thought it would. It's still so funny to
me that you're at a place where the focus is on stripping away the
frills of life and getting at the depths of the soul. (No offense,
but you're, like, the definition of frill.) Elijah really must have
done a number on you. God, you've always loved the ones who
look meek and mild, haven't you? (I'm thinking of your thing for
Michael Cera last year, obviously.)

Oh, and I was really moved (read: in tears of laughter) by your description of the conclusion of the orientation exercise. I worry, however, that saving the beard clipping is unsanitary (you didn't indicate what you did with it). I hope you discarded yours and washed your hands thoroughly.

The food here is outstanding. I'll tell you more about my friends soon, but I have to run to a meeting with my TF, the scintillating Susan.

I found those dresses you asked for. Expect your package in about two weeks. Anything else you want delivered? I'm charging it to Mum's card, so the heftier the better.

    From,
    Lael

To: All-staff <everyone@nymphettemag.com>
From: Wink DelDuca <wink@nymphettemag.com>
Subject: Miss Tulip
September 12, 1:12 p.m.

Salutations,

Wink here. Forgive me if this letter sounds delusional. I've just given a whole lot of blood at the Red Cross and I'm seeing stars, but nothing short of hospitalization could keep me from providing you with information about Miss Tulip.

As we all know (only too well), Miss Tulip dropped off the face of the earth on April 30 of this past year—the last day the site was updated. She lives on in our memories, eternally clad in a stunning red-and-white plaid skirt suit. My myriad emails to the domain holder have bounced back. My daily jogs in Riverside Park, where she was last photographed, have been fruitless (well, unless you count my ass, which now won't quit).

I don't really have much more info than that, but I do want you to know that we're working hard to track her down. I have a hard time believing that Elijah Huck decided to stop the blog just like that (it was a shoo-in for a bunch of other awards, after all), but he's notoriously difficult to get in touch with.

But we're not giving up yet, comrades. Miss T means too much to all of us for that. You never see her head, sure, but she really gets under your skin. Besides, how are we supposed to know how to dress without her stalwart example??

(Just kidding. I know we *Nymphette* editors all have our own beautiful and unique senses of style. But Miss Tulip really was—is? I'm not quite ready to start speaking about her in past tense—iconic.)

;)

Wink

Editor in Chief, *Nymphette* magazine

Nymphette is an online feminist arts & culture magazine for teenagers. Each month, we choose a theme, and then you send us your writing, photography, and artwork.

India Katz-Rosen
1025 Fifth Avenue, Apt. 9C
New York, NY 10028

September 12

India dearest,

We don't get grades here—just written evaluations for each class
at the middle and at the end of each semester. I think the first
round of comments is coming up soon. I'm not worried. All my
teachers love me. (I know I can tell you this without sounding
like a braggart.) It's the students I'm not so sure about. It's not
that they hate me, exactly, so much as they keep their distance
from me, like I'll infect them with my materialism or something.

By the way, I didn't tell you what happened to the student
lounge. It used to be in the basement of the dining hall, but one
night a little while ago all the seniors took the furniture and
created an outside lounge. It's funny, because they took the door
off its hinge too and propped it up in the grass, though of course
it's entirely useless.

The outside lounge is where the club fair was held this morning.
The second-years were all standing next to booths for the clubs
they run, chatting with the people milling around and deciding
which clubs to join. You'll find included in this letter a pamphlet
embellished with my annotations.

I lingered at the Guild table. It was the most impressive table,
wooden and heavy and round with a curvy pattern carved
around the edges. A gold lamp, not connected to any source of
power (its cord just lay in the grass like a dead snake), rested on
the table. Dean was the only one present. She sat in a stiff-backed

nineteenth-century wooden chair that looked out of place, to say the least, wedged into the damp grass. Dean Elliot, she of Quare Share lore (and my mentor! Though sometimes I doubt she remembers my name), was totally motionless and expressionless, hands crossed over her chest, not exactly moodily but with serious (and seriously enviable) 'tude.

I stood watching her, wondering if the dead expression in her eyes meant that she was a) made of wax, b) unspeakably bored, or c) daydreaming. But finally she caught my eye and wordlessly she beckoned me to approach. She did this without moving her face one bit, but somehow I just KNEW that she wanted me to come over. I did so.

"This is Guild," said Dean, gesturing to a small placard on the table. *Guild,* the placard spelled matter-of-factly in flowery script. "We're Quare's oldest and only theater troupe. It's a society of sorts. I'm master player this year, so it's my responsibility to recruit new members. We have an elaborate . . . process, I guess, of selecting people and then having them move up the ladder. If you're interested, our first meeting is this afternoon. Woolman Theater. The back half of the meetinghouse. During lunch. It's millet mountains today, but don't worry. It'll be worth it."

I debated for a moment. Not about the missed millet mountains (they're mounds of millet stuck together with egg substitute and spices and then baked, and they're alarmingly tasty), but about joining a CLUB.

You'll remember that I was a bit of a Joiner at Bowen. French Club, Movie Appreciation Society, Sewing Club, Bowen Urban Gardening (BUG), Bowen Feminists for Girl Power!, the *Bulletin,* and yes, the Dramatic Club.

But at Quare, I lie low. I don't speak unless spoken to. I don't volunteer details. I don't join in unless it's absolutely mandatory.

I'll admit that I'm *un peu fatiguée* of keeping my eyes down and my mouth closed. Not because I want to BELONG here, God forbid, but because I miss social interaction. But taking the first step—signing my name on the Guild interest list—gave me pause. Once my name was on that list, there was no backing out. I was on the grid. At Quare, I'm like a cat. I need to know I'll be able to escape whenever I need to. Signing my name would mean giving up that security.

But I did it. I signed the sheet.

So I'm writing to you from Woolman Theater, which is indeed at the back half of the meetinghouse (more on that later), waiting for the Guild meeting to start and using this activity—letter-writing—to avoid talking to people. It's a nice spot, with a great big stage and a long velvet curtain. They even have a fairly sophisticated light system. It's not as high-tech as the Bowen theaters, of course, but then again, Quare likes to kick it old-school. Also, there's only so much that the solar panels can do, I guess.

Meeting's starting. I'll keep you posted (literally).

Love from the farm,
Flora

P.S. I'm attaching my annotations on the club fair pamphlet.

Club fair pamphlet

- THE EARTH SOCIETY: How can we give back to—rather than take from—the earth?
  (Table featured a plate of quinoa-and-chocolate-cranberry cookies. Run by a gangly environmental hippie and a few barefooted cronies)

- LANGUEDOC: A group to appreciate the contributions of French artists, particularly the hippies living in the conservative south of France.
  (Run by hipsters, both intellectual and artistic. (You might be thinking that this is my type of club, right? I thought that too, until I noticed the emphasis on painting with menstrual blood. I'm a Francophile, of course, but not that much of a Francophile—I'll take the pastries and the shoes and leave the "period pieces," thank you very much)

- MAIN STREAM POTLUCK: An organization that cooks potlucks for Main Stream residents and Quares to mingle, because we believe that breaking bread together is the answer for mutual healing.
  (Run by activists. Gave out millet mountains to everyone who came by)

- MAKE LOVE NOT BOMBS: A club that discusses the ways in which safe sex and masturbation can curb cyclical violence.
  (Run by intellectuals with a good bit of activist participation. Filled wheelbarrow with condoms, vibrators, and spermicidal jelly)

- THE MUSES: A society for budding musicians of all stripes to come together and practice their craft.

(My neighbor Marigold hung around their table, probably because its leader is a cute harmonica-blowing hipster and not because she's semi-skilled on the banjo)

· RUN CLUB: The closest thing Quare has to a sports team, Run Club meets up weekly to jog the seven miles around the perimeter of campus.
(Led by a reedy second-year and some environmentalists, all of whom wear those five-toe shoes that are, like, the dorkiest things ever—and wouldn't they give you a serious toe wedgie?)

· GUILD: Quare's oldest and only theater troupe.
(Run by Dean Elliot, she of the perfect hair and awesome glasses. Featuring, inexplicably enough, intellectuals, artists, activists, environmentalists, and everyone in between)

To: Wink DelDuca <wink@nymphettemag.com>
From: Theodora Sweet <thee@nymphettemag.com>
Subject: Re: Miss Tulip
September 12, 9:49 p.m.

Wink,

Thanks for the update. I'm obviously just as upset as you are at Miss Tulip's disappearance. As much as I hate chalking up my decision to study photography at Stanford (undeclared as of now, but I'll keep you posted) to a white man's gaze of a female subject, it really was Elijah, and the entire blog, that made taking photos seem like something I'd want to spend the rest of my life doing.

I mean, I get that Miss T kind of has a cult following—not to say that we haven't spoken to people in, like, mainstream Kansas and

Utah who also read it religiously—but like you said, she touched us Nymphettes especially deep. And it's not even just the vintage clothes! I wear the first thing my hands touch in the morning, as you can probably tell. It's the whole thing. You just don't see things that are so goddamn tender anymore.

She was an empowered muse, that's for damn sure. God, I need to stop before I get too emotional in my ecology lecture.

Anyway, just writing to say thanks for persevering, and let me know what—if anything—you find.

Deuces,
Thee

Cora Shimizu-Stein
95 Wall Street, Apt. 33A
New York, NY 10005

September 12

Dear Cora,

Remember me?

Can you check with India to make sure she's getting my letters? I know we agreed that she would keep everyone else in the loop re: Quare, but something tells me she's shirking her duties. (Could Jasper, that idiot from Dalton, be to blame?)

Anyway, I thought I'd write to you. I miss you, and something exciting has happened. I'm imagining you reading this while on the elliptical at the gym in your apartment's basement. Or maybe you're in the steam room? (You're honestly the only person in the world who'd read a letter in the steam room—and that's exactly why I miss you so much.)

Yesterday morning I did something impulsive. I went to the farm to milk cows with Lucy (one of my neighbors) and Fern (another first-year).

The farm is actually quite nice. It's up past the orchard, and all the trees are full of fruit. You pick it off, just like that, and because they don't use pesticides, you can bite into an apple after just rubbing it a little bit. I felt a little bit awkward with Fern and Lucy, because they're both so gentle and well-meaning. Fern is dewy and soft-spoken with a long blond braid that she circles twice around her head and dots with daisies, and Lucy is a nudist who's nuts about animals. I mean, I'm a vegan 90 percent of the time (you know how I feel about my pastries, obviously), but I feel like I appreciate animals more in the abstract—I believe of course, that killing them for meat is murder, but that I don't necessarily have to roll around in mud with pigs. I feel big around both of them; maybe that's it. Not so much physically, but like I take up too much room or have too many things.

Once you get to the actual farm, there are some pastures with cows. Have you ever seen a cow in person before? Stupid question—of course you haven't. They're huge and very nuzzly, with pink nostrils covered in stubbly hair. I didn't want to stop petting them. And there are goats, too. They're much smaller, with wiry hair and little horns, and they bit our hands through their fences. Not hard, really, and it wasn't entirely unpleasant.

It was my first time at the farm, if you must know. When the rest of the class went up for a tour, I complained of cramps. But I wasn't even lying! Much.

When we were done milking the cows—I wasn't crazy about the idea of getting my hands dirty, so I just watched—Lucy, Fern, and I took off down the orchard, breaking into a run toward the bottom of the hill, because simply walking down it is nearly physically impossible. The sun was up, there was a nice breeze, and things suddenly didn't seem quite so bad.

The two of them ran directly into the two showers, so I had to wait on the small step in front of the communal bathroom. From my perch I watched the lights go on in people's cabins, one by one. Before long, Althea, my across-the-street neighbor, emerged from her cabin up the hill and took her morning piss on the grass, smiling up at the rising sun. (I'm sure India's told you about the peeing outside thing. At this point, it doesn't even faze me.)

I must have dozed off for a few seconds, because suddenly a pair of bright white sneakers was directly in front of me. I looked up to find Sam, a fellow first-year, with his puffy hair eclipsing the sun. He has a nose with a really high bridge—a Roman nose, if you will. He's Canadian, the only international student this year.

"Hi," he said. "Are you waiting for the shower?"

"Yeah."

He looked around like he was making sure nobody was watching. He whistled a few notes absentmindedly and then sat down beside me. I don't think I had ever talked to him before that morning (we make eye contact sometimes), but suddenly here he was: Popular Canadian Sam, just chomping at the bit to converse with me. It was eerie.

"I just had breakfast at Miriam's house," he said quietly, as though he were confiding in me.

"Why?" I asked.

"No real reason." He shrugged and stuck his feet out in front of him, luxuriating on the slab of concrete. I couldn't look away from his bright white sneakers. "She's inviting every first-year to breakfast in the next few weeks. I don't know why I got the first spot. Maybe Miriam just has a thing for Canadians."

I forced a laugh.

"I guess Canada really has embraced the Quare ethos," I said.

"Nah," Sam said. "It's the other way around. Quare copied us. That's why I'm right at home here."

I studied him. The thing about Sam is that he's NOT right at home here. He hates gardening because he doesn't like to get his hands dirty (and mumbles under his breath the whole time about the bacteria in the soil), didn't learn how to chop wood because he said he's too uncoordinated and he didn't want there to be a bloodbath, and almost gagged when he tried the lentil loaf for the first time. The other thing about him, though, is that unlike me, he's so goddamn CHEERFUL about not fitting into Quare, so everybody loves him for it. And the final thing about Sam is that he dresses like he's in his eighties: square glasses, slacks (sometimes plaid, sometimes brown or gray), and cardigans in somber patterns. And of course the blindingly white and vaguely orthopedic sneakers.

"Anyway, Miriam's house is amazing," he said. "It's got a pink refrigerator from the 1950s, and all the beds are gold. I think you'd like it."

"Gold?" I asked.

"The covers. And the headboards. It's like she's preparing for a visit from Louis the Fourteenth."

I laughed again. Look at me, being all sociable!

He pulled a book out of his satchel. "Have you been keeping up with *Jane Eyre*?" he asked. We're reading that for women's literature, and Pearl, our teacher, forces us to speak in British accents in class for authenticity. It used to be horribly embarrassing, but I've become used to it, mostly because I try not to speak in class at all (writing fifteen-page essays is more my jam).

I admitted that I was, in fact, keeping up with *Jane Eyre*. I didn't tell him that I'd read it before, though.

"I'm drowning," Sam said. "And Pearl knows it. I'm surprised I haven't been sent a gentle email yet. I mean, I'm not saying I DESERVE to be very kindly asked if I'm having emotional issues that are preventing me from doing my work, but if that's what has to happen, then I'll suck it up and take it."

"At least your British accent is good," I said. "When I try one, I sound like the biggest idiot—and my mum grew up in South Africa."

Cora, I swear, it just slipped right out. I'd sworn not to tell anybody any details about my life, and up till then I'd been perfect. I immediately stopped talking.

"South Africa?" Sam looked amazed, like that was the most exciting thing he'd ever heard. "I didn't know that."

Why would he have known that?

"Just until she was fourteen," I said. "After her dad died, her mom decided to start over again in the US. But the accent stayed."

I didn't for the life of me know why I was giving him so much information. Something about him hypnotized me—the square glasses, the white sneakers, the way he rubbed the bridge of his nose while he spoke.

"Sorry about your grandpa," he said. It was a Canadian "sore-y" that I nobly resisted imitating. "But I mean, that's pretty cool. We're Quebecois on my dad's side, and whenever I speak French, every actual French person judges me so hard, because Canadian French sounds like you're quacking."

At that moment, Lucy came out of the shower in a tattered white towel. I half-expected Lucy to drop the towel right then and there, which is what she does in her room next door (I'm used to her naked body now, but for the first few weeks catching a glimpse of her through the window was taxing), but she just smiled slightly and strutted off toward our cabin, her towel just grazing the bottom of her derrière. I waited until Fern, in a light blue bathrobe, followed her before I stood and gestured to Sam that it was my turn to use the shower. Sam quickly excused himself and disappeared into the other side of the bathroom.

But enough of all that. I want to hear about you! How is Bowen? And have you been to see your dad? I know Dr. Modarressi warned you that it might be triggering for you, given what happened last time you visited, but maybe you could call your dad? And this time make sure none of his financial convict buddies are listening in and leering at your Prada miniskirt. I think you'll be able to have a much more honest conversation that way.

You should totally get some pastries and take them with you if you ever go see him. You'll be a hit with all the inmates (even more so than when you wore your miniskirt, I mean). The number of that place on Seventy-fourth Street is 212.744.3100.

Some things you never forget.

Love from the farm,
Flora

Journal entry, afternoon of September 13

I felt a little better today. Having Sam helps. He's someone to walk to class with and sit with at dinner, and he has a cool style.
Sam outfits:

- *Oversized square glasses*
- *Suspenders (sometimes)*
- *Woolly cardigans (but he only ever wears them to breakfast and at night, because it's still pretty hot during the day)*
- *White grandpa shorts from the seventies*
- *Huge sneakers that squeak when he walks*

Flora Goldwasser
Pigeonhole 44
The Quare Academy
2 Quare Road
Main Stream, NY 12497

September 13

Flora!!!!!

You need to come home THIS INSTANT. If the terrible cell service and menstrual cloth girl weren't enough to merit your leaving, then SCABIES certainly is!!!! Do you want my mom to call a cab? We'll pay! I know you're too interesting for Bowen, or whatever the reason was that you left us for that shithole, but it has to be better than living in a HOVEL!

The only thing is that you might want to wait until next semester to come home, when that bitch Ms. Lancaster goes on maternity leave. The hormones must be impairing her brain function or something, because she's been failing people left and right. She gave me a B+!!!! I'm including my essay for proof that I'm not CRAZY. If you could send it back when you're done reading, that would be super.

Anyway, I have to go. My parents are fighting about my chances at Penn again, and I have to separate them before they murder each other.

  Love forever,
  India

India Katz-Rosen
1025 Fifth Avenue, Apt. 9C
New York, NY 10028

September 15

My dear India,

Okay, first of all, thank you SO much for writing me back and proving that you're alive. Lancaster isn't so bad, and a B+ isn't the end of the world, but I'll read your essay and tell you what I think.

Second of all, I didn't realize how weird and (strangely) cool Guild would be.

The first shocking thing: Althea, the one I saw peeing by her cabin the first day, is the apprentice of Guild this semester. The apprentice is the master player's right-hand woman, and it means she'll be assistant-directing the show that Dean (aka Jenna Lyons aka my mentor) will write, direct, and produce this spring.

Althea was sitting with Luella, a second-year with long, straight blond hair. She looks at you when she speaks and she's always smiling, even when nothing is particularly happy. You know that I usually abhor senseless jolliness, but in Luella's case, it works, somehow.

I chatted a little bit with Agnes, a fellow first-year. He's from Georgia. He has two moms—one of them is Tedra Louis (you know, the famous gender theorist who coined the term "gender warfare"?). So I guess it's no wonder he ended up at Quare. Agnes speaks all slow and Southern, and he never actually talks about his famous mom—even though everyone else does.

Dean mounted the stage suddenly. I didn't even see her come in, but she was suddenly up there, alone, ready to command the space.

"Is everybody here?" She looked around expectantly, black hair moving in one cohesive unit, and when nobody answered, she began. "I suppose having this meeting on millet mountain day wasn't the wisest choice, but eh. I guess it'll separate the wheat from the chaff, if you will."

I let out an appreciative chuckle for the wordplay, but nobody else made a sound.

(I've decided that Dean is my lighthouse: sophisticated, fashionable, and COOL. She's even scaring me less in our mentor/mentee meetings, during which I used to clam up, but lately I've been getting pretty confessional. I even told her about Mum and Daddy's separation.)

"This is Guild, everyone," said Dean. "I'm thrilled you made it. Especially delighted to see some new faces in the audience. First-years, where you at?"

I held up a hand, feeling like the geek of the world, but what else could I have done? Juna, Agnes, and this first-year girl Becca were also in the audience, and they raised their hands too, all a bit meekly.

"Wonderful. So. A quick rundown of what this is, how this works, et cetera. Guild is Quare's oldest and only theater troupe. We put on one or two shows per semester. Written, acted, directed, costumed, and lit by students. This is the real deal, kiddies. Parts were chosen last week for this semester's first show, written by our very own Michael Lansbury, and the next show will be done by yours truly.

"First-years, as tempting as acting sounds, it's important to remember that for your first semester, you won't act. Guild is not about acting. It's about producing theater. So what do first-years do, you might ask? You guys review. We believe here in Guild that good acting starts with good OBSERVING, and good observing is required for good WRITING. So once you've reviewed a show, you're golden. You're free to audition for plays. And only after that can you apply to write your own play. You can direct it, or you can ask for help. We're big on that here.

"There's no real hierarchy, but in the past all writer-directors have been second-years. It just takes that much time to cultivate the necessary experience. So I know that was a lot of information, but I think you'll realize that things in Guild work fairly smoothly. There's a lot of support. You'll sleep in each other's beds during tech week and pin each other's costumes two seconds before the show when you realize you gained three pounds from nervous pre-show eating. Okay, so this speech is getting pretty long, so I think I'll stop talking now. Does anybody have questions?"

Some people asked banal questions, I was too busy staring at Dean to pay attention.

Then Dean asked for two volunteers to review the first fall play, called *Pork Chop,* which goes on right around Halloween. She said she'll pick the better review—that's what she called it, the better one; I was shocked, because this was Quare, after all—and get it published in the *Quare Times,* the collaborative news co-op. I raised my hand, along with that girl Becca. Ugh.

Becca is the only other first-year from the City, and—as anti-Quare as I sound saying this—she's the actual worst. Well, maybe that's an exaggeration. There's just something about her that gets under my skin. Her parents live in Greenwich Village. She thinks that this somehow makes her special. She has enormous, unblinking blue eyes and wears feather earrings. Her chin recedes into her neck as she makes pretentious comments in class. This is major shell speak, I know, but what can I say?

In class, Becca gushes over how much she loved the article that was assigned the previous night, or how excited she is for the next elder circle (Miriam believes in intergenerational healing to combat our youth- and beauty-obsessed culture, which has replaced traditions that value wisdom and age). I spend too much time growing silently furious at Becca and her gushing. It's becoming unhealthy, how much I hate this girl. My teeth are grinding even as I write this. She is my sworn enemy, India. Worse than Priscilla Gubermeyer back at Bowen.

I'll stop bitching now. And I'll focus on the positive: Guild is cool. It's not like the other clubs at Quare. It seems edgy, fast-paced, even competitive.

It seems—dare I say it?—exciting.

Bisoux,
Flora

Miss Tulip blog post from last March

misstulipblog.com

HOME   SEARCH   ARCHIVES   PRESS   CONTACT

MEMORY JOG

<  >

Photos c/o Elijah Huck
Click to navigate through photo album

Miss Tulip isn't exactly the exercising type—she's too busy with her various social engagements, political protests, and academic pursuits to frequent the gym—but when this 1940s gym uniform came along, she felt called to go for a little jog in the park. Not Central Park, of course, which is always flooded with tourists, but Carl Schurz, a little gem on the Upper East Side. Miss Tulip jogged along the reservoir for about thirty minutes. Of course, she had to stop every few minutes to catch up with acquaintances, and by the end, had collected a whole flock of fellow joggers, all flipping off catcallers and chatting about the oppressive male gaze.

When Miss T wears this playsuit, she feels like an adolescent in 1944 who collects aluminum for the war and gets fresh with boys in the backseats of red cars. And if that weren't enough to put a spring in her step, the soft cotton—and the beautiful burgundy—alone would do it. Who needs Lululemon when you've got vintage?

THE LOOK: 1940s COTTON MOORE BRAND STANDARDIZED GYM UNIFORM (COLOR: ROSE PINK) WITH LINDA EMBROIDERED ON FRONT POCKET | | WHITE AND BLACK SADDLE SHOES | | ANKLE-LENGTH WHITE SOCKS | | ADJUSTABLE BELT AT WAIST | | BURGUNDY HAIR RIBBON | | BLAIR BOUTIQUE ACRYLIC SHELL SETTING: CARL SCHURZ PARK | | UPPER EAST SIDE

Elijah's interview in Nymphette magazine (September issue)

nymphettemag.com

| WORD | IMAGE | SOUND | SEARCH | JOIN | CONTACT |

NYMPHETTE MAGAZINE

Ask an Older Dude: Elijah Huck

Okay, so he's not THAT much older—nineteen—but Elijah Huck has already captured the minds, and, more so, the hearts of all of us here at *Nymphette*. Feminist? Naturally. Artist? Of course—have you seen his award-winning photo series, "Miss Tulip"? Wearing cuffed jeans, a bomber jacket, and his signature round glasses, Huck sat down with *Nymphette's* features editor, Grace Wang, to talk about his hair-care regimen, Miss Tulip, and muses.

Nymphette: *What's up?*
Elijah Huck: Not all that much, actually. I just finished a huge term paper, so I washed my hair for the first time in about two weeks. So there's that.

N: That's exciting. How often do you usually wash it?
EH: Well, it depends. Usually just a couple times a week. I'm not saying that's how often I should wash it, but that's pretty much what happens.

Hello! October's theme is LUST. For whom does your heart beat, Nymphettes? Let's see what you've got! Send your work to submissions@ nymphettemag .com.

ABOUT *NYMPHETTE*
Nymphette is an online feminist arts & culture magazine for teenagers. Each month, we choose a theme, and then you send us your writing, photography, and artwork.

N: Let's talk about "Miss Tulip." Readers want to know: What happened?
EH: That's so nice that you're a fan. Honestly, we—Miss Tulip and I—just got too busy to keep up with the blog this year.

N: There's no chance you'll tell us who Miss Tulip is, right? How about a hint?
EH: I wish I could say, but I can't. All you'll be able to know about her is what you can see from the neck down. Miss Tulip isn't supposed to exist in this world, or feel rooted to it in the form of just one person. But at the same time, she isn't lofty or merely an ideal, and I can confirm that she's just as real, and just as delightful, as she seems in the photos. Her privacy is her choice, and it's something we all have to respect.

N: I don't think anyone will be satisfied with that answer, but I can tell you're uncomfortable, so we can move on.
EH: Not uncomfortable! But yeah, not giving anything away.

N: Can you at least say if she's ever coming back?
EH: I will say that there's a possibility, but it's a small one. That's the thing about muses—you never know when they'll return.

N: It's clear when you look at all the pictures of Miss Tulip that you have a particular relationship to your subject. The gaze is adoring, like the way someone looks at his lover. Are you in love with Miss Tulip?
EH: Wow! That's quite a question. Let's just say Miss Tulip and I were—are—close friends.

N: I won't keep prying, but I don't believe you, and neither will our readers.
EH [laughing]: That's fine with me.

N: How'd you get into photography?
EH: That's a tough question. I guess I've always loved taking

pictures, but I didn't really understand how it could be an art in itself—like, I'd take pictures to remember stuff that was beautiful and unusual. Now I find myself gravitating toward things that are interesting: sometimes ugly, sometimes deformed, but I'll like the lines they make.

N: Are you professionally trained?
EH: Sort of? I went to this supersmall alternative boarding school in upstate New York, and all these artists who live in the area come through to teach classes—artists in residence, they're called. When I was a first-year—sorry, a junior—we had this super-rad dude come teach us how to take pictures. He had this thing where before we could even touch the camera, we had to learn how to see. The class was actually called "Ways of Seeing." A lot of staring at walls and trees and trying to read texture.

And then over the summer I started doing Chicago Arts, which is this program for teenagers into visual and performing arts; and I met a bunch of friends there who just wanted to talk about, like, making art all day. It's an amazing opportunity that they afford to young artists, and I learned a lot from them—and some of us ended up going to that same little boarding school upstate.

N: Do you want to be a photographer when you grow up?
EH: I thought this was "Ask an Older Dude"! Am I not supposed to be a grown-up already?

N: Do you feel like a grown-up?
EH: On some days. I recently went back home to Queens—I go to Columbia, so it's kind of a commute—to spend a few weeks with my mom, just because we're really close and I missed her. So I've been living in my childhood home, right next door to my childhood best friend, but still feeling kind of mature, I guess.

Well, there you have it, Nymphettes. Smart, stylish, AND caring.
Please try to restrain yourselves in the comments section.

And there, snaking just between the lines, was everything I
needed to hold on to the hope that he was coming for me after all.

Journal entry, afternoon of September 23

*After everyone went to sleep last night, I snuck into the library
and Googled Elijah, just for old times' sake. I haven't done it
since being at Quare, and as soon as I saw the interview, I was
immediately flooded with warmth. My thoughts:*

- *See! He DOES care for me.*
- *Why hasn't he written me yet? Or confirmed his December visit?*
- *I'mhismuseI'mhismuseI'mhismuse*
- *He's off being an artist. Of course he hasn't been in touch.*

*I read the line about not being meant to be rooted to this
world maybe fifty times, and then I turned off the computer and
hyperventilated for a while. The library was completely dark and
silent, and the computer I'd been using was warm.*

To: All-staff <everyone@nymphettemag.com>
From: Wink DelDuca <wink@nymphettemag.com>
Subject: Miss Tulip
September 24, 9:54 p.m.

Salutations,

Wink here with the weekly digest.

After we published Grace's piece yesterday, the comment section blew up, just as expected. I've been hearing from many of you editors, too, and it seems that everybody's on the same page: we want Miss Tulip back, and we want her back now. As you've read, Elijah seems pretty set on staying tight-lipped, but a girl can have hope, can't she?

As usual, we'll be meeting on Wednesday evening. Those of you who are local will be at the diner, and we'll Skype the rest of you in. We can drown our feelings in burgers and milkshakes and do some serious scheming. It's Rhonda's turn to buy.

;)

Wink
Editor in Chief, *Nymphette* magazine
Nymphette is an online feminist arts & culture magazine for teenagers. Each month, we choose a theme, and then you send us your writing, photography, and artwork.

Attempt 1

Elijah Huck
245 West 107th Street
New York, NY 10025

September 24

Dear Elijah,

I'm here at Quare.

It's just as bizarre as you made it out to be. And it's strange to think that I've only been here for less than a month. I'm already forgetting how to shop online.

~~Why did you decide not to come to Quare this year? Did it have anything to do with me?~~

Funny story! One of my neighbors, Marigold, was sitting next to me in the computer lab in the library and pulled up the latest issue of *Nymphette,* which as you know features an interview with you.

"Can you believe he *went* here?" she kept asking. "I'm such a huge Miss Tulip fan."

I tried to play it cool, and be all blasé ~~but I was having difficulty swallowing.~~

Attempt 2

Elijah Huck
245 West 107th Street
New York, NY 10025

September 24

Dear Elijah,

Everyone here nods and says, "This Friend speaks my mind"
when they agree with someone.

My roommate is Juna. She's okay, but very serious and I think
she hates me. There's an awful wood nymph girl named Becca
who thinks the proportions of sex are akin to an orange trying to
fit into a straw.

It's awful and I hate it. Can you come get me?

Attempt 3

Elijah Huck
245 West 107th Street
New York, NY 10025

September 24

Dear Elijah,

You would be so proud of how I'm adapting to Quare. I love how kooky and bizarre everyone is! I'm even embracing "no shell speak," though you teased me endlessly about not being able to do it when you told me about the rule last year.

That said, I haven't become ugly or unstylish. I'm maintaining relationships with my favorite Etsy merchants, who continue to update me immediately when they get something in that they know I'll like. I trust you won't tell anyone that I've been using the Internet like this when you come in December.

Attempt 4

Elijah Huck
245 West 107th Street
New York, NY 10025

September 24

Dear Elijah,

~~I want to bury my head in your neck and smell your flannel and wear your tiny round glasses but as a joke and everyone in Maison Kayser will look over and be like, Oh, those two again, they're so in love~~

The actual letter I sent Elijah

Elijah Huck
245 West 107th Street
New York, NY 10025

September 24

Dear Elijah,

I've been at Quare for about two weeks now, and I have to say that it's everything I thought it would be—and possibly more. I made a valiant effort to start off on the right foot (I even read the entirety of Naomi Klein's writings over the summer in addition to *Gender Trouble*), but I'm not exactly rolling in friends at this point. Between writing a loser of a poem during an orientation exercise and taking all the good stuff from the Free Store before everyone else got to it, I've established myself as the neighborhood oddball. A Boo Radley of sorts. Only much less creepy (let's hope).

Even so, it feels exciting. It feels like a new chapter, exactly what I need to clear my head from this past year, what with my parents and Bowen drama and the photo series. To be quite honest, I think the blog—in a certain way—saved me from thinking about all that other stuff. You could call it the perfect distraction.

I'm really looking forward to your visit. There are so many possible settings for Miss Tulip posts, and you can be sure I'm scoping them out!

Flora

Journal entry, evening of October 1

Sam and I have been sitting together at dinner this whole week, making snide comments about the Quares. Yesterday, after we circled up and sang the pre-meal song about letting life move and stir us, I stood to the side, as usual, waiting for the crowd to die down before getting food.

"You're always the last person to take food," Sam noted, migrating over to where I was standing to wait beside me. Today his high-waisted slacks were plaid, secured with suspenders visible under his red-and-brown cardigan.

"I don't do lines," I said, only half kidding. "They strike me as so plebian."

He laughed. "And you are . . . ?"

"A patrician, obviously."

"Obviously. Has anyone ever complimented you on your posture? You're like a ramrod."

I told him that they had, just once or twice. My heart was beating fast, but not Elijah fast, just like I'm-a-little-bit-excited-and-I've-missed-witty-banter fast.

We sat at a table with Juna. For dinner was Miriam's famous lentil loaf, which sounds much more disgusting than it is.

"Is this supposed to be so solid?" Sam slapped his fork on the mound of lentil loaf, which quivered gently.

"Again with the lentil loaf," I said. "You really have something against it. I think it's good."

"Oh, it's swell," he said. "Now we have some form of self-defense."

He looked around, then leaned forward conspiratorially.

"You never know when everyone is going to snap. They may

seem sedated with love now, but I don't want to know what's going to happen when they find out how much money you spent on that outfit."

I pushed his shoulder. Inside, I was beaming. There's nothing like someone noticing my outfit. Despite Quare's efforts to stamp this out of me, it is my DRUG.

"Stop it," I said. "I look the part. See? I'm finally starting to fit in."

He was kind of right, though. I was wearing a tunic with clogs, but the tunic was far from tattered. It was vintage DVF, for Christ's sake. And the clogs, painted with an intricate design depicting a Renaissance scene, were comfortable, sure, but they're those ones Daddy got me from Amsterdam on his "Amsterdam Dental Group Goes to Amsterdam" trip.

At that very moment, Althea and Michael Lansbury started doing contact improvisation right there in the dining hall. It's this form of dancing where you're always in contact, like sliding over each other's backs and rolling on the floor on top of each other.

Needless to say, I would never in a million years do contact improv.

"I think," I said, while everyone was still staring at Althea and Michael, "that once you've been here too long, you're sort of not fit to be around people anymore. You go off the deep end."

"Going off the deep end—that's kind of a perfect metaphor," Sam said. "Maybe going to Quare is like walking into a pond. Some of us are on the edge, just dipping our toes in from time to time. Other people are wading in, really getting their knees wet and getting used to the water like moms do, one segment of their bodies every fifteen minutes. Some people are actually swimming, doing those stupid flips in the water that always get water up your nose. And some people are, like, pegged under a rock at the bottom of the pond, just meditating. Those are the super-Quares." He looked meaningfully at the Oracle of Quare, seven feet tall and skinny, with

long, tangled yellow hair, then wearing a rainbow tie-dyed onesie and
heart-shaped sunglasses and holding Basilia over his head like in that
scene from The Lion King.

"Where are we?" I asked.

"Well." Sam leaned back in his chair. "It's hard to say, because
I've only known you for a month, Flo-Go, but I think you're a toe-
dipper. But more of a toe-dipper than you'd admit to being. Me, I'm
not putting my toe in that nasty shit. I'm, like, sunbathing on the
dock. SPF one hundred. I burn easily."

It's such a shame I'm not attracted to him, because he's so
funny, and I like talking to him. He really does remind me of my
grandfather: crotchety when he's hungry, uneasy around leafy green
vegetables. He mediates so easily between the Quares, who seem to
really like him—even though he makes fun of them all the time—
and people like me. I feel like all I do is laugh around him, and it's
been so long since I've laughed this hard.

"You two are such characters, but I don't think that's a fair
metaphor," Juna said, obviously using the confrontation strategy
of keeping her tone level and beginning with a lighthearted, non-
judgmental statement to remain amicable. But she had that pinched
look on her face that she gets when somebody says something she
doesn't agree with. "Quare takes some getting used to, but I think
you'll find that it's less homogenous than you think it is. Give it a
chance. Or maybe talk to the Oracle about it? His office hours are on
Wednesday nights, and if you're unhappy, it's really on you to address
it."

I'd thought that Juna and I had made strides in our relationship
ever since I had recently and vocally agreed with her that Quare
should do more to acknowledge that the school exists on land stolen
from indigenous people. But tension clearly bubbled below the surface
of her suggestion.

"I was talking to the Oracle the other day, actually," Sam said.

"He doesn't believe in condoms because they make sex meaningless. He looks like he'd give a great massage, if you're interested."

It sounds mean, now that I write it, but he really was joking. He was smiling at Juna the whole time, trying to form an alliance with her. Juna, though, wasn't biting.

"Thanks for the recommendation," she said, not unkindly, stacking her dishes and standing up. The back of her skirt was tucked into her underwear, but it would be shell speak to point it out to her, so I averted my gaze.

"My pleasure," Sam said easily.

"Well, I'll see you around, I guess," Juna said, and left.

Just because I have an ally now doesn't mean I miss India, Cora, and Lael any less. Sam is just someone who sits across from me in the library and emails back and forth with me to pass the time.

The emails Sam and I sent back and forth to pass the time in the library

To: Flora Goldwasser <fgoldwasser@quare.edu>
From: Sam Chabot <schabot@quare.edu>
Subject: Re:
October 2, 9:10 p.m.

I just found a long, curly black hair in my vegan oatmeal cookie. I feel like you'd know what to do with this information.

To: Sam Chabot <schabot@quare.edu>
From: Flora Goldwasser <fgoldwasser@quare.edu>
Subject: Re:
October 2, 9:15 p.m.

Spit it out, I guess?

To: Flora Goldwasser <fgoldwasser@quare.edu>
From: Sam Chabot <schabot@quare.edu>
Subject: Re:
October 2, 9:16 p.m.

Genius.

I thought I'd be cool with it, but this natural stuff is kind of wearing on me. I think I need a cigar.

To: Sam Chabot <schabot@quare.edu>
From: Flora Goldwasser <fgoldwasser@quare.edu>
Subject: Re:
October 2, 9:21 p.m.

If you're not a hippie, why are you at Quare?

To: Flora Goldwasser <fgoldwasser@quare.edu>
From: Sam Chabot <schabot@quare.edu>
Subject: Re:
October 2, 9:24 p.m.

Public school sucks.

To: Sam Chabot <schabot@quare.edu>
From: Flora Goldwasser <fgoldwasser@quare.edu>
Subject: Re:
October 2, 9:24 p.m.

Really?

To: Flora Goldwasser <fgoldwasser@quare.edu>
From: Sam Chabot <schabot@quare.edu>
Subject: Re:
October 2, 9:25 p.m.

Okay, maybe that's not the whole truth. There was a small incident last spring, and my analyst said it would be good for me to get out of Montréal for a while.

To: Sam Chabot <schabot@quare.edu>
From: Flora Goldwasser <fgoldwasser@quare.edu>
Subject: Re:
October 2, 9:26 p.m.

"Montréal." *Avec l'accent aigu.*

Also, you see an analyst?

To: Flora Goldwasser <fgoldwasser@quare.edu>
From: Sam Chabot <schabot@quare.edu>
Subject: Re:
October 2, 9:30 p.m.

Mais oui. Bien sûr.

To: Sam Chabot <schabot@quare.edu>
From: Flora Goldwasser <fgoldwasser@quare.edu>
Subject: Re:
October 2, 9:33 p.m.

I guess I don't know much about public school.

But seriously, that sounds hard.

To: Flora Goldwasser <fgoldwasser@quare.edu>
From: Sam Chabot <schabot@quare.edu>
Subject: Re:
October 2, 9:34 p.m.

"That sounds hard." The Quare motto. I feel like I hear that
fourteen times a day.

To: Sam Chabot <schabot@quare.edu>
From: Flora Goldwasser <fgoldwasser@quare.edu>
Subject: Re:
October 2, 9:34 p.m.

Sorry to be such a cliché.

To: Flora Goldwasser <fgoldwasser@quare.edu>
From: Sam Chabot <schabot@quare.edu>
Subject: Re:
October 2, 9:36 p.m.

That's okay. It was hard.

To: Sam Chabot <schabot@quare.edu>
From: Flora Goldwasser <fgoldwasser@quare.edu>
Subject: Re:
October 2, 9:37 p.m.

Can I ask you something? Why do you dress like you're eighty-five? Your cardigan today, for example. I think it's really cool and everything, but I'm curious.

To: Flora Goldwasser <fgoldwasser@quare.edu>
From: Sam Chabot <schabot@quare.edu>
Subject: Re:
October 2, 9:38 p.m.

I'm pretty sure that's shell speak. I could report you for that, you know.

To: Sam Chabot <schabot@quare.edu>
From: Flora Goldwasser <fgoldwasser@quare.edu>
Subject: Re:
October 2, 9:38 p.m.

Sorry.

To: Flora Goldwasser <fgoldwasser@quare.edu>
From: Sam Chabot <schabot@quare.edu>
Subject: Re:
October 2, 9:41 p.m.

I dress like this because I appreciate a casual, durable knit.

This is my leisure cardigan.

Maybe one day you'll see me in a more luxurious garment, but not here.

To: Sam Chabot <schabot@quare.edu>
From: Flora Goldwasser <fgoldwasser@quare.edu>
Subject: Re:
October 2, 9:47 p.m.

Sarcasm is violence, you know.

To: Flora Goldwasser <fgoldwasser@quare.edu>
From: Sam Chabot <schabot@quare.edu>
Subject: Re:
October 2, 9:47 p.m.

A quiet but deadly violence?

To: Sam Chabot <schabot@quare.edu>
From: Flora Goldwasser <fgoldwasser@quare.edu>
Subject: Re:
October 2, 9:48 p.m.

Nice riff on our Peace on Earth homework.

To: Flora Goldwasser <fgoldwasser@quare.edu>
From: Sam Chabot <schabot@quare.edu>
Subject: Re:
October 2, 9:49 p.m.

Don't act so shocked that I did the reading.

To: Sam Chabot <schabot@quare.edu>
From: Flora Goldwasser <fgoldwasser@quare.edu>
Subject: Re:
October 2, 9:49 p.m.

I didn't say I thought you'd actually DONE the reading.

To: Flora Goldwasser <fgoldwasser@quare.edu>
From: Sam Chabot <schabot@quare.edu>
Subject: Re:
October 2, 9:51 p.m.

Harsh, but fair. Just as a patrician should be.

Allison's legendary birth email

To: Faculty, staff, and students <everyone@quare.edu>
From: Allison Longfield <alongfield@quare.edu>
Subject: birth
October 5, 8:44 a.m.

Dear Friends,

As some of you might have heard, I gave birth yesterday afternoon to a healthy and wise child, Olive. Inspired by our dear friend Meghan, who's in Sudan this year on a Peace Corps mission, I thought I'd share some highlights from my birth with the community.

I was lucky enough to be in my birthing spot—the garden—when my water broke, splashing into the soil and reminding me of my connection to the earth. I squatted right where I was, between the onions and the zucchini, and allowed my body to sink into the ground. I closed my eyes and let the cool breeze tickle across my cheeks.

When I was certain that the contractions were real, I phoned my partner, who triples as my midwife and doula. He arrived in about thirty minutes, by which point the pain had become severe. Over the next hours, as many of you harvested crops around me while offering the occasional shout of encouragement and emotional check-in, I passed both blood and embryonic fluids, as well as a fair amount of fecal matter, into the soil (you're welcome for the fertilizer, capital-F Friends!). Luckily, my partner was, as always, incredibly attentive—kissing and even stimulating me as necessary to bring my blood pressure down.

When Olive finally arrived outside of my body, my partner snipped the cord that united us with a pair of gardening shears. The placenta, as well as the cord, is in a wooden box in our house; we invite everyone to come meet Olive and interact with the cord, if you've never seen one before.

Peace,

Allison
Peace Studies teacher, Quare Academy
BA, Hampshire College

Journal entry, night of October 8

Sam and I were walking back from the garden after shared work when we reached the dining hall. Without any warning whatsoever, he jumped onto a picnic table, swung himself onto the roof of the kitchen, and clambered up so that he was sitting on the tiles. I stared up at him, still dumbfounded.

"Come on up," he called down to me.

I didn't exactly want to go up there—climbing has never been my forte—but somehow I managed to pull myself, with a lot of effort and some tugging on Sam's part, into a seated position beside him. Sam was eating Panda Poop—the most sugary cereal Quare has; they're little balls of peanut butter and raw sugar—from the box. I have no idea how he got the box or where it came from.

"Welcome to my perch," Sam said. "I come up here to people watch all the time."

"But there are no people out," I said, looking around. It was gray and empty, twenty minutes before dinner, and the campus was deserted.

"You appear to be correct," he said. "So let's pretend there are people. Oh wait, there's Zev, walking across campus like he owns the place."

"He's sauntering."

"SAUNTERING?" Sam whistled. "Great work. A-plus. Gold star. Blue ribbon."

I started to laugh. "Cream of the crop. Cat's pajamas. The bee's knees."

I got a sudden urge to ask him something I'd wanted to know since the last week. "Can I ask why your analyst thought it would be good for you to leave Montréal for a while?"

Sam squinted into the horizon for a few seconds, eyebrows crinkling over his eyelids. "Sure, you can ask."

"Well, I'm asking."

He was silent for a few minutes more.

"You don't have to tell me," I said.

"No," said Sam. "I want to. Just give me a second."

I waited. I dug my hand into his Panda Poop and grabbed a handful. As soon as I began to crunch down, filling my mouth with alarmingly sugary peanut butter gunk, Sam spoke again.

"I mean, I wasn't molested by my aunt or whipped with a Gucci belt or orphaned at age ten and sent to live with my evil aunt and uncle," he said.

"Just because you're not Charlie Kelmeckis or Harry Potter doesn't mean your life hasn't been hard."

Sam swatted me with the cereal box. "Put a lid on it, Flora. It's my turn to talk now."

I swallowed a laugh. "Sorry. I'm trying to be an active listener."

"Can it," he said. "Anyway, I had my first anxiety attack when I was seven or eight, I think. We were driving over the Golden Gate Bridge on vacation, and I knew it was going to collapse. I knew it was going to collapse and that we were going to fall into the bay. It didn't, but we did have to pull over until I calmed down.

"By the time I was twelve, I was a full-blown nervous wreck. I worried about my own death pretty much constantly. I couldn't ride in cars or take trains or even leave my room very often. When I walked to school—because I couldn't go in cars, remember—I went the two-mile route, and I took all the back streets to avoid cars. I even wore a bike helmet and kneepads, no shit."

I nodded my appreciation for the gravity of the situation. I really WAS trying to engage in active listening. Sam didn't seem to notice. He was still looking at the horizon and the blue-purple-green-red mountains in the distance.

"So my parents took me to the first of many therapists, who put me on some stuff to help with the anxiety, and for about two years afterward I was a calm, happy, blob. I looked like one of those hovering things in a Zoloft ad. I gained about fifty pounds, which was okay, because I was so skinny before, and also I grew about five inches, so there was that."

"Was it happily ever after?" I asked hopefully.

Sam looked at me scornfully. "In your dreams," he said. "And I'm not done."

"Sorry. Go on."

"So after the Zoloft, I was pretty much your typical kid. The years went on, and I did more normal-kid stuff, like learn to drive, acquire a taste for old movies, and even enter into my very first relationship. Her name was Dorothy, by the way, and we were very much in love. But I'll save that for another time, because it doesn't actually have anything to do with this story. You following, Flo-Go?"

I nodded.

"So this is maybe eight months ago, at this point. I woke up one morning to the sound of my mom crying. I ran into the living room assuming that one of my grandparents was dead. But it turned out that it wasn't one of my grandparents. It was my dad. The police had found his parked car by the side of the bridge, and then they'd found his body on the ice below the bridge. We didn't even know he was depressed. My mom says he must have decided to do it very recently, because he'd just been told that his business was going to have to file for bankruptcy."

Sam swallowed hard. My heart was racing, and I felt like crying and throwing up. I didn't know what to do or say, so I just grabbed Sam's cold hand and squeezed.

"After that, I stopped taking the anxiety meds pretty quickly. I felt like they were preventing me from, I don't know, experiencing my grief to the fullest extent. I don't know why that's something I felt I

had to experience—an obligation to my dad, I guess. So I began to
spiral. And pretty soon, when I couldn't stand the sadness, I began
to obsess over other things. I got really into my music and started
writing songs. I wasn't sleeping at all, or eating, which weirdly gave
me superhuman-like energy. This went on for a few weeks, but when
you're not sleeping or eating, that's enough time for you to pretty
much lose it.

"My mom was like, 'We're going back to the shrink,' but I was
like, 'Why? I'm doing great.' It was like I was caffeinated without
ever needing to eat, drink, or sleep. What's wrong with that? So we
made a deal: I'll go, but first I'm going to perform at this open mic
that my cousin Bobby hooked up for me. I was convinced that this
was going to be my big break, that some big-shot person was going to
be in the audience and see that I was the next Buddy Holly."

"My God." I knew where this was going. My palms were even
sweating a little bit.

"So the days before the performance, I didn't sleep—even less
than usual, I mean. I practiced nonstop to make the song even
more genius than it already is. I got to the place early, like, five hours
early, and play some more backstage. My memory of this is pretty
blank from here on out, actually, so you'll have to watch the
YouTube video next time you're on the computer. All I remember is
wearing one of my dad's old suits—which was superbaggy, because
of the weight loss—and trying to sing at the same high pitch as
Frankie Valli."

He was silent. I was silent.

"Were all your friends there?" I asked.

"Nope. But it spread pretty quickly around school. Someone
filmed it. Obviously. Because it's on YouTube."

"Did you watch it?"

"Yeah."

"So that's why you're here."

"Pretty much. I wrote a heart-wrenching essay to get in here, and I guess they ate it up."

"But you're on . . . stuff?"

He nodded. "Antidepressants twice a day, sleeping pills every night, Xanax when I need it. I try not to use it, even though it feels fucking awesome, because I feel like after other stuff, I can take it from there."

I nodded. "Thanks for telling me all that stuff. That's really horrible."

He shrugged. "It's a little easier now. But sometimes it hits me, you know?"

"I know."

"Your turn."

I shook my head. "My parents divorced recently, which was hard, but hardly traumatic."

"You're from a broken home, Flo-Go? No shit. I didn't realize that about you."

We sat in contemplative silence for a few minutes, until the dinner bell rang out below us and I jumped about three feet in the air. The sound was amplified because of our position, and we scampered off the roof before anyone could see that we'd been up there. Climbing is encouraged, probably—to explore our hierarchical differences or whatever.

Reader, does it seem obvious what I'm setting up for you here by including these exchanges with and reflections on Sam? At this point, in October, I did have the beginning threads of expectation: despite the fact that I was still blinded by my love for Elijah, I found myself thinking more and more about Sam at times usually punctuated by longing for Elijah: in the shower, before bed, while taking long solitary walks. I wasn't attracted to Sam, not really, but something about him made my breath turn shallow, if only because I recognized something of myself in him, something I thought only existed outside of Quare.

Postcard from Elijah, maddeningly vague and putzy, decorated with Cindy Sherman's Untitled Film Still #21 (1978)

Flora Goldwasser
Pigeonhole 44
The Quare Academy
2 Quare Road
Main Stream, NY 12497

october 10
dear flora,
hope quare is treating you well / not sure if dec. will happen / but will keep you posted / don't forget to smile / or just stare intently / cindy sherman self-portraits forever —e

Journal entry, late night of October 12

    Got an Elijah postcard. My chest immediately tightened, and my heart felt like it was close to exploding. Of COURSE he sent a Cindy Sherman postcard; he's always loved her, and the fact that he said Cindy Sherman forever to me makes me feel like he might love ME. My arms and legs are shaking. I love him so freaking much. I'm in the library, reading old Miss Tulip posts and looking for evidence that he does love me HE DOES LOVE ME DOES HE LOVE ME

misstulipblog.com

HOME   SEARCH   ARCHIVES   PRESS   CONTACT

GREEN WITH ENVY

<      >

Photos c/o Elijah Huck
Click to navigate through photo album

The only redeeming feature of the cold that's descended onto
the city is that it's finally time to break out the serious winter
gear. And there's nothing Miss Tulip loves more than sweater
dresses—preferably tailored to a T (if you don't have a tailor, find
one immediately). Warm knits are perfect for self-expression; on the
wintry landscape, they're sometimes the only things we see. Nobody
quite understands the power of a dress like Miss Tulip; I tease her
about the fact that she has a different dress for every five degrees
Fahrenheit. ➡*He did tease me about this, made me feel like one of those
women whose husbands love them so much and shower them with jewels and
pretend to begrudge them but really love them so much and would be super
lost without them.*

— Tulip

The gorgeous moss green isn't even the best part of this hooded wool dress. The magic is in the details. It falls to the mid-lower leg for optimal warmth, and its pale flora-shaped buttons set off the deep hue of the coat. The platform boots Miss T chose to wear on her feet aren't *technically* from the fifties, but sometimes you've got to let the seventies in. ➡ *Shows that he thinks of me as versatile, admires the fact that I'm not just ONE THING but contain multitudes, just like Walt Whitman said.*

Oh, and a word about the setting: New Brighton, Staten Island. They just opened an ice cream shop that has two vegan flavors. If you can brave the crowds of NYU students, you deserve the vegan ice cream of your choice. Miss Tulip met a few friends after attending a demonstration for animal rights at a nearby artisanal grocery store. ➡ *Always loved that I'm mostly vegan, said so few people actually practice what they preach and that I was refreshing, would thrive at Quare.*

THE LOOK: FIFTIES | CASHMERE COCOON SWEATER DRESS (COLOR: MOSS GREEN) | | BLACK STOCKINGS | | PLATFORM ANKLE BOOTS | | VINTAGE PERSIAN WOOL BLACK HAND MUFF–CLUTCH COMBINATION (COURTESY OF GRANDMOTHER TULIP)
SETTING: SINGLE-FAMILY HOME | | NEW BRIGHTON, STATEN ISLAND

Attempt 5

Elijah Huck
245 West 107th Street
New York, NY 10025

October 13

Elijah,

~~WHAT THE HELL DO YOU MEAN, YOU'RE NOT SURE
WHETHER OR NOT YOU'LL BE ABLE TO COME IN
DECEMBER???~~

I was thinking about the poem we used to talk about, the Emily
Dickinson one about a volcano that's really about her vagina.
And how when you told me that, I didn't believe you. And how
you were like, "You have to pay attention to the language. It's
all figurative." And how I was like, "You shouldn't sexualize
Emily like that." But then you told me that she wants us to—that
that's why the innuendo is there in the first place, so we can
think of her in that way without her having to explicitly state it:
I AM A SEXUAL BEING. Because, you know, she was Emily
Dickinson, and she looked kind of like a spinster platypus. Lately
I've been feeling like Emily, placing innuendos and hints all over
the place for you to find, like a scavenger hunt, or something.
And you come so close to finding all the pieces, but there's that
one that's missing, and neither of us really knows what or where
it is.

I was thinking about how we were in Margot Patisserie when
you said this, probably drinking coffee, and it was probably
a Thursday afternoon, and I probably was waiting for you to

ask me if I wanted to go for a walk, and I probably would have
agreed.

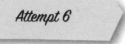

Attempt 6

Elijah Huck
245 West 107th Street
New York, NY 10025

October 13

Dear Elijah,

It's like that poem, "Along the Sun-Drenched Roadside," by
Rainer Maria Rilke. The poem you said was your favorite poem,
and the one that's now my favorite too. The guy passes by this
trough of sparkling cold water, but he can't drink it in normally.
He has to let it seep in through his wrists, because drinking would
be "too powerful, too clear."

And it's a love poem, really, because the last stanza goes, "Thus,
if you came, I could be satisfied / to let my hand rest lightly, for
a moment, / lightly, upon your shoulder or your breast." The
message being that the smallest things, the "unhurried gesture[s]
of restraint," are so perfect and satisfying in themselves.

It's like how when you caught my gaze for a minute—"lightly,
for a moment, / lightly"—or brushed your hands against mine,
and I got tingles ~~in my underwear~~ up and down my body, it was
so, so much more meaningful than if you had just reached down
and kissed me, because isn't the anticipation of the thing always
better than

Attempt 7

Elijah Huck
245 West 107th Street
New York, NY 10025

October 13

Dear Elijah,

In the words of Beyoncé, "Why don't you love me when I make me so easy to love?"

The letter I sent to Elijah

Elijah Huck
245 West 107th Street
New York, NY 10025

October 13

Dear Elijah,

One of my favorite things to do here is canoe alone. You know how much I love my alone time (remember how Wednesdays were my introvert days, and I'd refuse to talk to anyone except sometimes you?), but it's so scarce here—they really schedule us within an inch of our lives with shared work, nonviolent communication, and electives. So sometimes I just escape to the pond with a few books and my parasol (and, if I'm being honest, the dark chocolate truffles my friends send me from the city) and spend the afternoon floating. I've only been attacked by bugs a couple of times; usually it's perfectly beautiful.

It's almost like I don't know what to do with myself here. I haven't really settled into any role like I had at Bowen: I'm nobody's friend (well, I kind of have one friend, actually), nobody's sister, nobody's muse. It's a precious time, I guess, the predefinition stage, but also a disorienting one. Maybe that's why I'm clinging so furiously to my old stuff—dressing in all my old clothes, clacking on my typewriter until my roommate groans and leaves the cabin to study elsewhere. It's really the only thing reminding me of who I really am.

I'd love to hear about your sophomore year!

Flora

To: Faculty, staff, and students <everyone@quare.edu>
From: Miriam Row <mrow@quare.edu>
Subject: Re: birth
October 13

Everyone,

I know you'll join me in congratulating Allison on the birth of her child, as well as thanking her for demystifying the process of childbirth.

On an unrelated note, I'd like to make a request: the Oracle mentioned that the package room is looking rather crowded. To ensure that everyone feels comfortable in this space, please request packages from friends, family, and vendors off campus only when absolutely necessary.

I invite you to come speak with me if this presents a problem for you.

Blessings,
Miriam

QUARE TIMES

The Quare Academy Student News Collaboration,
October 15

QUARE SHARE DELIGHTS AUDIENCE

By Shy Lenore

To those of us who were at Quare since first year, Quare Share—a start-of-school tradition featuring student talent in both classes—is nothing new. For others, it's a chance for students to see what their new peers are made of.

Dean Elliot, master player of Guild, Quare's oldest and only theater troupe, hosted this year's Share; it's tradition for master player to serve as emcee.

"Oh, it was a blast," Elliot said. "All the kids did such a neat job."

One of those "kids," as Elliot, a second-year, called them, was Marigold Chen, a first-year from San Francisco. Chen performed Eminem's "Lose Yourself," much to the delight of her audience.

"I first sang the song last year, at my old high school," she said. "Everyone was kind of shocked and then I became known for it."

Here at the Academy, Chen was bombarded with applause.

And so was Agnes Surl, another first-year from outside of Atlanta, GA. Surl, who organized the largest Atlanta Moth story share, told the audience about a cross-country road trip with an alcoholic uncle.

"[Surl] was sensational," said Alice Jackson, a second-year. "I haven't laughed that hard in a long time."

GOT WATER? STUDENTS DISCUSS MEANS OF TRANSPORTATION

By Juna Díaz

We all know it's a good idea to stay hydrated, but on a campus that's long outlawed plastic bottles, what's a person to do?

Perhaps the most prevalent trend for transporting water is the Nalgene bottle.

"I don't go anywhere without my Nalgene," said Clive Daniels, a second-year. "It's the perfect size, and it hardly ever spills."

Others, however, are partial to

the aluminum bike bottle, whose ergonomic shape and handy keychain makes carrying it simple.

"It keeps the water nice and cool, too," said Fern Hastings, a first-year. "It also fits perfectly in the little water holder on my bike."

Most ubiquitous, for hot liquids especially, are Mason jars; students are often seen drinking soup, tea, and coffee from them.

"Mason jars are the bomb diggity," said Dean Elliot. "I have at least four in my A-frame at any given time."

Long explained that there is a crucial difference between Mason jars and other similar jars with which they are often confused, such as the Ball jar.

"Balls are ideal for canning," she said. "If you're making jam, don't even consider using anything but a Ball."

For some, neither the Nalgene nor the aluminum, and neither the Mason nor the Ball, appeals. One student's unusual choice—a Pastis 51 French antique jug made of glass—may be nifty, but gets her occasionally into trouble.

"I keep dropping it, because there's not really a handle," said Flora Goldwasser, a first-year. "It's almost been really bad a couple of times."

SOCIETY BY SAM
By Sam Chabot

Sources have confirmed that an unseemly shower run-in (she was showering; he wasn't paying attention) served as the beginning of the romance between LW and GH. According to the source, her music makes him come alive, while his obvious passion for permaculture gets her going.

Chabot is a first-year. This is his first humor column.

The Quare Academy
Midterm Progress
October 16

Student: Flora Goldwasser
Year: First

WOMEN'S LITERATURE
Instructor: Pearl Bishop
Credits Earned: 5.0

It would be an understatement to call Flora Goldwasser an "outstanding" student. She's deep, sensitive, creative, and a joy to have in class. Her comments, insights, and interpretive ability for literature has touched and impressed all of us. Her reading of the red room in *Jane Eyre*, for example, as a gaping vagina both illuminated Brontë's original meaning and provided us with a jumping-off point to discuss "literature of the womb" in other works.

It's a thrill and an immense pleasure to have her in class, and I'm looking forward to all the work she will continue to do. On a more personal note, my family and I have immensely enjoyed having Flora on our dinner prep crew on Thursday nights. She makes a mean vegan peanut butter cookie!

ENVIRONMENTAL STUDIES
Instructor: Gabriel Cohn
Credits Earned: 5.0

Flora is a brilliant and thoughtful student. When she participates in class, her ideas are important contributions, benefitting the entire class. The other students value her comments, and her work ethic sets a good example for the entire class. I especially enjoyed her analytical essay on Cronon's "The Trouble with the Wilderness," and I even photocopied it to share with the entire class.

WORLD ISSUES I
Instructor: Jaisal Veerasuntharam
Credits Earned: 5.0

Flora's written work has been outstanding, some of the best I have encountered in terms of comprehension of the material, critical thinking, and technical proficiency. She possesses a deep understanding of all topics we covered in our first unit, Global Capitalism. (Even though she sympathizes with Paul Krugman more than some of her peers would like!)

There are many options for raising the level of expectations for her, if she is interested in being pushed further. I hope that she will accept at least a couple of more difficult assignments in the weeks ahead.

PEACE ON EARTH
Instructor: Allison Longfield and Gus Phillips
Credits Earned: 5.0

Flora is a deep thinker and provides an outspoken perspective on a number of the difficult issues we cover in Peace on Earth, a class that examines structures and models of nonviolence throughout history and culture. Her ability to connect past course work and experiences, the readings assigned, and others' contributions to class discussion is exceptional. Her essay on Gandhi and King was both nuanced and thorough, prompting me to reflect on ideas that I had previously held without question.

I hope she will continue to set an example to other students by being able to change her mind as she becomes more informed.

FRENCH
Instructor: Yvette D'Arles
Credits Earned: 5.0

Flora is an excellent student whose French language proficiency puts her at the highest level of Quare students. Her beautiful accent and impressive written work have urged me to request that she work with a couple of students at a lower level on their grammar and expression. I am happy to say that she has acquiesced.

CALCULUS
Instructor: Gail Jacobsen
Credits Earned: 5.0

Flora is a superlative student who works hard, thinks deeply, and does not let anything slip by. Her work is beautifully done and well thought-out. Flora is working at a good pace that she would do well to keep up for the duration of the semester.

Amsterdam Dental Group
1243 Amsterdam Avenue
New York, NY 10027

October 18

Flora,

Your father has received your midsemester progress report in the
mail, and he commends your excellent performance and urges
you to "keep up the good work"! He was considering sending
chocolates, but I advised him that perhaps flowers were a more
prudent choice (it's warm for October, and I didn't want you to
have a mess on your hands). So I called the flower place, but they
don't do deliveries in Main Stream. Nonetheless, congratulations
on your well-earned success!

    Sincerely,
    Linda Lee Lopez, Receptionist

Cora Shimizu-Stein
95 Wall Street, Apt. 33A
New York, NY 10005

October 20

Corset,

Sam is in love with Marigold.

At first he wouldn't admit it, but every time she comes and sits
with us in the dining hall or he happens to be next to her in class,
he gets all fidgety and trips over his words.

"How's Marigold?" I asked him on our way to World Issues this morning, sort of teasing.

"I assume she's fine," said Sam. He kicked a rock with the toe of his white sneaker, and we both watched it sail far away. "Why do you ask?"

"Because you like her."

He put his arm around my shoulders and breathed in the quilted shirt I was wearing, one of the only cute items in the Free Store that week. I'd cinched it with a black belt to keep it from billowing open in the passing breeze.

"What, was this your grandmother's?" he asked. "It smells like Boca Raton."

"How do you know about Boca Raton?"

He shook his head. "I'm from Montréal, not Siberia. I'm hardly *provincial*, Goldwasser. Give me some credit, please."

"Actually," I said, "I'm pretty sure it was Pearl's. Every time she sees me wear it, she gives me this squinty look like she definitely recognizes it but doesn't want to bring it up."

Sam nodded. "That's like the time I saw Zev in my boxers. First I was like, 'I hope you washed those,' but then I was like, 'Wait a minute. How did those end up in the Free Store?'"

"Why don't you just go up and talk to Marigold?" I asked, trying to catch him off guard.

His lips flew open. "And say?" he asked finally.

"I don't know," I said. "It doesn't matter what. Just make contact."

Sam doubled over and wailed in pain. "I'm bad at this," he said.

"She won't like me. I'm nothing special, if you really think about it. I doubt she even knows my name."

I rolled my eyes. "She obviously knows your name," I said. "There are sixteen people in our class."

"Okay, so she knows it."

"Have you ever kissed anyone?" I asked.

He stared at me. "Haven't you ever been to Jewish summer camp?" he asked.

"Do I look like I went to Jewish summer camp?"

He laughed. "Okay, so no. But kissing is a full-fledged activity. You pretty much sign up for it along with basket weaving and tennis. Have you ever been kissed?"

"It's not very classy to kiss and tell."

I might have sounded confident, but my heart was racing.

"You might even call it déclassé," he said.

There was a pause. He wiggled his eyebrows at me, but I just shook my head.

"I keep forgetting that you went to an all-girls school," Sam said. "*Boeing*. Was that what it was called?"

I threw my head back. "BOWEN," I corrected. "It's a fancy private school, not a midsize commercial jet. You should write about Marigold in your column. 'Society by Sam.' That would be so romantic."

It's still funny to me that Sam writes for the *Quare Times*, because it makes him such a Joiner, you know?

By that time, we'd arrived at World Issues, and I'd gotten out of answering his question.

Oh, Cora. Bowen did us no favors in this department. We can conjugate Latin verbs all the livelong day, but when it comes to boys, we're illiterate.

Later that night, I took a good look at Marigold when she and I were brushing our teeth side by side in the communal bathroom. Silky hair, soft lips, and the most perfect complexion I've ever seen. I've been fighting the urge to borrow her (all-natural, of course) skin care products that have lined the shelves in the bathroom this entire semester. I could totally see why Sam would like her, not just because she's beautiful, but also cool in that way that doesn't announce itself too annoyingly.

That's major shell speak, but still. Sam and I are being rebels and not participating in the "no shell speak" rule. So there.

Virginally yours,
Flo

Lael Goldwasser
Harvard College
2609 Harvard Yard Mail Center
Cambridge, MA 02138

October 20

Lael,

Well, whoop-de-doo. The first time I hear from Daddy in weeks, it's through Linda Lee Lopez, and it's about my grades (well, narrative comments—we don't get grades here). Because of course he doesn't ACTUALLY care about anything besides my transcript.

Maybe he's trying. But he's going to have to work a little bit harder than *this*.

Flora

PAGE SIX

Lili Shimizu Gets Posh Wall St. Apt.
in Swift Divorce
By Helena Brown
October 17

Lorne Stein, former power attorney serving a twenty-year sentence for conspiracy, fraud, and money laundering at the Federal Correctional Institution at Sandstone, in northern Minnesota, has split with his so-called "geisha girl," Lili Shimizu.

The Japanese-born ex-supermodel Shimizu will keep the couple's six-bedroom duplex at 95 Wall Street, which they bought for $6.8 million in June of last year.

Stein, once known as the "king of the Financial District," has replaced the queen of his now six-by-eight castle: he dumped Shimizu, reportedly over the phone, and is rumored to be dating fellow Sandstone inmate Gillian Zenk, charged with embezzlement.

Shimizu and her daughters, aged sixteen, ten, and eight, are left to nurse their wounds on Wall Street.

According to a source, "Lorne was happy to let Lili keep the apartment. It's not like he can use it from where he is."

Cora Shimizu-Stein
95 Wall Street, Apt. 33A
New York, NY 10005

October 20

Cora my love,

I just read the article. India sent me the clip. Helena Brown is
such a jerk for writing that. And to call your mother a "geisha
girl"? So shamefully racist. Promise me you won't pay any
attention to what idiots like her say about your family. It will
blow over in one week flat. I promise.

Did you ever go see him, by the way? Your father, I mean. If
you're going to go, I would go sooner rather than later. Northern
Minnesota isn't anywhere you want to be going past November.

What does Dr. Modarressi say about all this?

   Please remember that I love you,
   Flora

India Katz-Rosen
1025 Fifth Avenue, Apt. 9C
New York, NY 10028

October 25

India,

At dinner last night, as the whole school was circling up in the
dining hall, I found myself next to Dean Elliot. She told me
that starting in November, she's directing a play of her own,

one she's been writing since the summer. It's called *300 Years of Mourning*.

She said, "You should audition. Later this week. We can meet beforehand and run lines, if you want."

So we did. Today.

I got there early, because from Pine House it's only a five-minute walk to Woolman Theater. Pine House is where Gus Phillips, who teaches Peace on Earth, lives. All the teachers get their own houses on the fringe of campus, and when it's too cold to go outside, we usually have classes in their living rooms. Some of them are nice and make us hot chocolate and tea. Gus is one of the nice ones. Once there were a few condom wrappers stuffed between Gus's couch cushions. People wouldn't shut up about it for ten years afterward. (So much for sex positivity, am I right?)

Anyway, I was at Woolman Theater a little early. It was a pretty bleak walk over. There's no snow yet, but all the leaves have fallen off the trees, so everything looks heavy and gray. I hadn't been alone in the theater since the first Guild meeting, so it was a little weird to have it all to myself, all empty and dark and just a little bit sad.

When Dean arrived, her satchel overflowing with papers and books, she looked perfect, as usual, in a satiny black dress with a crocheted lace collar. I think I'd seen the dress in the Free Store, but without the collar and the white buttons going down the front, so I wondered if she'd sewn them. Her loafers were black and shiny too, just like her hair.

Dean said, "I'm glad you made it. I'm sorry I'm late. The fucking printer in the library was being a bitch."

I nodded, because I've had experience with the library printer too. It's ancient and takes about forty days to print one sheet of paper.

I told Dean that I hadn't been waiting too long.

She strode toward the stage and swung herself up onto it in one single hop, letting her legs dangle.

"So it's called *300 Years of Mourning,*" she said. "Mourning with a *u*. It'll make sense once you read it. It's Victorian and kind of wacky. I'm just deciding which . . ." She was shuffling around in her satchel. "Okay, I think I've got it. This is the part where the main character's, Elizabeth's, younger sister, Fanny, acts like kind of a brat. Fanny's whole bit is that she's obsessed with the guppies in the fountain outside. So do you want to skim the script and then read for me?"

I read the script. It was funny, definitely odd. I was wearing my cream-and-green knit skirt suit, so I felt a little too dowdy to be playing a seven-year-old girl, but I had no choice but to go with it.

"Are you ready?" Dean asked. "I'll read for Elizabeth."

Here's what I remember of the first lines of script:

ELIZABETH: Fanny, come inside for dinner. Cook's been calling you for ages.

FANNY: I've already got my dinner. It's right here in the fountain!

Dean stopped me.

"That was good. I like the way you read. Most people don't

pronounce the words enough, but you've got a nice, slow tempo."

She studied me up and down.

"The only problem is that you read it like you're a ninety-five-year-old grandma. You're all bent over and crooked, like a fucking C."

I fell all over myself, apologizing.

"Don't apologize. Just do it right next time."

I swallowed and tried again.

"Okay, now that we've established that you can pronounce words and stand up straight, I need a little more emotion," coached Dean. I liked that she was blunt, but it didn't make me any less scared of her.

"Like this?" I tried to put passion into the line like I did when I played Hippolyta in *A Midsummer Night's Dream* back at Bowen.

"Not feeling it," Dean said, shaking her head, and I panicked that she would send me away. "You're supposed to be performing, for heaven's sake. Can you change your voice a little bit? Like, the tone and the volume? Right now what I'm getting is like the color of the sky outside right now."

I got the picture.

So the next time I read the line, I went all out. I screamed and stomped my foot. I wasn't even humiliated, actually. I just really, really wanted to please Dean.

But Dean just laughed. "That's supposed to be emotional? This is a wacky play, Flora, not *Anne of Green* fucking *Gables*."

I was close to tears at that point, but there was no way I was showing Dean that. I filled my lungs with air, and before she knew what was happening, I burst out anew: "NO!" I wailed. "THOSE ARE MY GUPPIES! NOBODY CAN TAKE AWAY MY GUPPIES! I-I-I'LL THROW MYSELF OUT THIS WINDOW, I SWEAR I WILL!"

Not sure how else to convey Fanny's despair, I threw myself on the ground, beat my fists against the floor, tossed myself this way and that, flung my limbs into the air like I was being electrocuted. When I was done, I lay on the floor, panting, a bit dazed that I had done something so crazy.

But it had worked. Dean was laughing, and she continued to laugh for what felt like three solid minutes.

"Totally overdramatic," she said. "There it is. Thank you. You accessed your inner crazy. Insanity is the way to go for you, I think. Sometimes it is, especially for the people who seem as though they have it all together."

I got to my feet, seeing stars.

We kept reading. We read every line perhaps twenty times, until my voice was hoarse and my arms and hip bones were bruised from all the thrashing on the floor and against the stage. When Dean was finally satisfied, she reached into her leather satchel and extracted a Mason jar filled with tinted liquid. As she unscrewed it, I realized it was alcohol, and I looked left and right to make sure nobody was around. The theater was silent, cozily thrumming with heat; even the hard-backed pews, lined with thin cushions, looked inviting. But there was the minor matter of the abstinence pledge we'd all signed in September, after all, and that was enough to make me squirm.

Dean chugged from the Mason jar for a few seconds and then held it out to me, gulping.

I accepted it and stared down into it. It was slightly cloudy, and I wasn't crazy about putting my mouth to it, but Dean was watching me, so I took a small sip. It was repugnant and burned on the way down, doubly irritating because my throat was already scratched raw from all the screaming.

I must have made a face.

"It's moonshine," said Dean. "Louis makes it right on the back porch of his A-frame, no shit. It's good, right?"

My esophagus felt scalded, so I just nodded and handed the jar back.

Then Dean told me I could go, and she said, "Between you and me, I think you've got Fanny in the bag."

As I walked from Woolman Theater to my hovel, where Lucy and Benna were somewhat inexplicably curled up on our couch together in front of the woodstove, whispering sweet twin nothings into each other's ears (and I didn't even have Juna to commiserate with, because the few times I had tried to make snide comments to her, she had just stared at me, Quare-eyed), my elation dimmed just slightly. I know I should be happy, what with all the praise from my teachers and Dean, but I'm starting to wonder if it's all kind of empty. I mean, as cool as it can be here, I miss you guys. A lot.

Love,
FMG

To: Elijah Huck <ehuck@columbia.edu>
From: Dean Elliot <delliot@quare.edu>
Subject: visit?
October 25, 4:11 p.m.

Hey, dude,

How's it going, home slice?? We never talk anymore. And you don't have any excuse: I'm a second-year now, so we can actually email.

You promised you'd come visit this fall and see all the teachers. I told them about how we've known each other forever through the Chicago Arts summer session and they're all, like, "Wow, we really miss that guy." Plus, a disturbing number of first-years have been fangirling over you ever since the latest of issue of *Nymphette* hit computer screens everywhere (classy move to not name Quare, btw).

So what gives?
D

To: Guild <guild@quare.edu>
From: Dean Elliot <delliot@quare.edu>
Subject: "300 Years of Mourning" cast list
October 26, 4:11 p.m.

Elizabeth / Dean Elliot

Gregory /Michael Lansbury

Paul / Gary North

Calliope / Althea Long

Susanna / Luella Lookman

Carlos / Shy Lenore

Fanny / Flora Goldwasser

Lael Goldwasser

Harvard College

2609 Harvard Yard Mail Center

Cambridge, MA 02138

October 26

Lael,

Jesus Christ, I just had the worst and weirdest interaction with that girl Becca Conch-Gould, who's my neighbor on one side. We're in Guild together, and after I got Fanny and she didn't, she's been super cold to me in the dining hall and in class.

But then tonight, just now, she knocked on the door to my hovel. When I opened the door, she was standing there in the moonlight, arms crossed at her chest.

I was in there alone (Juna was at a meeting for the Feminist Underground, which she always invites me to, and although I considered going for once this time—just to see what it was all about—I ultimately decided that I had too much reading), so I invited Becca in. She sat on the floor, against Juna's bed, and not wanting us to be on different levels, I sat on the floor against my bed. We faced each other. It goes without saying that Becca and I are not friends; we've probably had three short conversations in the two months (!) that I've been here.

"Is everything okay?" I asked finally, after she'd pouted at me for thirty seconds.

She let out a beleaguered sigh.

"I'm sorry," she said. "There's just something I have to get off my chest."

"Go for it," I said. My heart started to pound.

"The part," she said. "I mean, I didn't see you read, so it's possible that you were really good, but a few of us have been studying acting for years, and it's a little bit unbelievable that none of us got parts."

I blinked at her. It was one of those moments that was so surprising that it felt, actually, entirely expected: this bug-eyed, chinless girl with *feather earrings* accusing me of playing the system, or whatever, and taking parts from those who were more deserving.

"Okay," I said, not sure what else to say.

"I just wanted to say that we all get that you're superspecial and everything"—a mocking grin curled at the corners of her lips; clearly she was amused by her own biting wit—"but that doesn't mean you're entitled to special privileges. I thought I'd bring this up with you directly rather than let it simmer."

I stared at her. Lael, I thought I was going to punch her out. One of my hands actually rose automatically, but I gripped the side of my bed instead. And the way she kept reiterating her own maturity, manifesting in her ability to be directly aggressive rather than keep her petty bullshit to herself!! It was unbelievable, really.

"What do you mean?" I asked, struggling to control my tone.

She ignored my question and instead stood, presumably to leave.
She took a step toward the door, and then turned to speak again.

"It's clear that Dean feels bad for you because people think
you're really materialistic and everything," she said. Her voice
had now taken on a sickening sweetness, complete with an
innocent shake of the head. My stomach flipped over. "But you
get *everything*. People like you always get everything in the
outside world, and I guess you're allowed to have whatever you
want at Quare, too."

I jumped to my feet, seeing stars. Probably expecting me to deck
her, Becca lunged toward the door and opened it, hopping like a
cricket onto the porch but continuing to hold the door open. Her
eyes danced around my face. We stared at each other.

"You're really cool, Becca," I said finally. "So great. We should
hang out more."

Her face crumpled, then curled into a grin. My sarcasm—on our
first day, Miriam had spoken to us about Quare's no-sarcasm
rule, designed to promote vulnerability and sharing genuine
emotion—was proof of my inferiority; this was what Becca had
been expecting all along. She shut the door, not a slam but close
to it, and sprinted back to her hovel. *Trip, trip, trip,* I chanted in
my head, but she didn't so much as stumble.

My body still feels funny.

I guess what's really getting to me is that I honestly don't even
blame Becca for hating me. I have something she wanted; I
probably have lots of things that she wants, at least things that
make life easier for me in the outside world. But at the same time,

her accusation, her bitterness, turned my stomach. Something about the way she wears her anger and sadness on her face, in her words, disgusts me, and I'm not sure why. Maybe the thing is that it—she—makes me sad. Lael, I feel so torn. Half of me is still shimmering in the glory of getting this part, but the other part doesn't even want it anymore.

Love,
Flora

To: Dean Elliot <delliot@quare.edu>
From: Flora Goldwasser <fgoldwasser@quare.edu>
Subject: Re: "300 Years of Mourning" cast list
October 26, 5:10 p.m.

Dean! Thank you so much for the part. Can I get back to you on whether or not I plan to appear in the play?

To: Flora Goldwasser <fgoldwasser@quare.edu>
From: Dean Elliot <delliot@quare.edu>
Subject: Re: "300 Years of Mourning" cast list
October 26, 5:59 p.m.

Just so you know, Flora, the part of Fanny came down to you or either of two first-years—Juna and Becca. I decided that Juna and Becca weren't ready for it. So while you're up onstage, playing Fanny, which I've rewritten and tweaked especially for you, there are going to be some people in the audience who aren't rooting for you.

We like to say, "This is Quare, so everybody roots for everybody," but that's pretty much bullshit. The thing about Guild is that it's the only society on campus where it's okay to be a little bit competitive—to admit that we're not all equals at everything, and that some of us rise to the top because we're that much better. In a school of thirty-four students, competition doesn't work very often—not with grades or sports or anything like that—but in the case of Guild, it's our lifeblood.

I shouldn't be telling you this, but at the end of the semester, the master player picks a new apprentice for the spring. And getting this parts means you're in the running for apprentice.

To: Dean Elliot <delliot@quare.edu>
From: Flora Goldwasser <fgoldwasser@quare.edu>
Subject: Re: "300 Years of Mourning" cast list
October 26, 8:12 p.m.

Were you in Guild as a first-year?

To: Flora Goldwasser <fgoldwasser@quare.edu>
From: Dean Elliot <delliot@quare.edu>
Subject: Re: "300 Years of Mourning" cast list
October 26, 8:25 p.m.

I was. And my first-year fall, I auditioned for my first play, just like you did. I lost the part to Michael, whom they decided to dress up as a girl rather than cast me. God, I was devastated. But then I auditioned for the next play, and I got a part, and then another, and another. And I'm planning to do more theater next year, at the University of Chicago (assuming I get in—I'm telling people I applied there early decision because I think jinxing is witchcraft).

Talk to Susan María Velez, who's going to be the playwright in

residence next term, if you ever decide to get into writing. She'll
also be the Guild faculty adviser.

You can do this, Flora. People are going to like you. To tell you the
truth, nobody cares how deep or pure or Quare you are. They care
about liking you, and they like you if you make their reality even a
little bit better—more entertaining, funnier, smarter. *That's* what's
real. I like your style, Flora. You're different. Don't compromise that
to fit in here.

To: Dean Elliot <delliot@quare.edu>
From: Flora Goldwasser <fgoldwasser@quare.edu>
Subject: Re: "300 Years of Mourning" cast list
October 26, 8:29 p.m.

I promise that I'll try not to!

To: Flora Goldwasser <fgoldwasser@quare.edu>
From: Dean Elliot <delliot@quare.edu>
Subject: Re: "300 Years of Mourning" cast list
October 26, 8:27 p.m.

There's one more thing. For years, Miriam has begged the Guild
master player and apprentice to write and submit plays to the
Young Innovators' Promise Awards—YIPA, they're called, for
all sorts of literary and visual arts. If someone at Quare wins
a YIPA gold medal, the entire school gets recognized by the
government as a charter for the arts, or some shit like that,
and its ranking goes through the roof. That means more people
apply, fewer get in, and its tuition soars, which means of course
that it becomes richer. It's a money game, at the end of the day.
That's why they're so insistent that we win, though they'd never

breathe a word of this to any student. And they know that the Guild master player and apprentice are more likely to win than members of Languedoc or whatever, with their menstrual blood paintings.

I'm only telling you this because if you want to submit a play, you should start thinking and writing as soon as possible.

India Katz-Rosen
1025 Fifth Avenue, Apt. 9C
New York, NY 10028

October 28

Dear India,

Cora's not writing me back. Can you bug her, please?? Or at least let me know how she's doing?

I've been in the Free Store all day. It's my favorite place north of Harlem.

What is this place, you might ask? It's in the attic of the Art Barn, and it's where old clothes find new owners. It operates on the premise of the gift economy: nobody charges, and nobody pays.

All this to say that if you're willing to sort through some nasty junk, there are pretty neat clothes to be found, totally free of charge.

A sampling of the contents of the Free Store as of October 22

- A pair of sagging gray tights with holes in the crotch and down the legs

- A pair of cracked leather shoes with droopy tongues but awesome laces
- A suede vest with fringe and a little cowboy logo
- A khaki jacket, made for light spring, size 2X
- A pair of lime-green hot pants
- An assortment of thick socks
- A pair of Rollerblades, size five
- A tweed dress, slightly frayed but magnificent
- An A-line navy wrap skirt with a thick red seam (tried it on, a little tight but it's a go)

I'm not sure how into Halloween people here get (some people seem to celebrate it by dressing up in wild costumes every day, but because of "no shell speak" we're forbidden from commenting on any of it), but I'm sure getting into it. Do you remember when we—you, Cora, and I—went as Nancy Drew, George Fayne, and Bess Marvin?

I'm still a little pissed that you guys made me be Nancy and ask for the candy on all our behalves.

Anyway, Sam and I are going as Suzy Bishop and Sam Shakusky from *Moonrise Kingdom*. Sam has one of those beaver hats (fake, of course), and obviously I have a mod pink dress and knee socks. Sam is such a blast.

Climb ev'ry mountain,
Flora

To: Dean Elliot <delliot@quare.edu>
From: Elijah Huck <ehuck@columbia.edu>
Subject: Re: visit?
October 29, 2:13 p.m.

Hey, D,

I want to come. I really do. I miss you, dude. But things are kind of complicated. I do have some time later in the semester. Did I tell you about that girls' school—the tutoring gig? It's a long story.

E

RETURN TO SENDER

Emma Goldwasser
82 West 17th Street, Apt. 2B
New York, NY 10011

October 31

Mum,

I haven't heard from you in a few weeks, so I wanted to write and let you know how things are going. Today is Halloween (as you can see from the date), and it was fun to get into costume.

Please write to me whenever you can. I'm curious to hear about your new apartment.

Love,
Flora

PS: Did Daddy send you my midsemester report?

Lael Goldwasser
Harvard College
2609 Harvard Yard Mail Center
Cambridge, MA 02138

November 1

Lael,

I'm still shaking from what just happened.

I've just about had it with meeting for worship. I think it was sent from the devil just to torture me. But let me back up.

Meeting for worship is mandatory. It's every Wednesday for an hour, right at the end of classes. Half an hour of silence. No knitting, no journaling, no reading. We straggle in from women's literature, sit on hard-backed pews, and try to get in touch with the great beyond. Quakers believe in direct communication with God, that every person should speak her own truth; there are no preachers or rabbis or reverends. It's very beautiful, and all that, but have you ever tried to sit in silence for half an hour?

It's really hard.

Usually I watch people. I watch the ropes of drool that slither out of Althea's mouth when she falls asleep on her pew (because they can't exactly outlaw napping, though it is discouraged). I watch the people who get creepy smiles with their eyes glazed over. I watch Gabriel, the environmental studies teacher, and his wife, Sarah the baker, hold hands when they think nobody's looking. I imagine Sam, who's excused from Meeting for Worship because he sometimes uses the hour to talk on the phone with his analyst back in Montreal. Sometimes I manage to daydream a little, despite the hard pew pressing into my spine. The minutes always drag by, but usually it's halfway bearable, even kind of calming and nice.

But not today.

Today, twenty minutes into the meeting, Juna stood up to speak her truth. People are allowed to do that, you know—stand and speak their truths. She was wearing a dress that was three different, yet equally abhorrent, shades of yellow. She looked like a penis turned inside out.

"I've been thinking about shell speak," she said. People always begin their comments with "I've been thinking about . . ." because it's not normal to barrel right ahead into a thought without any preamble.

"It feels weird to me that we're working to create this community of, like, decreasing the value of physical appearance, yet it doesn't seem that we're all equally committed to that," she said. "I feel disheartened when people bring relics of the empire, like fancy shoes and designer clothes, into Quare. I thought Quare would be an escape from all that. We're trying to build this radically inclusive community where we're judged for things other than our clothing, and being reminded of the premium that the outside world places on appearance hinders that work."

I was sitting there, barely breathing. *She was talking about me.*
She thought I was the empire. I could feel everyone's eyes on me,
looking at me but pretending not to. It was all so obvious. And
BECCA! She was trying hard to hide her smirk from me, but
her cheeks still pulled her entire lower face up, making her look
deranged.

And I was royally pissed. My hands started to shake. I looked
down at the outfit I chose this morning: a white short-sleeved
blouse tucked tastefully into a vintage wrap skirt. Black DKNY
stockings. Suede boots with a half-inch heel. I had stared at my
reflection in the mirror this morning and felt like a young woman
trying to make it in the male-dominated world of publishing in
the 1960s, and I'd felt damn good, like a real vixen.

My heart was thudding so hard that I could feel it in my earlobes.
As soon as Juna sat down, smug and self-satisfied, I stood up
shakily, grabbing on to Lucy's shoulder for support. My toes
were clenched inside my boots. Everyone looked up at me
expectantly, their eyes trained on my face. Their greasy hair fell
in stiff blocks, glasses sliding down their noses, chapped lips
open wide. Their unwashed clothes emitted a smell so strong
that it was visible. I would never say this to anyone but you, but
I couldn't help feeling that despite their holier-than-thou values
and righteousness, I was better than they were. Emboldened by
Dean's email (I've included it), I felt SPECIAL. I looked out at
the sea of flannel and Mason jars and Birkenstocks with socks. *I
am superior,* I thought, *because I am all that and more.*

There's nothing quite like being angry and also being sure you're
right.

"No one's placing undue premium on clothes besides you,"
I said. My voice was shaking so badly that I had to take a few

deep breaths. It was dead silent. Some people looked away, while others looked up still, bleary-eyed. "It's really that simple. If you want Quare to be a place for everybody, then you have to accept everybody who's here, whether or not they wear harem pants or wash their hair."

I paused to smooth my hands over my skirt. The words flooded my mouth so fast that I could hardly speak quickly enough to get them all out.

"Wearing nice clothes isn't shell speak. Shell speak is judging people for what they're wearing. It's totally counterproductive to subtly prioritize dressing without care to rebel against the rest of the world, where dressing well is prioritized, because you're just flipping the pressure. Not caring what you look like in no way makes you superior. You're not better than I am because you're too pious to put on something that looks like you put any effort into it at all. That's not what a radically inclusive community looks like."

My knees were shaking so much that I could barely stand still. My stomach was fluttering all over the place. Instead of sitting back down in the pew, I snatched my yellow peacoat, swung it around my shoulder like a cape, and strode out of the meetinghouse, my suede boots clicking on the wooden floor with each step. I pushed open the heavy doors and stepped outside, letting the door slam shut with an angry boom behind me. I was still royally pissed, but now I was filled with adrenaline. I felt like a badass, but a sort of melancholy badass.

It's hard for me to explain to you why I was so agitated and antsy. What Juna had said using her stupid "I" statements and nonviolent communication technique was infuriating. And how she'd clearly judged me as inferior because I wasn't exactly

like her, how they'd all stared at me and politely averted their
eyes, made me irate. But even though each of those things was
making me angry, neither of them was really the reason. It was
something larger than the sum of its parts. I felt vindicated, sure,
but also cheap somehow—not as good as I thought I'd feel on
the cusp of my outburst. I'm just guessing here, but maybe it was
because I felt that somehow making such a concerted effort *not*
to fit in was actually, well, not letting me fit in. Sounds obvious, I
know, but it still hurt. It's like this: my prior vision of myself was
of someone mysterious, the Elegant One who floats in her own
orbit. But after Juna's comments, it seemed more like I was just
the Shallow One—the one everyone scorns.

I was in such a bad, desperate mood that I felt like crying.
Outside the meetinghouse, I walked over to a patch of newly
sprouted wildflowers and sat down. And I did cry, a little bit. I
wanted to go home, not back to my cabin or back to Daddy's
shack, but to West Seventy-Ninth Street. The people with insipid
smiles on their faces in the meetinghouse are not my people. You
and India and Cora are my people. I haven't been around my
people in a long time.

Then came anger at more people than just the Quares. I was
furious at myself for wanting to come here at all, just to impress
stupid Elijah, who writes me three sentences on a postcard and
won't even say for sure whether or not he's coming to Quare at
some point; furious at Mum and Daddy for LETTING me leave
Bowen, when any psychologist could easily tell that I was just
trying to escape my crumbling home life, or whatever; furious at
Quare for accepting me when they knew I wouldn't fit in here;
furious at India and Cora for getting to stay at Bowen . . . even
furious at you, if I'm being perfectly honest, for graduating and
going to college.

So I was sitting in the wildflowers, quietly steaming and crying into my black stockings, when someone came and sat down next to me. I didn't look up, just felt the presence of the body beside me.

But then my curiosity got the better of me, and I lifted my head.

It was Dean, in high-waisted mom jeans and a flannel button-down. She didn't say anything, just sat down next to me, her knees bent up.

Of course, I was a sniffling mess, so I sucked the snot back into my nose and wiped my eyes with the sleeves of my peacoat. She didn't say anything for a while.

"How are you?" she finally asked.

I grunted noncommittally, because I didn't trust my voice.

"Meeting for worship was hard for me at first too," she said. "I was raised Presbyterian. The preacher talks to you, and then you get to go home. Being your own deliverance is tough. A lot of things come up."

"It's not that," I said. "It's what Juna said."

Dean was silent for a few seconds. "Was it?" she asked.

"What do you mean? That's what I was responding to in there."

She nodded slowly. "So Juna was talking about you," she said.

"Yes."

"How do you know?"

I threw up my hands in frustration, not even caring that I was showing a very déclassé side of myself to Lighthouse Dean.

"Of course she was talking about me," I said. "I'm the only one who wears . . . what she said. And I always see her giving me these looks of pity, like, 'Isn't it sad that you think you need to wear nice clothes to be accepted?' Not that other people aren't constantly judging me also."

"How do you know?"

Was she serious?

"It's the way they look at me. The way they don't talk to me unless they have to, and the way they raise their eyebrows when I walk by."

Dean nodded some more.

"So you're making every effort to get to know them, too," she said, "and it's failing because they won't give you the time of day. I see. That makes perfect sense."

My mouth opened. She was starting to sound like . . . you, to be perfectly honest.

"Flora, why are you at Quare?" Dean asked.

I couldn't tell her the truth. I just couldn't. I felt like the biggest fool in the universe, crying into the flowers about being at this ridiculous place—a place I'd come for the cool little baby bird I'm in love with.

"I . . . well . . ." I started to say.

"Don't worry about it." Dean laid her arm lightly against mine, sending an electric shock through my body. "All I'm saying is that you have to give them a chance if you want them to give you one. It goes both ways. Decide to like them, and they'll decide to like you."

My heart was still pounding, but now it was with mortification. I still thought I'd been wronged, of course, but now it didn't seem so black and white.

"You're really not that different than they are," Dean said.

I scoffed openly.

"Really," she said. "When you think of yourself as so different, you become so different. All you'll be able to think about are the ways that you're an outcast."

I took a few deep breaths.

"What if I like being different?" I finally asked.

"Well, then you have to accept the consequences," she answered, but not in a mean way. In a firm and gentle way.

"Okay," I said.

"Okay," she said.

A pause.

"Look," Dean said, pointing at the sky, "the sun's finally out."

It did feel a bit warmer, but I was still wiggling my half-frozen toes around. Those boots I got on Madison Avenue weren't exactly warm (though they are adorable, and I stand by—and in—them).

"Take my socks," Dean offered. She shook off her mud-caked farm boots and then stripped off her deliciously thick wool socks. Her feet were pale and shocked looking, as though her skin itself were squinting in the sunlight.

I accepted the socks. They were still warm from her feet, soft and fluffy and glorious. I jokingly offered her to trade, but of course she didn't take my stockings.

I stuffed my boots back on, not caring that they looked ridiculous over the socks. She sat with me until the meeting was over and people streamed out. Lucy and Fern shot us a suspicious look, but I didn't care.

O Dean! O lighthouse!

Love,
Flora

To: Cora Shimizu-Stein <cshimizustein@bowen.edu>
From: India Katz-Rosen <ikatzrosen@bowen.edu>
Subject: weird experience
November 3, 9:02 p.m.

Hey, babe,

I'm emailing because my mom confiscated my phone. She says I have to do well on my math test tomorrow or no more shopping. She's actually camped out on the bench outside my room right now to make sure I'm studying, but she can't tell from where she is that I'm emailing you and not Dr. Bergman.

ANYWAY, the weirdest thing happened to me this afternoon. Remember how I said the debate team was going up to Columbia for an invitational? Well, we went—we lost big-time; what else is new—and then Stacy, Onitra, Vivienne, and I went to that café in the student center. Alfred Hall, or something like that. You know, the glass building on Broadway and 115th?

Well, we got our muffins and coffee, and were looking for a

place to sit—the place was absolutely packed with students and professors—when whom do we see but Elijah Huck?

Of course you remember Elijah the history Tutor. Flora wouldn't shut up about him last year, especially because he was actually HER Tutor and they met one-on-one all those times to talk about her essays on St. Francis of Assisi or whatever. I mean, I guess he's kind of cute (actually, I think he looks like a baby bird: it must be the beaky nose, feathery blond hair, and round glasses), especially for Bowen, but in the real world, he's kind of meh. I was actually surprised at how meek he looked surrounded by guys instead of just Bowen girls.

Anyway, as I brushed by his table with the girls, he looked up at me. I swear, we must have made eye contact for about fifteen solid seconds, until I finally just eked by him and made my way to another table. But the look he gave me—it was so bizarre, like he was trying to suck my soul out of my eyes or something. We've never spoken, obviously, and I don't even know if he knows I go to Bowen. Besides, didn't he quit or something? This year, all the Tutors are women, I think. But anyway, it was bizarre as fuck.

Okay, I should probably go study for math before my mom comes in here.

Oh yeah, also, hi, Flora. I know you still periodically check my Bowen email (God, can you believe some friends DON'T share passwords?) for Bowen gossip and will probably read this when you're home for Thanksgiving break. Sorry I called Elijah a meek baby bird. But you can't really deny that that's EXACTLY what he looks like.

xx!!!

Letter from Lael

Flora Goldwasser
Pigeonhole 44
The Quare Academy
2 Quare Road
Main Stream, NY 12497

November 7

Dear Flora,

Dean sounds like my cup of tea. She'll do in my stead. Plus, she has a point about feeling different from everyone else. I think you have this romantic idea of yourself as a Grace-Kelly-dress-clad outcast—an image no doubt fueled by Elijah, or whatever, and his creepy yet adoring gaze—but remember, Flora: all that is *just your shell*.

LMAO.

I also want to raise the question of your true motives for being at Quare. I mean, yeah, you're there primarily because of Elijah—that much is clear—but what if something in your subconscious wanted you to go there for other reasons too? What if what you're telling India and Cora—about Bowen being stifling, about wanting to prove to yourself that you can stick this out—is actually, well, kind of THE REAL REASON? After all, how hard would it have been to simply change your plans and just return to Bowen after finding out that he wouldn't be going to Quare this year?

Maybe it's crazy. But all the stuff you're trying to prove to Elijah—that you're an adventurous and wild and up-for-anything type of gal—what if you're actually trying to prove it to YOURSELF?

My point is, you don't have to have a plan for how Elijah reacts to your being at Quare. You're there, and the more I hear about it, the more I'm sold that it's kind of *exactly* where you need to be right now. You're not going anywhere. Not on my watch, anyway.

Also, I'm not sure if you knew this, but Mum moved a few weeks ago. Not far, though. Just a few blocks south to be closer to Washington Square Park (because we both know how much she thinks she loves nature). I wrote her new address on the back of this paper. Ignore the psych notes. We're learning about confirmation bias. Go figure.

What do you want for your birthday, by the way? I know you said that birthdays aren't celebrated at Quare, which I suppose makes sense from a philosophical standpoint, but it's still depressing. So if none of your friends there are giving you anything, my gift had better be top-notch—better than the typewriter last year, even.

From,
Lael

Flora Goldwasser
Women's Literature
November 8
Short response: Toni Morrison's *Beloved*

> *At Sweet Home, Sethe is milked as though she is a cow; this abuse*
> *contorts her both emotionally and physically as she becomes stamped*
> *and imprinted inside and out. After being raped, Sethe thinks to*
> *herself, "I am full of . . . two boys with mossy teeth, one sucking on*
> *my breast the other holding me down, their book-reading teacher*
> *watching and writing it up" (83). Morrison paints the boys as carnal*
> *and carnivorous, and they leave an emotional imprint, one that stays*
> *with Sethe two decades after the fact and continues to mutilate and*
> *distort her body. Being milked brings a literal change in shape, one*
> *that is deflated and sucked out, and so it is somewhat paradoxical*
> *that Sethe says that she is "full of" the experience. Morrison's play*
> *on words reveals that Sethe harbors a poignant memory that lingers*
> *long after her abuse. In effect, Sethe is still "full of" being emptied—*
> *literally and figuratively.*

COMMENTS

Fascinating stuff, Flora. You're suggesting that Sethe's rape
forces her very shape to change, and I think you're on to
something. When something is taken out of Sethe—as you say,
she's "milked as though she is a cow"—she in fact becomes
"full" in a way that seems to defy logic. What are other ways
in which violation—the little thefts to which women-bodies,
particularly those marked for racial violence, are constantly
subject—actually fill us up? And with what tools, feelings, and
thoughts do they stuff us? To whom do these thoughts and
feelings actually belong?

India Katz-Rosen
1025 Fifth Avenue, Apt. 9C
New York, NY 10028

November 11

India dear,

We're swimming in apples up here. All the trees are bursting
with them, and they're incorporated into every dish in every
meal. Apple pancakes, applesauce, apple casserole, apple pie,
apple and quinoa salad, apple and kale stir-fry, apple-infused
potatoes, apple fritters, apple muffins, seitan with apples, apple
slaw—you get the picture. Some people are talking about
bobbing for apples, but the thought of sticking my head in a
barrel that everyone else's heads have also been in makes me
want to dry heave.

But you'd be proud of how far I've come. I've even dismantled
my mosquito net. Mostly it's because there are no mosquitoes
past September, but it's also because I've made peace with the
fact that there are bugs in the world, and they will do what they
do. It's very Quare of me, actually.

I told Dean about the itching, by the way. We meet every other
week for her to check on my progress. She's always swaddled in
an enormous felt green coat with random squares of yellow and
white felt sewn onto it. It's a great coat.

She never runs out of things to talk about (her favorite talk
shows, the vintage bicycle she's repairing, the healing properties
of various herbs), but I stay quiet when she asks about me—
unless, of course, she threatens to serenade me with a private
concert unless I say something, and that's when I start bringing
up things like my relentless itching.

Dean offered to make me a balm, for which I was really grateful. It was really goopy and messy, but, boy, did it work. I rubbed it all over my body after showering, swung myself around naked in the cabin when I was alone (and had closed the makeshift curtains) to dry it a bit, and then put on clothes. In two days the only evidence of my itching are the ribbons of skin on the floor of our hovel.

Oh, also, I submitted my review to Dean a few days ago, but I haven't heard anything yet.

Cross your fingers that she approves!

Better go. It's time for my dinner prep shift. What are we making, you might ask? Applesauce and tofu cakes.

Also, question: Do you think it's too much to wear my 1920s vintage cloche hat—the flowery one that secures under the chin—to pick apples on Sunday? There are some kids from Main Stream coming for the fall festival in a few days, and I don't want to scare them.

"Love and other indoor sports,"
Flora

To: All-staff <everyone@nymphettemag.com>
From: Wink DelDuca <wink@nymphettemag.com>
Subject: Miss Tulip
November 11, 7:08 p.m.

Nymphettes,

Yesterday I got to wondering if there isn't something we can do about Miss Tulip's disappearance. Is Miss T in danger? We can't know for sure. I'd love to be able to make MISSING posters with her face, but obviously, we can't do that: Miss Tulip doesn't show her face, and it would be hard to make MISSING posters with her headless body—just her milky white neck, her tousled curls . . . but I digress.

But that gave me an idea. What does everyone think about screening photos from Miss Tulip's all-time great shots onto T-shirts? They'll look great over slacks. I took the liberty of asking Thee, and she's on board.

We'll be voting on which ones should be made into shirts. Come to Wednesday night's Google Hangouts with your favorite in mind.

Here are the ones I'm plugging for:

http://www.misstulipblog.com/to-kill-a-mockingbird-schoolteacher-dress.html

http://www.misstulipblog.com/jackie-kennedy-all-pink-everything.html

http://www.misstulipblog.com/green-and-white-gingham-culottes.html

http://www.misstulipblog.com/knit-green-dress-big-gold-buttons.html

;)

Wink
Editor in Chief, *Nymphette* magazine
Nymphette is an online feminist arts & culture magazine for teenagers.
Each month, we choose a theme, and then you send us your writing,
photography, and artwork.

Lael Goldwasser
Harvard College
2609 Harvard Yard Mail Center
Cambridge, MA 02138

November 11

Dear Lael,

Okay, okay, fine, maybe you have a point, and Quare is really about me and not Elijah. I'm giving it until the end of the semester anyway, so don't work yourself up about it. And I really am giving it a fair shot.

Case in point: dish crew was—dare I say it—fun tonight. It helps that Sam shares my shift. Usually there are some people lingering over tea in the dining hall, but by the time we're done with the dishes, it's emptied out except for a few students on the couches, doing homework, playing their instruments quietly, or sketching in their journals. That makes it easy for us to sweep and mop the main eating area. I sweep, and Sam mops. He says it's a good way for him to achieve definition in his upper arms. I don't know how to break it to him that upper-arm definition might not be in the cards—and I won't break it to him either, because I don't have any particular desire to mop.

So we were standing there, me getting the dirt out of the way and Sam moving the sudsy mop all around, doing a pretty terrible job as always because we're both weak, lazy, and chatty.

I told him I was glad he'd finally made contact with Marigold, whom he's in love with. They've been staying up really late singing through the whole Beatles repertoire, and even though I've felt the tiniest bit left out, I wasn't about to tell Sam that.

He waved the mop ineffectually over the floor. "The power of song," he said. "If you see me with a guitar, the myopia becomes charming."

I quietly conceded his point.

"You seem down," he said.

"What?"

"You always do."

I always seem down?

"Seriously," he said. "You strike me as a sufferer."

"Thanks?"

"It's a compliment." He swung the mop haphazardly. "I feel like I couldn't ever be friends with someone who isn't at least a little bit tormented."

"What do you think I'm tormented by?"

"Irrelevant." He wagged the mop at me. "But you're definitely suffering."

After that, Sam was whisked away by Pearl to sort the compost, and he came back shaken and pale.

"I just spent half an hour knee deep in moldy lettuce and black eggshells," he said. He had to sit down for a minute to recover.

I shuddered. "Thank God Pearl knows I'm not cut out for compost," I said. "You've got to assert yourself, Sam."

"I think it builds character actually," he said. "All the complaining is just to entertain you."

On my way back home from the library last night, I walked by Marigold and Sam singing again in Marigold's hovel, on the floor, the door wide open. They were sitting cross-legged in front of the burning woodstove, facing each other, Sam with his guitar and Marigold singing and smiling at him in her daisy crown. If Sam were wearing slightly nicer jeans and ditched the square glasses, they would have looked like an Anthropolgie ad. I didn't want them to see my watching them, so I ducked my head and ran into my own cabin, where Juna was waiting to softly chide me for my head scarf collection having spilled over onto her side of the dresser.

Sorry for the self-pity. I promise I'm done now. Write me back with your own woes!!!

Love,
Me

To: Flora Goldwasser <fgoldwasser@quare.edu>
From: Sam Chabot <schabot@quare.edu>
Subject: TG
November 15, 11:12 p.m.

I forgot to ask—are you going home for Thanksgiving?

To: Sam Chabot <schabot@quare.edu>
From: Flora Goldwasser <fgoldwasser@quare.edu>
Subject: Re: TG
November 15, 11:33 p.m.

Yes. I am half-dreading it and half-looking forward to finally being
in a house with central heating and a cable connection.

To: Flora Goldwasser <fgoldwasser@quare.edu>
From: Sam Chabot <schabot@quare.edu>
Subject: Re: TG
November 15, 11:34 p.m.

Damn. I was going to ask if you wanted to stay on campus with me
and have a *Degrassi* marathon.

To: Sam Chabot <schabot@quare.edu>
From: Flora Goldwasser <fgoldwasser@quare.edu>
Subject: Re: TG
November 15, 11:35 p.m.

Just when I start to forget you're Canadian . . .

QUARE TIMES

The Quare Academy Student News Collaboration
November 22

SOCIETY BY SAM
By Sam Chabot

This week, a forgotten dinner prep shift turned sour when AS, the absentee in question, was seen at the beehives instead of in the teep. Sources confirm that AS became ornery when asked to join his cooking crew; he refused to take off his beekeeping outfit, insisting that it made him "feel like Queen Latifah in *The Secret Life of Bees*."

ALUM OF THE ISSUE: ELIJAH HUCK
By Juna Díaz

Ever since he graduated from Quare two years ago, Elijah Huck has been shaking up the photography world, first as an unofficial documentarian of the hipster élite at Columbia University and beyond, and next—and most poignantly—the creator of the blog "Miss Tulip," which has been reviewed in indie mags across the country.

Although Huck was unavailable for an interview, Miriam Row, Headmistress, informed the *Quare Times* that plans are in the works for Huck to visit campus for a three-hour photography workshop in December.

"Everyone is talking about the possibility of his visiting," said Marigold Chen. "It's cool that we have a local god at our disposal like this. Even if he doesn't end up coming, it's cool that he's a Quare."

To: All-staff <everyone@nymphettemag.com>
From: Theodora Sweet <thee@nymphettemag.com>
Subject: tees, etc.
November 22, 3:09 p.m.

Nymphettes,

I've been getting some great feedback for the tee designs I've
showed some people. You'd be shocked at the Miss Tulip following
in the Stanford freshman class!

So I finalized the designs and sent them off to the manufacturer.
They should be ready in a couple of weeks. I'll keep you posted.

Happy Thanksgiving, all!
Thee

To: Elijah Huck <ehuck@columbia.edu>
From: Dustin Crane <dusty_crane@vapenyc.com>
Subject: This afternoon
November 29, 7:33 p.m.

Dude,

I know we haven't hung out in ages—like, not since we were in
high school—so let's definitely do that at some point. I got all these
cool vapes from work, and if memory serves (spring break of
2008, fuck yeah), that is very much up your alley.

Crazy shit this afternoon. I got home at four to take my sister to
the dentist, and I swear I was about to swing by next door to see
if you were there—like, literally my hand was on the knob—when
this girl ran up out of nowhere and just, like, perched on your
top step. She was wearing this long pink coat that was, like, the

texture of stucco and one of those pink Jackie Kennedy circle hats or some shit in, like, the exact same color. And big black sunglasses. Is this ringing any bells??

We sort of, like, made eye contact through her glasses—like I said, I was on my way out—and she was all, "Oh, do you know if Elijah Huck still lives here?" and inside my head I was like, *Uhhh, Elijah is probably trying to shake this chick*, but instead I was like, "Yeah, he does, he'll be home in a few hours." She just stared at me for, like, a minute and then kind of, like, scurried away.

So if you don't know who she is or are trying to shake her for some reason, she definitely knows where you live now. Sorry 'bout that. Are you still a virgin, by the way? If so, my sister is single.

OK, peace out,
Dusty

To: Lael Goldwasser <lgoldwasser@harvard.edu>
From: Flora Goldwasser <flora.goldwasser@gmail.com>
Subject: Mum
November 29, 11:41 p.m.

Dear Lael,

Let me start off by saying that I don't blame you in the slightest for spending Thanksgiving in Cambridge. Mum's was miserable.

I took the train into Manhattan and waited for Mum outside Grand Central, on Lex. It was freezing, and she was late. When I finally saw her rushing toward me in a heavy cashmere sweater, waving frantically, I staggered toward her with my heavy suitcase. We took a taxi to her place.

Mum has redecorated. She has pictures of impoverished, Great-Depression-era Appalachia all over her walls (don't ask me why): landscapes of big hollers and mountains, people with coal-smeared faces. The kitchen, which we both know she doesn't use, is teeming with pots and pans, some dirty, others clean.

"You're cooking now?" I asked her.

"Just a little bit," Mum said, rushing into the kitchen to open the oven. She peered inside as though this was how she usually operated (ha!). "My friend Nell is helping me."

Her friend Nell? Do you know of a Nell? Because I didn't.

"Who's Nell?" I asked.

"She's just a friend," Mum said, her head still buried in the oven. "She's an editor at, um, a big publishing company—I can't remember the name of it right now, but she can tell you all about it over dinner tonight."

Dinner. Tonight. I had somehow assumed that we'd go the usual route of Indian takeout and a Katharine Hepburn classic like *Adam's Rib*.

"You invited her over for dinner tonight?" I tried to hide my dismay, but it was hard. I was tired. I didn't want Friend Nell. I wanted naan and *Adam's Rib*.

"She's the one who gave me the recipe, so I wanted to have her over." Mum looked pained. "I'm sorry if you wanted it to be just the two of us."

It wasn't worth it to argue, so I said I was just tired from the crush of work right before break.

"Nell will be eager to hear about all your classes," Mum enthused. "She's an avid reader."

Funny that MUM didn't seem to be interested in any of my classes. She'd asked me barely two questions about Quare. It's to be expected, I guess, but still, you know how it rankles.

I went to change my clothes, and I guess I was so tired that I fell asleep on the bed in the guest bedroom, which is what I'll continue to call "my" bedroom until Mum makes any effort to make me feel welcome. The next thing I knew, someone was pounding on the front door.

"Nell is here!" Mum exclaimed, clapping her hands together like Katharine Hepburn herself had arrived. I staggered up and dragged myself into a seated position on my bed.

Mum opened the door to reveal a fantastically tall woman with thick hips and a long crooked nose. Her black hair was streaked with gray. By her side, barely grazing her knee, was a small boy. I stared.

"You brought Victor!" Again, the handclap. "Flora, come here and meet Nell and her son, Victor."

I hopped off my bed and made my way to the door. I shook her hand awkwardly. It was big, chapped, and dry. Then Nell pushed Victor forward, and I tried to shake his hand too, but it was tiny and limp. Victor buried his face in Nell's baggy pants and tried to blow a raspberry, only the fabric of her pants got caught in his mouth and he ended up gagging a little.

Mum ushered everyone into the kitchen. We actually sat at the table, a first. The pot roast she'd made was dry, but Nell quickly assured Mum that it was still edible—and besides, she was still learning.

"I'll come over next week and we'll do potatoes," said Nell, poking at the (undercooked) baked potato on her plate.

"Oh, will you? I would so appreciate it," Mum gushed. "Flora, isn't the food good?"

Obviously, I've been a vegetarian since I was ten, so I was just like, "Mum. It's murder."

She just blew out air through her nose.

There was a conversation, but I wasn't participating. I gathered that Nell had adopted Victor from Vietnam a few years before, and he was still adjusting to life in America. I also gathered that it was just the two of them—Nell and Victor, no life partner of any kind. Nell leaned her elbows on the table, didn't put her napkin in her lap, and belched liberally.

After dinner, Mum reached into the oven to pull out a burned pie. "Who wants dessert?" she asked, placing the pie on the table. Nell peered down on the pie, which was small and scalded looking. "Honey, did you forget about it or something?"

HONEY?

Nell reached for the knife and cut into the pie. Cherry filling oozed out. Mum knows I love cherry pie, so I was just about to thank her when Nell said, "Victor, look! Aunt Emma made cherry, just for you!"

AUNT EMMA? JUST FOR YOU?

Mum nodded bashfully, and I said nothing. I didn't have any pie. I just sat fuming, my legs tucked in front of me to form a barrier between me and Nell.

After dessert, Mum made tea. "Would you mind playing with Victor while Nell and I talk in here?" she asked. "He likes to look through my photography books under the coffee table."

You know when Mum asks a huge favor like it's a total

throwaway—like you'd be crazy to protest? Yeah. I didn't look at her. I just stormed into the living room.

Victor followed me with some prompting from Nell and Mum. Nell shut the folding door behind us. I yanked out one of the big books from under the table, and Victor sat sullenly on the couch, looking through it with a petulant expression. How many times had he been here before? I wondered. His tiny hands ran over the smooth photography paper with the deftness of someone who was deeply familiar with its contents. Victor's hair was all spiky, standing to attention at random angles. I examined it while I eavesdropped on Mum and Nell.

". . . wasn't sure whether it was a good idea to something something today . . ." Nell was saying.

". . . something something anyway . . ." was Mum's reply.

"Tall," said Victor. It was the first time I'd heard him talk. He speaks in a whisper-whine. He was pointing to a picture of the Twin Towers, a black-and-white shot that obscured the towers in fog.

"How long will Flora be here?" Nell was asking—whining, really. I perked up at the sound of my name.

"A few days and then something something and then something," Mum said.

Nell gave a satisfied-sounding grunt. "As long as something something something," she said.

"Don't worry," Mum answered, and they both laughed.

Lael, the indignity of it all! She and Daddy have been separated for, like, a minute!

Then Victor sent up a wail so sudden and loud that I jumped. He began to cry, first silently and then all at once dissolving into sobs. I just looked at him, unsure of what to do.

"Are you okay?" I asked, a bit stupidly.

When the wailing didn't stop, Nell came into the living room to collect Victor. "It's almost past his bedtime," she scolded, as though it were my fault. "That must be why he's cranky."

I just stared straight ahead.

When they'd gone, leaving a pile of dirty dishes in their wake, I cornered Mum in the kitchen.

"What's going on?" I asked.

"She's been a very good friend to me throughout the—" Mum began, but I cut her off.

"Mum. What's going on with Nell?"

Mum laughed that high-pitched laugh she does when she's nervous. I stared her down.

"Honestly, Flora, you don't have to be immature about it." Mum reached for the faucet and turned it on, facing her back toward me as she began to scrub the blackened pans. "We're good friends."

You know when Mum tries to make it sound like everyone else is ridiculous, and she's the only sane one?

"How did you meet?" I asked.

"Um . . ." Mum scrubbed intently. "The public library. I had gone to check out the newest Bill Bryson—by the way, have you ever read his work?"

I didn't dignify that with a response. (Obviously, I've read Bill Bryson.)

"We were waiting in line to check out our books, and Victor was there, so I asked about him, and she told me, and then she asked about *my* family, so I told *her*, and there you have it: we're friends."

"You don't have friends," I pointed out.

"Well, maybe I made one. Is that what you want for me? To be a lonely old woman, married to my work?"

"You work part-time," I told her.

Mum didn't answer for a long time. Then she resumed scrubbing the pan.

Lael, something is going on between Mum and Nell. I'll get to the bottom of it and write back.

Enjoy Cambridge, you lucky duck!
F

To: Lael Goldwasser <lgoldwasser@harvard.edu>
From: Flora Goldwasser <flora.goldwasser@gmail.com>
Subject: Mum!!!
November 30, 8:17 p.m.

Lael,

Can you please pick up your cell phone for once? I have major news. It's confirmed: Mum and Nell are . . . something. Together.

But first, let me tell you what happened to me and Victor.

The day after Thanksgiving—small and simple with me, Mum, and

Grandma and Grandpa—Nell was nowhere to be found. It was as though she'd evaporated. I didn't bring her up for fear that my mentioning her would somehow summon her.

It was like old times. Mum and I went our separate ways during the day and met up at night for takeout and a Hepburn movie. Yesterday I spent the day with Daddy in Rye, which—unbelievably—could have been worse: it was almost nice to sit in silence and read with him and look out onto the Long Island Sound. I had finally convinced myself that Nell was out of the picture until yesterday, when Mum got a phone call in the morning. She was still in her robe and slippers, sipping her coffee at the kitchen table.

"Well then!" she said in that fake chipper tone once she'd hung up. "That was Nell. She and I are going to a movie. She's picking me up at noon."

And that's when my stomach turned to stone, because we both know that *Mum hates going to the movies during the daytime.* When it's bright out, she's outside taking photographs. Period. And yesterday was sunny, no chance of snow. Cold, but Mum likes that.

"You don't go to movies during the day."

"I do sometimes."

I didn't bother to respond. We both knew she was lying.

Nell pounded on the door at a quarter to noon. I didn't answer, and she kept on pounding. Mum was in the shower. I should have been pissed, but honestly, I was annoyed at Mum, so I was looking forward to her being out of my hair. I planned to hit up a few places that sell things I can never get at Quare: silk scarves, real pastries, suede shoes, vegan ice cream . . . you get the picture.

When Nell was still pounding on the door at 11:47, I crawled off the couch to open the door. There was Nell in all her glory, sweeping curves and hard eyes. I'm telling you, she must be over seven feet tall. And there, at her side, cowering, was Victor. He was emitting muffled sobs into Nell's pants, and when he came up for air, he left a splotch of liquid that Nell didn't seem to notice. I pitied the people who'd be sitting next to Mum, Nell, and Victor at the movies.

We stared at each other. Finally I pointed at Victor. "He likes movies?" I asked.

Nell frowned. I glared. When Nell opened her mouth to speak, Mum emerged from the bathroom wrapped only in a towel. Nobody seemed to find this unusual, and the implications of that realization sent a shiver crawling down my spine.

"You and Victor are going to spend the afternoon together," Nell explained as though I were stupid or hard of hearing or both. She waited for Mum's approval.

Mum nodded giddily. Rage boiled in my chest. It was all I could do not to reach out and strangle Nell.

"We hardly know each other," I managed.

"So you'll get to know each other," said Nell.

I looked down at Victor's tear-streaked face. His mouth was twisted in a gruesome display of woe, and his hair was spikier than it had been when I'd last seen him. His cheeks were bright red, and his eyes were squeezed firmly shut. His eyelids were all puckered and wet.

"Come and keep me company while I get dressed," Mum said to Nell. "Flora, why don't you make a plan with Victor?"

It wasn't a suggestion. So while Nell went off with Mum to get dressed, I forcibly removed Victor from the doorframe and tugged him over to the couch.

"What's the matter?" I asked, trying to be comforting. I would cry too if Nell were my mother, but I wondered if something more specific was wrong with him.

Victor just hid his face and wailed all the harder. He sat on the rug, his face between his knees. I tried to be tender—it wasn't his fault he was so miserable, after all—and rubbed his back a little bit, at first awkwardly but then getting into a good rhythm.

"Your mum won't be going away for long," I comforted him, not sure if that was good news or bad news to him. I guessed it was the latter, because he kept weeping piteously. "I'm not sure what you want me to tell you," I said. "Do you want to watch TV? Does your mum let you do that? Even if she doesn't, you can watch whatever you want, okay?"

He was still crying when Mum and Nell snuck by and crept out the door. Mum mouthed, *Thank you*, as though her gratitude elevated her to the status of Pope Francis, but I pretended not to see her.

"Victor," I said sharply, "you need to tell me what's wrong if you want me to help you. Are you hungry? Thirsty? Have you eaten lunch?"

He shook his head to all three questions. I wondered if he still wore diapers. Surely six was too old for diapers, but I thought it was better to be safe than sorry.

Just in case, I picked him up and put him on the couch, feeling his little derrière quickly. It was dry. I breathed a sigh of relief and turned on the TV. He didn't seem to care for cartoons. Or real housewives. Or singing competitions. Or the Food Network. Finally I just let him cry, went to the kitchen, and cut up an apple. I added a little dollop of peanut butter and brought the plate over to him.

I was about to scream in frustration when he just looked at the plate and cried, but it sort of got to me. I remembered being so young and so upset, feeling like nobody could help me. Being trapped in my own misery.

So I tried again. "Victor, tell me what is wrong." I tried for a stern but loving tone.

Finally he spoke. "M-m-my ear h-h-h-hurts," he bawled.

His ear? I had no idea what that meant, but suddenly there was a problem I could try to fix. "Let's go to the doctor," I said, swinging into action and grabbing my coat and wallet.

In the subway I swiped twice, once for myself and once for Victor, succeeding at activating the turnstile but, in my hurry, causing Victor to walk straight into it at neck level so that his head snapped back. He was too dazed to react, I think, so I pulled him through and kept moving, hoping the transit police wouldn't come running to arrest the both of us. His mouth was in a surprised little O shape from the turnstile incident, as though he had been too shocked to cry. People were staring.

Victor's legs are shrimpy, and he was holding us up in a major way, so I finally hoisted him onto my back. He gripped my neck, strangling me, until I barked, "Hands on my shoulders, mister." I felt like we were in an action movie, swinging through the crowds and racing up the subway steps—and nearly bursting my lungs in the process—to the walk-in clinic in Midtown.

The receptionist just folded her arms over her chest.

"You don't look like his guardian," she snapped.

I briefly explained the situation, telling her that I was just babysitting. She shook her head.

"We need consent from his parent or guardian," she said. "Otherwise, we can't help you."

I looked down at Victor. He had melted onto the floor and seemed to be humming to himself, hands over his ears.

"Give me one second," I said.

I called Mum perhaps fourteen times, until I finally got to her, hissing about interrupting the movie, and then Nell, who provided her consent and insurance information. The receptionist frostily handed me the forms. Obviously I didn't know anything about him besides his name and age, so I left a lot of the form blank or scribbled in my best guesses. Victor clutched my arm like I was his savior.

The doctor felt Victor's glands and took his temperature before looking in his ears and confirming an acute ear infection.

"You should have brought him in sooner," Dr. Sayeed scolded. "It looks like this has been developing for over a week. Hasn't he been complaining of pain for days?"

"He's not mine," I tried to explain, but Dr. Sayeed was busy writing a prescription.

"I'll give him drops today, but you'll have to pick this up from your pharmacy," she said, handing me the piece of paper.

We walked out of the clinic hand in hand, a bit deflated but relieved. The drama had thinned, and I scoured the horizon for a Duane Reade. It was starting to snow as we headed toward the subway. I bought myself and Victor each a huge pretzel (I figured we deserved it, after the morning we'd just survived), and we sat on a bench, munching contemplatively. His little chest fell and rose defiantly. When he had settled down sufficiently, I quickly squirted the drops into his ear, a sneak attack, and he accepted them with a self-indulgent sigh.

"Do you see a lot of my mum? Um, your aunt Emma?" I asked him.

Victor nodded sorrowfully. "Uh-huh. They kiss good night," he said. "On the lips."

Needless to say, I didn't finish my pretzel.

Lael, Mum is a late-in-life lesbian. And she chose NELL. There are a million and one cool, hip lesbians in New York—in this neighborhood alone!—who could have become our new stepmothers, and our genius Mum chose NELL.

We have so much to discuss when I see you in December. Are you sure you can only be home for a week?

F

To: Flora Goldwasser <flora.goldwasser@gmail.com>
From: Lael Goldwasser <lgoldwasser@harvard.edu>
Subject: Re: Mum!!!
November 30, 11:54 p.m.

Oh my God. That is so, so rich. It almost makes me wish I were home to experience it with you.

Almost.

Did I tell you what Mum said to me when she came up for parents' weekend?? (Honestly, I was surprised she even remembered when it was, but I guess I shouldn't be so shocked—she'd never miss an excuse to talk loudly about the evils of apartheid—*which she experienced firsthand*, she never fails to add, never mind the fact that she was WHITE—with all her other former classmates whose kids are at Harvard now.)

Anyway, we went shopping for something for me to wear to the holiday a cappella concert, and she would NOT stop talking about my weight. I mean, literally every college freshman gains a bit of weight. This is hardly news. And you'll see when I come home over winter break that it's not even that dramatic. But, like, would it occur to her to not make a huge deal about it? I mean, her entire profession is dealing with pregnant women, so you'd think she'd have learned a little tact.

Ugh. I feel like we're both being extra tough on Mum, even though if we really think about it, Daddy's to blame for the dissolution of their marriage: he's the one who gave up even trying to work things out, choosing instead to sleep at the office more nights than not just to avoid Mum's wrath.

But don't even get me started on Daddy. He calls me for ten minutes a week, asks me about my grades, and then says he has to let Ginger out. God, it's disgusting how he treats me like a little A-making machine. I mean, you should know: he does the exact same thing to you, Miss Quare superstar.

Anyway, Nell sounds like a nightmare, and you're my hero for sticking it out this weekend. I owe you a private concert.

To: Lael Goldwasser <lgoldwasser@harvard.edu>
From: Flora Goldwasser <flora.goldwasser@gmail.com>
Subject: Re: Mum!!!
December 1, 12:04 a.m.

Do you know anything by the Shangri-Las? Sam and I got super
into them the week before break.

To: Flora Goldwasser <flora.goldwasser@gmail.com>
From: Lael Goldwasser <lgoldwasser@harvard.edu>
Subject: Re: Mum!!!
December 1, 1:23 p.m.

Didn't I tell you that the group specializes in Georgian and Balkan
music?

"Sam and I . . ."

To: Lael Goldwasser <lgoldwasser@harvard.edu>
From: Flora Goldwasser <flora.goldwasser@gmail.com>
Subject: Re: Mum!!!
December 1, 1:27 p.m.

Don't make fun of me!!!

To: Flora Goldwasser <flora.goldwasser@gmail.com>
From: Lael Goldwasser <lgoldwasser@harvard.edu>
Subject: Re: Mum!!!
December 1, 1:29 p.m.

I'm not. I'm happy you have a friend.

To: Lael Goldwasser <lgoldwasser@harvard.edu>
From: Flora Goldwasser <flora.goldwasser@gmail.com>
Subject: Re: Mum!!!
December 1, 1:47 p.m.

So am I, to be honest. We're thinking of throwing a little party
(doo-wop soirée, we'd call it) to celebrate the music of the 1950s
and '60s. But Juna overheard us planning a playlist and was like,
"I don't get why you'd want to romanticize the 1950s like that. Like,
we still have bobby socks and casual homophobia."

To: Flora Goldwasser <flora.goldwasser@gmail.com>
From: Lael Goldwasser <lgoldwasser@harvard.edu>
Subject: Re: Mum!!!
December 1, 1:59 p.m.

I mean, I guess Juna does have a point.

Also, only you would go to a place like Quare and find someone
else who's also into weird fifties shit. God.

To: Lael Goldwasser <lgoldwasser@harvard.edu>
From: Flora Goldwasser <flora.goldwasser@gmail.com>
Subject: Re: Mum!!!
December 1, 2:01 p.m.

It's really quite something. He's also been known to walk with
a cane, but then he got called out for ableism (a fair criticism, I
must admit—to have been using it as a fashion accessory when so
many differently abled people genuinely need them to get around).

Also, I did something kind of crazy the other day. I'll explain next time you call me.

To: Flora Goldwasser <flora.goldwasser@gmail.com>
From: Lael Goldwasser <lgoldwasser@harvard.edu>
Subject: Re: Mum!!!
December 1, 2:03 p.m.

This better not involve Elijah.

To: Lael Goldwasser <lgoldwasser@harvard.edu>
From: Flora Goldwasser <flora.goldwasser@gmail.com>
Subject: Re: Mum!!!
December 1, 2:09 p.m.

He's not returning my calls, Lael! What else was I supposed to do? NOT investigate? I was going to tell you, but then I remembered that you're on your whole Flora-is-at-Quare-for-her-own-reasons-not-Elijah kick and thought better of it. Please don't hate me.

To: Flora Goldwasser <flora.goldwasser@gmail.com>
From: Lael Goldwasser <lgoldwasser@harvard.edu>
Subject: Re: Mum!!!
December 1, 2:12 p.m.

For God's sake, I don't HATE you. You are a damn fool, though.

To: Dean Elliot <delliot@quare.edu>
From: Elijah Huck <ehuck@columbia.edu>
Subject: coming soon . . .
December 3, 10:43 p.m.

D,

Sorry about Thanksgiving. I was moving back to school and pretty
much just ate some potatoes with my mom. It was a pretty sad
affair. But you win. My classes end next week. When's best for me
to come?
E

Part II

To: India Katz-Rosen <ikatzrosen@bowen.edu>
From: Cora Shimizu-Stein <cshimizustein@bowen.edu>
Subject: umm??
December 8, 4:37 p.m.

The weirdest thing ever happened on my way home from school today.

You know how now they make all the drivers park on Seventy-ninth now? So I'm crossing the street to find Dominic, who was maybe fifty feet away, when I see this girl coming toward me. She has all this curly brown hair just, like, piled on top of her head and a tweed coat with huge shoulder pads. And these eighties acid-wash jeans. She was so Sloane Peterson in *Ferris Bueller's Day Off* that it hurt.

I stopped so I could decide whether or not the eighties look was working for her, and if so, I would ask her where she got the jacket she was wearing to tell Flora, when I noticed that underneath the jacket, she was wearing a T-shirt with an image printed on it. I think she saw me looking, so she pulled open her coat a little bit more, just flaunting the shirt. So weird. We were in the middle of the street at this point—it was like everything was happening in slow motion.

It was a picture of a girl's body, just the neck down, but, India—I could have sworn that it was FLORA'S body. I'll admit that I didn't get a perfect look, but it was eerie. The girl in the picture was wearing those ESCADA by Margaretha Ley gingham culottes that

Flora definitely has, and a black turtleneck tank top that she would so wear, and I think I could even see some brownish-red curls just before the picture cut off—which, you know, is *Flora's hair*.

Is Flora a T-shirt model now?
Core

To: Faculty, staff, and students <everyone@quare.edu>
From: Miriam Row <mrow@quare.edu>
Subject: Angel Walk
December 13, 4:06 p.m.

Dear Friends,

I'm delighted to announce that this Friday—the last day before winter vacation—we will be holding our annual Angel Walk in place of shared work. How it works is as follows: everyone who wishes to participate will meet on the soccer field at 4:10 p.m. After the Oracle introduces the activity, we'll form two parallel lines. With your eyes closed, you'll be guided to the start of the line and be shepherded down the middle to get loved on. Those on the edges will be chanting, singing, swaying, and heaping non-shell-speak-related praise onto whomever is walking with her eyes closed down the line.

Remember, if you'd rather not participate, there will be absolutely no judgment—only love.

Infinite blessings,
Miriam

To: Grace Wang <grace@nymphettemag.com>
From: Wink DelDuca <wink@nymphettemag.com>
Subject: new fans
December 13, 4:49 p.m.

Grace,

You have to move to New York. No more of this Chicago bullshit.
I've been wearing the shirts nonstop for days, and every time I
leave the house, people stare. Like today, when I was walking
home from school, this girl—she probably went to Bowen or
Fairfax or something; I always forget how much it must suck to
go to a uniform school until I see those unfortunate polyester
kilts—was practically salivating. I almost told her where she could
get one for herself, but before I could give her my business card,
she sprinted away from me into a big black car. It's a shame that it
was as cold as balls, so I was wearing a coat—she didn't even get
a glimpse of the #BRINGBACKMISSTULIP on the back.

Anyway, for next month's Ask an Older Dude, I'm thinking we do
a profile on Michael Cera. Think we can snag him? He's definitely
Nymphette material. Have you read his latest piece in the *New
Yorker*?

;)

Wink
Editor in Chief, *Nymphette* magazine
Nymphette is an online feminist arts & culture magazine for teenagers. Each
month, we choose a theme, and then you send us your writing, photography,
and artwork.

To: Elijah Huck <ehuck@columbia.edu>
From: Dean Elliot <delliot@quare.edu>
Subject: Re: visit
December 13, 7:18 p.m.

DUDE. Yes. How about the eighteenth (this Friday)? I can skip
shared work (aren't you happy you graduated?) and take out the
van to come get you.

To: Dean Elliot <delliot@quare.edu>
From: Elijah Huck <ehuck@columbia.edu>
Subject: Re: visit
December 14, 12:02 a.m.

Sounds good. There's actually someone there who I'm hoping to
surprise (again, it's a long story that has to do with the shit from
last year), so if you could keep this on the DL, that would be much
appreciated.

To: Elijah Huck <ehuck@columbia.edu>
From: Dean Elliot <delliot@quare.edu>
Subject: Re: visit
December 14, 12:11 a.m.

God, yes. I wouldn't tell anyone. You're kind a big deal now, E. I
mean, at least in the indie-photography circuit. I wouldn't want a
sex riot to break out preemptively. I've read your *Nymphette* profile,
after all. I know the score.

Program for Dean's play, December 17

Guild fondly presents

300 Years of Mourning

written & directed by Dean Elliot

CAST OF CHARACTERS

ELIZABETH / DEAN ELLIOT

GREGORY / MICHAEL LANSBURY

PAUL / GARY NORTH

CALLIOPE / ALTHEA LONG

SUSANNA / LUELLA LOOKMAN

CARLOS / SHY LENORE

FANNY / FLORA GOLDWASSER

Guild, established in 1966, is the only and oldest theater troupe at Quare. Its members are: Dean Elliot (master player), Althea

Long (apprentice), Michael Lansbury, Gary North, Lia Furlough, Jean Noel, Shy Lenore, Solomon Pitts, Luella Lookman, Peter Wojkowski, Heidi Norman-Lester, Flora Goldwasser, Juna Díaz, Agnes Surl, and Becca Conch-Gould.

When I first sat down to write *300 Years of Mourning*, I found myself searching for a story about possession: why we want what we want, and the lengths we are willing to go to acquire it.

I soon found myself writing about redemption, about the journey back to grace, about the things we lose—and gain—along the way. America on the brink of the Industrial Revolution seemed the natural setting for such a story, and I selected the town of Chicago for its rich and layered history (it's also where I grew up).

300 Years of Mourning is about America, sure, but it's also about a family, a haphazard cluster of individuals who must make different peaces with the same tragedy. I learned as much from my cast as they did from me, if not more, and I am eternally grateful for their ready willingness to take risks and go with them. —DE

India Katz-Rosen
1025 Fifth Avenue, Apt. 9C
New York, NY 10028

December 17

Dear India,

Dean's play is over!

And I'm apprentice for next semester!

She announced it after the play was over, in front of everyone.
I was still in my Fanny outfit (starchy navy Victorian dress that
Dean sewed and that I'm definitely going to wear in my daily
life), so it was kind of hard to bow and hug her and everything. I
wouldn't say I've ARRIVED, or anything like that, but it feels so
nice. I can write a play for next semester!

I just need something to write ABOUT. You know that plot isn't
my strong suit. Sam congratulated me about a thousand times
at the small cider-and-peanut-butter-cookies after-party, even
though Marigold was right beside him and kind of scoffing to
herself. Whatever. Later that night we—just Sam and I—hung
out in the Art Barn until after eleven, talking about how weird
it is that our first semester here is almost over. All of the dark
Art Barn paintings from the Art and Activism elective looked
so creepy. We made up backstories for all the weird eyeballs and
bleeding heads. We had a long conversation about the Dionne
quintuplets (Marie, Annette, Yvonne, Émilie, and Cécile, the
French Canadian quintuplets from the 1930s who all survived
into adulthood).

I know what this sounds like. You know how dear the Dionne
quintuplets are to me, and I wouldn't discuss them with just anyone.
And Sam ISN'T just anyone. But I'm not attracted to him at all—
and I think I've told you that he has an enormous crush on Marigold.
I feel like myself with him, but also like I can be more than just
myself. You know? We have so much fun together.

Not, of course, as much fun as I have with you and Cora. I'm
so excited to see you (less than a week!). What's the first stop?
Maison Kayser? Beacon's Closet?

   Love,
   Flora

To: Dean Elliot <delliot@quare.edu>
From: Elijah Huck <ehuck@columbia.edu>
Subject: here
December 18, 3:34 p.m.

D, I'm here at the train station. You coming?

Lael Goldwasser
Harvard College
2609 Harvard Yard Mail Center
Cambridge, MA 02138

December 18

Lael!!!

I'm in the canning station, quietly hyperventilating. Elijah is
here. HERE!! I'm sorry if my handwriting is shaking all over the
place.

Let me start from the beginning.

Today was the last day of school before winter break. Apparently
it's a tradition to do what's called the Angel Walk. Basically,
everyone—faculty, staff, students, and residents—forms two
long lines, facing each other, on the soccer field. So we're all
standing there, chanting and swaying and singing (or, in my case,
swaying and mouthing), and the person at the top of the line,
either the right or the left, is whisked off by the Oracle of Quare,
who's holding a burning stick of sage.

He instructs the person to close her eyes, waves the sage stick
in the outline of her body, and then guides her to the lines,
where she is received and then shuttled down. It's the job of the

people on the edges to caress and whisper praise to whomever is journeying down the line. The first person to go was Fern, and it took forever, because everyone loves Fern.

We sang Quare tunes all the while. When Fern was finally at the end—people wouldn't release their death grips on her—she dissolved into a happy puddle on the ground, basking in the sunshine. Pretty much everyone was there, but I didn't see Dean. As the line shuffled up, I began to dread my turn. You know how I hate gratuitous touch. I toyed with the idea of refusing to go, but then I got over myself and let the Oracle of Quare lead me a few feet away. It was hard to keep my eyes closed and he breathed warm air into my face and outlined me with sage, which made me cough and gag a little bit. He chanted something in guttural Sanskrit or Hebrew or something—God, it was all I could do to keep it together—and then sort of clucked in either ear a few times.

Going down the line was actually a lot easier than I thought. I won't bore you with the details, but maybe my classmates do like me a little bit more than they let on—or maybe everyone was just a little high on sage. But one by one they clutched me, whispered non-shell-speak-related praise into my ears, and then gently shepherded me down the line. At first I tried to keep my head from touching anyone else's, because I had spent all morning perfecting my victory rolls, but after a while I just sort of gave in to it.

Some hands were familiar—Sam almost made me burst out laughing by grabbing me close, like I was a hysterical Scarlett O'Hara and he was Rhett Butler, and I'd know Lucy's sandpapery hands anywhere—and some I couldn't place.

When I finally got to the end, I was a tiny bit disappointed to be finished, even. I felt light enough to want to collapse on the ground like the others who had gone before me, but before I sank down, I opened my eyes to make sure that prior to my nubby pink coat making contact with the ground there wasn't a huge puddle below me.

But the minute I opened my eyes, I was face-to-face with the baby bird himself.

Elijah freaking Huck.

Dean was standing right beside him, the sun blocking her dark eyes behind her enormous glasses. Dean and Elijah had obviously just arrived from somewhere. Dean was holding car keys and Elijah held a small duffel bag. He looked just the same as ever: bomber jacket, cuffed jeans, delectable round glasses. And his face, so pale and earnest and adorable.

We looked at each other for about ten seconds. His lips were slightly parted. I can only guess at the shock on my own face. I turned and sprinted toward the garden. That's where I am now: the little storage hut lined with rows and rows of preserves and canned tomatoes.

I can't leave. Send help.

XOXO,
Flora

Lael Goldwasser
Harvard College
2609 Harvard Yard Mail Center
Cambridge, MA 02138

December 19—morning

Lael,

I know we always said we'd tell each other immediately when
it happened. And I'd never break a promise to you, so I'm
telling you: it happened. Last night.

I feel so weird and empty and kind of sick to my stomach.

He's gone. He didn't say good-bye or anything. He left the guest
cabin at, like, five in the morning, when I was still half-asleep and
gripping the wool blanket with my knees. When he was standing
in the doorway and slipping his shoes on, he told me we'd see
each other at breakfast, but when I made my way from the guest
cabin to the dining hall this morning, all bleary and mussed,
Dean told me he had already left. Like, for home.

I'm writing to you from a back table in the dining hall, but I have
to go pack now. For home. I don't know why I'm writing to you
if I'm going to see you in, like, four days, but oh well. I'm so, so
tired.

Also, for some inexplicable reason, Elijah left behind Miss Tulip
fan mail. It was all together in a packet under the bed in the guest
cabin. I read it all without really reading it. It felt like it wasn't
even meant for me in the first place.

　　Flora

Attempt 8

Elijah Huck
245 West 107th Street
New York, NY 10025

December 19—night

Elijah,

Was it something I did? I mean, to make you leave without
saying anything to me? Such as "good-bye," for example? Or
that maybe you loved me?

Or maybe how, when it was over and you scooped me from
behind and buried your head in my neck and it was like you were
drinking me in, not through your mouth or even your wrists, but
maybe by just lining yourself against my back, but then you got
up and closed the bathroom door because the guest cabin has its
own bathroom and I thought it was such a luxury

Attempt 9

Elijah Huck
245 West 107th Street
New York, NY 10025

December 19—night

Elijah,

I've always been in love with the way you look at me, like I'm the most interesting girl in the world. And last night you treated me like I looked so good, tasted so good, *was* so good. And then you left, even though I'm here at Quare, which I thought you were supposed to love, even though I'm surrounded by dirt and lentils and

Transcript of Sam's conversation with the Oracle of Quare, taped on Sam's cell phone, December 19

THE ORACLE: Greetings, my child. Make yourself at home.

SAM CHABOT: Oh okay. Is the chair supposed to . . . ? Sorry. It's really dark in here. Got it.

O: You good?

SC: Yeah, I'm good.

O: Before we begin, I'd like us to laugh together for three minutes.

SC: Laugh together? I'm actually leaving pretty soon.

O: Laughter meditation. It's the best medicine.

SC: We just . . . laugh?

O: Yes. I'll start. Join in whenever you feel comfortable. Remember, I can't see you. [Laughs]

SC: [Laughs] Are we done now?

O: [Laughs]

SC: Hello?

O: Okay. [Sound of glass breaking] Oh fuck. I'm sorry. Just give me a second.

SC: Take your time.

O: Just one—okay. I'm all ears. What's on your mind?

SC: I, uh, just wanted to get something off my chest. About what happened this morning.

O: Ah yes.

SC: And I was hoping for a bit of advice.

O: I don't give advice, friend. I just listen.

SC: Oh. Well, what good is that?

O: Please begin.

SC: Okay. So as soon as I got to breakfast this morning, I knew something was off with Flora. Everyone was saying good-bye and just hanging out and stuff, but Flora wasn't saying anything. She was staring off into space and, like, writing a letter or something, but desultorily. And her hair was a mess. Yesterday she was wearing victory rolls, or whatever they're called—you know that hairstyle from the forties where there are these two big, like, rolled sections of hair on either side of your head? So I asked her, "How's it going?" and she just looked straight through me.

So I coaxed her for a little bit, and people around us came and went, and then, at a certain point, tears just started streaming out of her eyes. But her expression didn't change at all. It was kind of scary. So I just grabbed her and hugged her for a little bit, but she wriggled away from me.

O: Uh-huh.

SC: I kept asking, "What's wrong? What's wrong?" but she kept saying, "Nothing; I'm fine." Finally I led her out of the dining hall and into the kitchen. I know she likes jasmine tea, so I started boiling some water. And the second I turned my back, she said something really quietly about Elijah—you know, that guy who went here and was just on campus visiting Dean? I gather that he's kind of famous, which explains why all the first-year girls were wringing their hands and looking at each other when he showed up. I mean, *I've* never heard of him, but I guess that's not saying a lot.

I asked her to repeat herself maybe a hundred times, but she just wouldn't. I mean, it didn't take a genius to realize what had happened. He hurt her—and it didn't even matter now.

So I was like, "I'm going to break his face."

She freaked out. "No! No! You can't!"

O: That's a good impersonation of Flora.

SC: But I was like, "Why not?" And she goes, "It's not worth it. He's already left. And besides, he didn't do anything."

O: Uh-oh.

SC: The way she said it just GOT to me, you know? This son of a bitch comes here, hurts her, and then is going to get away with it? That just didn't seem right to me.

O: And how do you know he took hurt her?

SC: Well, let me back up for a minute. I've known about Elijah since Saturday night, when Flora and I were hanging out in the Art Barn after her play. Things got all confessional, and it came out that she's here because of this random guy who was her history tutor at her fancy private school, which sort of means that he was her teacher, back at Bowen. You probably knew him when he went here, right?

O: I won't say.

SC: They became superclose, and she was super into him, but he could never love her because it was forbidden since he was her Tutor, or blah, blah, blah. And that's why she's here—because he went here, and she thought that maybe he'd be able to love her if she followed in his footsteps. Like he was supposed to ride in here and sweep her off her feet because she decided to be all crazy for a year. She said, "I'm here because I want to be," but I could see she was just telling herself that. And then when he showed up here, she freaked and bolted from the Angel Walk. And I didn't see her until the next morning, at which point she was a teary mess and he was gone. So I put two and two together. She kept saying he didn't take advantage of her, and that everything was consensual, but you can be consensual and still be an asshole.

So I went to go find him. I realize in hindsight that I might have been running. So I sprint away, and Flora's chasing after me, yelling at me to stop, and everyone is looking at us. The whole thing was surreal. I think I, like, barreled into someone. There were all these people on the porch of the dining hall, and they all stared like we were crazy.

I asked them, "Where is he?"

And Jaisal goes, "Where is who?"

"Elijah."

She gestured up the hill. "He was up there earlier."

So that's where I went. Flora was right behind me the whole time. It was like I was in some action movie. I sailed over the fence to the farm like it was nothing. And then we both stopped, and we were breathing so hard, like we had just run a marathon.

But I was on a roll. I started yelling. I was like, "ELIJAH, SHOW YOURSELF, YOU FUCKING COWARD!" But he wasn't there. I went into the barn, but there was no one there. Then I looked down, and there's this red bandanna just, like, fluttering in the wind. It took me a few seconds to remember that it was what Elijah had been wearing yesterday, tied around his neck. It's, like, what are you, a border collie?

O: [Laughs]

SC: And Flora immediately starts giving me shit for doing this. She's like, "I told you not to do this. What if he had been here?"

And I was like, "If he had been here, I would have broken his face." But then she got angry.

She was like, "Can't you just stay out of it?"

I mean, I was surprised. I'm her only friend here, I'm pretty sure. I'm kind of like the Quare mascot, but Flora doesn't really talk to people all that often. So I told her that I thought Elijah should pay, and she just lashes out at me, like, "I can take care of myself."

And at this point I'm mad, so I'm like, "Spare me the bullshit." I'm like, "What the fuck happened between you two? For fuck's sake, Flora."

I kept trying to get an answer out of her about whether or not she thought she was going to be okay, and finally she eked out a yes.

But the way she said it was just so meek, like her voice was coming from somewhere behind her and she was listening to it just like I was.

We had some words after that. I maybe offhandedly accused her of not participating in her own life. In hindsight, that was the wrong move. She was pissed. She was all, "FUCK YOU! I DO PARTICIPATE IN MY OWN LIFE. I'M DEEPER THAN YOU THINK I AM! I HAVE RESERVES OF INNER STRENGTH!"

After she lost it on me, we were quiet for a few seconds. I feel like it was good for her to let that out. Because then she started laughing, and I laughed too. We walked down the hill, talking about other things. She wasn't really feeling all that much better, I could tell, but I felt like I had to let it go or she might snap my head off.

She left for winter break about half an hour ago on the shuttle to the train station. I didn't want to leave on bad terms, so I went and sat in her cabin while she packed, and she was polite and all, but I could tell she was still pissed.

So now I don't know what to do. Do I report this? Do I bring this up again? What's your advice, sage?

O: My job isn't to give advice.

SC: Oh. I forgot about that part. Aren't you going to tell me what you think about any of this?

O: No. You already know what you have to do.

SC: I do?

SC: Hello?

SEMESTER TWO

To: Faculty, staff, and students <everyone@quare.edu>
From: Miriam Row <mrow@quare.edu>
Subject: Welcome back!
January 18, 9:02 a.m.

Dear everyone,

I hope you all had restful and rejuvenating winter breaks. I look forward to hearing about the projects you tackled during your time off.

I'm delighted to let you all know that Allison will be returning to teaching this semester; her partner, artist in resident Daniel Longfield, will be entering paternity leave. Also joining us this semester is Sinclaire O'Leary, a first-year most recently from Seattle, Washington. Sinclaire is an avid gardener and artist who writes beautifully about growing up in Ireland. She will be living with Marigold Chen

Which brings me to my next point: I'm less happy to report that Becca Conch-Gould has left us. Although Becca reports that she was not unhappy here, she feels that she is more suited for a different environment. We are holding Becca in the light and thank her for taking care of her needs.

In other news: we welcome the addition of several new laptop computers from a generous donor; these have been placed in each first-year cabin to allow for quicker communication among students and faculty. First-years still may email only within the Quare email server.

Blessings,

Miriam

To: Faculty, staff, and students <everyone@quare.edu>

From: The Oracle <oracle@quare.edu>

Subject: Re: Welcome back!

January 18

Greetings Quarelings,

Thought I'd follow up this lovely welcome with our first weekly menu of the new year! As always, all items are vegan unless otherwise indicated, and gluten-free alternatives are always provided.

MONDAY: cranberry oatmeal / millet mountains / kale and tofu stir-fry

TUESDAY: lemon muffins / lentil stew / peanut noodles

WEDNESDAY: grits / spicy chickpeas and quinoa / roasted vegetable pizza

THURSDAY: oatmeal party / three-bean chili / pasta party

FRIDAY: bialys / baked potatoes / Mexican rice and beans

SATURDAY: buckwheat pancakes and assorted brunch / curry

SUNDAY: tofu scramble and assorted brunch // orange bean soup

And just as a reminder, we eat at the hours of eight, twelve, and six. Out of courtesy to our cook and our dinner prep team, we ask that you arrive on time.

One last thing: my "office" hours this semester are Tuesdays from eight to eleven p.m. in the confession booth at the back of the meetinghouse. I can't wait to love you!

Love,

The Oracle

QUARE TIMES

The Quare Academy Student News Collaboration
January 22

WE ASKED: QUARE, WHAT DID YOU DO OVER BREAK?
By Gary North

Juna Díaz: "I worked with the native community in my hometown of Santa Fe, New Mexico. I interned for an organization that's trying to empower native artists through microloans."

Althea Long: "I grew melons in cardboard boxes in my garage."

Dean Elliot: "After finishing college applications, you mean?"

Michael Lansbury: "I did a lot of queer theater in Columbus, Ohio."

Agnes Surl: "Sleep. And some tutoring."

Marigold Chen: "Urban gardening in Oakland."

Dexter Holliday: "I helped this really old woman write her memoirs."

Shy Lenore: "I translated for Mexican and Russian immigrants at a law firm in New York."

FIRST-YEAR STUDIES, CAMPAIGNS AT SEA
By Benna Williams

Pete Seeger died in 2014, but he's far from forgotten: namely, his boat, the *Clearwater*, still makes regular journeys up and down the Hudson River. This spring, first-year Zev Londy will embark on a four-month expedition.

"I think it'll be a lot of singing Pete Seeger classics, learning about marine biology and ecology, and journaling," Londy said.

Not only will Londy have the opportunity to get environmental science hands-on, but he'll also be reading the literature of the sea for an English credit. Although he will have to take a math class at a local college over the summer, Londy insists that the slight inconvenience is worth the payoff.

"I can't think of a better way to honor the legendary Pete Seeger," Londy said.

Miriam Row, Head of School, explained that she encourages students to take time away from the Academy in order to explore their passions.

"I'm thrilled that so many of our students are able to step away and then step back in with renewed vigor," she said.

PEACE ON EARTH CLASS VISITS LOCAL COMMUNE
By Robin Cruz

You've probably heard of Paradise Farms. It's a twenty-minute drive from campus, an intentional community devoted to artistic expression and communal living. To kick off the semester, Allison Longfield's first-year Peace on Earth section made the short journey in everyone's favorite vegetable-oil-powered van to check it out for themselves.

"It's rare that we see a model of communism that's really working," said Juna Díaz. "It was heartening to see firsthand that the tropes we hear about alternate economic systems are just that: tropes."

SOCIETY BY SAM
By Sam Chabot

Visiting alum Golden Boy proved himself to be less the artistic wunderkind and more the Enormous Asshole when he "fucked and ducked" on a first-year in December.

Reader, as you can tell, this is where everything explodes.

THE NEW YORK TIMES, JANUARY 22
Style Section

At Boarding School, No Talk of Physical Appearance
By Nadia Levkov

This fall, Miriam Row, Headmistress of the Quare Academy, a prestigious peace- and environmentalism-focused boarding school of thirty-four students in Main Stream, New York, welcomed students new and old to the thirty-acre campus, which includes an organic farm and orchard. Noticeably absent on that September day was the usual talk of new summer tans, haircuts, and clothing purchases.

Ms. Row, who like the Quare Academy itself is Quaker, gave an opening speech in which she explained the logistics of "no shell speak," a guideline that recommends that faculty, students, and staff refrain from commenting on one another's physical appearance.

"Quare is a radically inclusive community," she said. "One of the things we can do to ensure that kindness reigns here is to practice baseless love, and not to judge each other or even comment on how we look."

Emmaline Parker, a Quare second-year (the boarding school is unique in that its students are in the eleventh and twelfth grades), was jarred upon arriving from a private school in Boston, Massachusetts.

"It was a huge adjustment," Miss Parker said. "You realize how easy it is to comment on someone's outfit or their hair when you've just met them. 'No shell speak' forces you to go up to someone and say, 'Hey, tell me about what inspires you.'"

Psychologists have long studied the effects of negative adolescent self-image, including comments directed at oneself ("my thighs look so fat in these shorts"), but Ms. Row explained that the Quare guideline applies to neutral, and even positive, remarks.

"It places an undue premium on physical appearance," Ms. Row said. "If you say that my hair looks good today, tomorrow I'll be worried about it looking the same way in order to please you. At Quare we look for things that are deeper."

Instead of shell speak, Ms. Row suggests that students give compliments such as "You're a superhero!" or "Your inner beauty is shining."

Gus Freeman, a first-year, is the son of Reginald and Christine Freeman, who own a designer consignment boutique in Philadelphia, Pennsylvania.

"Gus came back home for fall break and asked us not to talk about others' clothing, at least in a way that detracted from the person they were underneath," Ms. Freeman said. "It was a wake-up call that our family was going too far toward the shallow end of things."

Quare has a long tradition of churning out well-adjusted graduates—30 percent of the average graduating class goes on to Ivy League schools, University of Chicago, and Stanford, with other graduates choosing among private liberal arts colleges such as Wesleyan, Swarthmore, and Oberlin.

"Students come back to Quare and thank us for this guideline," Ms. Row said. "They tell us that 'no shell speak' has empowered them to jump into life, to go down to the deepest levels and find the most powerful lessons of all."

To: Flora Goldwasser <fgoldwasser@quare.edu>
From: Miriam Row <mrow@quare.edu>
Subject: meeting
January 22, 1:12 p.m.

Flora,

Please stop by my office as soon as possible. You may skip your afternoon classes to do so. Your teachers have been informed that you'll be absent.

Blessings,
Miriam

Flora Goldwasser
Pigeonhole 44
The Quare Academy
2 Quare Road
Main Stream, NY 12497

January 22

Flora!

I'm not into writing letters like you are, but something's gotta give. Send a sign—honestly, any sign at all—that you're alive and well. I'm THIS close to calling the office to make sure you're still on campus (and you know I have that weird thing about talking on the phone).

Honestly, you didn't seem right over break. I know you chalked it up to stress, but I know how you are when you get stressed—you head to Maison Kayser, not the white walls of your bedroom (minimalism is in, I know, but can you say *psych ward*?).

Write me, okay?

Cora

Juna's letter to her girlfriend, Theodora Sweet, donated by Juna to this collection (Spoiler alert: Three years post-Quare, Juna and I are now close friends)

Theodora Sweet
1330 Corrida De Agua
Santa Fe, NM 87507

January 22

Baby,

Do you mind it when I call you that? It feels natural on the page, just like you feel in my arms.

I don't need to tell you again how awful and scary it was to leave you in that airport. These past six weeks have been nothing short of incredible, and I say quite seriously that I never want to lose you. And I know we're keeping this open, but trust me when I say this is the best thing that's ever happened to me.

Just as I expected, shit hit the fan pretty immediately when I got back to Quare the other day. *Quare Times*, a cheery little student-run cooperative quarterly that covers the goings-on on campus, published its first issue the other day. Well, this issue wasn't so cheery: it came to light that Elijah Huck—maybe you've heard of him; he's like the wet dream of every sixteen-year-old girl in knee socks—was a major asshole to Flora Goldwasser, or something, at the end of last semester. (Wait, of course you've heard of him. Even if you weren't a photographer for *Nymphette*, it would be impossible to avoid him in the world of up-and-coming photographers, right?)

Anyway, Flora just happens to be my roommate.

I told you about her, right? The one who has fully embraced neither the ethos nor the pathos of Quare?

Well, she's destroyed, and I don't know WHAT to do. She's been sitting on her bed placidly for the past hour. In a housecoat and a silk turban. (That's shell speak, I know, but I felt it necessary to paint the picture.)

To be honest, the guy who published the commentary about their encounter in the *Quare Times*—Sam, who's, like, her only friend here—is a little dick for doing that so publicly. I mean, he didn't go into specifics, or anything. And he certainly didn't allude to sexual assault—*fucked and ducked* is the term he used, which leads me to believe that Elijah, well, fucked and ducked on her. Sam so majorly fucked up. And that's another piece of it, too: I don't want to participate in the toxic sort of callout culture, the kind in which those who make mistakes are shunned and vilified rather than, well, engaged in conversations about their choices. But every time I think about what he did—what a violation of privacy it was, and how Flora must feel—I want to scream and cry, or possibly both at once.

I don't know their history, but Flora is clearly devastated. Now that it's come to light, we have no choice but to rally around her. What are your words of wisdom? Put that Stanford Feminist, Gender, and Sexuality Studies education to good use (even if you ARE taking a semester off, you can still be a dutiful member of the department).

Love,
June bug

To: Faculty, staff, and students <everyone@quare.edu>
From: Juna Díaz <jdiaz@quare.edu>
Subject: new moon women's circle
January 22, 4:42 p.m.

Dear everyone,

As we are sure the recent events in today's *Quare Times* upset everyone, we welcome all female-identifying people to partake in a new moon women's circle to debrief and support members of our community who are hurting. For those of you who aren't aware, for generations circles of women have met on or around the new moon to hold space to discuss and revel in one another's wishes, dreams, and intentions. This is a practice familiar to people of many cultural backgrounds. If you would like to join, please be in the Art Barn at eight p.m. tomorrow night.

Sincerely,
The Feminist Underground (Juna Díaz, Shy Lenore, Althea Long, and Heidi Norman-Lester)

To: All-staff <staff@quare.edu>
From: Miriam Row <mrow@quare.edu>
Subject: SENSITIVE MATERIAL
January 22, 4:59 a.m.

Dear all,

I'm writing to update you about a sensitive situation involving Flora Goldwasser.

As you all know, Sam Chabot's column in the welcome-back issue of *Quare Times* suggested that Flora had been sexually active, possibly in an emotionally destructive way, with Elijah Huck on campus this past December. Yesterday I met with Flora and Sam, both separately and together.

Sam expressed remorse at his impulsive decision to write the column, which, though it declined to go into specifics, certainly suggested that there had been nefarious behavior on Elijah Huck's part. Sam apologized to Flora, but she—perhaps understandably—refused to meet his eye. I used my nonviolent communication training to coach the pair through identifying feelings and needs. Both were somewhat resistant to the process. When I dismissed

Sam, I asked Flora about the validity of his words. She was quite resolute that things are fine between her and Elijah. Her body language, however, seemed to suggest that the opposite is true.

Please keep all this in mind in the coming weeks. I let Flora know that all she had to do was ask for an extension or an exemption, and it would be granted without issue.

Finally, in light of the nature of the published commentary, I have decided to step in and overrule the current process of publication for *Quare Times*, which as you know is completely student-run and edited horizontally, with no editorial board. From now on, however, I will require that the final copy be reviewed by Allison Longfield, interim adviser, prior to publication in order for the newsletter to continue to receive funding. Moreover, Sam Chabot will be meeting with me and the entire nonviolent communication team every week for the next month for intensive sessions.

Do not hesitate to get in touch with me if you would like to discuss this further.

Blessings,
Miriam

Minutes
New Moon Women's Circle
JANUARY 24
Benna Williams, Secretary, Feminist Underground

8:00 p.m.: People slowly arrive in the Art Barn. We have turned out the lights and laid blankets on the floor. The moon is visible through the glass roof.

8:05 p.m.: People continue to arrive. Fifteen or so are present.

8:07 p.m.: Juna Díaz begins a soft rendition of "Where There is Light in the Soul." Women join hands and sing together.

8:10 p.m.: Lucy Williams asks if we should begin. Juna replies that we are waiting for one more person.

8:12 p.m.: Juna excuses herself. Althea leads the group in a soft rendition of "This Little Light of Mine."

8:17 p.m.: Juna is still not back. Benna, Lucy, and Shy consult in the corner. Counted seventeen present.

8:23 p.m.: Door opens. Juna walks in with Flora in tow. She is covering her mouth ~~with the sleeve of her cream-colored cable-knit sweater.~~

8:23 p.m.: Juna guides Flora to a spot on the floor. Flora sits. She takes a candle and holds it in her hands. She stares into the candle.

8:25 p.m.: Juna begins to speak. She explains that we are all here to heal from recent events and asks the group to do a check-in. She clarifies that we are not here for any reason in particular—just to start the semester in an intentional way.

8:26 p.m.: Check-in begins. Women share feelings of hurt, fear, and empathy. It is clear that these comments are directed at ~~Flora~~ what Sam published in the *Quare Times* earlier this week about Elijah's having "fucked and ducked" on Flora. Nobody knows what to make of this statement.

8:32 p.m.: It is Flora's turn. She chooses not to speak.

8:45 p.m.: Flora still looking into candle.

8:46 p.m.: Juna asks Flora if there is anything she would like to express. "It's a safe space."

8:47 p.m.: Flora: "Sam shouldn't have done that."

8:47 p.m.: Lucy: "Is that all?"

8:48 p.m.: Juna gently asks Lucy to give Flora her space.

8:48 p.m.: Lucy: "It was so wrong of Sam to do what he did, but now that everyone knows what happened, we can support you. Look at it that way." Lucy goes on to say that even though many of the assembled women have had strong feelings of admiration for Elijah in the past, they accept their primary duty—as feminists—to support Flora. Lucy says that even though the encounter was consensual, Flora is still completely entitled to feelings that range from rage to depression.

8:48 p.m.: Juna changes the topic, asks how the Feminist Underground can better support all women at Quare in the coming semester, particularly those who are most marginalized (queer and trans women, women of color, immigrant women, survivors of sexual assault, poor women).

8:50 p.m.: Heidi suggests a revamped Feminist Underground support network that stands with survivors of sexual assault informally rather than involving the administration, which can be an intimidating process.

8:52 p.m.: Juna agrees, asks how that would be possible. What about any sexual experience, positive or negative? How can we be more open about those? Support all women in their experiences?

8:53 p.m.: Benna answers that maybe the key is to normalize discussions about safe sex and consent.

8:54 p.m.: Juna asks if anyone in the room has experiences with emotionally charged sexual experiences that he or she wants to share.

8:55 p.m.: Lucy says she is going to "name it." "Flora, are you comfortable sharing your experiences?"

8:56 p.m.: Flora says no, not right now.

8:57 p.m.: Final refrain of "Where There Is Light in the Soul."

*Email from Dean to Elijah, published
here with Dean's permission*

To: Elijah Huck <ehuck@columbia.edu>
From: Dean Elliot <delliot@quare.edu>
Subject: WTF???
January 25, 3:42 p.m.

E,

What the fuck is going on? What the fuck happened between you and Flora last semester? You need to provide some clarity, because I have absolutely no idea what's going on.

D

Flora Goldwasser
Race in Writing
January 28
In-Class Reflection

PROMPT: In Alice Walker's *The Color Purple*, what do Celie's messages to God reveal or illustrate about her relationship to the divine?

In The Color Purple, *Celie tells her story in missives to God; her life, which she lays before us, is both a confession and a prayer. Alice Walker places this prayer in stark opposition to sex: although prayer allows Celie to author her own narrative, sex is not so much a choice as it is a transaction that involves Celie and her husband, Albert. Despite her unfair treatment by Albert, who by any account is an abusive husband, Celie, socialized to not only accept but also expect his abuse, remarks only that he "do his business . . . [and] go to sleep." This economic relationship that Celie has with sex, located in her use of the word "business," makes sex into a transactional rather than a spiritual experience and disables any sense of autonomy awarded to her through her frequent prayer.*

COMMENTS

Thoroughly engaging work, Flora. You seem to be suggesting that for Celie and Albert, sex is more of a transaction—you call it an "economic relationship [to] sex"—and less a space of true connection. Sex becomes about giving and taking (what Celie must provide; what Albert can acquire) rather than sharing. Astute observation! How does society provide a framework for such an understanding of sex? —Pearl

To: Flora Goldwasser <fgoldwasser@quare.edu>
From: Sam Chabot <schabot@quare.edu>
Subject: sorry
January 28, 5:20 p.m.

Flora,

I know you're not talking to me right now, and I get it. I'm feeling a lot of guilt about what I did, and I think we should talk one-on-one (without Miriam) about it.

I'm so sorry. I meant to hurt Elijah, not you. I wanted to ruin his reputation, not compromise your privacy. I see now that I was stupid. I feel like such an idiot. It was impulsive. I'm honestly at a loss.

But I know I've put you in a horrible position, and all I want is to talk to you about it.

Write back if you ever feel like it.
Sam

Journal entry, night of January 28

I feel sometimes like I'm still in that stage, that half of a second between stubbing your toe and feeling the pain, which is almost worse than feeling the pain because the anticipation of the thing is sometimes way more profound than the thing itself.

But then other times it comes rushing in so fast that I have to sit down wherever I am, sometimes directly on top of a snowbank, and even when the cold makes my derrière go numb, I can't get up,

*because getting up means moving forward through a new space and
time where this new reality exists.*

　*And then there's all this anger. God, it's RAGE. I will never
forgive him. I feel gutted, and then I feel like I'm stuffed with so
much ANGER that I'm not even hungry. And you know what?
Maybe anger is healthy. Maybe anger is okay. Maybe my anger will
be strong enough to catapult me all the way back home.*

As you can see, I was a melodramatic little mess. But really, can
you blame me?

Cora Shimizu-Stein
95 Wall Street, Apt. 33A
New York, NY 10005

January 28

Cora!

I'm so sorry I've been absent. Mea culpa!

A quick update: I almost didn't recognize Juna when I got to
campus. Gone are the colorful woven tops and flowing prairie
skirts. She now has a cropped haircut, thick-framed glasses, and
a pair of corduroy trousers. She looks like a teenaged communist
circa 1960.

I asked her why she decided to cut her hair.

"I'm a budding Marxist," Juna explained breezily.

Do all Marxists have short hair?

"That's interesting," I said.

She hasn't abandoned all her flowing things, but there are a good number of shapeless black smocks and grim trousers now in the mix.

To make matters worse, she won't stop trying to talk to me about this and that—it's almost creepy, like she's trying to get dirt on me, or something. Like she's on assignment for the FBI.

There's also a new girl, Sinclaire. She has an Irish accent and lots of long, long black hair and pink rain boots. I don't think I've heard her say ten words yet, but she's pretty intriguing, in a Wiccan sort of way.

Would you mind scanning and sending me copies of all the letters I wrote to you guys last semester? I'm doing a project and need to piece together some details I think I forgot.

Thanks, and I'll keep you posted!

Oh yeah, I'm sorry I was so weird about the whole Elijah thing over break. It still feels super weird, and it's hard to talk about the way it ended, even with you . . . and you wouldn't believe how people here are carrying on about it (it's a long story, and I have to run!).

Love,
Flora

To: Dean Elliot <delliot@quare.edu>
From: Elijah Huck <ehuck@columbia.edu>
Subject: Re: WTF???
January 29, 1:15 a.m.

What the fuck? How do you know about me and Flora?

To: Elijah Huck <ehuck@columbia.edu>
From: Dean Elliot <delliot@quare.edu>
Subject: Re: WTF???
January 29, 1:17 a.m.

It's all over school. Here's a photo of what was published in the
Quare Times last week.

<attachment: quare-times.jpg>

To: Dean Elliot <delliot@quare.edu>
From: Elijah Huck <ehuck@columbia.edu>
Subject: Re: WTF???
January 29, 1:22 a.m.

Who the fuck is Sam Chabot?

To: Elijah Huck <ehuck@columbia.edu>
From: Dean Elliot <delliot@quare.edu>
Subject: Re: WTF???
January 29, 1:24 a.m.

First-year. Flora's friend. Everyone on campus is talking about it.
Flora's a complete fucking mess.

To: Dean Elliot <delliot@quare.edu>
From: Elijah Huck <ehuck@columbia.edu>
Subject: Re: WTF???
January 29, 1:25 a.m.

It's complicated between Flora and me.

To: Elijah Huck <ehuck@columbia.edu>
From: Dean Elliot <delliot@quare.edu>
Subject: Re: WTF???
January 29, 1:28 a.m.

Yeah, it really does look that way, doesn't it? She's seventeen, Elijah.

To: Dean Elliot <delliot@quare.edu>
From: Elijah Huck <ehuck@columbia.edu>
Subject: Re: WTF???
January 29, 1:30 a.m.

I know. I know. I really didn't mean to hurt her. It's just hard.

To: Elijah Huck <ehuck@columbia.edu>
From: Dean Elliot <delliot@quare.edu>
Subject: Re: WTF???
January 29, 1:33 a.m.

Whatever, dude.

Lael Goldwasser
Harvard College
2609 Harvard Yard Mail Center
Cambridge, MA 02138

January 29

Lael,

It was all a lie. Everything. Elijah. Our connection. Miss Tulip.

I don't think I've eaten solid food since coming back from winter break, so forgive me if I seem a little bit out of it. I *am* a bit out of it, to tell you the truth. I just keep thinking about Elijah. Obsessively. And now about what everybody is saying happened between us, and how that isn't what happened at all—it's different and horrible in its own way. "Fucked and ducked" is how Sam put it, but it's just so reductive, and I feel like I'm never going to be able to look Sam in the eye again. Because I AM SO FUCKING MAD AT HIM. And I told him EVERYTHING the night before, too. In the Art Barn after Dean's play. And for him to do that—I just can't. I can't even write about it. It makes me too upset. I'm literally shaking with rage. Maybe I'll take up running, or something. God, I HATE him. I HATE HIM SO FUCKING MUCH. I feel like Bertha Mason from *Jane Eyre*. Next thing you know, I'll be setting his bed on fire and haunting him every night.

And sure, he says that his goal was to get back at Elijah and ruin his reputation, not mine, but my God, how fucking dumb can a person be? Everyone knew that Elijah had come to see me. Everyone could clearly tell that I was the unsuspecting, innocent little FUCKING first-year.

The night the article was published, I went to the computer lab when everyone had gone to sleep and searched on YouTube for the embarrassing performance Sam gave after his dad died—the one that made him the object of ridicule at his high school. And it really was bad, Lael. He's wearing a tuxedo that's too big for him, for one. And he tries to do an *Annie Hall* impression in the middle of it. I'm waiting for the right time to disseminate the video to the entire school to exact revenge. I was going to do it that night, actually, but after I drafted the email and linked to the video, I just couldn't bring myself to press send.

I'm just too fucking classy for this shit.

And I know that over break I told you the outline of what happened between Elijah and me, but I feel like I'm still trying to swallow it down, if that makes sense.

Love,
Flora

Journal entry, night of January 29

The worst thing is that I can't stop replaying it. I didn't black out or have an out-of-body experience. I REMEMBER what happened, and I can't stop remembering it.

I remember his coming to stand beside me when we circled up for dinner, and I remember him laughing gently into my ear when we started to chant the simplicity song. And I couldn't believe it, that he was really here to see me after all and take the last picture in the Miss Tulip series. I didn't want to seem too eager, or anything—I was Quare now, I was cool—so I didn't mention the picture; I figured that would happen the next day.

I remember how he tweaked my victory roll hairstyle and shook his head like he couldn't believe it either, even though he was the one who'd come to surprise me—that's what he said. He'd come to SURPRISE me. He'd come in December, just like he'd mentioned he might, and he was seeing me at Quare, and everything was going according to the plan.

I remember how he whispered in my ear to come to his guest cabin after my roommate had gone to sleep, and how, with a pounding heart, I gathered everything I wanted to wear into a bundle and crept into the communal bathroom at midnight, and how when I pulled on my lace underwear, my legs were shaking and my toes were ice.

I remember putting on a coat and slipping into my clogs because it's a long walk to the guest cabin and the night was frigid and still.

I remember arriving and pausing at the door, knowing that once I knocked, once I crossed the threshold and crept into the warmth (he had a strong fire going, as I knew he would), I was starting and ending and entering and leaving all at once.

I remember leaving my shoes by the door.

I remember the slight smile on his face when I took off my coat.

I remember him patting his bed, covered in one of Miriam's guest quilts, and I remember sliding onto it, careful not to let my nightgown ride up. I remember hoping he couldn't see the eyeliner I'd smudged around my eyes, because I suddenly felt embarrassed about showing up to him like this—a painted woman.

I remember talking for a long time—him talking, mostly, in a little whisper, about how he thought I was the most fascinating girl in the world, and how everyone across the country agreed with him.

I remember how he leaned in to kiss me, and I remember that his lips felt slightly cold, but soft, and also incredibly hot.

I remember him taking off his little round glasses and setting them gently on the bedside table.

I remember how slow he was, tracing my stomach and ribs with two fingers and sighing and saying it was the softest thing he'd ever felt (thanks, Embryolisse Lait-Crème Concentré).

And kissing my collarbone, nibbling slightly, making me giggle.

I remember thinking that this—Elijah's loving me, or at least wanting to—was the only thing I'd ever wanted, and how now that it was happening—actually happening—I could only watch it, as though I were one of the moths fluttering around the light.

I remember him asking, like the good feminist he is, before taking off any of his clothing or mine. I remember nodding. I remember meaning it.

I remember placing my wrists on his chest and it feeling warm.

I remember wanting him to see the little space between my breasts and my waist.

I remember the surge of wetness and wondering if my lace underwear would have to be dry-cleaned.

I remember wanting to dive under the covers when he unhooked my bra but instead sliding under him and wrapping him around me and tracing his back with my fingernails.

I remember us laughing.

I remember him telling me I was beautiful, over and over, and interesting, again and again, and special, and my body reacting—like opening and expanding. (Ew, I'm making myself want to vom.) He called me a swan.

I remember falling asleep, and at four in the morning I remember him grabbing me closer from behind, and feeling the warmth of his breathing on my neck, and my eyes opened, and I looked at the wall for a few seconds and thought I saw God.

Ugh, I can't believe I just WROTE that. I'm such a freaking cliché. Who am I even BECOMING?

It's also so weird, because I thought I was kind of becoming someone else, all these months that I didn't see him. I mean, I was still waiting for him, obviously, but, like, I was changing on my own, too. And then he came back and it was like I was my old self again, which felt both comfortable and a little strange.

But then he LEFT. He left me in the guest bed while he brushed his teeth and staggered into his clothes, and the space where he had been lying was still warm. And he threw all his stuff into his little bag and opened the door, letting a gust of cold air in that sent me shivering underneath the quilt again.

"Elijah?" I asked, trying to keep my voice from shaking.

He paused in the doorway.

"Aren't you going to stay for the day? So we can take the last Miss Tulip picture?"

He turned around to face me, and I immediately saw on his face that things were very, very wrong. He wasn't smiling, for one, and in fact looked pained, like he was trying to find a good way to tell me that my grandmother had died.

"I don't think that's a good idea," he said.

I didn't want to ask him why not, but it came out anyway, in a thin gasp.

He just shook his head. "I don't think I can do this, Flora," he said.

"Do what?"

He took a deep breath. "See you." Another breath. "Be with you."

"Why not?" My throat felt swollen to three times its size. I crawled into the space between the reality of it happening—his leaving me—and my understanding it. I detached myself completely.

He closed the door, securing himself inside with a dull thud, but he still didn't face me.

"It's complicated. This . . . what we did . . . it's all complicated."

"Complicated? How?" Now my throat was really closing, and my face felt hot enough to explode off my neck.

He wasn't looking at me. His head faced the closed door, and he peered desperately out the window, where the sun shone meekly. He didn't want to be in this room with me. His bags were packed; his coat was on.

"I didn't mean for this to happen. I'm so proud of you for being here. I'm sorry for confusing you." He delivered these three lines with three twists of his neck, none of which awarded me eye contact.

He pushed the door open again, letting in a patch of sunlight for a second, and then let it close behind him.

And then I was alone, and the room looked hollow and gray, and I couldn't decide whether to laugh or sob. I chose neither, and instead swaddled myself in the quilt and stared at the dark ceiling.

I didn't realize I was still naked—I'd been naked! In bed with a BOY!—until I put one foot on the cold wood floor. The fire had gone out late the night before, and he hadn't lit another.

I feel so used. He took everything he wanted—photos, sex—and BAILED. I can't shake the feeling that he signed up for the Tutorial thing just to find a swanlike sixteen-year-old muse. My throat is as tight as a fist again. I'm not even that swanlike, if you really think about it. My neck is of average length, I think. And I guess I'm pale, or whatever, but lots of people at Bowen are pale. Why did he seek me out? Was it my shoes?

I almost can't blame Sam for writing the thing. I was a complete fucking mess after Elijah left. But whenever I think of him writing that thing in the Quare Times, my chest gets all shaky and I need to sit down. It's okay. I don't really need him as a friend. I have Lael and India and Cora, but I can't possibly tell India and Cora any of this—they just would never understand it, because they still think the only reason I'm at Quare is because Bowen wasn't interesting or exciting enough. Nobody will understand this. I did write India a long letter, explaining everything, but I never sent it, because she just wouldn't get it, you know? She'd be all, "Why are you letting this skinny hipster guy ruin your life?"

Over winter break, when everyone saw me all disheveled, they were like, "Don't go back to that place! Bowen will take you back in a heartbeat!" But honestly, I've never felt more sure of something. I don't even know why—Quare should be the last place I want to be right now. But I can't just fucking leave because of what he did to me. I'm not going anywhere.

Attempt 10

January 29

Elijah Huck
245 West 107th Street
New York, NY 10025

Elijah,

This is what I wrote in my journal last April: "Just as I've loved you since before I knew it, I'll love you beyond when I stop knowing it. I want to get closer to you than skin."

Well, we got closer than skin. But maybe not. Can you ever get past your skin? Did we get past ours? Even when you were asking and I was saying yes, YES, always yes?

Flora Goldwasser
Elective: Feminist Forms
January 29
Short response: "Girls with Eating Disorders"

Roxane Gay's short story "Girls With Eating Disorders" associates abuse with foolishness, disturbing our notion of the traditional trauma narrative. In the story, the protagonist, Peter, dates solely women with eating disorders: "He preferred the tall girls who hovered around 105 and spent most of their time sucking their bodies toward their spines." Peter's misogyny is evident; this is nothing new. It is the depiction of Vivian, Peter's current anorexic and bulimic girlfriend, which disturbs

our notion of trauma: Vivian is not just an innocent victim, but also
a fool.

After she prepares a milk shake and drinks the whole thing, Gay
writes that Vivian "lovingly rubbed her hands over her food baby belly
and waddled around. She smiled for a brief moment as she imagined
what she would look like if she were pregnant with Peter's baby and
how she would raise that baby to be skinny and beautiful."

Vivian's shallowness and vapidity are evident; rather than address
or even recognize her serious eating disorder, she focuses on her one-
day baby's weight in a half-baked way. Vivian is a one-dimensional
character whose disease turns her hollow rather than complex: it is all
we see of Vivian, perhaps all there is to her at all.

At the end of the story, Vivian and Peter agree to have "a
tiny little baby," and Vivian is overcome with fondness for Peter.
Even though he talks with his mouth full, and Vivian "f[inds] this
repulsive," she resolves to withhold judgment, deciding: "Life was
repulsive." Vivian seems to surrender here to the nastiness of life—
her eating disorders; her possibly abusive relationship with Peter,
who emotionally manipulates her; her messy, secret escapades in the
bathroom with other women—and she chooses to live it anyway,
somewhat foolishly, merely because of the attention Peter gives her.
Vivian trades everything she has—happiness, dignity, and even her
physical body—for Peter's approval. She is the ultimate brainless,
mindless fool. Should we then pity her?

COMMENTS

Flora, you seem to be suggesting that Gay draws a line
between victimhood and foolishness. Gay's choice to portray
Vivian as a fool for trading "dignity" for "Peter's approval"
rather than as a victim, as you argue, "disturbs our notion of
trauma," which typically isolates and insulates the victim from
any blame. Does Gay impose a hierarchy on foolishness and

victimhood? To me, both seem equally disempowering: to be cast as either a hapless victim or an utter fool (as though for allowing herself to be taken advantage of) denies women both autonomy and agency to write their own narratives. —Pearl

To: India Katz-Rosen <ikatzrosen@bowen.edu>
From: Cora Shimizu-Stein <cshimizustein@bowen.edu>
Subject: Flora
February 1, 9:18 p.m.

Babe,

I just got a Flora letter. She's avoiding the topic altogether. We need to get to the bottom of this. You didn't get the letter, did you? The one that was supposed to explain everything but mysteriously disappeared in transit?

Cora

To: Cora Shimizu-Stein <cshimizustein@bowen.edu>
From: India Katz-Rosen <ikatzrosen@bowen.edu>
Subject: Re: Flora
February 1, 9:20 p.m.

No, I never got the letter!! Don't you think I'd tell you if I had?! Blanca's on the lookout. It's like I'm waiting for a college acceptance letter, or something.

UPS shipment form for the vending machine

UPS   FEBRUARY 4

ATTN: CITIZENS' VENDING
PHONE: (800) 764-0912

DELIVERY NOTIFICATION
            INQUIRY FROM: PIRANHA VENDING, LLC
            506 CENTRAL INDUSTRIAL DRIVE
            MARLOE, MICHIGAN 48315

SHIPMENT TO: FLORA GOLDWASSER
            PIGEONHOLE 44
            THE QUARE ACADEMY
            2 QUARE ROAD
            MAIN STREAM, NY 12497

SHIPMENT NUMBER   889766

ACCORDING TO OUR RECORDS, 1 PARCEL WAS
DELIVERED ON 02/04 AT 1:12 P.M. THE SHIPMENT WAS
SIGNED FOR BY F. GOLDWASSER AS FOLLOWS:

FLORA M. GOLDWASSER

To: Flora Goldwasser <fgoldwasser@quare.edu>
From: Pearl Bishop <pbishop@quare.edu>
Subject: your essay
February 4, 8:42 p.m.

Flora,

I just took a look at the first draft of your Roxane Gay essay. I wrote some comments on the paper, but I thought I'd reach out to ask: Is there anything you'd like to discuss?

I'll also add—and I'm not sure if you're aware of this—that I hold a PhD in adolescent psychology, and Miriam has asked me to step in to see if you'd like to come to her office and have a chat—the three of us. Please do let me know.

Pearl

To: Pearl Bishop <pbishop@quare.edu>
From: Flora Goldwasser <fgoldwasser@quare.edu>
Subject: Re: your essay
February 4, 9:56 p.m.

Pearl,

I'm okay, thanks!

Flora

To: Miriam Row <mrow@quare.edu>
From: Juna Díaz <jdiaz@quare.edu>
Subject: Flora
February 5, 4:03 p.m.

Dear Miriam,

As you know, Flora's been going through a tough time lately. I've
taken it upon myself as her roommate to schedule an appointment
for her at Planned Parenthood in Woodstock for this Wednesday
afternoon. Would you be able to drive us there (it was their only
opening for weeks)? She's still pretty down-seeming, and I'm
wondering if someone there would be able to talk to her about any
emotional or physical feelings she's been having.

Thanks,
Juna

My application for an independent study

NAME OF APPLICANT: Flora Goldwasser

FACULTY ADVISER: Susan María Velez, playwright in
residence

STUDENT MENTOR: Dean Elliot, master player of Guild

GENRE OF PROJECT: Playwriting; performance art

DESCRIPTION OF PROJECT: I will be writing a play that
incorporates performance art. Loosely speaking, the
play will be about Ursula, a girl from a private school in
Manhattan who gets pregnant in her junior year and is sent
to a community for wayward teens in rural Pennsylvania.

There, she's dared to deflower the innocent, virginal Caleb in order to win the approval of her classmates, into whose secret society she's desperate to be admitted.

GOALS FOR THE PROJECT: The play will be about an hour long, and actors will perform it at the end of the semester.

TIME PER WEEK DEVOTED TO PROJECT: ten hours

Letter from Juna to her girlfriend, Thee, published here with Juna's permission

Theodora Sweet
1330 Corrida De Agua
Santa Fe, NM 87507

February 6

Thee,

I told Flora about my sexuality last night. It feels good to finally be able to tell people. After these past six weeks, I feel so empowered. We were talking about this celibacy pledge that's been going around among the guys in a show of solidarity with Flora. Sam Chabot—the guy who wrote the thing in the Quare newspaper—was one of the first to sign it, but I'm of the mind that he's just trying to get into this other girl's—Marigold's—pants. After all, what's more irresistible to a girl than a guy who doesn't want to sleep with her—and for *feminist* reasons, no less?

"Don't you think we should give Sam a little credit?" Flora asked, in a rather Stockholm syndrome-y way. Or maybe she was being sarcastic? We were lying in the dark, both in our beds; it's really the only time that I sense Flora feels she can be vulnerable.

Oh, Thee. I don't want to be *annoying,* and play psychiatrist to Flora (if you know anything about the psychiatric field and its historical treatment of women, particularly women of color, you know it's not a pretty picture). But I wish I could help her, you know? I just hate that she's suffering in silence. What Elijah did, and what Sam did, make me so mad I could break something.

But anyway, back to our conversation.

I honestly thought no, we shouldn't "give Sam a little credit," but I decided to modulate my tone out of respect for her healing process.

"I suppose I am being harsh," I allowed. And then, because it seemed like an in: "It's been an odd time for me to be thinking about men."

I'd really set her up for that one. Flora asked why that was.

I took a breath. "I've begun to have some questions," I said.

"About Sam?" she asked.

"About me," I said. "About my sexuality." I tried to keep my tone light, but I think my voice wavered a little bit. It IS hard to tell people—you were right.

Flora didn't really say all that much, however. She's still in the trance she's been in for the past two weeks, the one where she sits on her bed, wearing her silk turban and doing her homework (sorry, ugh, shell speak again). Like, all day. Besides, I get that I've been presenting as more queer these days, so it's possible that she wasn't exactly shocked.

Still, I was emboldened by her response. I felt a yearning to reach out to her, to let her know that I was still thinking about what happened between her and Elijah. I really do feel for her, if Elijah hurt her, as Sam certainly implied he did. I've even stopped checking the Miss Tulip site for updates—in protest.

"Can I ask you a question?" I said.

"Sure?"

I had to choose my words very carefully.

"Are you ready to talk about what happened when Elijah visited?"

She answered, though, immediately.

"No," she said. "I'd really prefer not to discuss it. And I'd really appreciate it if you'd stop talking to people about it."

"Who have I been talking about it to?" I asked, taken aback.

"You know," she said. "The Feminist Underground."

I'll admit that I resented that, a bit. The Feminist Underground is a grassroots project designed to support all women, but I guess, now that I think about it, we have been the tiniest bit, well, *aggressive* in our support of Flora in this particular case. I mean, I'm proud of the way we've been encouraging her to narrativize her experience outside of the neat framework that the assault/consent dichotomy presents. But in the moment, I just wanted her to tell me what exactly had happened. I just wanted to know so that maybe she could begin to heal. My nonviolent communication skills are getting so much better! I just wanted to help!

"Flora," I said, struggling to stay calm, "I know better than anyone that it's easier to deny something than it is to look it in the face. But one of these days, it's going to consume you."

"Juna," she said. The moment hung between us. "Fuck off."

I gasped quietly. Then I turned away from her and pretended to go to sleep, but really I couldn't sleep all night. I feel so conflicted about this. Sam's accusation was so vague, but at the same time, he was Flora's best friend here—why would he have published a lie? Is it possible that indeed nothing happened between them? Why would Sam have taken a shot at Elijah's reputation like that unprovoked? Was the society article even about Flora?

I guess I just feel like *something bad* happened, you know? So I took the liberty of calling Planned Parenthood and scheduling her an appointment. It was really the least I could do. If she can't talk to me—and I'm her roommate!—then maybe she'll be able to open up to one of the medical and counseling professionals.

Miriam is driving us tomorrow afternoon—if Flora hasn't run off by then, I mean.

  Love,
  Juna

To: All-staff <staff@quare.edu>, faculty <faculty@quare.edu>
From: Miriam Row <mrow@quare.edu>
Subject: this afternoon
February 6, 7:18 p.m.

Dear Friends,

I know some of you were alarmed by the massive bang this afternoon. I'm writing to assure you that nobody was injured, and to explain that the noise was simply one of our first-years, Flora Goldwasser, transporting a vending machine (with the help of the Oracle and a few pieces of our heavy-duting lifting farm equipment) from the storage shed to her cabin. Although the machine did fall on its side—producing the bang in question—it fell into the bed of the truck and not, as many of you called me in various states of panic to suggest, on someone's head.

Blessings,
Miriam

To: Flora Goldwasser <fgoldwasser@quare.edu>
From: Juna Díaz <jdiaz@quare.edu>
Subject: meeting now!
February 7, 2:51 p.m.

Hey, Flora! We're meeting now—not sure where you went after Peace on Earth. Miriam and I are waiting by the van in the parking lot. Take your time, but we were hoping to be on the road in a few minutes!

Planned Parenthood®
Care. No matter what.

Planned Parenthood of Central and Western New York

Syracuse/Rochester area: 1-866-600-6886
Buffalo/Niagara Falls area: (716) 831-2200

Patient Data Form
PPCWNY Revised January 2014

Today's date _2/7/20—_

Patient Data Form
Please print

Goldwasser   _Flora_   _M_
Last Name   First Name   Middle Initial

Social Security Number _____   Date of Birth _11_ / _18_ / _—_   Gender/Sex _F_

Accurate contact information is critical for medical purposes and to notify you of abnormal findings. If attempts to contact you fail, you may be sent a certified letter.

Primary Address/Legal Residence	Day/Primary Phone
Street _Pigeonhole 44. 2 Quare Road_	(_____) _____
City _Main stream_	Type: Cell / Home / Work
State _NY_ Zip _12497_	Can we call? ☒ Yes ☐ No
County of residence _USA_	Can we leave a message? ☒ Yes ☐ No

Our envelopes do NOT say Planned Parenthood. May we send mail to the address above? ☐ Yes   ☐ No   (If no, you MUST provide an alternate mailing address for medical notifications.)

Secondary Phone
(_____) _____
Type: Cell / Home / Work
Can we call? ☐ Yes ☐ No
Can we leave a message? ☐ Yes ☐ No

Note to self paying patients: Services must be paid in full on the day of service or we will send bills to this address.

_____ Check here if you have completed the Consent Form for Use of Electronic Communication

Alternate Address (for medical notifications)
In care of _____
Street _____
City_____
State _____ Zip _____

Is there additional information that you would like to tell us about contacting you? _Mail is best._
Cell service is unreliable.

Do you have another source of health care?   ☒ Yes   ☐ No

Primary Language Spoken: (English) Spanish French ASL/SEE Chinese Japanese Other_____

Marital Status: Married (Single) Life Partner Divorced Separated Widowed Unknown

Student Status: (Full Time) Part Time Not a Student   Highest grade completed: 5   6 7 8   9 (10) 11 12   13 14 15 16   17+
                                                        Elementary Middle School High School   College   Post Graduate

Race: (White) African American Alaskan Native American Indian Asian Asian/Pacific Islander Multi-Racial Other_____ Unknown

Ethnicity: (Non-Hispanic) Hispanic

over
1 of 2
Confidential property of Planned Parenthood of Central and Western New York, Inc. ©

Planned Parenthood®
Care. No matter what.

Planned Parenthood of Central and Western New York

Syracuse/Rochester area: 1-866-600-6886
Buffalo/Niagara Falls area: (716) 831-2200

Patient Data Form
PPCWNY Revised January 2014

My Emergency Contact Information
Name __Lael Goldwasser__
Relationship __sister__
Phone number(s) (—) ————

Income
$_____ per _____ ☐ hours ☐ week ☐ month ☐ year
This supports _____ person/people, including me.

Pregnancy History
Number of lifetime pregnancies __O__
Number of live births __O__
Month/Year last pregnancy ended _____ / _____
Have you had Medicaid in last 2 years? ☐ Yes ☒ No

How did you hear about Planned Parenthood?

____ (1) Friend/family
____ (2) Website/internet search
____ (3) Advertisement (radio/print)
____ (4) Location is near me
____ (5) My insurance company

____ (6) I was a previous patient
____ (7) Another doctor's office or professional referral
____ (8) Yellow Pages
__X__ (9) Other __I was forced to come here__
__by my Marxist roommate__

Insurance
Please complete and provide electronic signature on the Payment Arrangement—Insurance Form during your visit.

If you have health insurance coverage, please present your health insurance card and a photo ID to the Patient Services Representative or Medical Clerk.

Theodora Sweet
1330 Corrida De Agua
Santa Fe, NM 87507

February 9

Thee,

Miriam and I took Flora to Planned Parenthood in the van today.
We both tried to be cheery—me especially—but Flora didn't say
one word to anyone on the car ride over. I mean, I get it: it was
hardly her choice; Miriam and I just about forced her, and I guess
it was easier to relent than to keep deflecting. She scribbled in her
notebook the whole way over.

"I think it's a great idea that we're going," I said, trying to be
helpful and cheerful. "It's always good to get to know your body
better."

Flora barely looked up from her notebook, but I detected a tiny
eye roll. I decided to let it, like pretty much everything she's
done and said in the last few weeks, slide.

Everything out the window was bleak and gray. Thee, I miss the
sun so much.

In the building, she silently accepted the forms and filled them
out. She didn't want anyone to come into the examining room
with her, even though I offered more than once. (I was so
grateful that you were there, holding my hand, when I got my
first pap smear over winter break!)

After, we went out for ice cream—Miriam's idea. It was freezing, so we sat inside this depressing little shop right off the highway. I got a chocolate cone with sprinkles, but half of it fell into my lap. Flora barely ate anything, though she did order a small cup of mango sorbet. She just twirled a coin around and around on the linoleum table. She was in this huge bulky cream sweater that she hasn't taken off in weeks, and these dirt-stained pink corduroy pants. (Again, excuse the shell speak.)

When we got back to campus, she and Sinclaire tinkered with the vending machine outside of our cabin. I don't know how their hands didn't freeze off. I watched them from inside at first, but I decided to go outside and chop wood in the shed right next to Sinclaire and Flora. I didn't eavesdrop, per se, but I did keep an ear out for anything interesting. But Sinclaire is dead silent—to be honest, she kind of freaks me out. She always wears these woolly animal hoods with ears on them and panels that swing down really low. GOD, I need to stop with the shell speak! I always try to be welcoming, as she's new, and invite her over all the time, but she usually just kind of shrugs and stares at me.

Later Flora came back inside and read all the back issues of *Nymphette* on her computer. I almost told her that you're a photo editor for the magazine—not that she would have really cared, to be honest—but I didn't want to interrupt her. She was reading so fastidiously. I hoped she wasn't reading any of the (many) articles that idolize Elijah, but it sort of just looked like she was researching DIY wrap skirts from my vantage point.

Now that you're taking a semester off, I think you've run out of excuses to not come and visit me. I don't care about the no-visitors policy. I need you. Now.

Juna

Part III

Onstage is the vending machine. One by one, spread out over the course of the play, students approach the vending machine and interact with it, silently inserting coins and collecting whatever falls out. No characters appear onstage; all speak into microphones backstage.

URSULA, *aside*

Today was one of the worst in recent memory. It's a good thing I know my rights as a patient, because like any good feminist, I refused to be weighed. Your healthcare provider works for you, you know.

I realize I sound like one of those too-cool teenage girls who skips school to dangle her legs in the river, or whatever. But believe me—my story is not that one. Right now I'm at Planned Parenthood. In the examining room. A nurse's finger is in my vagina. Well, not yet. We're still in that preinsertion stage, when you sit on the examining table in two ill fitting paper gowns and talk about girl stuff.

Person dressed in black walks onstage and sets up an examining table, which remains empty, and gynecological stirrups. She places a speculum at the foot of the table gingerly.

NURSE

So, Ursula, why are you here?

URSULA

It wasn't my choice.

NURSE

Oh! Your—is that your mother out there?

URSULA

No. My aunt.

NURSE

Okay . . . Let's see. When was your last period?

URSULA

Um . . .

NURSE

Just so we can know how far along you are.

URSULA

I'm not pregnant.

NURSE

Ursula, your—your cousin, I think she said she was?
She told me what happened.

URSULA, *shaking voice*

What?

NURSE

She told me about your situation. When you were
getting undressed.

URSULA

What situation?

NURSE

Nothing you say leaves this room, Ursula.

                        URSULA
What exactly did she say?

                        NURSE
She said that there was—a school retreat? With an
all-boys school? That there was an incident there,
and that you might be pregnant.

                        URSULA
To nurse: [Laughing] She told you that?

Aside: I was fucking with her.

                        NURSE
I'm not saying she got everything right.

                        URSULA
I'm literally a virgin. I don't know exactly what
you heard, but I'm not the kind of girl who gets
drunk on smuggled vodka and lets some random Lutton
Academy boy have sex with her on the top bunk of a
bunk bed in a cabin in Massachusetts.

Aside: Things pretty much went downhill after that.

And yeah. I was pregnant.

CUE LESLEY GORE'S "IT'S MY PARTY"

Readers, lest you think I'm dropping some sort of heavy-handed hint here, let me assure you that I was not pregnant. My play was a distorted mirror held up to my experience, in which I could recognize threads of myself—the desire to be admitted to a secret club, the confusion about sex—but which ultimately turned away at the critical moment from mimicking my life exactly.

To: Flora Goldwasser <fgoldwasser@quare.edu>
Cc: Dean Elliot <delliot@quare.edu>
From: Susan María Velez <svelez@quare.edu>
Subject: Application for Independent Study
February 9, 4:25 p.m.

Dear Flora,

I'm happy to let you know that you've been accepted to complete
an independent study in playwriting under my guidance. Are you
available to meet Wednesdays at eight p.m. (Dean, this includes
you)?

I took a look at your proposal, and I'm excited about the project.
I'm intrigued by the idea of an offstage play, and the use of the
vending machine looks promising. I'd like to meet as soon as
possible to discuss the timeline.

SMV

Lael Goldwasser
Harvard College
2609 Harvard Yard Mail Center
Cambridge, MA 02138

February 14

Dear Lael,

Happy Validation Day! That's what we're supposed to
call Valentine's Day here, so as to not prioritize romantic
relationships over nonromantic ones. I'm doing a bit better than
I was when we talked on the phone. You're right that he isn't
worth my time. A new project I'm working on (sorry to keep it

so vague) is really getting me going too. I had this realization that there's a lot I can't control—Elijah's behavior, for instance—but also some stuff that I can control. Like, I can still do things even though he doesn't love me. For some reason, that's a refreshing realization. I ordered a vending machine for the project, and of course I had no idea how to get into it!

But this new girl, Sinclaire, and I finally cracked it open the other day. We both cut ourselves a few times, but we were okay. Sinclaire is fascinated by blood, especially when it freezes while running down her wrists and congeals in a neat way.

"How horrible," Sinclaire kept whispering in her little Irish accent, but in a delighted way, looking down at her hands with fascination. She doesn't speak above a whisper, and she's whippet-thin, with long black hair and skin that's almost translucent, but she's as strong as an ox. She doesn't say a whole lot, but I feel calm around her. She Skypes her boyfriend at three in the morning, which breaks pretty much every rule: streaming, quiet hours, and romantic relationships.

The vending machine kept getting soot and grease all over our hands, but we buckled down and got it open. Girl power, and all that. She handed me stuff one by one, and I stocked it. It took me forever to decide on the configuration. I wish I could say more, but I'm keeping it hush-hush for now.

Love,
Flora

QUARE TIMES

The Quare Academy Student News Collaboration

February 15

CELIBACY PLEDGE CONTINUES TO GAIN SIGNATORIES

By Darcy Lu

A celibacy pledge that began last month continues to grow. At last count, the pledge, which hangs on the validation board in the teep, has twenty-six signatures out of thirty-four total students. Of the faculty, two have signed.

Michael Lansbury explained his decision to add his name to the list.

"Sometimes, something just wakes you up and helps you see the light," he said, but he declined to say what, exactly, that thing was. "I think it's good for us to take a step back and reevaluate the choices we're all making about sex."

Sam Chabot, whose statement at the top of the pledge reads, "We, the undersigned, pledge to remain celibate and tackle tough conversations about sex rather than tackle each other," started the pledge.

"I see it more as a stance of solidarity than anything political," he said.

Celibacy for nonreligious reasons is almost unheard of.

"It's almost similar to the 'no shell speak' rule," said Shy Lenore, one of the pledge's first signatories. "Sex is a very physical experience, and sometimes it can be helpful to take a break from all that in an intentional way once in a while."

GOLDWASSER VENDING MACHINE PERFORMANCE ART PIECE

By Heidi Norman-Lester

After a vending machine was delivered to campus earlier this month, it sat idle outside a first-year A-frame for three days before its new owner, Flora Goldwasser, cracked it open with the help of Sinclaire O'Leary.

An interactive piece, "Vending Machine, or Everything Must Go" asks that viewers approach the machine, which is plugged into Flora's cabin, insert a coin, and select any item—the hats, jewelry, scarves, bottles of perfume, tiny handbags, and the occasional pair of shoes of Goldwasser's—she wishes.

The piece, whose written component—a play to be performed at the end of the semester—is in the works, has already garnered media attention: the *Main Stream Press*, as well as the *Huffington Post*, recently interviewed Goldwasser. At all times of the day, members of our own community can be seen gathered around the machine, chatting with Goldwasser or inserting coins into the machine. Goldwasser has already restocked it three times.

"I don't really know what it's about," Goldwasser admitted. "I'm exploring the ideas of exploitation and sex, but perhaps in a way that isn't as clear-cut."

Particularly interesting to Goldwasser, who has spoken vaguely to media outlets of "sex and transaction," is the interactive piece of the project.

"Everyone on campus is taking from me, even though I'm offering these things up," Goldwasser said. "What the hell does that mean?"

SPOKEN WORD WORK-SHOP DELIGHTS SOME PARTICIPANTS, ANGERS OTHERS
By Jean Noel

This Wednesday, a group of traveling spoken word artists, Dâ Vinci and Michael Angelo, visited campus for a series of workshops with the spoken word elective class. Vinci and Angelo are professionally known as the Renaissance Men; their poetry concerns itself with themes of rebirth and impressionist paintings.

"The exercises they had us do were really cool, especially the one where they made us pretend to be whale penises," said Lia Furlough, a second-year. "I usually have such bad stage fright, but by the end of it, I felt really comfortable performing in front of everyone."

Other members of the community, however, felt that a few of the pieces that Dâ Vinci and Angelo performed contained misogynistic undertones.

"The birth scene, for instance, denigrates people who give birth, primarily women, and particularly those women who give birth in rural areas," said Juna Díaz, one of the students who walked out of the workshop prematurely. "This isn't to say the workshop was useless, but it struck me as slightly disrespectful."

SOCIETY BY SAM
By Sam Chabot

SC regrette beaucoup sa décision, et il espère que FG puisse le pardonner.

To: Benna Williams <bwilliams@quare.edu>, Lucy Williams
<lwilliams@quare.edu>, Fern Hastings <fhastings@quare.edu>,
Althea Long <along@quare.edu>, Darcy Lu <dlu@quare.edu>,
Heidi Norman-Lester <hnormanlester@quare.edu>
From: Juna Díaz <jdiaz@quare.edu>
Subject: supporting Flora
February 19, 9:02 p.m.

Hi, girls,

As founding members of and key players in the Feminist
Underground, it's important that we continually recommit
ourselves to supporting Flora. I know that the new moon women's
circle didn't go exactly as planned, so let's shift gears and go
all out in our support of this artistic expression. If you haven't
already, please come interact with the vending machine outside
of our cabin—and spread the word! I must warn you—and you've
probably observed this yourself—that Flora's been a bit testy
lately. I urge you to bite your tongues and just sort of sit with the
discomfort.

Yours,
Juna

To: Flora Goldwasser <fgoldwasser@quare.edu>
From: Sam Chabot <schabot@quare.edu>
Subject: hello
February 19, 10:07 p.m.

Are you ever going to talk to me again? Or at least let ME talk to
YOU so I can explain?

To: Flora Goldwasser <fgoldwasser@quare.edu>
From: Sam Chabot <schabot@quare.edu>
Subject: Re: hello
February 19, 10:19 p.m.

Hello? We're in the same room. I see you sitting on that window seat, drinking tea (illegally in the stone library, I might add).

To: Flora Goldwasser <fgoldwasser@quare.edu>
From: Sam Chabot <schabot@quare.edu>
Subject: Re: hello
February 19, 10:22 p.m.

Okay, I see that you're going to keep ignoring me. Marigold and I are going to make Mexican hot chocolate in the dining hall now, if you want some. We'll put the leftovers by the electric mixer when we leave.

To: Sam Chabot <schabot@quare.edu>
From: Flora Goldwasser <fgoldwasser@quare.edu>
Subject: Re: hello
February 19, 10:22 p.m.

Please stop emailing me. Thanks!

To: Sinclaire O'Leary <soleary@quare.edu>
From: Flora Goldwasser <fgoldwasser@quare.edu>
Subject: ughhh
February 20, 1:39 a.m.

Hey! Are you awake? There are a few things I need to stock in the machine right now.

To: Flora Goldwasser <fgoldwasser@quare.edu>
From: Sinclaire O'Leary <soleary@quare.edu>
Subject: Re: ughhh
February 20, 1:42 a.m.

sorry

skyping henry

but wait

his mother just came in and reprimanded him

(she is bulgarian

and looks like a gravy-faced ax murderer)

i'll meet you outside in five minutes

To: Sinclaire O'Leary <soleary@quare.edu>
From: Flora Goldwasser <fgoldwasser@quare.edu>
Subject: Re: ughhh
February 20, 2:02 a.m.

Thank you! And I'm so sorry about Juna—she always looks that scary when she's woken up. It's not your fault.

To: Flora Goldwasser <fgoldwasser@quare.edu>
From: Sinclaire O'Leary <soleary@quare.edu>

Subject: Re: ughhh
February 20, 2:05 a.m.

it was horrifying

her face reminded me of the time she found an inexplicable piece
of beef in the orange bean soup

"if this soup isn't vegetarian, someone's going to get it in the neck"

at least marigold is a heavy sleeper

even though she does have rowdy sexual intercourse in the cabin

To: Sinclaire O'Leary <soleary@quare.edu>
From: Flora Goldwasser <fgoldwasser@quare.edu>
Subject: Re: ughhh
February 20, 2:07 a.m.

Oh my God. With Sam?

To: Flora Goldwasser <fgoldwasser@quare.edu>
From: Sinclaire O'Leary <soleary@quare.edu>
Subject: Re: ughhh
February 20, 2:08 a.m.

no

gary

well, possibly sam

i try to shield my eyes though

but things are weird with you and sam

To: Sinclaire O'Leary <soleary@quare.edu>
From: Flora Goldwasser <fgoldwasser@quare.edu>
Subject: Re: ughhh
February 20, 2:09 a.m.

Yes. Very weird. It's complicated. We were best friends (or
something like that) first semester, but then he wrote the thing
in the *Quare Times*, and now I can't really look at him anymore.
He tried to tell me that he'd only written it to get back at Elijah
for being an asshole to me, or whatever, but that's a bit flimsy of
an excuse for my liking. And if he thinks a few French sentences
in the *Times* are enough to make me forgive him, he has another
think coming!!!

To: Flora Goldwasser <fgoldwasser@quare.edu>
From: Sinclaire O'Leary <soleary@quare.edu>
Subject: Re: ughhh
February 20, 2:11 a.m.

i smoked with sam and a bunch of others last weekend

he rolled a "j" (code-speak for "joint," code-speak for marijuana
thing)

i took just one inhale because peer pressure

peter fell asleep by the fire with his peen out

and it almost got burnt to a weenie crisp

but anyway. sam seems lost

the object of the feminist wrath

but he looks like buddy holly <3

i've done paintings of buddy holly <3

in one i used egg tempura that i made myself and he has a golden halo

my mum tried to hang it above her bed but my dad said no

To: Sinclaire O'Leary <soleary@quare.edu>
From: Flora Goldwasser <fgoldwasser@quare.edu>
Subject: Re: ughhh
February 20, 2:15 a.m.

I definitely see the Buddy Holly thing. The glasses, too!

Do you have a sustainability project partner yet?

To: Flora Goldwasser <fgoldwasser@quare.edu>
From: Sinclaire O'Leary <soleary@quare.edu>
Subject: Re: ughhh
February 20, 2:16 a.m.

no partner

i am the new girl

and i don't leave my cabin

but i want to build a garden

an english cottage garden

with roses

want to join me

f.g.

roses

just think of it

To: Sinclaire O'Leary <soleary@quare.edu>
From: Flora Goldwasser <fgoldwasser@quare.edu>
Subject: Re: ughhh
February 20, 2:19 a.m.

I'm in.

Also—holy shit—I was looking for some paper and found a note that must have fallen out of Juna's diary or something. (She also leaves letters between her and Thee in plain sight on her dresser, and let me tell you, they're not much better.)

"I'm scared shitless, because I can tell this isn't just puppy love. I saw right down to the place she keeps her fear and fury and I want to stay there forever."

I am laughing.

To: Sinclaire O'Leary <soleary@quare.edu>
From: Flora Goldwasser <fgoldwasser@quare.edu>
Subject: Re: ughhh
February 20, 2:24 a.m.

Sorry, that last email was really mean. I'm not sure what's gotten into me! Not a bitch, I promise.

To: Sinclaire O'Leary <soleary@quare.edu>
From: Flora Goldwasser <fgoldwasser@quare.edu>
Subject: Re: ughhh
February 20, 2:25 a.m.

I really hope I didn't offend you. . . . It's truly all out of love! I'm totally supportive of Juna's relationship with her girlfriend.

To: Flora Goldwasser <fgoldwasser@quare.edu>
From: Sinclaire O'Leary <soleary@quare.edu>
Subject: Re: ughhh
February 20, 2:30 a.m.

calm down, f.g.

i was just sewing a stuffed goat by candlelight and some yarn caught on fire

but crisis avoided

marigold slumbers on

the letter is hilarious

juna is so earnest and passive-aggressive at the same time

she once backhandedly accused fern of speaking in monologues

"have you ever thought about going out for *hamlet*?"

this must be about the theodora person

"thee"

they are in love

or whatever

"i want to stay there forever"

juna is sort of amazing

To: Sinclaire O'Leary <soleary@quare.edu>
From: Flora Goldwasser <fgoldwasser@quare.edu>
Subject: Re: ughhh
February 20, 2:33 a.m.

But I am bad for snooping. Also, she really does mean well. Every time someone comes close to me these days, I want to shove them away with all of my strength.

To: Flora Goldwasser <fgoldwasser@quare.edu>
From: Sinclaire O'Leary <soleary@quare.edu>
Subject: Re: ughhh
February 20, 2:34 a.m.

don't feel bad

that's what roommates do

i've found ungodly things in marigold's drawers

also she changes her menstrual cup in the cabin

and dumps the contents unceremoniously out the window

so i feel entitled to the odd snoop

i should sleep

good night, f.g.

Lael Goldwasser
Harvard College
2609 Harvard Yard Mail Center
Cambridge, MA 02138

February 21

Lael,

It's late at night, and I can't stop thinking about Elijah. I know I should stop thinking about him, because he's never going to write to me again or call me, or anything, but I just can't. I've thrown myself into my work, as I've said, but it still creeps up on me when I least expect it. I know I should be pissed at him. And I am. But I have to unlearn loving him first.

You know when you're reading a book and two characters fall in love, and the author tries really hard to make you understand and feel the love between them? I feel like that trying to get you to understand how I felt when I used to think about him. From the moment I first met him, I felt like if he would only love me, if he would only choose to love what I could offer him, "I could die and that would be all right" (to quote Third Eye Blind). But then he DID accept my offer, and I've never felt so hollow and creeped out in my life. I wanted him to absorb me, or maybe I wanted to absorb him, I'm not really sure which.

In the words of the Shangri-Las, "What's a girl supposed to do?"

Flora

To: Elijah Huck ehuck@columbia.edu
From: Dean Elliot <delliot@quare.edu>
Subject: hey
February 24, 10:14 a.m.

you need to take responsibility for your actions. flora is. she's
doing a performance art piece that everyone's talking about. i'm
proud of her.

To: Dean Elliot <delliot@quare.edu>
From: Elijah Huck <ehuck@columbia.edu>
Subject: Re: you
February 24, 12:01 p.m.

I feel bad if Flora is upset, but what happened—in my eyes,
anyway—is pretty much none of anyone's business but ours. So
if you could get off your high horse and let me know what the
hell is going on at Quare, or why that idiot wrote the thing in the
newsletter, that would be much appreciated. Thanks.

Transcript of the NPR piece on Vending Machine
by Hugo Lauer

From *Vending Machine*, A Lesson About Selling Ourselves
March 5 8:53 PM ET
HUGO LAUER

▶ LISTEN TO THE STORY
All Things Considered
+ Playlist

HUGO LAUER, HOST: Before I boarded my train from Grand Central Station to a two-track station in small-town Main Stream, New York, I was hungry. Instead of dishing out five dollars for a bag of pretzels, I headed to a vending machine to get my fix, my one and only vice: a Twix bar. Here at the Quare Academy, though, an arts-and-justice boarding school of thirty-four students, vending machines just got a whole lot more complicated.

ALLISON LONGFIELD: So how can we end cycles of oppression? Well, it's similar to what we're doing here at Quare: interrupting racism, ageism, sexual discrimination, ableism. . . .

LAUER: That's Allison Longfield, who teaches Peace on Earth, an introduction to peace studies, at the school. I sat in on her class this morning and learned all about structural violence. The students at Quare are engaged and serious, and despite the ease of cracking jokes about the abundant kale in the dining hall, it's clear that they're doing important work. But back to the matter at hand: a curious vending machine on campus that everyone's talking about.

FLORA GOLDWASSER: As you can see, all you have to do is insert a coin and make your choice. . . .

LAUER: And that's Flora Goldwasser, a first-year—the equivalent of the eleventh grade—at Quare. We're standing outside her A-frame cabin, which overlooks the enormous Quare Pond, still thick with ice in most parts. Flora's the creator of *Vending Machine, or Everything Must Go,* a performance art piece that debuted at the school last month. In the machine are trinkets, cosmetics, and clothing directly from Goldwasser's own cabin.

GOLDWASSER: There are my cat-eye sunglasses, my French glass water jug, a pair of suede Carel flats. . . .

LAUER: Whenever a row is emptied of possessions, Goldwasser and a friend crack the machine open. She shows me how it's done.

(SOUND BITE OF BANGING AND POUNDING)

GOLDWASSER: So we've gotten really good at using these tools— Oh, wait, Sinclaire, could you grab this for a second?

(SOUND BITE OF JANGLING)

GOLDWASSER: And now I'm putting some jewelry in this row, because it ran out really fast.

LAUER: What makes this story more interesting still is that Quare was most recently profiled in the *New York Times* due to its curious "no shell speak" policy. Students sign a pledge not to talk about physical appearance—and that includes objects like the ones in Goldwasser's machine. And that, for Goldwasser, is where part of the activism lies.

GOLDWASSER: I was surprised when I found out that we couldn't talk about how we look on the outside, because I'm from Manhattan, and making comments about other people's clothes and bodies has always been normal for me. Plus, I've always loved shopping and going to thrift stores to find treasures like this.

LAUER: Goldwasser's holding up a pair of old-fashioned binoculars.

GOLDWASSER: But the Oracle—have you met the Oracle of Quare yet?—teaches us every week, in spirituality seminar, this thing about baseless love, this love that doesn't have to be earned. Baseless love is what "no shell speak" is trying to accomplish. But after last semester, I've started to wonder if baseless love exists—or if even when we think we're experiencing it, what's really going on is a transaction.

LAUER: That's a lot to consider.

GOLDWASSER: I'm incorporating all these ideas into an actual play, and that'll hopefully have more of a narrative.

LAUER: In all the interviews she's done, which at last count is seven, with every paper from Quare's student news cooperative to *New York magazine*'s "The Cut," Goldwasser's been tight-lipped about the exact genesis of the project, saying only that it has to do with themes of sex—and all relationships—as transactions.

Many have compared Goldwasser's project to Emma Sulkowicz's *Carry that Weight,* a performance art piece by a Columbia student who vowed to lug her mattress around campus until her rapist was expelled from the university. Goldwasser, however, unlike Sulkowicz and other activists who have achieved notoriety on college campuses, isn't talking about sexual assault at all. I asked Flora: What do you make of comparisons between you and Emma Sulkowicz?

GOLDWASSER: While I'm flattered, I have to point out that the comparison is not exactly merited. The key difference between Emma and me is that she's a survivor of sexual assault, and I'm not. I think that it's important for the conversation around my project to stay focused on the idea of transaction rather than assault. It's an enormous problem in our society when survivors can't be heard, so the last thing I'd ever want to do is distract from that narrative. What I'm trying to do with my project is to add nuance to the dichotomy of transgression and consent. Because what happens if you consent, but sex still feels like an economic exchange where you're selling parts of yourself in order to get somebody else's love or approval?

I've been thinking a lot about this quotation that's been wrongly attributed, actually, to Sylvia Plath. We talked about it in my Feminist Forms elective. It goes, "Girls are not machines that you put kindness coins into until sex falls out." I think whoever said it is speaking to a really important point: that sometimes what looks like free will, or even liberation, is still just a transaction.

We have to believe all the stories women tell about their bodies and experiences. Of course, saying that runs into issues of privilege, too—because I'm white and wealthy and able-bodied and all that, more people are bound to listen to and believe anything I say.

I also want to be really careful about making this a quote-unquote "women's issue." People of all genders, including men, struggle with narrativizing their experiences and feeling around sex.

LAUER: Goldwasser's given us a lot to consider, which is good given the name of this program, but now there's a student approaching the vending machine. I'd tell you that he was wearing a beanie, ripped jeans, and an oversized hooded sweatshirt with an enormous star design on it, but that, of course, would be "shell speak."

GOLDWASSER: Hey, Agnes. How's it going?

AGNES SURL (Student): Pretty good. Can I . . . ?

(SOUND BITE OF COIN BEING DROPPED INTO MACHINE)

LAUER, to SURL: What'd you choose?

SURL: I nabbed the sunglasses. Some guys would say they're effeminate, but I think I can rock them.

LAUER: That's Agnes Surl, by the way. His mom—one of them, anyway—is Tedra Louis, the famous gender theorist who coined the term "gender warfare." But I digress.

Miriam Row, the head of school, has been quoted at length about "no shell speak," the campus mandate. I caught up with her outside of the dining hall, where students, faculty, and residents—including playwright in resident Susan María Velez, who's advising Goldwasser's independent study—eat all their meals.

MIRIAM ROW: You know, I obviously support any and all means of artistic activism. I'm proud of Flora for taking a risk. She's one of our most fascinating students.

LAUER: Where do you see the "no shell speak" rule fitting into all this?

ROW: Well, every student comes to Quare with a different level of awareness of the concept of "shell speak," and a different level of participation in what I like to call "stuff-ness": a general preoccupation with material things rather than ideas. I see this project as a negotiation between perhaps the two identities Flora occupies—pre-Quare and post-Quare. I see her desire to get rid of all this stuff as an impulse to embrace what's inside as opposed to what's outside.

LAUER: But when I found Goldwasser by the pond, still tinkering with her machine, she wasn't sold on the idea of the binary that Row presented.

GOLDWASSER: I think that a lot of times we paint this contrast between what's shallow and what's deep—or what's accessory and what's core. But it's not that simple. Am I a holier person because I've chosen to get rid of everything? What about the fact that people are taking these things—purchasing them from me? I've been talking to my roommate about this a lot, actually, and we still have no idea.

LAUER: Goldwasser says that her favorite time to work is in the middle of the night.

GOLDWASSER: I think the most clearly between two and three in the morning. I used to be such a morning person—up by eight—but now I'm all about the middle of the night. The darker the better. I'm still deciding whether that says anything about my attitude toward aesthetics, or whatever.

LAUER: Hugo Lauer, *All Things Considered*.

END MUSIC.

A few days after my interview with Hugo Lauer aired, I checked my pigeonhole to find a stack of fan mail. I was surprised, to say the least, but not altogether fazed by the response. I felt, with *Vending Machine,* the type of focus I'd never felt before and have rarely felt since.

Flora Goldwasser
Pigeonhole 44
The Quare Academy
2 Quare Road
Main Stream, NY 12497

March 7

Dear Flora,

I don't know if you remember me, but my name is Wendy Watson, and I'm in ninth grade at Bowen. I always thought you were cool when you went here, but now I think you're even cooler! It's so awesome that you're doing the vending machine project. I just think it's the coolest thing ever.

Would you be interested in coming to speak to Bowen Feminists for Girl Power! at some point (I'm the secretary of the club this year)? We'd love to hear you impart some feminist wisdom.

Thank you,
Wendy

Flora Goldwasser
Pigeonhole 44
The Quare Academy
2 Quare Road
Main Stream, NY 12497

March 7

Dear Flora,

My name is Joelle Jackson, and I heard your piece on NPR. I
was so impressed by the vending machine! I've definitely gone
through the experience of feeling like my body was a vending
machine—the kindness thing you were saying with Sylvia Plath
(even though she was misquoted) is exactly it. I am working on
my own project where I'm from (Birmingham, Alabama), and I
was wondering if you would want to come see it when it's done.
If you write back to me, I will give you all the details.

Best wishes,
Joelle

Flora Goldwasser
Pigeonhole 44
The Quare Academy
2 Quare Road
Main Stream, NY 12497

March 8

Dear Flora,

I wanted to tell you a funny story about something my friends and

I did after hearing about your vending machine. I am in the tenth grade at a public school in Des Moines, Iowa, and my friends and I are tired of being taken advantage of by boys. We are also against the fact that vending machines in our school are constantly stocked with foods that are bad for us. So we broke into the school late at night and replaced all the junk food with our belongings. We got in huge trouble, but we made a statement.

Please write back! Or at least send your autograph.

Love,
Judy Lincoln, Sandra Nimes, and Clara O'Keefe

Flora Goldwasser
Pigeonhole 44
The Quare Academy
2 Quare Road
Main Stream, NY 12497

March 9

Flora,

Way to go. Sticking it to the man! I had a feeling this was what you might be doing. Have you heard from Elijah yet? I'm sure he's heard your interview on NPR. I feel like he's the kind of person who listens to *All Things Considered* religiously.

Obviously, I'm hardly wise in the ways of love (need I remind you that my lips have yet to meet those of another?), but my instinct says you'll get over him. Maybe not right this second, but very soon. You didn't know him, Flora, and he didn't know you.

It's exactly what you said it was: a transaction. The only thing to do now is blaze on ahead.

Love,
Lael

Flora Goldwasser
Pigeonhole 44
The Quare Academy
2 Quare Road
Main Stream, NY 12497

March 9

Flora,

Holy shit!!!!! We heard the thing on NPR. Are you SERIOUS? You need to call me RIGHT NOW—I mean, whenever you get this letter. India is here, and we're freaking out. Use the headmistress's phone or something if you don't have service! She'll definitely let you now that you're a CELEBRITY!!!!!

Also, a quick piece of news: Do you remember Jasper, that Dalton boy who India was really into last year? Well, right after you left, we went away for MLK Day weekend to the Hamptons, and at the last minute he and his friends decided to come over, and she totally hooked up with him in the indoor pool. Not hooked UP, hooked up, but made out with him . . . hardcore. Then Zachary Brunelli started throwing pool toys at them, and they snuck into the pool house, where I'm assuming they finished the deed (though India says that a lady never kisses and tells— but I'm calling bullshit, am I right?).

Anyway, things at Bowen are sucky as usual. PSAT bullshit. College bullshit. APUSH bullshit. Calc bullshit.

But I want to hear about you. Call us!!

> Love & other indoor sports (remember when you signed off like that?),
>
> Cora

Flora Goldwasser
Pigeonhole 44
The Quare Academy
2 Quare Road
Main Stream, NY 12497

March 9

Dear Flora,

My name is Wink DelDuca, and I'm the editor in chief of *Nymphette*, a feminist teen magazine for girls, boys, and everyone in between (we like to think of ourselves as the teen answer to *Ms.*). We, the editorial staff, were moved by the piece about you on NPR, as well as the myriad other articles and interviews we've gotten our hands on. We'd love to interview you at some point in the future. We'll be in touch!

> ;)
> Wink

Amsterdam Dental Group
1243 Amsterdam Avenue
New York, NY 10027

March 9

Flora,

Your father listened with great interest to the segment on
National Public Radio on which you were featured. He expressed
dismay that he had not heard about any of this until now. He
hopes you will call him as soon as you get the chance. He just got
off the phone with Miriam Row, who seems to have succeeded
in assuring him that you are not, and have never been, in any
immediate danger.

  Kindly,
  Linda Lee Lopez, Receptionist

To: All-staff <staff@nymphettemag.com>
From: Wink DelDuca <wink@nymphettemag.com>
Subject: vending machine girl
March 9, 3:07 p.m.

Hey, gurls,

I'm sure you're aware that the feminist message boards have been
all a-twitter (and by a-twitter, I mean they've lit the fuck up) about
feminist performance art's newest darling: Flora Goldwasser.
Haven't heard of her? She's the totally radical chick who's pulling
an Emma Sulkowicz (well, sort of) at her boarding school upstate.

Check out the piece here to see what the buzz is all about: http://
www.npr.org/from-vending-machine-a-lesson-in-the-idea-of-
transaction.

Nymphettes, unite! We need to be at the forefront of this. This is
exactly where we should pounce—she's really adding nuance to
the idea of consent.

Grace, I'll put you on possibly contacting her for a Latest
Obsession? And hey—while you're at it, see if she wants to write
for us. I wrote to her after the NPR piece aired, and, believe it or
not, snail mail seems like the best way to go (the school is way up
in the boondocks).

In other news, the Miss T tees have really taken off. Sales have
skyrocketed. Soon we'll be able to hire a full investigative team to
find her! (Kidding . . . mostly.)

;)

Wink

Editor in Chief, *Nymphette* magazine

Nymphette is an online feminist arts & culture magazine for teenagers. Each
month, we choose a theme, and then you send us your writing, photography,
and artwork.

Journal entry, early morning of March 10

God damn it. Sam run-in.

*I was walking back to the hovels after dinner. It was dark—a
black soup night, as Sinclaire calls them. Sam caught up with me and
cornered me on the footbridge. It was so dark that I didn't realize he
was there until he was standing right in front of me. His eyes were all
glowy and scary behind his Buddy Holly glasses.*

He was all, *"Flora, a word?"*

And I just said, *"WHAT?"* Because honestly, I was getting sick of this whole thing—his moping around, begging me to forgive him.

He was clearly scared of me in that moment, because he jumped back.

"It's okay," he said. *"I just wanted to ask how you were doing."* He touched my shoulder. I almost screamed.

"Sam, I'm sorry, but I'm still upset," I said, trying to stay calm. I shouldn't have apologized, I know, but it just slipped out.

He repeated the same thing he always says about how he'd been meaning to hurt Elijah, and he'd never hurt anyone (meaning me) this badly, and he feels horrible, but he just wants to know what happened because we were such good friends and . . .

"You seem to already know every detail," I snapped, *"so why are you even asking me?"*

His face looked all stricken.

"I don't know what it's going to take for you to forgive me," he said. *"I have no idea why I did that. Seriously, it defies explanation. I can't even come up with a good excuse."*

He reached out for me—to hug me or smother me, I don't know—but I turned and ran to my cabin, slipping and sliding across the footbridge and cutting my heels on the spiky brush.

I have half a mind to send that email linking to the embarrassing video, the one that's sitting in my drafts folder. But I don't know. I'd feel so dirty, I guess, doing that.

To: Sinclaire O'Leary <soleary@quare.edu>
From: Flora Goldwasser <fgoldwasser@quare.edu>
Subject: omg sam
March 10, 2:21 a.m.

Sam confrontation. It was bad. I ended up running back to the hovel and cutting my feet. So that's why you saw me dressing my wounds on the porch.

Just thought I'd let you know. If you wanted to come work on the machine, that's where I'll be.

To: Flora Goldwasser <fgoldwasser@quare.edu>
From: Sinclaire O'Leary <soleary@quare.edu>
Subject: Re: omg sam
March 10, 2:34 a.m.

horrible

he is being a huge gonard

be there in three

To: Flora Goldwasser <fgoldwasser@quare.edu>
From: Dean Elliot <delliot@quare.edu>
Subject: play
March 10, 9:14 p.m.

Email me the latest draft of your play by tonight so I can prepare for our meeting with Susan.

Also, I'm sorry I haven't been as present for you as I could have been. I know Elijah (obviously), but I'm here, you know, if you ever want to talk about any of this.

To: Dean Elliot <delliot@quare.edu>
From: Flora Goldwasser <fgoldwasser@quare.edu>
Subject: Re: play
March 10, 9:20 p.m.

Elijah was not very nice to me.

To: Flora Goldwasser <fgoldwasser@quare.edu>
From: Dean Elliot <delliot@quare.edu>
Subject: Re: play
March 10, 9:22 p.m.

I know. So what happened?

To: Dean Elliot <delliot@quare.edu>
From: Flora Goldwasser <fgoldwasser@quare.edu>
Subject: Re: play
March 10, 9:27 p.m.

When he came to campus in December, we had sex. In the guest
cabin. And then in the morning he seemed all distraught, and left
and avoided me and kind of ended things between us (I guess it's
not like they'd ever really begun), and I felt like he'd just . . . used
me, or something, and I let myself be used because it didn't occur
to me to do anything else. And then Sam did that boneheaded
thing, which was seriously fucked up because it violated Elijah's
privacy and mine. And I feel weird because he's kind of famous, or
whatever, and I feel like part of the reason people are supporting
me (at Quare, at least) is that they're so caught up in the whole
scandal and not because of me, per se.

To: Flora Goldwasser <fgoldwasser@quare.edu>
From: Dean Elliot <delliot@quare.edu>
Subject: Re: play
March 10, 9:37 p.m.

Okay. Got it.

Elijah is really weird about all this emotional stuff. I obviously don't
know the details of what happened between you two last year, but
I'm sure it was fucked up. It's not your fault that he jumped ship so
suddenly. It was shitty of him to turn away from you like that. You
deserve someone who sticks around. He can be such a freaking
Sadboy.

But people are supporting YOU, and it's not because Elijah is
known. They're supporting you because YOU'RE reclaiming your
body, YOU'RE doing an amazing art installation, and YOU'RE
growing and changing a fucking ton. Maybe you haven't figured
everything out quite yet, and maybe you'll have to swing all the
way to one end before you swing back to the middle, but YOU'RE
getting there.

You're golden, Goldwasser.

Cora Shimizu-Stein
95 Wall Street, Apt. 33A
New York, NY 10005

March 11

Dear Cora,

Things here are crazy—I guess junior year is wild everywhere.
Papers, tests, you name it. Thanks for being so sweet and

concerned, but you really have nothing to worry about. (And I'm hardly a celebrity!) I think I'm really coming into my own here (ew, cheesy, I know). And you should see my cabin: there are practically no decorations. I'm like a nun now. Just call me Sister Goldwasser.

OMG, I just can't re: India and Jasper. And Zachary Brunelli is such a dickhead.

And believe it or not, Quare now requires two history seminars in the second year, so instead of getting rid of World Issues II: Conflict and Resolution and replacing it with US Narrative History, we're doing both. Did I mention how busy I was?

Gotta run, but please write me about the visit to your dad. . . . I want to know everything about the Channing Tatum prison guard! (Did you see his gun? Ha-ha.)

> All my love,
> Flora

Attempt 11

Elijah Huck
245 West 107th Street
New York, NY 10025

March 15

Elijah,

~~Fuck you~~ Why did you

To: Cora Shimizu-Stein <cshimizustein@bowen.edu>
From: India Katz-Rosen <ikatzrosen@bowen.edu>
Subject: everything
March 16, 4:12 p.m.

You're not going to believe this.

I just got back from Emma Goldwasser's apartment to look for
all the stuff Flora's borrowed from me over the years and never
returned. Flora's room is so depressing—I feel like she took all the
stuff she really likes with her to school, so all that's left is some
random art on the walls and her old textbooks and stuff. Not what
her room should look like at all.

So I was rifling through the closet, looking for this one black belt
I never got back, when a shoe box tumbled down and flew open.
About forty letters spilled out, so I sat on her bed to put them back
in.

Then something caught my eye: Elijah's name. Elijah Huck.

It was the letter to us—only Flora never mailed it. It wasn't even in
an ENVELOPE. I'll let you read it in person, but here's the deal: she
was low-key obsessed with him, and it kind of seems like he didn't
give THAT much of a shit about her. If anything, he was obsessed
with somebody named Miss Tulip, who was, like, Flora's alter ego
or whatever. Also, he's an emotional virgin. And he's why she went
to Quare. And he's why she's different now.

After I had absorbed this information, I reread all the letters Flora
sent us. Plus the ones she sent Lael. It didn't exactly take Nancy
Drew (throwback to that Halloween, by the way) to figure out that
the guy who Flora's vending machine project is based on is Elijah
Huck. It's really the only possible explanation. He showed up at

Quare at the end of last semester—we know that much. He must have been such a major asshole to her. He really, really hurt her. And that's all we need to know, honestly.

I say we find the bastard and take him out.

Part IV

My interview in Nymphette magazine (March issue)

nymphettemag.com

NYMPHETTE MAGAZINE

Latest Obsession: Flora Goldwasser
By Grace Wang, Features Editor

If you haven't heard of her by now, you're about to. Our latest obsession is Flora Goldwasser, a junior at the Quare Academy in Main Stream, New York. *Nymphette* sat down with Goldwasser to talk about her bomb-ass performance art piece, *Vending Machine, or Everything Must Go,* a reflection on sex and transaction.

NAME: Flora M. Goldwasser (Editor's note: Flora doesn't divulge what the *M* stands for. We find this to be extremely badass –GW)

AGE: Seventeen

HOMETOWN: New York, New York

Hello! April's theme is RISK. What have you put on the line, Nymphettes? Let's see what you've got! Send your work to submissions@ nymphette.com.

ABOUT *NYMPHETTE*
Nymphette is an online feminist arts & culture magazine for teenagers. Each month, we choose a theme, and then you send us your writing, photography, and artwork.

WHY WE'RE OBSESSED: Flora built a performance art piece that addresses sex and transaction. *Vending Machine, or Everything Must Go* is an interactive piece that invites its audience to select and pay for one of Flora's items, all of which line the shelves instead of snacks.

FEMINIST HEROINE(S): Ruth Bader-Ginsburg and Audre Lorde

WHAT'S YOUR END GOAL WITH *VENDING MACHINE, OR EVERYTHING MUST GO*?: "I'd love to continue it for as long as possible—as long as I still have stuff to get rid of. I'll keep some clothes, but I'm trying to sell everything else."

ARE GIRLS LIKE VENDING MACHINES?: "No. I don't think we are. Or at least we don't have to be. You can certainly have stuff and not be a vending machine, and you can have sex and not be a vending machine. But I do have a hunch that everyone might be exploiting everyone else all the time."

DESCRIBE YOUR SENSE OF STYLE IN THREE TO FIVE WORDS: "It would have always been 'Jacqueline Bouvier Kennedy Onassis.' But now I'm not really sure."

To: Guild <guild@quare.edu>
From: Dean Elliot <delliot@quare.edu>
Subject: auditions for "vending machine" play
March 18, 7:32 a.m.

Hey, guys*,

We'll be having auditions for Flora Goldwasser's play, tentatively titled *Everything Must Go*, on Monday afternoon. Haven't heard of it? Do you even go here? Do you even live in this world?

Enjoy the weekend. Be at Woolman Theater at four p.m.
DE

*I know there's historically been some resistance to the term *guys* because not all of you identify as guys. But it's a nongendered term of endearment, and I'm going to keep using it.

Lael Goldwasser
Harvard College
2609 Harvard Yard Mail Center
Cambridge, MA 02138

March 19

Lael,

Yesterday, after doing a phone interview with this reporter from
the Bard College student newspaper, I ran into my sort-of friend
Agnes. He was taking out the compost, his post-dinner job,
and I walked with him up the hill and all the way to the garden.
He's really easy to talk to—just laid-back and Southern and
everything. We're also in Guild together.

As he was dumping the compost from the bins into the huge piles
in the garden, he was lavishing me with praise—saying how I'm
the darling of Quare now and a feminist icon and all that. I just
blushed (you know how I hate to be complimented) and tried to
change the subject. It was weirdly warm out, so we sat on the two
swings on the swing set and just talked.

"So you're famous now, right?" he asked.

I rolled my eyes. We were both swinging slightly, and when he'd
go up, I'd go down, and vice versa.

"God, hardly," I said. "It's a niche audience."

Agnes nodded sagely.

"But you get fan mail," he said. "The darling of the teen feminist
scene."

"It's not about *me*," I said, gesturing. "People just like to see
their experiences reflected in art. And I think most people can

identify with feeling like their relationships, and sex and stuff, are just transactions."

"I've felt that way," he said. "And you're right. It's nice when art reflects reality."

"It's weird, though," I said. "I feel like people from the outside look at me—this girl who goes to Quare and is selling all her stuff and doesn't wash her hair as regularly as she used to—like I must be a certain way, like, this young radical making this grand statement, when I really don't feel like I'm like that at all."

The whites of his eyes were all glowing and warm in the moonlight. I noticed for the first time—in the dark, weirdly enough—that today he was wearing not harem pants, as I had first assumed, but a patchwork skirt that grazed the middle of his hairy calves.

"People must assume stuff about you all the time," I said.

He laughed. "The name alone," he said. "People decide I'm an eighty-year-old woman before they've even met me."

"Is it hard?" I asked. "Like, where you're from?"

"You mean to be the black son of two lesbians in the American South?"

"Yeah."

"A little," he said. "Atlanta's not bad. But it's much better when I travel to the New York area with Tedra. She goes every few months to work on the book she's writing with Jasbir Puar. There, I feel like I'm almost boring."

I nodded. "But if you had grown up in New York, you wouldn't have a Southern accent."

"Or Southern charm." He cocked his head, and his hair swung down around his chest.

I was flirting, a little bit. We stared at each other for a minute, and then I looked away.

"Tedra's the one who . . . ?" I asked uselessly.

"Gender warfare," he confirmed, nodding. "Her claim to fame. She always gets kind of pissed when people only ask her about that, because that was her thing in the eighties. Now she's much more into homonationalism."

"What's that?"

He cocked his head at me. "Do you really want me to explain it to you?"

"Another time," I agreed. "My brain is kind of all over the place."

"Better to be all over the place than stuck in one mode? Maybe?"

"Yeah, I think so."

Crickets. Literally. My heart was beating really, really fast. I wasn't sure what to do.

He decided for me, luckily, checking his watch. "Shall we?" He stood from the swing and arranged his skirt around his knees.

I stood too. We walked through the garden to the first-year cabins. Nobody was outside. The trees were all big and rustling above us. Agnes walked me straight up to my door.

"Should I walk you home now?" I asked.

He laughed.

"I think I can find my way," he said. "Thanks for the offer."

He leaned in and gave me a quick hug. His back was strong and hard beneath his white T-shirt. I stood in the doorway until he reached his own doorstep. On his porch, he turned to look at me once more and then gave a slow salute.

I laughed and shut the door.

Juna was a mound in her bed. Hearing the door close, she straightened up. Her hair was all over the place.

"What was that?" she asked groggily.

"Just Agnes," I said. "He walked me home."

She smiled widely and wiggled her eyebrows. "I approve," she said.

So. Agnes. Thoughts?

Love,
Flora

Attempt 12

Elijah Huck
245 West 107th Street
New York, NY 10025
March 20

Elijah,
I'm working on putting together all the documents that help make sense of this year. I'd love it if you could send me a few things of yours.

Attempt 13

Elijah Huck
245 West 107th Street
New York, NY 10025

March 21

Elijah,

Last night I dreamed that you were in my bed with me, just
sleeping next to me, hardly even touching me at all, with just
our feet all overlapping like a Jenga tower. And your feet were
slipping away and out of mine, I could feel it, so I grabbed on
tighter. And when I woke up, my knees were around the blanket
and my toes were cramping.

To: Dean Elliot <delliot@quare.edu>
From: Flora Goldwasser <fgoldwasser@quare.edu>
Subject: auditions
March 21, 8:19 p.m.

Hi, Dean,

Thanks so much for all your help at auditions today! I'm really
happy with the way it went, and I'm also sure that Althea will
stop being miffed about some of the similarities between her and
Sister Athena—I mean, honestly, they're not THAT striking, and
Sister Athena is obviously the hero at the end. I actually think
that Althea would make a really GOOD Sister Athena, if she can
get over herself. And Juna, too, should really play Miranda, even

though I think she was a little bit shocked by the references to budding Marxists.

In terms of the other parts, I think it was really good that you had them read from both the beginning and the middle. Michael Lansbury did a really good Lorne. For Caleb, it's coming down to Agnes and Shy. We can talk more about this with Susan on Wednesday also.

What are your thoughts?
Flora

To: Flora Goldwasser <fgoldwasser@quare.edu>
From: Dean Elliot <delliot@quare.edu>
Subject: Re: auditions
March 21, 8:34 p.m.

Good calls. Agnes has got to be Caleb—Shy just really doesn't have it in him.

You'll be Ursula, right?

I'm also attaching the Young Innovators' Promise Awards application. Do it. Now.

To: Flora Goldwasser <fgoldwasser@quare.edu>
From: Sinclaire O'Leary <soleary@quare.edu>
Subject: tonight
March 22, 2:04 a.m.

still skyping henry

althea is definitely upset about the play

i saw her hmmphing all over the dining hall

"i don't BUY hanes; they're made with slave labour"

& marigold and zev have been in my cab ferking all night

i'm in the art barn

i like it at night here

To: Guild <guild@quare.edu>
From: Dean Elliot <delliot@quare.edu>
Subject: cast list, "everything must go"
March 22, 5:11 p.m.

Ursula / Flora Goldwasser

Caleb / Agnes Surl

Lorne / Michael Lansbury

Sister Athena / Althea Long

Miranda / Juna Díaz

If you didn't get a speaking role, don't fret. You'll be interacting
with the vending machine onstage and moving the set around.
Everyone will see you. You'll be a star.

The Quare Academy
Spring Midsemester Progress Report
March 22

Student: Flora Goldwasser
Year: First

RACE IN WRITING
Instructor: Pearl Bishop
Credits Earned: 5.0

Race in Writing is a course devoted to exploring the ways in which literature deals with racial identity and subverts racism. Students begin by reading *The Color Purple* and *Their Eyes Were Watching God* and end the course with stories by Amy Tan, Colson Whitehead, and Chimamanda Ngozi Adichie.

Flora continues to turn in thoughtful work—her essay on *The Color Purple* was brilliant—and beyond the classroom, I'm continually proud of her as *Vending Machine, or Everything Must Go* moves into the spotlight. I look forward to working with Flora for the rest of the year to find more ways to integrate her activism into her academic work. —PB

ENVIRONMENTAL BIOCHEMISTRY
Instructor: Bass Foley
Credits Earned: 5.0

Although last semester Flora preferred not to accompany us on trips to Quare Pond and the forest (I was the assistant teacher that term), this year she has been active and engaged. Her work has remained high quality. I sense, too, that Flora's peers have begun to respond extremely well to her, especially in light of her recent activism. I sense a deep friendship between her and Sinclaire O'Leary, a new student whom Flora has kindly taken under her wing. While I am thrilled that Flora's newfound popularity is the case, I am keeping an eye on her, and I urge Flora to speak to me or Miriam—or her adviser, Pearl Bishop—if she needs to talk. —BF

WORLD ISSUES II: PEACE AND CONFLICT
Instructor: Allison Longfield
Credits Earned: 5.0

Flora's work has remained high quality. Moreover, I am delighted to see that she has stepped into a Quare sense of being; her activism inspires and moves us. I understand that there has been minor tension between Flora and Juna, her roommate, but I am confident that both young people have the tools to sort things out. —AL

It seemed, for the first time in months, that things were finally looking up. It wasn't that the hurt about Elijah had fully dissipated, or even really softened: when I thought about him, I still felt the familiar weight in my abdomen, the pain radiating through my chest.

Yes, I still felt that Elijah had hurt me, but I no longer loved him in the same way that I had before. Part of this was a matter of distraction; other things demanded my attention. But it wasn't the mere quantity of other things to think about. *Vending Machine* and my friendships began to surpass Elijah in importance, and as they grew, his image shrunk slightly, like a softball soaring away from me across a field.

But the story isn't over yet.

To: Cora Shimizu-Stein <cshimizustein@bowen.edu>
From: India Katz-Rosen <ikatzrosen@bowen.edu>
Subject: we're on!
March 22, 8:19 p.m.

Okay, so after EXTENSIVE stalking (and you don't want to know
what else), I got his address: he lives off campus, right on
Broadway and 107th. There's no way I can do it tonight, but let's
meet right after Calc tomorrow afternoon. This is gonna be SO
GOOD.

To: India Katz-Rosen <ikatzrosen@bowen.edu>
From: Cora Shimizu-Stein <cshimizustein@bowen.edu>
Subject: Re: we're on!
March 22, 11:18 p.m.

Hell yes. Let's tape the confession on your phone—mine has been
sucking lately, and we can't afford a new one right now (shit's
going down with my mom's account—I'll explain in person).

CORA: If you're listening to this, we've made it to Elijah's building on Broadway and 107th street. We haven't gained entry yet, but we're working on it.

INDIA: We should add that it's raining a lot, so we're standing under the awning. The rain is freezing. We're also kind of wet, because our Uber driver—Dustin was his name, and let the record note it—refused to take us all the way. He'll be getting two stars and a snarky review.

CORA: An old woman is walking toward us, but— Oh, is she coming in here? Nope, she just went into some Thai restaurant.

INDIA: I could really go for some tofu pra ram right now.

CORA: Should we, or . . . ?

INDIA: Let's get the confession first.

CORA: You're right. Eyes on the prize.

INDIA: You have the apartment number, right?

CORA: Yeah. Obviously: 12C.

INDIA: Just double-checking. You don't have to be rude.

CORA: I just sometimes feel like you invade my judgment space.

INDIA: Your JUDGMENT space? Who are you? Flora?

CORA: That's not funny. You know I've been in therapy.

INDIA: Oh yeah. Sorry. Wait! Is she—?

CORA: Hi! Are you going in—?

(SOUND OF DOOR OPENING)

INDIA: Thanks!

(SOUND OF ELEVATOR DOOR OPENING)

FEMALE VOICE: What floor?

CORA: Oh. Yeah, you already— Yeah. Twelve.

(SOUND OF ELEVATOR DOOR CLOSING)

FEMALE VOICE, *on the phone:* Yeah? Elijah? I'm coming right up.

INDIA: *indistinguishable*

(SOUND OF ELEVATOR DOOR OPENING)

CORA, *softly:* India! Hang back.

INDIA: We need to stop this. What if he's going to hurt her?

CORA: Just wait. India. Wait.

(SOUND OF DOOR OPENING)

ELIJAH, *to the other girl:* Hey, Juliette. Come on in.

(SOUND OF DOOR CLOSING)

INDIA: Okay, let's just rehearse one more time. We knock on the door, say we're students writing an article for the *Spectator,* and see if we can ask him a few questions.

CORA: Right.

INDIA: We lead into it slowly.

CORA: Good. Now we wait. Ah! India! Stop!

INDIA: What? I have to wring out my hair.

CORA: Not all over the floor. Wait, also, what if he recognizes us?

INDIA: Well, he clearly thought he knew me that day in the coffee shop in October or whatever. So I was thinking we'd pretend to be students. I mean, neither of us was in his Tutorial section at Bowen. And he was only there twice a week. And we HAVE cleverly disguised ourselves in non-Bowen clothes.

CORA: Right.

INDIA: I think we should go in now.

CORA: Fine. I still think we should wait, but whatever.

(SOUND OF KNOCKING ON DOOR)

JULIETTE, *from inside*: Did you hear that?

ELIJAH, *from inside*: What?

JULIETTE, *from inside*: Someone's at the door.

ELIJAH, *from inside*: Who is it?

CORA: Uh—your, uh, your neighbors.

(SOUND OF DOOR OPENING)

ELIJAH: Hello?

INDIA: Hi. We live just down the hall—we're students writing an article for the *Spectator*. Could we ask you a few questions?

ELIJAH: Uh . . . what's the article?

JULIETTE, *from inside*: Who is it?

ELIJAH, *to Juliette*: Just—just some people down the hall.

JULIETTE, *from inside*: Invite them in!

ELIJAH: Would you like to come in?

INDIA: Thank you!

(SOUND OF DOOR CLOSING)

CORA: Wow, this is a nice apartment.

INDIA: I like the tapestry. Did you get it in upstate New York?

CORA, *whispering*: India.

ELIJAH, *laughing*: Thanks! I actually did get it upstate, around Woodstock.

JULIETTE: Hi. I'm Juliette.

INDIA: Wow. You're really pretty.

JULIETTE, *laughing*: Thanks.

CORA, *whispering*: India.

ELIJAH: So, you girls live down the hall?

CORA: Yeah. We just moved in a few weeks ago.

ELIJAH: Oh. Uh, cool. And you go to Columbia, you said?

INDIA: Yeah! But we just started this semester. We transferred from, uh, Vassar. You're a sophomore, right?

ELIJAH: Yeah.

INDIA, *to JULIETTE*: Are you his girlfriend?

JULIETTE, *laughing*: I'm his sister, and I'm twenty-five. Anyone want some wine?

CORA: We'd love some, thanks.

ELIJAH: Cool, cool. And what were you saying about an article?

INDIA: Okay. We're writing an article about the sexual norms on campus and were wondering if you, as, uh, someone who is male, would give us your take.

ELIJAH: Do you have a more specific question?

CORA: Have you ever hurt a girl so badly that she's rendered mute for months, save for the occasional fake-chirpy letter?

ELIJAH: What are you talking about?

INDIA: Do you have something to hide?

JULIETTE: Elijah? Do you know these girls?

ELIJAH: Of course not. No.

CORA: And what were you doing the night of December 18 of this year?

ELIJAH: What?

JULIETTE: Excuse me?

INDIA: What were you doing the night of December 18?

ELIJAH: I have no idea what you're talking about. I was—I wasn't—

JULIETTE: I don't know if I like where this is going. . . .

INDIA: Nobody asked *you*.

ELIJAH: Um, maybe you could—

CORA: Why aren't you answering the question?

ELIJAH: I, uh—this is ridiculous. Is this about Flora, or something?

JULIETTE: Who's Flora?

INDIA: I've never heard that name in my life.

JULIETTE: Hey, I think it's best if you guys leave.

INDIA: So you're denying it, then?

ELIJAH: It would be great if you could go now.

CORA: Not before we give you a taste of your own medicine. Here.

(JULIETTE SCREAMS)

INDIA, *screaming*: Her blood is on your hands! *Aside, into the microphone:* The blood is symbolized by the red wine.

ELIJAH: Oh my God. What the hell?

JULIETTE, *now calm*: Do you have any seltzer? It'll come off.

(SOUND OF DOOR OPENING)

ELIJAH: Please don't ever come back here.

(SOUND OF DOOR CLOSING)

CORA: So there you have it. He's in denial. No surprise there.

INDIA: I mean, I guess it WAS asking for a lot to think he'd confess to everything. But if you really think about it, his denial has to mean something.

CORA: Good work, Inds.

INDIA: Okay, bye!

To: Elijah Huck <ehuck@columbia.edu>
From: Dustin Crane <dusty_crane@vapenyc.com>
Subject: Weird shit
March 23, 5:12 p.m.

Hey, dude. I just pulled over (I'm Ubering on Wednesdays now for some extra cash) to give you a heads-up. I just drove these two chicks to about two blocks from your apartment. I lied and told them I couldn't get closer because of the rain because I wanted to give you a heads-up. The shit they were saying in the car was crazy. Something about getting you to confess to abandonment or something? I don't know, dude. Just don't open the door.

Sent from my iPhone

My application for the Young Innovators' Promise Awards

THE YOUNG INNOVATORS' PROMISE AWARDS (YIPA)
APPLICATION FORM
MARCH 25

The Young Innovators' Promise Awards (YIPA) are the oldest and most prestigious form of recognition for young artists and writers in the United States. We welcome your submission and encourage you to keep creating even in the likely event that you do not receive an award. We aim to notify you of the status of your application by the first of May.

NAME: Flora Goldwasser
CONTACT INFORMATION:

> Flora Goldwasser
> Pigeonhole 44
> The Quare Academy
> 2 Quare Road
> Main Stream, NY 12497

CATEGORY: Writing
GENRE: Dramatic Script
TOTAL LENGTH: Fifty-two pages
SUMMARY:

When sixteen-year-old Ursula Webber gets pregnant on a retreat with her elite private school in Manhattan, she is shipped off to the Convent of the Illuminated Eye, a farming community for wayward teens in rural Pennsylvania.

If it weren't for a certain soft-spoken, Emily Dickinson–reading, virginal drug addict named Caleb, Ursula would be on the next wagon out of the Convent. Her mission—to deflower Caleb, born of a dare by the convent's secret society, to which Ursula is desperate to be admitted—soon takes over her life, eventually prompting her to realize that sex is more complicated than she'd initially expected.

This play is unique in that it is told completely in voice-over: actors stand offstage and speak lines—either dialogue or asides—into microphones. The set changes frequently, however, as noted in the script. Most prominent, the play involves the performance art piece *Vending Machine, or Everything Must Go*, which has recently gained media attention.

PLEASE ATTACH A SHORT (20- TO 25-PAGE) SAMPLE OF YOUR
WORK. NOTE THAT THE SUBMITTED MATERIALS WILL NOT BE
RETURNED.

Lael Goldwasser
Harvard College
2609 Harvard Yard Mail Center
Cambridge, MA 02138

April 1

Lael,

I don't even know where to begin.

After closing night of Luella's play (I've been busy with my
own project, so I just stage-managed), Juna decided to have a
Guild party. I agreed that a party was what everyone needed, and
Juna immediately began scribbling on a napkin. Things between
us have been the slighest bit tense since the whole "fuck off"
incident for which I actually feel really bad given how supportive
she's being, but she's been laughing at herself more and more
in rehearsals for my play, for which rehearsals began the other
week, so we're not on as shaky ground.

"No smoking weed or drinking alcohol, obviously," she said.
"I'll tell Gary he can make cupcakes if he wants, but I'll advise
him strongly against it. And I'll make some cookies after the
dining hall empties out from dinner tonight, and we can serve
bubbly cider with the stuff from last year."

"Sounds good," I said.

Juna was barefoot, in an oversized black flannel shirt and just white underwear on the bottom. She looked like a character in a movie, one who walked away from a steamy sex session without an ounce of self-consciousness.

"I hope it won't make it worse if Sam comes," she said.

"It's okay." I tried to keep my tone light. "Things are bad already."

"God." Juna pranced about a little bit more. "You and Sam were destined to be friends. God, I can't think of anyone else who would be your best friend."

Which sounds mean when I write it, but when Juna said it, it was really quite tender, in a surprising way.

"I do have Sinclaire," I said.

Juna stood in front of the mirror, propped up against the dresser, and studied her bare legs, turning this way and that.

"You do," she said. "But, like, Sinclaire is weird and quirky in this totally charming way. With Sam, it's more a match, because he's more . . . prickly. An acquired taste. An outsider."

"And that's how you see me?"

"Well." Juna smirked. "It's how I DID see you. Last semester. Now you're pretty much the darling of Quare."

"Thanks to Sam."

She didn't deny it. "What he did was wrong," she said, shrugging, "but are you going to stay mad forever?"

I gaped at her. Juna, of all people, should haven been the last person to suggest forgiveness, especially for a crime as heinous as Sam's.

"You're kidding, right?"

She shook her head. "I'm not saying all should be forgotten," she said. "And I've gone back and forth on this. But practicing radical forgiveness can feel pretty amazing. It gets complicated when you take into account the gender politics, of course, but I don't know. It's worth considering."

"Don't hold your breath," I said.

Our cabin isn't big enough for six people, let alone sixteen, but that was okay, because we were all right with being suffocated, and also we weren't all in there at one time. It was a nice night out, and people flooded onto the steps and the patch of grass outside, just talking and snacking on refreshments. Juna played a tape of some classical Mexican singer as loud as it would go, and thanks to Gary's pot brownies stored safely underneath my bed to regulate access, people began to dance to the music. Juna turned off all the lights except for the fairy one in the corner, basking everything in the dusty light, and the music really was catchy.

I wandered over to the top of Juna's dresser, which was filled with plates of food, and picked up something chocolate, not sure if it was something Juna had made or a second batch of brownies Gary had concocted (he'd been in and out of the kitchen all night, running in with more food—who knew he was such a good baker?). It was warm inside the cabin, so instead of looking for Juna to ask her, I bit into it. It was delicious.

Then I started to dance with Agnes, a little bit, and when he started to rub his pelvis on mine through my blue satiny flapper dress, one of the last things I'm planning to put in the vending machine, I didn't pull away. My brain was on a seesaw, flying up and floating down as the weight on either end shifted. I laughed loudly, and Agnes persisted with his grinding, even nuzzling his face into my neck and the top of my shoulder. I thought about kissing him.

Agnes shouted something into my ear, but we kept on dancing, banging into the bedposts and the dressers and people and just laughing. Outside the window, people were dancing and laughing and talking just outside the cabin. All was right in the world—except with Sam. I'd still have to figure out that situation. Every time I thought of him and what Juna had said, my muscles stiffened, a little, until Agnes shifted into me at a different angle, at which point I laughed and loosened up again.

But then I was sweaty, and I pried myself away from Agnes and pushed past people to move toward the exit of the cabin. I stumbled down the steps—coordination was suddenly difficult— and collapsed onto the little stump outside the A-frame.

That's when I caught sight of Sam. He must have been standing inside the cabin, directly in front of the window—my vision was off, and I couldn't quite tell where things were—but I didn't remember seeing him go in.

I stood shakily and mounted the steps, with no plan other than to say hello and be a good hostess. For some reason I was feeling benevolent. Inside was hazy. People staggered all over and lounged on the floor and the beds—my bed, Juna's bed. I convinced myself that it didn't bother me that people's dirty feet were on my clean sheets or that their greasy hair was rubbing into my cotton pillowcases. Rae and Jasmine were sitting on my bed, backs pressed up against the wall, just talking, and sure enough, Sam was standing with his face to the window, sipping from a Mason jar of coffee and sliding his bare foot over and over again on the smooth panel of wood on the floor—this piece of wood that's an anomaly, black and shiny and not like the dusty, splintery panels that cover the rest of the cabin.

The corners of Sam's mouth twitched when he saw me.

"Hi," I said, unaware of the sound of my voice.

"Hey," said Sam, taking another sip of coffee.

"Should you be drinking that this late?" I asked. "With your insomnia, I mean."

Why was I trying to reconcile with him? Lael, I have no idea.

"It's decaf."

"Oh."

I tried again. "You don't want anything to drink?"

"Like alcohol?"

I nodded.

He shook his head.

We were silent.

"Are you having fun?" I asked.

"Not really. I'm not into this whole scene. You know, merrymaking. Look." He gestured around at the chunks of tinfoil littering the floor, the empty Mason jars and bottles stationed on every available surface. I hadn't noticed it before he pointed it out, but it gripped me, suddenly, that Juna and I were responsible for this. I'd become one of those suburban kids who throws raucous parties when their parents leave town, the kind who stays up into the wee hours of the morning shoving pizza crusts and beer bottles into garbage bags. "The detritus of revelers makes me anxious."

"Then why did you come?" I grabbed the wall for support.

"I didn't want to sit in my room alone." This with a touch of bitterness, which he covered up by swishing the coffee around in his jar.

"Sam," I said. "I might be able to forgive you one day."

I was being so benevolent! But he just stood there, refusing to look at me and drinking his coffee. A twinge of annoyance shot through me. I was planning to forgive him; shouldn't he be a little bit happier?

"Of course you'll forgive me," he said. "Things have never been better for you. You're Quare now."

"What? I'm not Quare."

He stared at me for a minute.

"You don't get it, do you?" he asked.

"Maybe I don't. Why don't you enlighten me?" Now *I* was annoyed.

"Flora." He took a long, reluctant breath. "Just look around."

"What are you talking about?"

"You're becoming just like them."

I could hardly breathe. "You don't know anything about me or what I'm doing," I snapped. Suddenly the music stopped, and we were the only ones talking in a room that had gone dead quiet.

Everyone was staring, so I wrenched Sam's arm, marched him
outside like he was a disobedient fourth-grader, and dragged
him behind a tree. It was so dark that I could only see the faint
glimmer of his eyes.

"You listen to me," I seethed, angrier than I'd ever been.
Adrenaline surged through my limbs, and my arm shook. "Don't
you ever imply that what I'm doing is fake. Maybe you're jealous,
or whatever, that people are rallying around me now, but you had
no right to create this messy situation for me."

Sam punched the tree. Then he recoiled in pain, bending at the
knees and shaking his hand out. When he stood straight again, he
was almost screaming, but in a whisper.

"I have no excuse," he hissed. "It's the most fucked-up thing I've
ever done. Jesus Christ, how many times can I apologize? I was
your FRIEND, Flora. It really upset me to see you all catatonic
after he left. He was a flaccid putz, but he really got under your
skin, didn't he?"

I just nodded. I was trying not to cry, because yeah, Elijah was—
and is—a flaccid putz. I get that now. But it still really hurt to
think about him.

"I think what you're doing is great, but it kind of seems like
you're pandering to the Quares, or something," he said. "And
they're all eating it up. I just want to make sure you're not trading
trying to please one person for trying to please all these people."

I gaped at him.

"ME?" I asked. "What about YOU? You're the one who
pretends to hate it here, but in reality you're performing for
them, complaining about everything and being all neurotic.

You're a character, just like everyone else here is."

He shook his head. "But it's not the same bullshit deepness."

"BULLSHIT DEEPNESS?" I screamed, no longer caring who heard. "YOU CREATED THIS WHOLE THING! I AM AN ARTIST OUT OF NECESSITY!!!"

My head felt light, suddenly, and I felt the unmistakable urge to dance. I pulled myself away from Sam and went to find Agnes. It was easy: he was shouting something about the Mexican singer to everybody in his immediate vicinity, and I grabbed him and thrust against him as the music swelled. To be honest, this is all a little hazy, but I do remember that when I tired of that, tired of the Agnes smell seeping into my nose and Agnes pressing up into my derrière, I detached myself from his hips and went in search of Juna to tell her that we were out of bubbly cider and that someone—preferably someone who hadn't gotten high on the brownies—should run to the dining hall and fetch some more snacks.

Juna didn't appear to be in the cabin, so I pushed my way down the steps—past non-Guild people swinging and dancing and shouting—and looked around. Sam was gone, but Juna wasn't outside either, so I turned back around and returned to the cabin.

There's no real place to hide in there except for the tiny crawl space where Juna and I keep our folded-up suitcases. And then I saw it: outside the crawl space were our bags, flung every which way by the person who had tossed them aside to force her body into the little cellar. I dropped to my knees and inched toward the crawl space, struggling to stay focused and wobble in a straight line. I parted the legs of the people blocking the doorway, and then I opened the cellar door. And there, folded up as tight as could be, knees at her mouth, was Juna.

"Juna?" I shouted, competing with the music. The words were like marshmallow fluff oozing from my mouth. "Come out!"

Juna's head was shooting back and forth. I searched in the darkness for Juna's hand, quickly feeling her pulse to make sure that she was stable, and with considerable effort I heaved her out of the crawl space. Juna sank against the wall of the cabin, her eyes tightly closed, head grazing the wall where it sloped down low.

"What's wrong?" I managed, putting my mouth right next to Juna's ear so that I could be heard without having to shout.

Juna was quiet for a minute, and then she screamed, "I ATE THE BROWNIE!"

Then she began to hyperventilate, choking and coughing and sucking in air like a vacuum cleaner. But then she fell still. "I'm not even that far gone," she said, suddenly calm. "I just feel so light, like I'm going to pass out." I thought about calling someone else over to address the situation, but then I realized that I was as capable of handling it as anybody else.

"It's okay!" I shouted at her. "It can be fun!"

"NO!" Juna screamed, doing a shimmying motion on the floor, legs splayed, flopping open like two big flounders. "I . . . DON'T . . . DO . . . THIS!!!!!"

She was so distraught that I didn't know what to do. I leaned in and hugged her, thinking that maybe the pressure of my body on hers would be calming. Her body was firm, stable. She wore a black crop top and high-waisted black pants, her Marxist party outfit evidently. A strip of her flat stomach was visible between the top, which really covered only her breasts and some of her

ribs, and the pants, and her eye makeup was smudged with sweat
and tears. She was earnest. She was a good roommate. She was so
intentional that I leaned in and kissed her lightly on the mouth.

That's right. I kissed JUNA! My roommate! A girl (woman?)! I
mean, whom the fuck am I even ATTRACTED to?

But I was even more surprised when Juna, despite her disheveled
state, kissed back.

We kissed for a while, making out sitting against the cabin wall.
Juna's lips were soft, her hand light on my thigh. She pulled my
hair, slightly, which felt oddly nice. It wasn't like kissing Elijah—
it was better. Juna didn't cup my face in her hands like he did,
and she smelled different too, but it was kind of fun, her breath
in my face and her little tongue darting in and out. And I felt a
different, more interesting stirring, my body warmer and kind of
softer around the edges. I didn't want to stop.

Oh my God. I guess I'm queer, or whatever. Is it normal to have
these random surges of attraction to other girls?? God almighty.
My freaking LIFE right now.

Finally Juna pulled away.

"Bed," she croaked.

I jumped to attention, glad for a task, and cleared her bed of
people, who got up haltingly, resentfully. Then I heaved Juna up,
deposited her into the bed, and tucked her in.

"Party's over!" I shouted, shutting off the record, and people
began to swarm out, mumbling that they still wanted to dance.
Juna was a deflated mound on her bed. But my own bed was
stripped naked. Someone, I realized, must have taken my blanket

outside. I let out a huge sigh and headed out to find it, probably caked with dirt. The scene had emptied out, but there, sitting on the stump, was Sam. I stopped short when I saw him.

At this point, my head was pounding and my body felt like syrup.

"Sam," I said.

He turned to look up at me.

"Flora?" he asked.

"Do you have my blanket?" I worked to keep warmth out of my voice.

He looked around in confusion for a second.

"Oh," he said. "I think I'm sitting on it."

He lifted my blanket out from under him. I accepted it and wrapped it around my shoulders, suddenly cold.

"The vending machine looks cool from this angle," he said.

I followed his gaze. The machine DID look pretty cool, all lit up and glowing and thrumming in the middle of the night.

"The shoes," he said. "You're selling them."

He was referring to the pair of suede Carel flats he'd once complimented.

"Yeah," I said. "Everything must go."

"Why?"

I shook my head. "Every relationship is a transaction. Or something like that."

"So you have to choose? It has to be that you either keep everything for yourself, or sell your things one by one?"

I sort of threw up my hands. "I guess so," I said. "I mean, with Elijah, it was like I had to choose. He only liked me because I fit some ideal of hip beauty for him to photograph, and once he got all of me . . . I guess, he left. Even YOU just liked me for my style, probably."

He laughed. "No, I didn't. I liked you because you were cool and smart. It was cool that you were different, and stuff, but I'm that way too. Besides, it was kind of the least interesting thing about you."

He made room for me on the stump. I hesitated. Then I sat.

"Flora," he said.

"Sam."

"What happened with Elijah?"

"Nothing." I said it before I thought about it.

Sam reached out to me. He tried to put his arm around my shoulders, but I wriggled away from him. In one fluid motion, I shirked the blanket, kicked off my sneakers (ignoring the stabbing pain in my leg), and ran for the lake. I know—I'm not the type of person who keeps running away (at least physically), but for some reason my skin was jumping and I needed to move. So I ran. Pebbles stabbed the soles of my feet. The wind bit my cracked skin, but I ran anyway, feeling oddly liberated.

I couldn't stand the weight of myself anymore. I wanted to go deep.

I reached the dock and scampered onto it. The wood was soft and scattered with bird shit, but I didn't care so much about that. The water was murky and filled with algae. I might as well disappear, I thought.

I dove in headfirst.

It took my body a second to process the shock of the cold, and in that second I started swimming, pinwheeling my arms and hurling my legs as fast as I could, in random directions. The dirty water stung my eyes, but I kept going because it was dangerous to stop. In my haste I swam right through a tangle of algae. I didn't take the time to detach it, instead plowing ahead with the plant attached to my head, winding itself into my mouth and eyes. In the water, I could amass weight easily. There was nothing to it.

But then Sam's voice broke in. "FLORA!" he screamed. "You're going to die!"

I flipped up my middle finger underwater, knowing that the surface was too black to make it out. I paused for a second and laughed, sending out a muddy gurgle. Then there was a splattering behind me. I suspended myself in a doggy paddle and spun around to look. It was Sam, from the neck up at least, his hair a depressed little halo. One shoe burst up to the lake's surface, and he let it float away. He was spluttering. He was irate, and I began to paddle away faster, laughing in spite of myself.

"FLORA!" Sam shouted. "Stop! Swimming! Right! Now!" He slapped the water, producing muddy fireworks. "If you don't stop swimming, I'll"—he searched for a threat—"call the National Guard!"

I began laughing uncontrollably at the thought of uniformed soldiers, all blocky haircuts and military-industrial complex swooping onto the Quare campus to rescue me, Flora, from the depths of the Quare Pond. Would Miriam offer them quinoa cookies? Would the Oracle encourage them to tap their chakra points for extra strength? I paddled over to the side of the pond.

"Fuck off!" I called back merrily to Sam. He followed me close behind—he was a strong swimmer, somewhat surprisingly— and waited until I had crawled out of the water, struggling and heaving, to effortlessly crawl out himself. My satiny dress, coated in mud, stuck to me and immediately formed a clingy, icy blanket. My bare feet dug into the rock- and stick-covered ground, collecting a new layer with every step, and my thigh hammered out in protest, but I had done it. I had jumped into the pond. I had gone deep.

I staggered toward my cabin, Sam stomping behind me. People who hadn't yet gone in for the night were on their porches, staring, but I didn't even care. At the last minute I used my final burst of energy to swerve, throwing Sam off course, and headed toward the communal showers.

"FLORA!" Sam roared, and I finally turned to face him. Absolutely everyone on their porches was agog. In the distance, a cabin door opened and Agnes's face appeared, then disappeared. The door squealed shut.

"What?" I challenged him. I stood in the entrance to the showers, shivering and chattering so hard that I could barely form words. "This is me, Sam. I really don't have that much to give you anymore."

I ran crying into the showers, slipping and sliding on the wet wooden floors. I fell to the ground and my knee cracked, hard, but I got up and finally made it into a shower. I kneeled down. Still in my ruined clothes, I reached up and turned the shower onto the hottest setting, even though I knew it would take a minute or two to warm up from ice-cold.

I bent my head and bawled. I was so fucking tired.

Sam appeared in the doorway to the shower. He stood there, watching. His hair dripped with muddy water, and there was a leaf stuck to one of his cheeks. His face didn't bother me so much anymore, just made my stomach hurt.

"I know you don't have anything else to give me," he said quietly. I cried softer so I could hear what he said next. "But I still love you."

Lael, as cheesy as it was, that's really what he said.

The shower got steaming hot, and he helped me clean off and get warm. I didn't take off my bra and underwear, obviously, but he did help me wring out my dress and hang it on the line outside. Once I climbed into bed, we talked for a while about a bunch of little things. And he offered to sleep over, but I told him to just go home. I'm still mad at him, of course, but the anger is starting to thaw.

Because, Lael, what is life if we can't forgive people after we note the way they've messed up? Am I being a total pushover? Am I being a bad feminist who's forgiving a guy for violating her privacy only after he jumps into a pond to rescue her?

In any case, Sam and I decided to blow off our morning class. I'm probably going back to bed when I finish this letter, actually. I'm too tired to wrap this up in a meaningful way. Sam loves me. And that's something, I guess.

F

To: Miriam Row <mrow@quare.edu>
From: Ash Tree Willis <awillis@quare.edu>
Subject: last night
April 2, 7:42 a.m.

Miriam,

I'm writing to fill you in on an incident that occurred last night between two of our first-years, Flora Goldwasser and Sam Chabot.

At around one in the morning, I woke to a frantic tapping at my door. As you know, when I'm on duty, I sleep on a cot in the infirmary, so it took me a minute to orient myself. As soon as I did, I opened the door to find Agnes Surl waiting for me. He explained that there had been an incident involving Flora Goldwasser and Sam Chabot and the pond. I followed him through the second-year cabins to the pond.

And what I saw there was incredible: just as I arrived at the scene, Sam Chabot and Flora Goldwasser staggered out of the pond—it was forty degrees, mind you—and ran toward the communal showers. This seemed like a dangerous situation to me, so I followed them. It seemed that Flora had been trying to thwart Sam, or evade him in some way, but we both finally caught up with her inside the bathroom. I hung back, just out of sight, while he delivered an impassioned little speech, ending with "I love you." I recalled what had happened at the end of last semester and quickly ascertained that this was a complicated dynamic.

I listened hard for sounds of physical intimacy and, if so, to suggest that they get a good night's rest before making any choices about sex, but all I heard was Sam helping to clean, dry, and warm Flora. I dashed back to the infirmary, procured a few extra blankets and two mugs of tea. Sinclaire O'Leary and Marigold Chen, Flora's neighbors, helped me carry everything. When I arrived, Juna, Flora's roommate, was sleeping soundly (still in her clothing, however, which was somewhat troubling). Upon seeing me for the first time—or noticing my appearance; before, the two had been focused on each other—Flora and Sam seemed surprised and not entirely welcoming. I announced that I was, as always, available to talk. But my voice trailed off as I fully absorbed the state of their cabin: plates and dishes strewn around the floor, candles melted onto every surface, clothes flung about— piled on top of Juna, even.

I quickly realized that this was the cabin of two individuals undergoing a very rough time. The last time I had seen the cabin was at the beginning of last semester, during lice checks: I remember it as the neatest space on campus. But it was clear that Sam and Flora wanted to talk to each other, not me. So I deposited the blankets and the tea and left them there, Flora sitting inside of her bed and Sam at the end of it. I have notified their morning teachers that they will probably not be at shared work this morning.

Moving forward, I think it's important that we check in with Flora, Sam, and even Juna on a more regular basis. If Flora, for example, feels uncomfortable talking to her adviser, Pearl, then I will offer myself, and perhaps bring in Dean Elliot, Flora's mentor, with whom I noticed Flora shares a special connection.

I will be in touch about a plan of action for the coming days.

Warmly,
Ash Tree Willis, RN
School Nurse
The Quare Academy

To: Flora Goldwasser <fgoldwasser@quare.edu>
From: Sinclaire O'Leary <soleary@quare.edu>
Subject: Sam
April 2, 9:52 a.m.

omg

i am doing a big lol

sam loves you

platonic soul friends

the platonic part i am assuming to be true

come weed with me at four

the garden (of ur soul) needs tending

To: Sam Chabot <schabot@quare.edu>
From: Flora Goldwasser <fgoldwasser@quare.edu>
Subject: Juna
April 2, 3:13 p.m.

I still feel like shit, by the way. Have you gone to any classes? I'm
too lazy to come find you.

But I need to tell you about this morning.

When I woke up, all the windows were still open, and so was the door, inexplicably. I felt as though someone were knocking on the front of my skull like it was a door knocker. Juna was lying on her side without any blanket at all, her arms wrapped around her body and her knees to her chest. She was so still that I worried for a moment that she was dead. It was almost eight, which meant that we had half an hour to get to breakfast.

Did I tell you that I kissed Juna last night? I knew that we would have to discuss it. We were both HIGH, but just because it's JUNA, and she needs to talk through every little thing, I geared up for a chat. If I'm being honest, kissing Juna was fun, but I obviously didn't want to DISCUSS it with her, or anything.

When I next opened my eyes, I found Juna standing over me, shrugging into a sweater. The litter and stray jars—"the detritus of revelers," was that what you called it?—was swept into tidy piles by the door, sorted as only Juna would by each item's destination: compost bin, recycling, dining hall.

"We missed breakfast," said Juna without a trace of hangover in her voice. "I have some cereal under my bed, if you want. Unless they ate it all yesterday."

"I'm okay." I yawned, turning over again in bed. "I'm not really hungry, anyway." Then I closed my eyes.

When I opened my eyes again, Juna was sitting on the edge of my bed. My eyes jerked open as Juna lay a hand on my arm underneath Agnes's bomber jacket. (Somehow I had acquired a layer of people's coats as blankets. Don't ask.)

"We need to talk," Juna said.

See? But I can't even be mad at her. She's just so goddamn earnest.

Juna took one of those deep Juna breaths, "Last night was kind of like a dream," she said.

"You mean like a nightmare?"

Juna shook her head. "No. Not like that. I mean, it's almost as though it didn't happen. I don't remember much of it."

"Not much happened," I said. "You were scared because you were high for the first time, and then we, um, kissed for a bit, until you kind of fainted, and I helped you get into bed. Your coordination wasn't the best it's ever been."

Juna pressed her face into her hands. "I can't believe I got *high*," she said. "I broke the abstinence pledge. I'm a deviant. Oh my God. I'm no better than YOU."

She shot me a sad smile to let me know that she hadn't really meant her insult.

"You're not a deviant." I struggled to push myself up onto my elbows. "Deviants don't feel guilty about stuff like that. Stealing cars, maybe, but not accidentally eating a pot brownie."

Juna patted my arm gratefully, but I could tell that she was still beating herself up a little.

"Anyway." She smoothed herself down onto the bed beside me and reached her hands all the way above her head, giving me a close view of her bristly hairy armpits. "I didn't know you liked girls, Flora."

I wanted to slap the coy smile off her face. But gently, you know?

"I'm not really sure of anything right now," I said.

"So what was last night about?"

"Drugs? Youth? Reckless impulsivity?"

Juna smirked. "Be serious."

"What do you mean?"

"I don't know. I have a hard time believing that it meant absolutely nothing. We can talk it through, if you want."

My head was pounding.

"No, thanks."

Juna looked miffed. "So what do you want to do from here?"

"Move on."

"I don't know if I can forget about it," Juna said. "I don't know how I feel at all. Are you going to tell people?"

"Maybe," I said.

"Well, good." Juna straightened up a bit. "I mean, I do have my long-term open relationship. But in any case"—here she caressed my arm for a few seconds—"I'm glad we've debriefed."

I collapsed back into bed.

And haven't left since.

You?

Flora

To: Sinclaire O'Leary <soleary@quare.edu>
From: Flora Goldwasser <fgoldwasser@quare.edu>
Subject: Re: Sam
April 2, 4:11 p.m.

Oh God. I'm assuming he meant platonic. I tried to act natural in an
email to him and worry that I failed miserably. SOS. I'll be at the
English Cottage Garden in five.

To: Flora Goldwasser <fgoldwasser@quare.edu>
From: Sam Chabot <schabot@quare.edu>
Subject: Re: Juna
April 2, 5:02 p.m.

You kissed JUNA?

That's hilarious.

I just stopped by your cabin, but you weren't there. I got the feeling
that you were probably in the garden, or something, but I figured
I'd let you do your thing and we could talk later.

Want me to tell Juna I confessed my love for you last night?

To: Sam Chabot <schabot@quare.edu>
From: Flora Goldwasser <fgoldwasser@quare.edu>
Subject: Re: Juna
April 2, 5:54 p.m.

Yes, please. Also, about that . . . am I right to assume that you
meant platonic? Like, no physical attraction whatsoever?

We should probably be having this conversation in person, with a moderator trained in nonviolent communication, but the only issue is that I don't want to do that.

To: Flora Goldwasser <fgoldwasser@quare.edu>
From: Sam Chabot <schabot@quare.edu>
Subject: Re: Juna
April 2, 6:07 p.m.

God, yes. I'm not attracted to you in the slightest. Let's be platonic lovers. Good?

To: Sam Chabot <schabot@quare.edu>
From: Flora Goldwasser <fgoldwasser@quare.edu>
Subject: Re: Juna
April 2, 6:09 p.m.

Good.

Mum and Nell's wedding invitation

You are invited to join
Emma & Nell
for a celebration of our love and commitment
on May 22 at 5:30 p.m.
at Washington Square Park, Manhattan.
A picnic will follow in the same location.

This is an interactive occasion. Please bring one (and only one) vial of sand for the communal portion of our ceremony.

Dress is casual. As this is an outdoor gathering, please be advised that grass, mud, wind, or a light drizzle may also be in attendance.

RSVP to emmanellinlove@gmail.com.

Flora Goldwasser

Pigeonhole 44

The Quare Academy

2 Quare Road

Main Stream, NY 12497

April 10

Flora,

No way are you "dating" someone who you're not going to even kiss. Of all things! Work that Pauline Trigère crepe dress and seduce him, for Christ's sake!!! Also, Jasper just asked India to interschool prom over iMessage—she should say no, right? I mean, obviously she should say no, but the little bitch has been debating actually *going* with him for about four days nonstop. I'm like, are you drunk? The only thing he has going for him is that he's already being recruited by Princeton to play squash—and that's about it.

The other thing I think I should tell you about is that we had a little run-in with your friend Elijah the other day. We just ran into him (in his apartment building, actually . . . it's a long story). We casually brought up your name, playing it cool, obviously, but he seemed kind of confused, to tell you the truth.

Oh, and another thing: my mom just got free tickets to Hawaii (don't even ask how—she's dating this seventy-year-old loser who's superrich or whatever), and she says that you, India, and I can have them. So what do you say? Maui in July?! Let me know ASAP, 'cause otherwise I'm asking Jasper (kidding).

Love,
Cora

To: India Katz-Rosen <ikatzrosen@bowen.edu>
From: Cora Shimizu-Stein <cshimizustein@bowen.edu>
Subject: Flora
April 12, 9:22 p.m.

India!!!

I'm practically panting with excitement. Do you remember that girl who was wearing the shirt that I thought was Flora, and you told me I was crazy?

Well, LOOK WHO'S CRAZY NOW. (Hint: not I.)

I was doing some homework at Coffee Dean & Tea Leaf on Eighty-third and Third to avoid going back to my house this afternoon (my mom's meeting with the whole legal team), and who walks in but THAT SAME GIRL? The *Heathers* one in the eighties shoulder pads and all the curly black hair just stacked on top of her head. We locked eyes—she's superpretty, with this olive skin and really deep green eyes and a really long bony nose that just works—and I knew she recognized me, too. I looked down at her outfit, and sure enough, IT WAS ANOTHER FLORA SHIRT. This one was really unmistakable—the Jackie Kennedy outfit (you know, the nubby apricot dress with the matching apricot coat).

And then, right on her heels, before I could wave her over, walked in this Asian girl with ANOTHER Flora shirt under a striped cardigan. This one was Flora (now I'm positive, as you'll see) in a red-and-white plaid skirt suit. WHAT THE HELL WAS GOING ON, right?

She clearly saw me staring, but she played it cool, asserting her dominance. The two of them ordered their coffees and pastries and chose a table not far from where I was sitting with my calc homework. I kept shooting them glances over the top of my computer. Something was telling me that this was key—that they knew something we didn't about what happened to Flora.

I waited fifteen minutes. They took all these papers out of their briefcases (!) and laid them on the table. There were photos all over the pages, but I couldn't really tell what they were of. When it was time, I took a deep breath, smoothed my skirt (how embarrassing that I was still in my Bowen uniform), and walked over to them with as much confidence as I could muster.

"Hi," I said, holding out a hand. The Asian girl shook it hesitantly, but the one with all the hair just kind of stared at me. "I'm Cora Shimizu-Stein, and that's my friend on your shirt."

This certainly got their attention. They shot each other a glance that fell somewhere between terrified and excited. They seemed to be communicating telepathically.

"I'm Grace," the Asian girl said.

"Wink," said eighties McGee. She still didn't shake my hand.

As soon as she said her name, I knew exactly who she was: she's the wunderkind editor of that teen feminist magazine, *Nymphette.*

She's been profiled in *The New Yorker* and does interviews with, like, *Mirth* magazine.

"Maybe you're confused," Grace said. "These shirts are of Miss Tulip. You know? The website?"

It rang a bell. Remember what Flora wrote about in her letter, about that creepy blog Elijah had of her?

"Oh right," I said. "Well, Miss Tulip is my best friend."

They looked at me, unsure as to whether or not I was unhinged.

"What's her name?" Wink asked. A challenge.

I hesitated. "Flora Goldwasser," I said finally. I mean, it's not like they'd know who she was, right?

Well, wrong.

They gaped at each other. Wink had finally lost her cool.

"Vending machine girl?" she said. Her voice was shaking all over the place.

I nodded.

"Your friend is Flora Goldwasser, vending machine girl, who's also Miss Tulip." Grace's eyes were shooting around in her head. A few crumbs from her blueberry muffin shook off of her lips.

"Miss Tulip?" I asked.

Grace gaped at me. "MISS TULIP," she practically screamed. "THE GIRL ON MY SHIRT. FEMINIST STYLE ICON."

Oh right. This was all in the letter. To be honest, I didn't really understand what they were so excited about—I mean, OBVIOUSLY

Flora is a feminist style icon. So I just nodded and smiled.

"Wait, let me get your number." Wink took out her phone and handed it to me. I typed it in. She texted me so I'd have hers, and then I left. They're superdown to help us do something . . . no idea what yet.

Oh FUCK, I have to go—my sister's crying. But call me. Something huge is happening!!!!
Core

To: Dean Elliot <delliot@quare.edu>
From: Elijah Huck <ehuck@columbia.edu>
Subject: Flora
April 12, 10:21 p.m.

Could you please just ask Flora to call me? I feel like she'd be more responsive if it came from you.

A few weeks ago, two deranged girls came to my APARTMENT. So it's safe to say we need to talk.

To: Elijah Huck <ehuck@columbia.edu>
From: Dean Elliot <delliot@quare.edu>
Subject: Re: Flora
April 12, 10:53 p.m.

Dude,

I've been getting your messages and emails. I don't really feel like talking to you, so I'm not planning to call you back anytime soon.

As to your request, that I force Flora to contact you and take

ownership, here's the deal: she HAS taken ownership. You're
the one who hasn't. Call her yourself if you want to talk to her. It
seems like you're kind of used to getting other people, like your
sister and maybe now even me, to fight your battles for you. Well,
not anymore.

I care about Flora. We've been working closely on her play, which
I'm fairly certain is going to win big at YIPA this year. To be honest,
I don't know why things fell apart with you and Flora, and I don't
really care. I'm all about Flora now.

I hope you figure your stuff out as best you can, but it's not any
more hers than it is yours. To be honest, what you guys had
(have?) doesn't even really have anything to do with this anymore.
If that was over here, then this is over there. You dig?

Peace out,
Dean

Letter from Elijah

Flora Goldwasser
Pigeonhole 44
The Quare Academy
2 Quare Road
Main Stream, NY 12497

April 13

Flora,

I'm not really sure what's going on, but I wanted to check in. I
listened to the interview you gave on NPR, and I'm really proud
of you—what you're doing is awesome.

The other week, these two girls came to my apartment, and I think it had something to do with the radio piece, or something with one of the blogs. Now, I get that you're not spreading this, so I can hardly blame you for that. But still, I'd hate for my reputation to be compromised because of that ridiculous piece in the *Quare Times*. I think we both understand that what happened between us was much different than a "fuck and duck," whatever that even means. So I'd really appreciate your doing anything possible to contain these rumors.

Fondly,
Elijah

Attempt 14

Elijah Huck
245 West 107th Street
New York, NY 10025

April 15

Elijah,

I'm realizing more and more that the reason I feel sick when I think about you (and us) is that maybe I'm hungry. My insides feel scooped out like a pumpkin.

Or am I still too full, even after giving all this away?

There's either not enough or too much inside of me—that's what I'm trying to say. It's not sex's fault, per se. It's not your fault (not entirely, I mean). It's not my fault. I didn't get pregnant. It wasn't assault.

~~At what point did you start to actually like~~

And how exactly was it different—really, actually different—than a "fuck and duck"?

Flora Goldwasser
Pigeonhole 44
The Quare Academy
2 Quare Road
Main Stream, NY 12497

April 16

Dear Flora,

Did you get Mum and Nell's wedding (oops, "celebration of love and commitment") invitation? It's absurd. I've met the woman only once, and she was so preoccupied with the Suze Orman special that we couldn't have even a halfway decent conversation about her work. I was the one asking her the questions, prying answers out of her, for God's sake—and which one of us is the future stepparent?

Can we sabotage, do you think? God knows Mum won't listen to any of our reasons that Nell sucks (bad table manners, has no interest in us whatsoever, gives off serious bad energy), so I think our only option is to set fire to the park—that, or torch Mum herself (kidding, sort of). In any event, forget the vial of colored sand: I'm bringing coal.

Your sister,
Lael

To: all-staff <everyone@nymphette.com>
From: Wink DelDuca <wink@nymphette.com>
Subject: everything!
April 17, 7:11 p.m.

Comrades,

Big things are happening here. In brief: it's come to light in the
past few days that Elijah Huck is Flora Goldwasser's ex-paramour,
and Flora Goldwasser (also known as our friend Vending Machine
Girl) is none other than Miss Tulip herself.

It's a lot to process, I know. A lot of you hold Elijah dear; a lot of
you want to sleep with him; many of you see him as a voice (a
snapshot?) of our generation. We editors—primarily Grace Wang
and I—will be in New York this weekend, planning our next move.
I've been in contact with Flora's two best friends, and they're
great—more than willing to help out.

;)

Wink
Editor in Chief, *Nymphette* magazine
Nymphette is an online feminist arts & culture magazine for teenagers. Each
month, we choose a theme, and then you send us your writing, photography,
and artwork.

Lael Goldwasser
Harvard College
2609 Harvard Yard Mail Center
Cambridge, MA 02138

April 20

Lael,

Tonight after rehearsal for my play, we—the cast and some other friends—ate dinner on the couches in the dining hall, stir-fry and brown rice. After dinner we passed around some Quare cereal. Panda Poop and Mesa Sunrise, along with a stuffed bag of cruelty-free chocolate chips that we'd found smashed against the bottom of a ginormous tub of peanut butter. The Mesa Sunrise was as bland as ever, but with a few chocolate chips mixed in, it tasted just right, like cornflakes made for the purpose of transporting chocolate.

"I wonder if this stuff exists in the real world," Agnes said, reaching into the box of Mesa Sunrise and taking a handful. "I've never once seen it in the grocery store."

We agreed that Mesa Sunrise must be manufactured at Quare, in the basement of one of the ethical farmers' houses.

"I used to hate this shit when we first came here," said Agnes. "It grows on you, though, you know?"

"Just like the people," I said before I could stop myself.

Agnes laughed. "You must have hated us so much at the beginning," he said.

"No . . ." I said, but it was obvious I was lying, and everyone burst out laughing.

They kept asking me to tell them my first impressions, so I did. They screamed with laughter when I told them about being scared to death of Dean and what I'd done with the beanbag.

"What did you think of me?" I asked the group, though I wasn't sure I wanted to know.

They were silent for a while.

"I thought you were lovely," Rae offered, "even though you looked like you wanted to melt into the walls."

"There is one thing. . . ." Benna said.

"Tell me!" I urged.

"There was a small rumor that you scrubbed the heels of your suede Steve Madden boots with a toothbrush every night in the fall," she said quietly.

Another hush. Then we all screamed with laughter.

"That's true!" I yelled. "I did do that!"

"I know," Rae said, throwing an arm around my shoulders. "I saw you in the bathroom, after you thought everyone had gone to bed, hunched over those damn boots with your toothbrush, like it was your job, or something."

It was a bit much, thinking about it. All the work to preserve the shoes, the posters, the typewriter, even! Not to mention the collection of retro sunglasses in nine different colors lined up on my dresser to be color-coordinated with each outfit.

But preserving all that was one of the only things I could control.

It's so crazy how far I've come.

Agnes walked me back to my A-frame. Oh, Lael. He's so cute and Southern and gentlemanly in the least sexist (and sexiest) way ever. Juna wasn't home, so I invited him inside. He stood awkwardly by the door. I bent down to pick up a pillow that had fallen off my bed, and when I straightened up, he was three inches closer to me than he'd been before. I jumped.

"Do you want to sit?" he asked, gripping the frame of my bed as though to stabilize himself.

I didn't comment on the fact that he was inviting me to sit on my own bed.

"Oh. Okay." I moved toward the bed. "What have you been thinking about?" I asked him, sitting down tentatively, only half-conscious of the fact that we were alone.

Agnes said, "I guess I've been thinking about all the types of privilege we don't necessarily think about: good looks, intelligence, height. Have you ever read the study about tall people being more successful?"

"The taller of two presidential candidates usually wins," I confirmed.

He laughed. And then, without any warning, he asked, "Can I kiss you?"

I gaped at him.

"Okay," I said finally.

He leaned in toward me and kissed me. It was such a sweet, soft kiss. His lips were smooth and warm. I mentally scanned my body: okay armpits, bad bra, dingy but passable underwear. At least my legs were both shaved and moisturized. Thank God for ye old nightly routine. Some things you just don't stop doing.

We kept kissing, perched on the edge of my bed.

Then Agnes's hand kind of migrated toward my shoulders. He stroked up and down my arms and played with my hair a little bit. I ran MY fingers through HIS hair too, as much as I could considering his dreads, and then rested my hands lightly on his chest. His hands kept moving up and down. When they got to my boobs, they would stop for a second and then keep going, like they were waiting for my permission.

"Want to lie down?" Agnes asked.

I wasn't completely sure I wanted to, but I agreed. So we lay on our sides, facing each other, and kissed some more. Agnes's shirt came off, just like that. His chest was so smooth. I wondered if he was naturally hairless or if he'd shaved his chest. He kept tugging at the bottom of MY shirt, but I didn't make any moves to take it off. When he finally started to tentatively pull it up from the bottom, I shot up and drew my legs into my chest. It was so weird, Lael. Agnes is superhot. And I'm into him. But I just couldn't do it.

"Sorry," he said, still horizontal. "I should have asked. And I forgot about Sam."

"Sam?" I asked.

"Yeah," he said. "Aren't y'all a thing now?"

Did I mention that Agnes is from Georgia? I love that way too freaking much.

I laughed. "No way," I said. "We're platonic lovers."

"Does that mean . . . ?"

"We're not physically attracted to each other, but we're sort of in love," I explained. "But we're not exclusive, or anything."

He mulled that one over.

"How is that different from being best friends?" he asked. "Aren't friends just people you love, but don't want to fuck?"

I shrugged. "Yeah, I guess it's not that different. It's all just language, anyway."

He laughed. "You and my mom should collaborate."

I smiled and looked away, suddenly embarrassed.

"So is this about . . . the thing . . . last semester?" he asked.

My chest got kind of tight.

"No," I said. "Not really."

He rolled over onto his side.

"It's about me," I said. "I think I'm taking a break from sexual stuff. For, like, a minute."

He laughed. "A minute," he said. "Is that right?"

"It's just that I'm still sort of getting used to my body again. And figuring out whom I'm attracted to, or whatever. Sorry."

He struggled up to a seated position beside me.

"Don't apologize," he said. "Please. It's okay."

I rested my temple on my knee so he wouldn't see the tears.

God, I need to get a grip. I don't know, Lael. Am I crazy?

Flora

To: Sam Chabot <schabot@quare.edu>
From: Flora Goldwasser <fgoldwasser@quare.edu>
Subject: this morning
May 1, 9:43 a.m.

Why weren't you at breakfast this morning??

I have huge news.

I fell asleep in Sinclaire's cabin (where was Marigold? With you?).
At an ungodly hour—maybe around six fifteen—someone knocked
on the door.

I lifted my neck with considerable effort and strained my body
to see who was at the door. It was Fern, in a long purple dress,
probably on her way to breakfast, cradling an envelope and
blinking fast.

"This was in my pigeonhole," she said. "It's addressed to you."

I accepted it and squinted to read it, feeling my brain shift in my
skull. It was from the Young Innovators' Promise Awards: a thick
white envelope with a fancy insignia in the upper left-hand corner.
It was only then that I realized that it was MAY. I tore it open,
letting the envelope fall to the floor, and slowly unfurled the letter.

Here's what it said:

DEAR FLORA,

IT IS OUR GREAT PLEASURE TO INFORM YOU THAT YOU HAVE
EARNED A GOLD MEDAL FOR YOUR PLAY, *VENDING MACHINE, OR
EVERYTHING MUST GO*, IN THE YOUNG INNOVATORS' PROMISE

AWARDS OF THIS YEAR. YOU SHOULD BE VERY PROUD OF
THIS ACCOMPLISHMENT. FOR 122 YEARS, THE AWARDS HAVE
RECOGNIZED TEENAGERS LIKE YOU FROM ACROSS THE COUNTRY.
BY WINNING AN INNOVATORS' AWARD, YOU JOIN A LEGACY OF
CELEBRATED AUTHORS SUCH AS JAMES BALDWIN, SYLVIA
PLATH, LUCILLE CLIFTON, LENA DUNHAM, AND ELIZABETH
BISHOP.

"What does it say?" Sinclaire was asking. "Flora, what does it say?"

I read it out verbatim.

Sinclaire screamed, the first time I'd heard her make a sound
louder than a whisper. So did Fern, who, I realized, had never left.

Sam, I won!!!

Juna Díaz
Pigeonhole 46
The Quare Academy
2 Quare Road
Main Stream, NY 12497

May 2

Dear Juna,

My name is Wink DelDuca, and I'm the editor in chief of
Nymphette magazine. Your girlfriend, Thee, suggested I get in
touch with you about an idea we had to collaborate on a project
to show our support of one of your peers, Flora Goldwasser.

It's a bit much to discuss via snail mail, but I understand you're allowed to make phone calls, so please give me a call at (212) ------- at your earliest convenience. I look forward to working with you!

;)
Wink

To: Faculty, staff, and students <everyone@quare.edu>
From: Miriam Row <mrow@quare.edu>
Subject: Exciting news
May 2, 2:18 p.m.

Dear Friends,

I'd like to extend my warmest congratulations to Flora Goldwasser, who just this morning was awarded a gold medal from the Young Innovators' Promise Awards (YIPA), the nation's highest honor for young artists, writers, and performers in the United States, for an excerpt from her original play, *Vending Machine, or Everything Must Go*. Flora will be traveling to Manhattan later this month to accept her award at Carnegie Hall.

Flora, currently the apprentice of Guild, will be performing the play on May 17. I strongly encourage the entire community to attend—I myself wouldn't miss it for the world!

Blessings,
Miriam

Amsterdam Dental Group
1243 Amsterdam Avenue
New York, NY 10027

May 3

Dear Flora,

Please accept this chocolate on behalf of your father, who congratulates you on your award but is too busy to make it to the ceremony. He is sure it will be wonderful, and he looks forward to hearing all about it when you come home for the summer.

Your father also asked me to remind you that he would like you to call him—and he will accept the charges, of course—as you come to decisions about college applications for next fall. He stressed to me that he would like to know immediately once you decide which schools you would like to visit this summer.

Fondly,
Linda Lee Lopez, receptionist

Lael Goldwasser
Harvard College
2609 Harvard Yard Mail Center
Cambridge, MA 02138

May 5

Lael,

Can you pick up the phone for once in your life? I mean, it was great to talk briefly after I found out I won, but you've been superMIA for the past few days. Is there a man or woman in the picture perhaps??

I just realized that the wedding is the same day (and the exact same time, now that I look at the event description again) as the Carnegie Hall thing, so I just called Mum to let her know that I'm missing the actual wedding ceremony and that I'll try to come after the ceremony if I have time to do that before heading back up to school.

She sounded really hurt, and I felt bad, but what can I do? Should I skip the award ceremony? I'm a bad daughter, I know, but it's not like Mum has been mother of the year, either.

Advice, please?

Flora

To: Cora Shimizu-Stein <cshimizustein@bowen.edu>, India Katz-Rosen <ikatzrosen@bowen.edu>, all-staff <everyone@nymphettemag.com
From: Wink DelDuca <wink@nymphettemag.com>
Subject: Idea
May 6, 9:21 p.m.

Thanks, Cora, for the heads-up about Flora's big win. It gave me—and Grace—an idea about what's going to go down. I just got off the phone with Juna, who's a student up at Quare, and discussed all the details with her.

The ceremony's on May 22 at Carnegie Hall, right? Well, what if we gathered together as many Nymphettes as possible—and you two, obviously—and did a rally when Flora gets back to campus later that night? Juna, our Quare contact, said the Feminist Underground is planning a separate rally specifically for sexual assault survivors, so this one would be more of a generalized show of support for all women, all of their bodies, and all of their stories. Any sort of reclamation.

I'm thinking full rally spirit. Chants? Candles, as it'll be evening?

It'll be called the *Nymphette* Storm. Let's raise hell, maybe see what this school is all about, do our march, and peace. Natalie, you'll contact news outlets? And, Thee—can we count on you for photos to make sure the whole thing goes down in history?

;)

Wink
Editor in Chief, *Nymphette* magazine
Nymphette is an online feminist arts & culture magazine for teenagers. Each month, we choose a theme, and then you send us your writing, photography, and artwork.

To: Wink DelDuca <wink@nymphettemag.com>; all-staff <everyone@nymphettemag.com>; Cora Shimizu-Stein <cshimizustein@bowen.edu>; India Katz-Rosen <ikatzrosen@bowen.edu>
From: Theodora Sweet <thee@nymphettemag.com>
Subject: Re: Idea
May 6, 9:34 p.m.

I'm so down, it's not even funny. I can fly in from Santa Fe on the morning of the twenty-second.

Anyone want to help me ask my girlfriend to move in with me for the summer when we're done?

Thee

To: Dean Elliot <delliot@quare.edu>
From: Elijah Huck <ehuck@columbia.edu>
Subject: Re: Flora
May 7, 6:13 a.m.

D,

I think I should come talk to her in person. My finals end the
twenty-first. So I'm thinking the twenty-second. Want to give me a
ride from the train station, or am I still too irrelevant in your book?

E

To: Elijah Huck <ehuck@columbia.edu>
From: Dean Elliot <delliot@quare.edu>
Subject: Re: Flora
May 7, 9:56 a.m.

E,

I'll be there. But if she doesn't wanna talk to you, I'm taking you
home.

D

Flora Goldwasser
Pigeonhole 44
The Quare Academy
2 Quare Road
Main Stream, NY 12497

May 7

Flora,

Don't even give it a second thought. Go to the Carnegie Hall ceremony, and stop by the park if you have time when it's over. Seriously. We both knew Mum was going to act offended, but you've worked so hard for this, and it would be such a shame to miss it. I'll hold down the familial fort until you can get there.

Love you, and congrats again,
Lael

PS. There indeed might be a woman in the picture . . . remember my teaching fellow, Susan? God, what is it with us Goldwasser girls and authority figures? (Sorry, too soon?)

My play's program, May 17

It was recently brought to my attention that for the first month at Quare, I scrubbed my Steve Madden boots with a toothbrush (whose? I'm never telling) in the gender-neutral bathroom after my roommate had gone to sleep.

Things are a little bit different now, to say the least. After my "sexual debut" at the end of my first semester and the ensuing emotional crisis, I decided to get light. I launched *Vending Machine, or Everything Must Go,* an interactive performance piece in which many of you have participated. Along the way, I've found a robust, if unlikely, community.

I've become preoccupied with buying and selling. When you watch the play, you'll doubtless have myriad questions: What does the vending machine mean? Am I—is Ursula—the machine itself or the stuff inside (I'm still grappling with this one)? Are we ever more than the sum of our saleable items? Why are none of the actors onstage? And, maybe most important, why does the play end in such an awkward, non-ending type of way? —FG

Guild fondly presents

Everything Must Go

written & directed by Flora Goldwasser

CAST OF CHARACTERS

Ursula / Flora Goldwasser

Caleb / Agnes Surl

Lorne / Michael Lansbury

Sister Athena / Althea Long

Miranda / Juna Díaz

Guild, established in 1966, is the only and oldest theater troupe at Quare. Its members are: Luella Lookman (master player), Flora Goldwasser (apprentice), Michael Lansbury, Gary North, Lia Furlough, Jean Noel, Shy Lenore, Solomon Pitts, Luella Lookman, Peter Wojkowski, Heidi Norman-Lester, Juna Díaz, and Agnes Surl.

To: all-staff <everyone@nymphettemag.com>, Cora Shimizu-Stein
<cshimizustein@bowen.edu>, India Katz-Rosen <ikatzrosen@bowen
.edu>
From: Wink DelDuca <wink@nymphettemag.com>
Subject: preparations
May 18, 7:50 p.m.

Okay, we're on. Grace and I are in charge of the banner. Cora and
India, you're on transportation. Everyone else: rest your voices,
because this is going to be one hell of a reclamation rally!

In terms of dress: this isn't a slut walk, per se, but I wouldn't be
opposed to showing a little skin. Do what you're comfortable
with, obvs, but don't be afraid to go all out! We see this as being
centered around supporting both Flora and her art activism, as
well as all women everywhere.

See you all at Grand Central on Friday.

;)

Wink
Editor in Chief, *Nymphette* magazine
Nymphette is an online feminist arts & culture magazine for teenagers. Each
month, we choose a theme, and then you send us your writing, photography,
and artwork.

Carnegie Hall program

THE YOUNG INNOVATORS' PROMISE AWARDS
May 22
Medal Ceremony

2:00 p.m. Medalists arrive at Carnegie Hall

2:30 p.m. Rehearsal begins

3:00 p.m. Students proceed to holding room

3:30 p.m. Guests arrive

4:00 p.m. Introduction: Head of YIPA; video of winners

4:30 p.m. Keynote speaker: Lena Dunham

5:00 p.m. Awarding of medalists

5:30 p.m. Ceremony concludes

I had to miss classes (just Nonviolent Communication and World Issues II) to catch a train to Grand Central. Luella, Guild master player, brandishing her acceptance to Hamilton, where she planned to major in theater, begged to come with me—now that she knew where she was going to college, she said, there wasn't much use for her to be in classes—but Miriam, of the opinion that learning is not for college's sake but for life's sake, disagreed, and I was just as happy to go alone. I've always liked train rides, and it's nicer to be able to look out the window without anybody bothering me.

"Now, you'll come right after the ceremony is over, right?" Mum asked on Thursday night on the phone. "Just hop on a train?"

I told her I'd do my best. I felt evil, but the thought of Mum and Nell marrying still made me all panicky. I mean, at this point, it wasn't even personal. The fact that Mum was marrying ANY-ONE less than a year after the divorce was finalized made me want to throw up.

Mum paused. "If you're sure . . ." she said. In the background I could hear Nell's low, urgent voice saying something about a salad. "We're knee-deep in wedding planning. And we're praying for good weather. Nobody likes wet sand." She laughed too loudly.

I could tell from her tone that she was trying to make it up to me, everything from this past year, and when my throat got tight, I told her I had to go.

It wasn't too hard to decide what to wear, because my closet was looking pretty sparse post–vending machine. I'd saved my apricot Jackie Kennedy shift dress, the nubby one, for reasons un-known; it just never felt right to stuff it in the machine with all the other things. So I zipped it up, ran a comb through my hair, dabbed some blush on my cheeks, and headed out the door. The dress, I realized, standing in direct sun, had certainly seen better days: today the fabric looked worn, covered with a dusty film that I tried to hop and shake off on my way to the van.

The Oracle was headed to Poughkeepsie to visit a friend, so he took me there to catch a train into Manhattan. The station was absolutely still. As the Hudson Valley flew by, I read a book and looked out the window. The train filled up slowly, people filling the empty spaces around me, and I found myself, as I had been on all previous breaks from Quare, fascinated by the little details that made them "normal": leather bags, shoes with heels, hair slicked back with gel.

And then I was there—back in Grand Central Station. I swarmed into the main hall with everyone else who had been on my train, but as they dispersed, I stood in the middle and looked up at the ceiling like a tourist. People were everywhere around me, laughing into their cell phones and shouting to one another in various languages. The ground felt like it was buzzing. I took a sharp inhale and pulled out my one remaining pair of sunglasses—a classic pair of big and black ones—from my bag, sliding them onto my face. Everything still looked gold.

The ceremony was slated to begin at five o'clock in the afternoon, but the information packet had instructed us to arrive at two for a dress rehearsal. It took me a second to get my bearings, and I exited to Forty-second Street and started walking north, and then west to avoid Times Square, which feels like an assault in the best of circumstances.

And there it was, finally, Carnegie Hall: palatial and majestic, stretching over a few blocks in its grandeur. It was positively crawling with people too, and it took me a second to trace the line of awardees stretching down Fifty-seventh Street, shuffling forward desultorily. I had time, I realized. The line of young innovators stretched to the deli two blocks away. Even if I joined the end of the line now, it would be at least a twenty-minute wait. But then I looked down. My shoes—white Oxfords with a slight heel—were falling apart. And not only that, but they were smeared with dirt and smelled a little bit like manure.

Most of the female recipients and a handful of the males were wearing some variation on a prom dress, or what I imagined to be a prom dress: lacy, fluffy, paired with bright shoes with spiky heels. Obviously *I* would never wear any such thing, so it wasn't much help, but the clock was ticking, so I spun on my flimsy heel and searched the horizon for a store, any store.

Much to my dismay, I found only H&M, home of the Little Lacy Thing. I shuddered. Not only because I prefer to think of my style as more vintage, but also because of the articles that Jaisal and Allison had made us read, about the abominable conditions to which workers in factories producing clothes for inexpensive stores are subjected. But I was already opening the door by that point, and heading over to a rack of little lacy things. I caught sight of myself in a wide mirror in the middle of two racks of short shorts. My hair! My face! I clutched at the bird's nest that had taken residence on my head. It had been a while since I'd last looked in the mirror—or maybe the mirrors at Quare were kinder than those illuminated by fluorescent lighting. My hair, over decent shoes, was the most important thing to take care of, I realized. The dress was in good shape, and as long as it wasn't stained, it would have to do.

So I dashed back outside and took a few deep breaths. Surely one of the prom girls in line would have a comb. I walked down the street again. Carnegie Hall came into view, and I made my way to the back of the line, trying not to stare at my fellow awardees. Almost every winner had his or her parents in attendance. Many had two: a plump father and a blond mother, or a plump mother and a bald father, both beaming and squinting to read the pamphlets about visiting New York City that YIPA had sent in the mail. I wasn't jealous, exactly; in fact, I felt lucky to be alone. I wouldn't have wanted Mum dabbing her finger in her mouth to smooth my eyebrows or Daddy fighting his urge to read the newspaper he'd stuffed into this briefcase rather than make conversation with any of the neighboring families.

The girls on the line were shiny. Their eyes glimmered under thick layers of eyelashes that I guessed had been made possible by Maybelline; their hair was sparkly, chemically straightened, falling in thick curtains at their shoulders. And these were supposed to be artists—young innovators? How did they all have time to apply glitter to their cheekbones? Most girls wore heels, and almost all of them, except for the serious-looking ones in suits, wore big shiny dresses, or even little lacy things that had the same effect. Almost all had bare arms.

I said, "Excuse me," and pushed my way through the crowd to find the end of the line. I knew I must smell, at least a little bit, and I hoped that there would be a ladies' room that I could use in Carnegie Hall to give my armpits a quick douse.

I found the end of the line, finally, in front of a building two blocks away from Carnegie Hall, and joined it unceremoniously. The girl directly in front of me was slightly plump, a tall girl with a long curtain of straightened blond hair and enough glitter on her face and dress so as to be spotted from space. The light bounced off her in such a way that I had a hard time looking at her for more than one or two seconds at a time; she was like a vampire. The girl was with just her mother, a short blond woman in a pantsuit.

"Where are you coming from?" the mother asked me.

I wasn't sure what to say. "Ulster County," I said finally, but that didn't feel right, exactly, so I said, "Well, Manhattan, originally."

"We're from Columbus, Ohio," the mother said, her daughter still silent and avoiding looking at me. "We drove through the whole night, and after this we're driving back, because her high-school graduation is tomorrow morning." She jabbed a long red fingernail at her daughter.

"Wow," I said.

"We got a little nap in this morning, but I'm afraid I might doze off during the ceremony," she confessed, then burst out in a snorting laugh. "Anyway, what'd you win for?"

"A play."

"She got a silver medal for a drawing she did. Charcoal. You should see our white sofa. She's going to RISD in the fall. Where are you going?"

"I'm just a junior," I said.

"Oh, right, right." The mother waved her hand in recognition. "That's great. Good luck with the college process. Now *that's* a real accomplishment: they should give out awards to any parent who survives college applications."

We made a bit more small talk, me feeling like a toad the entire time, and then the line began to move rather quickly. I showed the attendant the confirmation that had been sent in the mail and was swept inside the cool, expansive lobby. Inside the lobby, parents were ushered to the right and students to the left, where we were fed into what turned out to be the famous cavernous auditorium with a brightly lit stage and stressed-out people rushing around setting up podiums and handling clipboards. We took our seats and waited to be told what to do. It was air-conditioned in the room, a nice relief, but my perspiration dried and left me cold. One of the stressed-out men explained the order of events: the opening video made by the First Lady of the United States; the message from the president of the awards; the actual awarding of medals; the keynote speaker's address; the closing video and remarks; and the final bow.

I sat next to two girls from New Orleans, each in a dress with a wide skirt and a gaping back that dipped to the little crevice just before their derrières. I felt horribly frumpy in my light wool dress.

"Ask her what she won for," the blond one said to me, talking about the brunette one.

"Oh. What did you win for?" I asked the brunette.

She gave a deep-throated laugh. "It was a sculpture."

"That's nice."

"Ask her what it was a sculpture *of*."

"What was it—"

"A vagina." She was proud of it, and spat the words at me like a challenge.

"Whose?" the blonde prompted eagerly.

"Mine."

I offered a feeble laugh, even though I didn't find it that funny. She was fake, this girl, trying to be edgy and racy when really she just wanted my approval—or not my approval, probably, but somebody's.

"I like your dress," the blond girl said to me, trying again.

Shell speak! I just mumbled, "Thanks."

I didn't know what was wrong with me. I used to be so friendly.

I was glad when the two Louisiana girls gave up on me and rushed off together into the holding room, once we were released, which is the private upstairs portion of Carnegie Hall, before the ceremony began. It's structured like a museum, with pictures on the wall and little placards explaining the event they depict, in two ornate rooms into which all the awardees spilled.

In the holding rooms, everyone immediately either clustered into a friend group or slunk to the walls, awkward and alone. I didn't have any friends, so I made myself comfortable on the floor. The cliques had been established effortlessly. Vampire-suit-wearing artists; the quiet, nerdy novelists; the shiny girls, probably sketchers or sculptors; the ironic-glasses-wearing hipsters, maybe photographers or lithographers; gawky young boys in too-big suits and draping ties, definitely computer animators.

One thing that Quare didn't have were the little flutes of sparkling cider that were floating around. They were twinkly and bubbly, and people took them with two fingers and drank with their pinkies up.

And then I saw them: the coolest group, floating together as though their shoes rested on a cloud rather than the red-and-gold carpet, each more perfect than the next. Just three shiny girls and one towheaded guy, sipping sparkling cider and laughing as though they were royalty. I saw them only from behind: the girls' defined calf muscles, the guy's casual suit. They occupied their own corner of the holding room, and the rest of us kept a good ten-foot radius, allowing them to soak up each other's excellence.

"That's them," someone said breathlessly beside me.

I looked over to find a girl a good four inches shorter than I, in a bowler hat and a shift dress. Her mouth opened slightly as she stared at the group.

"Who?" I asked.

"The portfolio gold-medal winners," the girl said. "I've been watching them since freshman year. They're the best writers and artists in the country."

I remembered this portfolio prize vaguely from a pamphlet I'd received: they had won the biggest, most impressive awards, for a whole portfolio of work rather than a single one, giving them the chance to meet in a small group with Lena Dunham and the First Lady.

"What?"

The girl nodded seriously. "It's the highest honor. And they've known each other since seventh grade, since they were brought together as winners when the first awards ceremonies opened up to them. They go to Miami every year for YoungArts, do the same writing and art camps during the summer, and in a week or two they'll come here again for Scholastic."

"You know them by name?"

"Lauren, Matilda, Thomas, and Bex," she listed without hesitation. She gestured to each one as she said the name too, her nail-bitten finger hovering in the air for a second as she pointed to each in awe.

I took a good look at the sparkly people. They were outfitted in glitter, but refined glitter, no hem too short and no bulges at the hips or stomach. The girls' legs, all lean and propped up in modest heels, shone, and their hair fell in sleek layers around their soft faces, illuminated by the gentle lighting. Stiletto heels were jammed onto their feet in a way that could only be miserable, but the girls stood easily, perfectly balanced as they joked and imitated and carried on—the lone boy was less remarkable, but there was something endearing about him still, something childish, and they took turns reveling in his fleeting attention. Their eyes shone with the knowledge that they were on top of the world, the group that ruled this scene of young writers and artists. I searched in myself for jealousy but found only a weird brand of pity. To have meant to lose; to be special meant to be constantly on the verge of being unremarkable.

My philosophical musings were cut short by an astounding realization. I had been staring at them for so long that I was shocked not to have seen it before. Wait! It was Becca Conch-Gould! Not Bex, this creature with chiseled legs and blue eyes surrounded by lashes coated in mascara, but Becca, the quiet, fringy thing from first semester—the one who wore dingy feather earrings, sucked up to the teachers, and confronted me in my cabin after I'd gotten the part in Dean's play. I was sure of it.

She had changed enormously in the five months since I'd last seen her, but Becca still had that jittery look about her, those cricket eyes that hummed and thrummed with anxiety. Now those eyes were beautifully made-up, yet immutably freaky. But now she was pure sex appeal, shimmying up to Thomas and sipping Perrier. I was close enough to them now—I had shuffled forward, I realized, dangerously close to the outside of the ten-foot radius they demanded—to hear their conversation, about that time a young Philip Roth look-alike had asked for Lauren's number at a hotel in the Bahamas over spring break, and what was the hilarious literary reference that she had spouted back at him . . . ?

I made my approach, figuring I had nothing more to lose.

"Um, Becca?" I asked tentatively, painfully aware of my unkempt hair and greasy face.

Becca broke her gaze with Matilda and slowly, glacially, turned to glance at me, at which point her eyes flicked away again. But then she stopped. Turned again, just as slowly. She looked me up and down, her eyes slow with confusion. For what felt like five minutes, the entire clique—and then the entire room, practically, as though it took its cue from these four—was silent as Becca stared at me, taking in my dusty pink Jackie Kennedy dress and beaten shoes and glossless face. It was obvious that she knew who I was—we'd seen each other only five months ago—but this new shiny Becca clearly loved the drama of the slow reveal.

"Flora," she said slowly. "Oh my fucking God, I thought I would never see you again! This is Flora," she said, turning to her friends. "She's basically the reason I left Quare— *you* know, the hippie school upstate that was my inspiration for my novel—after my first semester. When I was cut from Guild, I realized that I could never compete with people like that." She flung her head back and laughed uproariously. "True artists!"

I was too shocked to say anything, partially because the last time I had seen her, Becca was wearing knit leggings, no makeup, and earrings she described as "funky," and partially because she considered me—*me*—to be a true artist. When had that been true? When Dean had cast me, when she had crowned me apprentice? That seemed so quaint now, so humble, in the dinky old Woolman Theater as opposed to Carnegie Hall. A world away. Somewhere that was out there, and *out there* was not *in here,* with shiny Becca and Lauren and Matilda and Thomas and even the whispery social climber who was panting quietly beside me, clearly beside herself to be in the presence of loyalty.

Becca kept talking. "God, I can't believe you stuck it out at Quare for the whole year," she said. "I mean, you're made for the place, because you're so quirky and artsy and all, but I can't imagine staying there for both years—after one semester I was ready to get out. I'm naturally competitive, I guess, and I could sense that the school was going to stomp all over me. But has the class gotten really close? Are things superincestuous? Oh my God, what happened to Agnes? I had the hugest crush on him."

I said, "A little bit incestuous, yeah."

"I was sort of lucky, because after Quare I ended up at Chapin, and it's all girls, but of course there are boys from Collegiate, which is sort of a fun challenge . . . but I'm talking too much, aren't I? What did you win for? I never asked you."

"A play."

"Of course. I should have known. You'll be master player next year, won't you? Well, that's great. I won for my novel, which of course isn't as impressive as a play. A play is a performance, and a novel is . . . a rumination, I guess. A play is brilliant. You've got to accomplish everything with, like, dialogue and actions, none of your own self-obsessed narration."

I watched her lips move, prattling on and on as her friends laughed politely and sipped cider. And suddenly there it was, naked as the toes poking out of Becca's high-heeled shoes: *me*.

Rather, my old self. And not only my old self, but India and Cora and the rest of my friends. It was just a glimmer—surely we were never so hollow or even so shiny—but it was there nonetheless, in the shape of Becca's hand around her cider flute and the way Lauren's quad muscles stuck out slightly from underneath the hem of her blue dress. Bex, for all her pretentiousness and annoyingness, had found her place.

My place.

"You should come to our after-party," Bex said. "My parents are staying at a hotel, and they don't mind how many friends stay over. I've got people coming from Bowen and Fairfax and Chapin, but also, like, Westwood and Collegiate and Parker for some variety. We moved out of Greenwich Village over the summer—my parents thought it had lost its character. Now we're on Eightieth and Park, and the apartment is literally a dorm room, but I'm going to push all the furniture to the sides of the living room so there's enough space to dance. There's going to be wine and cheese—oh wait, Matilda, did you get your new fake yet?"

Even in that cramped, dark holding room, the city felt huge. There was room here, streets that careened over hills and buildings that stretched up into the sky, competing with the clouds. And there were people here, people like Bex and the social climber in the bowler hat and the girl in the shiny gold gaping-back dress and the pantsuit mother. Even I felt hollow here, like there was nothing left in me.

There were a few people I wanted who weren't gouged out inside but heavy, anchored. And a little bit mangled, sure, but at least rooted.

"I'm sorry," I said, "but I have to go."

Bex just stared. "Right now?"

"Yes."

"But, Flora, you'll miss the ceremony! Lena Dunham is coming! You won't get your medal!"

I gave one last smile, turned on my worn heel, made my way through the crowd of young innovators, down the grand staircase, past the anxious, clipboard-wielding man (he dogged me for a bit, imploring me to stay), past the throngs of parents waiting eagerly in the lobby. I pushed open the heavy door and walked into the sunlight.

I sucked in air, fresh air, and looked at delis and shops and bakeries. The sun slumped lazily in the sky. It was a nice time in the late afternoon, when the sun wasn't quite as hot as before. It was still warm, but I now felt comfortable. When I was outside, I didn't notice so much that I smelled.

Horses waited in a line by the entrance to the park on Fifty-ninth Street and Fifth Avenue, all muzzled up and hooked to carriages. Tourists swarmed them, touching their faces, feeding them apples and carrots as the horses swished their tails and stomped their heavy feet. There were people everywhere, mostly with cameras. I wanted to sing, because I didn't have a camera, and I had never had a camera. I kept walking, past the fancy hotels and mobs of people. On my way to the Columbus Circle subway stop, I paused for a minute in the spot where Elijah had photographed me for the first time. The air felt thick and warm, and kids shouted and shrieked in the background, clambering on all the rocks at the entrance to the park.

I looked down at my body. My dress! I'd been wearing the same exact dress, albeit with its matching apricot coat. Today I laughed and threw my hands in the air.

"Move," someone grunted behind me, pushing me slightly.

I scampered down the subway steps and pressed my back against the wall as I waited for the 1 train. A man with a homemade drum set around his waist played wildly, trying to make eye contact with me, not threateningly, just with a huge grin. I fished a dollar bill out of my wallet and handed it to him as I got on the train.

"Beautiful, beautiful," he said, and I didn't know if he was talking about me or my dollar.

The crowd heading downtown on Friday afternoons is generally young, and today was no exception: people in gauzy dresses and jean jackets, cell phones flashing at their waists. The train thundered to a stop at Fourteenth Street, and I pushed my way out, checking my watch. I had about ten minutes, but I didn't want to show up empty-handed. As soon as I got to ground level, I sprinted south, dodging throngs of NYU students to make it to the first little grocery I saw. I quickly selected a bouquet of multicolored tulips and paid the shrunken woman at the register before dashing out. By the time I could see the Washington Square Arch, it was 5:33, and I realized then that I had no idea where, exactly, in the park the ceremony was being held. I came to an ungraceful stop, my heart pounding and my dress sticking to my sweaty back.

I fished my cell phone out of my purse and called Lael, willing her to pick up. Of course she didn't: the ceremony had already begun. I forced myself to take a deep breath and slow my mind. They had to be here somewhere, right? The park wasn't that big. I began around the outside edge, scouring every small group—the wedding, Mum had told me on the phone, would be limited to very close family and friends, meaning a group of about thirty people—for a judge (Mum decided that having a rabbi wasn't important to her, and Nell, an atheist, felt uncomfortable with religion being part of their union) and multicolored sand.

Sand! I froze. I hadn't brought sand. Instead I'd shown up late, with a bouquet of flowers—the wrong thing, the wrong time, the wrong family. Dumb, dumb, dumb. I considered tossing the flowers into a gutter but resisted the urge. Instead I sat on a bench and began to cry slow, pitiful, snaking tears. I'd wanted to surprise Mum, to show her that I still cared about her and wanted her to be happy, but now the entire thing felt useless: I'd missed the ceremony, and now I was missing the party, too. When a young couple passing by eyed me, concerned, I slipped on my sunglasses again and crossed my legs daintily. Elijah had shot me here, too: it seemed he'd shot me everywhere in the whole city. What had I been wearing? It didn't matter, it only mattered that he had seen me and positioned me until I looked just right. Just fucking right.

I didn't even like him, now that I thought about it. Sure, if he were standing in front of me, I'd feel the familiar clenching in my stomach and the tremor in my hands, but my body was practically conditioned to do that. He'd been there, shiny and new when my family was crumbling, and he'd offered the perfect escape from my old life: do something wild; get someone to love you. It was stupid, all of it. I was stupid. The tears came faster.

And now that I'd been recognized *officially,* invited to Carnegie Hall and paraded around as one of the best artists in the country, that felt hollow too, another form of Elijah appreciation. They didn't know me. Nobody did.

I don't know how long I sat there, weeping tears of rage and self-pity and disgust, before I felt a cold hand on my shoulder. I screamed and threw my elbow up, like we'd learned in self-defense classes at Bowen. I didn't make contact, but I leapt to my feet and scrambled to get my purse, not even looking at my attacker.

"Flora!"

I stopped what I was doing. It was Lael, in a light blue sundress. Her hair was loose and curly around her shoulders. I gasped and rushed into her arms. They felt warm and fleshy. I buried my head in her shoulder and breathed in her familiar scent.

I was still sobbing when we started to hug, but by the time I released her from my grip, we were both laughing.

"Wait," she said, holding my shoulder with one hand and ripping my sunglasses off my face with the other, "have you been CRYING?"

I nodded. "I couldn't find you," I said lamely.

She shook her head. "We were just over there." She gestured toward the center of the park. "But the ceremony's over. It's past six."

"So everyone's gone?"

Lael laughed. "Oh no, of course not. Mum just sent me to pick up compostable paper plates, because the ones Nell's mom brought are plastic."

"Let's go." I grabbed her hand and we threaded our way to the park's exit.

"You're here so early," Lael said. "What happened?"

I told her the whole story as we walked to the closest D'Agostino. I yammered on about all the things I'd discovered as Lael selected and paid for the plates, and I was still talking as we reached the park again. The sun was lower, just slightly, but heat still rose off the streets, and my arms felt toasty. Lael, who'd been nodding and asking questions the whole time, stopped suddenly in front of a grassy expanse. I stopped talking and looked. There was the picnic, maybe twenty yards away: Mum, in a long red dress and her hair piled on top of her head, laying out food, guests smoothing blankets; Nell on her back in the grass, smiling at the sun, her white shorts-and-top combination directly touching the grass. At first I didn't see Victor, but then I spotted him crouched underneath the big plastic table, tiny arms wrapped around his legs.

"Look," Lael said. "There's everybody."

"Not Daddy," I said. "We should probably call him later and tell him we had fun."

We both laughed.

"Should we go over?" I asked when Lael still wasn't moving.

"One more minute," she said. "I'm surprised they don't see us."

Nobody was looking in our direction; they were all preoccupied with setting out food.

"Mum is probably one of the most frustrating people in the world," Lael said finally. "She says terrible things sometimes, and it usually seems like she cares more about herself than she does about us." She stopped uncertainly.

"But?" I asked. "Are you going to say, 'But she loves us'?"

Lael gave me a look.

"No," she said. "I'm not going to say that. She does love us, and we both know it. But what I wanted to say is that you get one family—one given family, I mean."

"So we might as well try to be happy?"

"Or, if not happy, at least we should try to be there," Lael said. "Just show up for each other, you know?"

"I agree," I said. "Maybe Nell isn't as bad as we think she is."

"That remains to be seen," Lael said, "but I think we owe her more of a chance than we've given her."

"Look how mature we're being," I said.

"It's about time we grew up," she said.

I took her hand.

"Shall we?"

We walked over to where the group had assembled. As soon as Mum saw me, she ran over, almost tripping over her dress. She was barefoot—I wasn't sure if she'd had on shoes to begin with. I fought against rolling my eyes, and accepted her hug. She smelled like she'd always smelled, but now I detected something muskier, like sweat.

"You came," she wailed, gripping me tighter. "Nell, look who's here!"

Nell straightened up and saluted me, a smile glimmering on her lips. I forced myself to smile and wave at her.

I handed Mum the flowers, which she cooed over and arranged on the table. Lael set out the plates, and Mum called everyone over to get food. As I was spooning roasted potatoes onto my plate, I felt a slight tickle on my shin. Thinking it was a bug, I yelped and I yanked my leg away (I'd come a long way, but not, evidently, far enough).

From below the table came a tiny giggle, almost inaudible. I peered underneath the table and found Victor still crouched, now with a devious grin on his face. I arranged my dress around my thighs and bent to face him. Under the table it was dark and shadowy, a good ten degrees cooler than it was outside of it.

"Hi, Victor," I said softly.

He didn't speak.

"I guess we're siblings now," I continued.

He let out a cackle.

"How are your ears?" I asked. "Any more infections?"

He cackled again, really getting into it. His hair looked longer; now it grazed the tops of his ears.

"Hey, do you think we'll ever have a conversation?"

He shook his head, still grinning. I smiled in spite of myself.

"Okay," I said. "I guess we'll check back in later."

He reached out with one tiny hand and touched my face, sliding his warm finger from my temple to my chin, then skittering across my nose. I forced myself not to smile. Victor was a serious kid; I didn't think he'd appreciate one.

When he was done, I got to my feet and wandered around, greeting a few relatives and Mum's friends, all of whom politely didn't mention the state of my dress, hair, or shoes. I managed to keep my potatoes down even when Nell grabbed Mum spontaneously and planted a huge kiss on her lips. And you know what? I didn't even have to try. I hadn't seen her and Daddy kiss in what felt like years. And now she and Nell were in love, never mind the amount of time that had passed since her divorce. *Just let her be happy*, I told myself. I hugged everyone good-bye, told Mum I'd call her about summer arrangements sometime soon, and took off.

By the time I arrived back at Grand Central, it was almost seven. I quickly bought a ticket and boarded a train. It was full of people heading to the country for the weekend: people with suitcases and sunglasses, talking just a little bit too loudly. I called the Quare office from my cell phone in the Poughkeepsie station and waited quietly, sitting on a step, my small purse beside me, for someone to come retrieve me. It was so quiet and so warm, dusky now, but not quite dark. Ten minutes later Allison Longfield's partner, Daniel, pulled up merrily and asked me a few questions about the ceremony; it didn't seem important to tell him that I'd skipped it, so I left that part out.

He parked the van by the office, and I climbed out. The air was fresh and summery even though the sun was pretty much gone. I put my palms up to the sky and walked across the field toward my A-frame. As I made my way toward the dining hall, though, faint yelling sounded in the distance.

HEY, HEY! HO, HO! PATRIARCHY HAS GOT TO GO!
HEY, HEY! HO, HO! PATRIARCHY HAS GOT TO GO!
HEY, HEY! HO, HO! PATRIARCHY HAS GOT TO GO!

I stopped short and looked up. A group of maybe twelve young women was proceeding down the soccer field, from the direction of the garden. The two in front were clearly the ringleaders: they carried an enormous glittering sign with the words WE SUPPORT FLORA painted on it in huge letters. They didn't seem to notice me cowering by the road. One of them, in a navy-blue suit with enormous shoulder pads and yards of curly black hair piled in clips all over her head, carried a bullhorn, through which she chanted her group's cheery slogan.

HEY, HEY! HO, HO! PATRIARCHY HAS GOT TO GO!
HEY, HEY! HO, HO! PATRIARCHY HAS GOT TO GO!

As they got closer, I made out a few more faces: a severe-looking Asian girl with feathery hair and enormous hoop earrings; a reedy girl in a baseball cap; a willowy redhead in what looked to be a prairie wedding dress. One girl, tall with a beaky nose, was naked, I realized suddenly, save for navy nipple tassels and matching blue satin booty shorts. A huge camera swung from her neck, dangling between her exposed breasts. They marched toward me, shouting all the while. The leader—the eighties girl—signaled to her group to change its chant as they rounded the hall, and they effortlessly fell into this second one.

ONE, TWO, THREE, FOUR! RECLAMATION IS WHAT WE'RE HERE FOR!

FIVE, SIX, SEVEN, EIGHT! NO MORE VIOLENCE! NO MORE HATE!

ONE, TWO, THREE, FOUR! RECLAMATION IS WHAT WE'RE HERE FOR!

FIVE, SIX, SEVEN, EIGHT! NO MORE VIOLENCE! NO MORE HATE!

On and on they went, keeping a slow march. And they were headed toward me again, their WE SUPPORT FLORA sign shimmering and swaying with the motion, their eyes fixed on some point above my head. I was so shocked that I stood stock-still, a tremor flashing through my entire body.

I looked to my right, but what I saw next was more shocking still: all eight female students in my class, each harnessed in a sophisticated criss-cross of rope, dragging my vending machine across the field. All were on their hands and knees, and all strained and heaved. A group of Quare onlookers—from here I could make out Thomas watching nervously from the side; Gus, Gary, and Agnes trying to push it from the back; Peter and Solomon down at the girls' level, coaching them as they strained against their ropes. A laugh bubbled up in my throat, but I swallowed it down.

CLAIM OUR BODIES! CLAIM OUR RIGHT!

OUR ART IS HOW WE FIGHT!

CLAIM OUR BODIES! CLAIM OUR RIGHT!

OUR ART IS HOW WE FIGHT!

The vending machine progression was nearing the protestors now. Benna and Fern, the two hauling the most of the weight, were both drenched in sweat. The vending machine grunted forward, pulling up tufts of grass in its wake. The two camps, which had come within perhaps ten feet of each other, paused and sort of nodded in agreement. Suddenly the Asian girl, one of the leaders of the chanters, motioned for everyone to be quiet. Everyone fell silent.

"THERE!" she shouted.

But she wasn't pointing at me. Instead it was to something behind me. I spun around.

Elijah.

We were almost face-to-face. It took my brain a few seconds to unscramble the image, piecing together a whole from the sum of its parts. Fluffy hair. Tiny round glasses. Flannel, even in late May. Cuffed jeans. He stared down at his Converse. He wore, as always, a slight smile.

By this point, we were in the middle of the soccer field. I was surrounded: the Quares to my right, these protestors to the north, Elijah to the south. Everyone went dead silent. I spun back around to study the group of protestors. The lead girl, whom I instantly recognized as Wink DelDuca, founder and editor in chief of *Nymphette* magazine, stood panting before me, bullhorn slack in her hand. My gaze traveled from her fitted blazer to her high-waisted slacks. What appeared to be a monocle hung from her waistband, swaying gently in the breeze. And then behind her—India! Cora! Huddled at the back, as though not sure what they'd gotten themselves into. India gave me a shy wave and motioned to me that we'd talk later. I wagged my fingers at them.

I turned to Wink.

"Heather Duke?" I asked feebly, trying to make a joke.

She just stared at me. "What?" She wasn't annoyed, exactly, but the word came out shrilly.

"From *Heathers,*" I explained. "The 1988 cult classic. You look just like Heather Duke."

She smiled.

"Oh," she said. "Of course."

There was a long pause. Everyone stared.

"I'm Wink DelDuca," she said.

"Flora Goldwasser."

"Also known as Miss Tulip?"

I shrugged. "Sometimes."

She cleared her throat.

"Flora," she said, "we've come here today to support you and your art."

Everyone, including me, swiveled to look at Elijah. He stared down at his shoes.

"Thank you," I said.

He looked up at me. My neck got hot.

Click. My neck snapped over to the side, where the nearly nude beaky girl peered at us from behind her big black camera.

Wink's mouth opened. But before she could speak, I turned to the Quares.

Benna and Fern, drenched in sweat and spent on the ground. Dean, clearly trying to contain herself, standing off to the side in pink rain boots. Lucy and Juna, their arms folded, looks of indignation on their faces.

"Elijah," I said, turning again to him, "I forgive you."

"Wait, did he assault—" this indignant squawk from Juna.

"He didn't," I said. "But what he helped me realize is that I'm supertired of selling parts of myself in exchange for love from other people." I fixed my gaze on him again. His face lacked expression, or maybe I just couldn't read it. "I'm not really Miss Tulip, or at least I can't be her all the time, and I'm never going to really, truly be Quare, either, no matter how good it makes me feel for people to see me that way. I ended up giving you what felt like everything. But it's not. I have so much more. And there has to be some way we can meet in the middle, if we ever want to be friends."

His face broke out into a smile.

"The middle," he said. "I like that."

"I'll be waiting for you in the middle," I promised. And then, when he didn't budge: "Elijah, please go now."

His face sagged.

"I wish I could be the kind of guy who's good at this," he said.

"Good at what?"

"Sex. And stuff." He looked around, suddenly aware that everyone on the field had their eyes trained on us.

Dean's email flashed into my mind: *He can be such a freaking Sadboy. Elijah is really weird about all this emotional stuff.*

"No, Elijah," I said. "You're fine at sex. That's not the issue here." I paused. "Wait. Are you trying to win me back, or something? Were we even together?"

He laughed. "I've realized that I'm in love with you," he said. "I think I knew I was all along."

His face beamed out at me, shiny and expectant, the corners of his mouth upturned. And right then it turned my stomach. All of it: the cuffed pants, the small, round glasses, and most of all, the naked expectation. It was the way he was looking at me, the way he'd written letters apologizing for using me all so that he could have me back again—a me who wasn't really even me at all.

"I want you to leave," I said.

"What?" He didn't believe me, and that's why he was still smiling, his palms turned toward the dark sky and dipped down to me.

"Leave," I said.

The smile dripped off his face. *Click. Click.* I wanted to rip the camera out of naked girl's hands, but I forced myself to fix my gaze on Elijah, who had now shoved his hands into his pockets.

"Okay," he said finally. He started to walk away. Everyone on the field silently watched him, breathing in unison. As soon as he'd walked maybe twenty paces, my heart began to race.

"Wait, Elijah!" I called out.

He stopped in his tracks, and I jogged over to him.

"I want to shake your hand," I said. "No hard feelings. Really. I just—*can't* right now. Maybe ever."

He reached out. I reached out. We shook hands slowly. His hand was chapped, but delicate, not too calloused. Slightly warm. The familiar tingles were there, but as soon as they'd washed over my body, they were gone. I released his hand. He nodded once and then turned and took off. I exhaled.

Sinclaire sent up a tiny cheer that Juna quickly quelled by slapping one paw onto hers. She had staggered up to a kneeling position.

"Wait just a minute," Juna said. "What exactly happened between the two of you?"

I shook my head. "It's complicated."

Juna stared up at me in disbelief. "Really?" she asked.

"Really," I said. "Juna, thank you. I should have been thanking you all semester. You were a better person, and a better friend, to me than I was to you. You are way kinder and more patient than I ever gave you credit for, and your integrity is rare. But I'm sorry. I'm sorry that you've been so supportive of someone who doesn't exist."

"What do you mean?" she demanded.

"I mean, this past semester, I've become this weird, deep Quare celebrity. And before this semester, I was Miss Tulip, and she was all of *your* heroes." I pointed at Wink and the people who'd come from *Nymphette*. "And I was really only Miss Tulip so I could be *his* muse." I gestured at Elijah, who was slowly disappearing. "I feel happy with the vending machine project, but it doesn't really get at everything I am. I don't really feel that I have to sell everything I own."

I pulled Juna into an embrace. She was still roped to the machine, so I bent down to her level. We hugged for a good thirty seconds. "Aww," someone—I couldn't tell who—cooed.

I reached down and untied my little white shoes. I stepped out of them and onto the grass. It was soft and warm from the sun, slipping between my toes. I wiggled them. In the distance, a bell sounded. The dinner bell—but dinner had happened hours ago. Everyone's neck snapped to the side, wondering who would ring the dinner bell at such an hour.

But I wasn't wondering.

I locked eyes with India, standing off to the side in olive skinny jeans and black wedges, then looked over at Cora, locking arms with her, holding on for dear life. It was hilarious to see them here, with rhubarb growing in the background and Benna and Fern sweating on the ground beside them. Immediately the three of us burst out laughing. I ran over to them, clutching at them both, all three of us falling over with hysterical laughter. It didn't matter that everyone was watching. As soon as we could breathe again, I released my grip. The bell was still ringing gently.

"I'll be right back," I told them. "I just have to do one thing."

Everyone looked around at each other, not sure what to do. Nobody moved.

Except for me. I sprinted across the field, my dress tight around my knees, and reached the dining hall, panting.

And that's when I saw him, right on the kitchen roof, sitting with his legs propped up on the gutter and holding his guitar. His head was bent down, but his face tilted up, catching the light. He was straining to play a chord. Not getting it right, and repositioning his fingers and singing it again. As I got closer, his voice snuck to me, catching in my ears: "Puff the Magic Dragon." A box of Panda Poop was open next to him, and a few loose pieces of cereal had caught on the shingles.

He helped me up silently, not even laughing when I almost lost my balance and went crashing down to the porch below. A smile twitched at the corners of his mouth, but he clamped down on my arm until I was seated next to him, trying to remain solemn.

"Play it again, Sam," I said once I had adjusted my legs.

"Nice ref."

We smiled shyly at each other.

"You're here," I said.

"I'm here."

"Why?"

He just smiled, still strumming softly.

"What happened to the ceremony?" he asked, his eyes half closed.

"I left."

"Well, what about your medal? Don't you want to see your medal?"

"I don't care about it."

"Why not?"

"I didn't want to go to that swanky ceremony and some swanky after-party."

"Why not? You love swank."

"I don't care about my medal or Lena Dunham or champagne flutes."

"Okay. What do you care about?"

"I don't care about Becca or Elijah right now. They're the same to me. Both hollow."

"Do you care about me?"

I considered that for a minute. "Yes."

We were silent.

"Where are you?" I asked, sitting beside him and propping my knees up to my chin. I looked down to see that I hadn't shaved my legs before the ceremony, so I covered them with my skirt a little bit.

Sam was silent for a moment. "You won't believe this," he said, "but I think I'm underwater."

My eyebrows shot up. "You?" I asked. "You're in the pond?"

"Flora, I'm wearing fucking suspenders." He gestured down at himself. "At breakfast, I put soy milk in my coffee. Flax was involved at the oatmeal station. What else do you want from me? I'm Quare."

"You're not Quare," I said. "You wore those suspenders on the first day. Also, soy milk is the only type of milk Quare HAS. But anyway, I almost left my cabin without my shoes on, and I sprinkled chia seeds into my oatmeal, but doing Quare stuff doesn't make you QUARE."

"I hate to break it to you," Sam said, pressing his fingers over all his guitar strings, "but it sort of does."

"Yeah, I guess. Okay. Maybe we're Quare now. We're in a *different* pond, though. Maybe Sinclaire's there too. I need to think about that some more. But it's not about whether you're materialistic or, like, monastic."

"So what's it about, then?" Sam asked, laughing.

In the distance, down below, down at the field, where the three camps were still in a face-off, there came a loud cheer. We both strained to see what had happened. Juna, it seemed, had freed herself from her ropes and was now clutching a large bouquet of daisies. Beside her stood the pasty nearly nude girl. They kissed passionately.

"I hate to say it, but that girl's really growing on me," said Sam.

"I love her to death," I agreed.

But then! Juna had not in fact freed herself from the harness, and the sudden motion of leaping up destabilized the vending machine. It swayed and tottered for an interminable few seconds. Sam and I held our breaths. Down on the field, everyone watched it, frozen.

It toppled. The impact was solid, fatal. It lay on its side, defeated. Fern, who had rolled out of the way, raised her arms above her head, her expression indistinguishable. The Quares looked at each other, fretting and scurrying around the machine like ants dealing with a huge crumb. The Nymphettes stood, their arms crossed, not sure which chant would correspond to this recent turn of events.

We sat in silence for a moment, out of respect for the fallen machine. Then I bent down and rang the dinner bell again, a harsh chime that made even me jump a little. Everyone on the field turned and stared.

And then Juna was running toward us, scrambling up to the porch and mounting the picnic table. She smelled like peppermint and squeezed between us on the roof, panting, clutching my leg. On the field, Thee gave a little wave and shimmied her nipple tassels. We cracked up, then fell silent.

"I want suffering and sex and depression and panic attacks and death," I said finally, to the small group on the porch. "I want to FEEL things. I want to SEE things. I want to be heavy, and I want to be full. Maybe with things. Maybe not. I don't want to think about being materialistic, even if I am, a little bit. I want to know that it's okay to be ugly, and it's okay to be beautiful. I want you both to still love me tomorrow because I'm an old tree stump, wrinkly and chopped down but also rooted."

"A tree stump? That's some grand old ambition you've got." Sam laughed.

I swatted his face. Juna groaned.

"I want to be weathered by the storms of life. I want to be struck my lightning, and I want to grow despite of it. I want to do lots of my growing underground, spreading roots, and even if I'm dead, I'll be growing."

I rang the bell again and again and Agnes started running, and Sinclaire, and then Fern and Rae and Lucy and Benna, all sprinting up to the porch and climbing up, laughing and panting. There wasn't quite room on the roof, and pointy knees jammed into my shoulder blades. But I was on a roll, even as people pushed and shoved. India and Cora dashed up to the edge of edge of the dining hall, pointing and laughing nervously. I blew them a kiss.

I flung my hands out wide, and Sam grabbed them, still laughing. "My tree stump will drink in the pond water through its roots. This is the start of a beautiful friendship, and—"

"*Casablanca,*" he said. "Also, slow down. Let's not get ahead of ourselves. Tree stumps are hard to come by these days."

I wrapped my hands around Sam's neck and drank in the smell of them all, my beautiful friends. "I think," I said, "that I've already found one."

Note pinned to a tree outside my cabin, morning of May 23

> *I knew you would.*
>
> *Dean*